PRAISE FOR R
TRACY CRO

Praise for *What She Found*

"A deep dive that manages to be both grueling and masterful."
— *Kirkus Reviews*

"Readers will eagerly await Tracy's next outing."
— *Publishers Weekly* (starred review)

"The fact that there's a truly gripping mystery, full of corruption, murder, and scandal, at the heart of the book to push and propel our protagonist into new realms is just the icing on the cake."
— Bookreporter

Praise for *In Her Tracks*

"Gripping . . . Fans of police procedurals will hope Tracy has a long career."
— *Publishers Weekly*

"A warmhearted procedural about some ice-cold crimes."
— *Kirkus Reviews*

"Dugoni has produced one of his most shocking twists yet and Tracy, expertly developed over seven previous novels, is almost pared down here, in a refreshing, perspective-changing way."
— Bookreporter

Praise for *A Cold Trail*

Praise for *A Steep Price*

Praise for *In the Clearing*

"Dugoni's third Tracy Crosswhite novel (after *Her Final Breath*) continues his series' standard of excellence with superb plotting and skillful balancing of the two story lines."

—*Library Journal* (starred review)

"Dugoni has become one of the best crime novelists in the business, and his latest featuring Seattle homicide detective Tracy Crosswhite will only draw more accolades."

—*Romantic Times*, top pick

Praise for *Her Final Breath*

"A stunningly suspenseful exercise in terror that hits every note at the perfect pitch."

—*Providence Journal*

"Absorbing . . . Dugoni expertly ratchets up the suspense as Crosswhite becomes a target herself."

—*Seattle Times*

"Another stellar story featuring homicide detective Tracy Crosswhite . . . Crosswhite is a sympathetic, well-drawn protagonist, and her next adventure can't come fast enough."

—*Library Journal* (starred review)

Praise for *My Sister's Grave*

"One of the best books I'll read this year."

—Lisa Gardner, bestselling author of *Touch & Go*

"Dugoni does a superior job of positioning [the plot elements] for maximum impact, especially in a climactic scene set in an abandoned mine during a blizzard."

—*Publishers Weekly*

"Combines the best of a police procedural with a legal thriller, and the end result is outstanding . . . Dugoni continues to deliver emotional and gut-wrenching, character-driven suspense stories that will resonate with any fan of the thriller genre."

—*Library Journal* (starred review)

"What starts out as a sturdy police procedural morphs into a gripping legal thriller . . . Dugoni is a superb storyteller, and his courtroom drama shines . . . This 'Grave' is one to get lost in."

—*Boston Globe*

ONE
LAST
KILL

The David Sloane Series

Nonfiction with Joseph Hilldorfer

ONE LAST KILL

ROBERT DUGONI

THOMAS & MERCER

Text copyright © 2023 by La Mesa Fiction LLC
All rights reserved.

Published by Thomas & Mercer, Seattle

www.apub.com

Amazon, the Amazon logo, and Thomas & Mercer are trademarks of Amazon.com, Inc., or its affiliates.

ISBN-13: 9781662500213 (paperback)
ISBN-13: 9781662500206 (digital)

Cover design by Damon Freeman
Cover image: © Raggedstone, © Jeffrey T. Kreulen / Shutterstock;
© Robin Vandenabeele / ArcAngel

Printed in the United States of America

To Jennifer Southworth, Seattle Police Department
Violent Crimes Section, retired.
And
Alan Hardwick, Edmonds Police Department acting
assistant chief, retired. Private investigator, musician,
member of two successful bands, writer of novels.
Fisherman. Golfer. A true Renaissance man.
Thank you both for your service of many years.
I admire and respect you. Many blessings to you in your
retirement years.

PROLOGUE

November 1993
Seattle, Washington

Vic Fazzio had, on more than one occasion, been accused of being a vampire. During the years he worked patrol and the various detective divisions of the Seattle Police Department, he frequently arrived at the Public Safety Building on Third Avenue at two or three in the morning. He didn't aspire to be the first officer to arrive on his shift, usually by several hours, but he also didn't want to sit at home fretting about being unable to sleep and possibly wake his wife, Vera. His father had been an insomniac, only slept four to five hours a night, but he'd also died young, just seventy-two years of age. Got Faz to wondering if a person only had so many waking hours on this planet, and if each night his father couldn't sleep had shaved minutes off his allotted time, the way they said each cigarette shortened a life span.

Faz had quit smoking.

Staying asleep was another matter altogether.

He had tried hot showers, melatonin, reading, sex, and everything else short of prescription meds. Nothing seemed to work. His doctor explained that some people only needed a few hours of sleep a night. At least as a homicide detective, Faz had chosen the right line of work. When he and his partner were the "next up" detective team for a homicide, the phone could ring at any hour of the day or night—but usually very late or very early.

An adage in SPD's homicide section was: "Our day begins when your day ends." Macabre, certainly, but only because it was true. Faz didn't need to rush to a homicide—unless the victim turned out to be one of the undead, in which case you could count Faz out. Call Darren McGavin, from *The Night Stalker* television show, because Faz wasn't going anywhere near the supernatural, not without a good cross, silver bullets, and a bottle of holy water.

Early morning, Faz was reading a novel at the kitchen table and contemplating going into the office when the house phone rang. He made the sign of the cross, an old habit from his mother's side of the family to ward off bad news, and answered before the phone rang a second time and woke Vera.

"You sound like you're awake," his homicide partner, Taj Gibson, said.

"For an hour," Faz said.

"So the rumors are true, Fazzio. You really are one of the undead."

"I like to think of myself as one of the perpetually living," Faz said. "However, your being awake at this hour is an indication you don't have good news."

"Depends on how you look at it," Taj said. "At least we won't be bored."

"Laub call?" Faz referenced their new sergeant, Andrew Laub, who ran homicide's A Team.

"Like a ray of morning sunshine. Got a body on the Aurora strip. So cowboy up, put on your big-boy pants, and ride like the wind . . . or fly. Whatever you vampires do."

—

Half an hour later, Faz drove Aurora Avenue North, also known as State Route 99 and "the Aurora strip." The windshield wipers on his black Chevy Caprice slapped a steady beat, and Tony Bennett's smooth voice sang "New York State of Mind"—the cassette a gift from Vera. After Taj provided the address, Faz chose not to go downtown to sign out a pool car. He and Vera had recently bought a Craftsman house in Green Lake, north of downtown Seattle and closer to this presumed homicide.

The multilane thoroughfare's skyline was cluttered with telephone wires, traffic lights, and lighted billboards advertising massage and tanning parlors, tobacco shops, adult-only establishments, and hotels and motels. Many of the motels had been quickly constructed to house the anticipated throng of visitors to Seattle's 1962 World's Fair. In the intervening decades, Interstate 5 largely replaced the Aurora strip, and the motels and hotels lost business until economic blight set in. Those structures that had survived showed their age. Rooms were cheap and catered to the pimps, prostitutes, and drug dealers working the area. Like the motels, the women who walked the strip struggled to survive.

Many didn't.

Sometimes humans interceded.

That's when Faz got involved.

Faz drove into the parking lot of the two-story Tranquil Gardens Motel, a misnomer if ever there was one. He didn't see a single flower or leaf anywhere. He flashed his detective ID to a uniformed officer draped in plastic to protect against the persistent rain. As the officer wrote down the information on a log, Faz got a better, though not improved, view of the L-shaped, beige stucco motel. The rooms faced the parking lot, harsh light illuminating the landings

"This a pool car?" the young officer asked.

"Nah. Mine."

"Sweet." He directed Faz to the parked patrol cars, their pulsing lights reflected in puddles in the asphalt parking lot. Faz parked alongside a black Ford pool car. The automobiles were unmarked, but only to the general public. Those within Seattle PD could pick one out in an airport parking lot.

Laub lowered his driver's-side window. Faz turned down Tony Bennett and lowered his passenger-side window. They spoke across the bench seat.

"You got here fast." A gust of wind nearly swallowed Laub's voice and blew rain onto the passenger seat.

"The wife and I live in Green Lake," Faz said, the implication that he hadn't gone downtown understood.

"You spoke to Taj?"

"Said he's on his way." Gibson lived in Beacon Hill, and he had no doubt gone to the Public Safety Building before heading north. He'd be a while longer.

"We'll wait. No sense repeating myself." Laub raised his window and leaned his head back against the headrest. Faz closed his window and sat back, envious of Laub's ability to catch a few winks.

Faz had been elevated to Homicide within Violent Crimes just three months earlier and was still learning the ropes. The Violent Crimes Section encompassed the Homicide, Robbery, Gang, Fugitive Task Force, and Intel units. A captain ran the section, and lieutenants ran each unit. A sergeant supervised each of the four homicide detectives assigned to one of three teams. An additional detective served as each team's "fifth wheel." That detective would rotate into a Homicide Unit as detectives retired or left the team.

Fifteen minutes after Faz arrived, Gibson parked another black Ford alongside his Chevy. The three men exited their vehicles and took cover from the rain beneath the hotel's second-floor landing. Gibson wore his trademark porkpie hat to cover his bald head and chewed a toothpick, a nervous habit.

"Body is in a dumpster in the alley around the back, which is why I had the officers set the perimeter around the parking lot. I don't want any press snapping pictures," Laub said.

"Hotel owner bitch about the perimeter?" Gibson asked.

"Don't know and don't care," Laub said. "An officer is getting his statement."

"Fire department been here?" Faz looked around the parking lot.

"Left about fifteen minutes before you arrived. Engine number twenty-seven."

Faz took notes in a spiral notebook. He'd call and get the engine crew's report. The fire department responded to homicides, presumably in case the victim remained alive, and if not, to pronounce the victim dead. That was, more often than not, easily discernible. But the fire-fighters stormed the crime scene anyway, leaving their bootprints and fingerprints and sometimes stepping on evidence. On occasion they repositioned the body, which sent the medical examiner on a rampage. Nobody touched the body before the ME gave his papal blessing. In theory anyway.

Laub led them to the back of the building. At six foot four, Faz had to duck beneath a concrete staircase providing access to the second floor. A patrol car parked in the alley, sheets of mist falling in the shafts of light from its headlights. An officer, draped in the same opaque plastic poncho, stood alongside a battered dumpster against an unpainted concrete-block wall. Faz eyed the potholes and puddles in the asphalt. It was unlikely to yield a tire impression or a shoeprint, but he'd have the standby homicide detectives check anyway.

Faz shone his Maglite over the contents in the dumpster, which smelled of rotting food. He hadn't yet put on his N-DEX gloves and was careful not to touch the edges in case the killer had left prints that could be lifted. His light illuminated flat cardboard boxes and black, industrial-size garbage bags. A bare arm protruded between the bags, presumably attached to a woman's torso—though the emaciated limb and painted fingernails did not necessarily establish gender. The drug-gies, male and female, also walked the Aurora strip.

"Night manager found her when he dumped a bag of trash," Laub said.

"Dumping trash at this hour of the morning?" Faz said. "Seems unusual."

Laub nodded but didn't otherwise comment.

"Anybody get a statement yet?" Taj asked.

"First responder is interviewing him in his office." Laub made a vague gesture with his thumb. Faz put a star by the night manager's name to indicate the interview. "We'll know better when the ME gets here how and when she died," Laub continued.

"Know better?" Faz said.

Laub looked reticent to say more.

"What's going on?" Gibson said.

"This is the fourth woman we've found in this area in less than a year," Laub said.

"And there's speculation it's the same guy?" Gibson asked.

"The MO, strangulation, and the disposing of the bodies in dump-sters is consistent, but that's not the main reason for the concern."

"What is?" Faz asked.

"The brass is keeping this quiet for now, but the bodies were all cut in the same location, on the back of the left shoulder."

"Cut?" Gibson said.

"Carved," Laub said.

"What's the carving?" Faz said.

"That remains open to debate," Laub said. "The other three, it looks like two question marks facing one another, but I don't think that's it."

"What do you think it is?"

Laub exhaled a breath. "Between us? For now? To me it looks like angel's wings."

CHAPTER 1

Wednesday, July 8, Present Day
Seattle, Washington

Tracy Crosswhite shut her office door and moved quickly behind her desk, hitting the keyboard and bringing her computer screen to life. She typed her password into the system. Once logged in, she relaxed and removed her jacket, draping it over the back of her chair and storing her purse in the lower left-hand desk drawer.

She had used vacation days sandwiched around the July Fourth holiday for a long weekend with Dan and Daniella at a lodge on Hurricane Ridge in Olympic National Park. For four days she enjoyed fresh mountain air, glorious sunshine, hiking, swimming, and reading novels—to the extent Daniella allowed her the time. Her daughter, now officially a toddler, was on the go and more challenging than ever to corral. Vacations could be more exhausting than work, though Dan had ensured Tracy had time to relax.

She had needed it.

She was burned out and disillusioned after a missing person cold case evolved into an intense investigation of a corrupt Seattle drug task force in the 1990s. She exposed the task force, but the perpetrators were largely beyond justice, either dead or protected from prosecution by expired statutes of limitation. She didn't have enough hard evidence to prove others had taken drug money, though they had, including Chief of Police Marcella Weber. Tracy couldn't prove it, not in a court of law, but both women knew the truth, and they were now engaged in a volatile, tense standoff.

Tracy was late getting to work because Therese, Daniella's nanny, had called to advise of a flight delay back to Seattle from her home in Ireland. Therese didn't arrive at the house until nine fifteen that morning for the Daniella handoff.

Not that Tracy had been itching to get back to work. The sole member of the Seattle Police Department's Cold Case Unit, she felt not just disillusioned and frustrated, but also isolated. She missed the camaraderie of working active homicides with Faz, Del, and Kins. After a decade together, they had become a work family.

Tracy pulled black binders from her office shelves, the cold cases she had been pursuing before the extended holiday. She reviewed the files and her computer notes to refresh her recollection of where she had left each case before departing the office.

Her desk phone rang, an inside call. She was tempted to ignore it but didn't have that luxury.

"My office, pronto," Weber said. She did not sound happy.

Weber used to come down to Tracy's office on the seventh floor. She liked to project herself as a working cop first and a politician second. She liked to be seen by her force as one of their team. Since the two women's falling-out, however, Weber summoned Tracy to her inner sanctum on the eighth floor, usually using words like "pronto," "ASAP," and "now." A power play. Tracy's Violent Crimes captain, Johnny Nolasco, did much the same thing—a verbal reminder of who held the higher rank.

Minutes later, Tracy announced herself to Weber's assistant, who escorted Tracy into the police chief's office. Weber sat at her desk, the phone cradled between her ear and the shoulder of her French-blue short-sleeve uniform shirt that displayed four collar stars and a shiny gold badge. She motioned for Tracy to sit in one of two chairs across from her desk. Then she made Tracy wait, another power play. Tracy refused to check her watch or otherwise indicate she was annoyed. She was. Instead, she stared at Weber, a trick she'd learned from Dan when he took depositions and knew a witness was lying. He didn't argue. He didn't ask the question a second time. He just stared, which was unnerving.

Weber ended the call and hung up. "What are you working on?" she asked, forsaking pleasantries.

Tracy almost said, "My patience" but refrained. "Several cases with promising DNA evidence." Her answer mimicked Weber's instruction that Tracy focus on cold cases with "promising DNA evidence"—cases that had a better chance of being resolved. Weber needed numbers to justify her budget before the city council, which had slashed the police allocation during the past few tumultuous years. Violent crime predictably spiked, the homeless took over Third Avenue, retail shops closed or moved from King County because of rampant theft, and tourism tanked. The new mayor, Charles Garcia, was working to turn the city around, starting with more funding to hire more SPD officers, and he'd emphasized to Weber that she needed to back him up.

"I want you to focus on the Route 99 serial killer cases," Weber said, again without providing a reason or pretense.

"Any *one* case in particular?" Tracy asked, though she doubted Weber knew any of the serial killer's thirteen victims, all murdered between 1993 and 1995, when the killings stopped as suddenly as they had begun.

"All of them."

"Any reason you care to share?" Tracy said.

"It's a black mark on the department," Weber said. She paused before adding, "And I have word the *Seattle Times* is planning to run a series of articles to mark the twenty-fifth anniversary since the last killing."

Which couldn't be good news. In the nineties, the city's two newspapers had both been critical of the department's failure to catch the killer. Tracy had read the clippings in the cold case binders.

"I understand the new articles intend to rehash each case and highlight the task force's failings," Weber continued. "Given the decades it took for us to catch Ridgway, it doesn't make us look good." Gary Ridgway, the Green River Killer, had been convicted in 2003 of nearly fifty murders between 1982 and 1998.

"Serial killers aren't easy to catch," Tracy said.

"You caught the Cowboy," Weber said.

"I got lucky," Tracy said. Nabil Kotar, aka "the Cowboy," had earned his moniker because he hog-tied his five victims during a 2015 killing spree. Tracy caught Kotar in a motel on the Aurora strip. He was now serving multiple life sentences in the Monroe Correctional Complex.

"We need some of that same luck now," Weber said. "I want a fresh pair of eyes."

"Council still putting the squeeze to your budget?"

"Our budget," Weber said. "And squeeze or no squeeze, I want to say we remain active in our effort to bring closure to the victims' families."

Sounded like a well-rehearsed public relations statement. "There hasn't been a murder in twenty-five years," Tracy said. "Why poke a stick in the tiger's cage?"

"Because the families deserve closure. Have Melton run the DNA again." She referenced Mike Melton, director of the Washington State Patrol Crime Lab. "With DNA advances, maybe we get a hit."

Tracy didn't know what DNA Weber referred to. She understood the Route 99 Killer had worn a condom when he raped his victims while strangling them. The victims had black-and-blue marks on their throats and other telltale signs of asphyxiation—gray pupils with filmed-over corneas, and petechiae spotting their faces: tiny red dots from burst blood vessels caused by excess pressure. The fact that the killer used his hands only made the murders more chilling.

"We meaning . . . me?"

Weber smiled. "You are the Cold Case Unit, are you not?"

Tracy saw an opportunity to maybe make lemonade out of lemons. "A case this complex, with this much history, I'm going to need some help, preferably someone who worked the task force." Faz had worked that task force. He'd been a newbie to Homicide back then.

"You have the task force's files," Weber said.

"And you told me you'd get me help when I needed it. I need it, if I'm going to uncover anything before the *Times* runs that series of articles."

Tracy had dropped a gauntlet that she knew Weber could not ignore. The two women stared at one another, but Tracy had the upper hand. Weber needed to solve the killings more now than ever.

After a few seconds of silence, Weber capitulated. "I'll get you some help."

"Vic Fazzio worked that task force."

Weber picked up a pad of paper and jotted something down.

Tracy stood to leave.

"I'm told the story is coming out soon, on a weekend to get maximum circulation and readership. I'd like to shove that article up the *Times*' collective asses."

"Doesn't mean the killer is going to walk in and confess—if he's still alive and hasn't already been arrested."

"Get it done," Weber said. Tracy turned for the office door. "Or I'll find someone else to come into the office at ten in the morning after a long holiday weekend."

CHAPTER 2

Tracy left Weber's office with two things clear: Weber wasn't interested in making up, and she had a mole on the seventh floor keeping an eye on Tracy, including her daily comings and goings. Tracy wasn't the forgive-and-forget type either, but she did value her privacy. It pissed her off to know someone was reporting on her. She'd been tempted to appeal to Weber's motherly experience—the woman had grown children and could no doubt empathize with the unexpected things that could cause a parent to be late to work—but she wasn't about to give Weber the satisfaction of knowing she was getting under Tracy's skin.

Tracy tempered her anger with the hope she'd have the chance to work a case with Faz, who was like her older brother. Tracy thought so much of him she'd named Faz and his wife, Vera, Daniella's godparents. One hundred and ten percent Italian, Faz had taken to the role of godfather with a flair Marlon Brando would have envied.

Back at her desk, Tracy requested that the Route 99 serial killer task force boxes be brought from the vault to her office. While waiting, she tidied up the cases on which she had been working. On each of those half-dozen investigations, she awaited either DNA testing of clothes, records pursuant to subpoenas, or responses from other police agencies to which she'd made inquiries.

She opened her file drawer and pulled out the manila folders Anita Childress had given her. A reporter for the *Seattle Times*, Anita had approached Tracy a few months earlier and asked Tracy to find her mother, Lisa Childress, an investigative reporter for the now defunct *Seattle Post-Intelligencer*, who had disappeared in 1996. The manila files were four investigations Lisa had been pursuing when she had vanished. Anita had believed at least one of those investigations was the reason for her mother's disappearance. With the help of social media, Tracy had miraculously found Lisa alive in Escondido, California, though amnesia related to a blow to the head had wiped out her memory. Tracy believed that blow had been delivered by someone working the drug task force. She had reunited the two women. Both now lived in Escondido.

In addition to investigating the illegal activities of the Last Line drug task force, Lisa Childress had also been investigating three other potential stories: allegations by several young men that Seattle city councilman and mayoral candidate Peter Rivers had paid for sex when the men had been underage; corruption and graft within then mayor Michael Edwards's administration; and, most pertinent to Tracy's current assignment, the Route 99 serial killings.

Tracy opened that file.

Though Tracy had grown up well away from Seattle in a small town in the North Cascades, she and everyone else in Cedar Grove knew of the Route 99 Killer and the Green River Killer. Both had killed prostitutes and drug addicts, marginalized young women living on society's edge. But the Route 99 Killer had also murdered middle-class wives and mothers, and it had been those killings that had ramped up public outrage and stirred the hysteria. When the killings abruptly ended, it fueled rampant speculation across the Pacific Northwest that the killer had moved to new hunting grounds.

Based on her experience searching for the Cowboy, Tracy knew the pressure the police had been under to find both killers.

She bypassed newspaper clippings in Lisa Childress's file and stopped at photocopies of spiral notebook paper on which Childress had documented media briefings. Tracy knew from running the Cowboy investigation that a task force might, on occasion, provide details on the nature of the killings, the victims, or an FBI profiler's description of the killer—race, size, and possible background—to protect the public or generate leads. But task forces were also paranoid and feared releasing details of killings that could spawn copycat killers or false confessions.

In her notes, Childress had drawn what looked like two question marks facing one another. Beneath the marks, she had scribbled three more lines.

ʕ?

Angel's Wings

Carved Left Shoulder

Angel of Death

The information had never been released to the public, raising the question of how Childress knew it.

Tracy flipped to the last page of the notes and considered the five names Childress had scribbled. Suspects. Also information the task force had not disseminated to the media or to the general public, at least not at those briefings. Yet Childress knew the Angel of Death moniker for the Route 99 Killer, and the suspects. How?

The task force had a leak, someone with intimate knowledge of the evidence or the markings on the bodies.

Tracy clicked the keyboard and entered SPD's cold case database. The task force had been disbanded when the killer went dormant and remained dormant; the assumption was that the killer either had died or had been incarcerated for a different crime. Whatever the reason, he'd stopped killing, and his victims became cold cases.

The lead task force detective had been Johnny Nolasco, current Violent Crimes Section captain and all-around pain in Tracy's butt. Nolasco and Tracy had a long, sordid history going back to Tracy's time at the police academy, where Nolasco had served as one of her instructors. He'd been trying to get rid of her ever since, and he was the reason Tracy now worked cold cases instead of active violent crimes.

The task force's co-lead investigator and administrative officer had been Nolasco's partner, Floyd Hattie. Hattie's job had been to procure equipment, funding, and necessary manpower for the task force, as well as to seek priority from the crime lab and the medical examiner's offices. When Nolasco became the Violent Crimes Section's captain, Hattie had been assigned to train Tracy, SPD's first female homicide detective. Hattie chose instead to retire, but not before firing a parting shot saying, "I ain't working with no Dickless Tracy."

Moss Gunderson, another longtime detective now retired, had been given the impossible job of lead control officer. He was to keep on top of and organize the mountains of accumulated evidence and make it easily accessible to task force members. Below Moss's name was the name Augustus Cesare, who Tracy deduced had some cruel parents. Cesare's job, apparently, had been to work with Gunderson. That alone elicited her sympathy. Moss and Tracy also weren't on speaking terms. He was one of the detectives she had accused of taking money from the Last Line drug task force. Like Hattie and Nolasco, Moss was a self-indulgent ass. He could have been the leak.

Faz was one of the task force investigators. Del had been brought in sometime after he joined the Homicide Unit. Tracy didn't see either leaking information. The public information officer had been Blair

Bender. The PIO knew only what the lead investigator told him, and Tracy doubted Johnny Nolasco would have told Bender about the angel's wings.

The forensic pathologist had been a young Stuart Funk, King County's current medical examiner. Tracy didn't view Funk, who didn't talk much in general, as a possible leak. Someone in his office, however, could have been.

Tracy had already used federal databases to confirm that two of the five named suspects had been incarcerated in Washington State prisons at the time of the Route 99 Killer's final victims. A third suspect, Alex Bright, had moved to Georgia before those killings.

Tracy had run the two remaining names through the same federal and state databases. She did not receive a hit for Dwight Thomas McDonnel, meaning he had never been arrested for a crime or otherwise provided his DNA. She'd run McDonnel's name through other databases to determine where he had lived these past years, then searched to determine if there had been unsolved murders of young women in those areas.

The last man, Levi Bishop, had been incarcerated in Washington State for domestic abuse, a felony, after the task force had disbanded. He had spent six years at the Monroe Criminal Correctional Complex. Paroled, he had moved to Idaho. Tracy would check, but she doubted the task force would have remained disbanded if Idaho suddenly experienced a rash of killings of young women branded with angel's wings.

As a convicted felon, Bishop had been required to provide a DNA sample. Tracy would ask Mike Melton to run Bishop's sample through CODIS, an acronym for the Combined DNA Index System. The national automated system, developed in the 1990s, included DNA samples collected from criminal offenders, DNA found at crime scenes, DNA profiles obtained from unidentified human remains, and DNA voluntarily provided by family members of missing persons. The system had been relatively new when the Route 99 killings were at their apex and had, in the intervening years, become much more refined.

Tracy would have to bribe Melton, but even a bribe might not get priority for a twenty-five-year-old case. Melton and the Washington State Patrol Crime Lab were under a 2017 legislative order to oversee the DNA processing of some 10,000 rape case kits. King County had 1,600 such kits to process. It was a worthy challenge that stretched Melton's lab to its limits.

Tracy called SPD's liaison at the Washington State Office of the Attorney General and asked the liaison to search the Homicide Investigation Tracking System, or HITS, criminal database using search words like "angel" and "wings."

Half an hour later, the liaison emailed Tracy with paperwork for each of the Route 99 Killer's victims. In each file she scrolled to the section asking questions about the victim's lifestyle. Question 102 asked whether the crime had been "sex related." In all but one file, the fourth victim, the "no" box had been checked.

She scrolled to question 105 of the fourth victim:

Was semen found in body cavities of the victim?

1. ☐ No
2. ☒ Yes

That surprised her. She had understood no DNA material existed. A note had been typed below the box:

> Given the victim's occupation, the presence of semen may not be determinative of the killer and may be a mixture of several johns.

She scrolled back to the top of the form to determine the detective who had filled it out.

> Officer/Detective: Last Name: Fazzio, First Name: Vic

Someone knocked on Tracy's office door. She looked to the clock in the lower right corner of her computer screen. She'd been so absorbed in her work, she'd missed lunch.

"Come in," she said, thinking *speak of the devil*, though Faz was ordinarily not one to knock.

The door pushed in.

Johnny Nolasco stood in her office doorway. He looked like he was chewing nails.

CHAPTER 3

Tracy closed Lisa Childress's file and slid it beneath others, out of sight. She'd once said Nolasco could look like someone with a pointed stick up his ass, wincing with each movement, but his current expression appeared to be directed less at Tracy and more at his circumstance, which made her apprehensive. Nolasco clearly wasn't happy to learn his nemesis would be pursuing an investigation he had failed to close—and perhaps find his mistakes.

"Captain," Tracy said.

Nolasco stepped in. "Don't act like you don't know what this is about, Crosswhite."

"What is this about?" she said, toying with him.

He looked like he had swallowed what he was about to say, then said, "Chief says you're looking into the Route 99 killings and asked for help."

"Almost."

"Almost what?"

"Almost correct. Chief ordered me to look into the Route 99 killings, and I suggested Faz could help since he was on your task force."

Nolasco shut his eyes for a beat, a tic that could be unsettling. "Well, that might be, but Chief Weber didn't ask me to reassign Vic."

"No?" Tracy said, confused for a moment before the developing picture emerged.

"No," Nolasco said. "She told me to help you."

Her stomach clenched. Nolasco wasn't gloating, far from it. He had no doubt just deduced that Weber, well aware of Tracy and Nolasco's volatile history and general dislike of one another, was using him. Weber wanted the serial killer cases resolved, but if Tracy failed, Weber would want to place that failure directly on Tracy's shoulders. She likely presumed Nolasco would support any disparaging report that could hasten Tracy's departure out the SPD door.

Tracy fought against displaying her discomfort. "So how do you want to go about this?" she asked.

Nolasco scoffed. "You tell me. They're your cold cases."

In other words, he wasn't going to help her efforts to make him look bad. "Okay. I have some questions about the investigation," Tracy said.

"Let me stop you right there," Nolasco said. "If your questions are going to insinuate my task force failed in any aspect of this investigation, you can save your breath. I'm proud of the work we did. We did everything we could have."

"Except catch the killer," Tracy said, unable to resist, though she knew from her work as head of the Cowboy Task Force there was no "right" way to hunt a serial killer, just best guesses, hunches, and previously used techniques. A task force was not the glamour and series of dramatic breakthroughs depicted on television. It was day-to-day routine and mind-numbing drudgery. You couldn't predict what the killer would do, because serial killers weren't motivated by anger, greed, jealousy, profit, or revenge, which makes them the most bewildering, disturbing, and difficult to catch. They enjoyed killing and often saw their acts as fulfilling some higher purpose. Twenty-five years ago, catching them would have been even more difficult without the current advances in DNA testing and other forensic sciences, as well as technology like cameras on cell phones.

Nolasco did not verbally respond, but those jaw muscles looked to be crunching those nails again. Finally, he said, "I don't have much time."

Tracy offered him a seat, waited a beat until he took it, then said, "Did you have any solid suspects or leads?"

Nolasco took a breath and grimaced like the stick had jabbed him. "Four or five. I can't remember the exact number."

But he did remember. Tracy was certain the failure to catch the killer had eaten at Nolasco's enormous ego. It was the only investigation he and his erstwhile partner, Floyd Hattie, had failed to close. As Faz had once put it, "That's thirteen big matzo balls hanging out there."

Then Nolasco proved he remembered. "We eliminated two suspects because they were in prison on other charges at the time of the last killings. A third suspect had moved out of state, making him unlikely but still possible. We had one or two other suspects. Dwight something."

"McDonnel."

"Yeah. McDonnel. He'd never been convicted of a crime, but coworkers at his place of employment indicated he picked up prostitutes on the Aurora strip. We tailed him a couple of nights, but nothing came of it."

"Anyone else?" Tracy asked, not even pretending to be taking notes, which seemed to unnerve Nolasco. His gaze kept shifting from Tracy to the pen and pad of paper resting on her desk.

"Levi Bishop. I remember his name because of the jeans. I always thought he could be our guy. He got pinched for domestic violence. Beat the hell out of his live-in girlfriend and did six years. That was right around the time the killings stopped."

"What happened to him?" Tracy asked.

"He was paroled for good behavior and, as far as I can recall, left the area."

"To where?"

"Don't know."

"You didn't check?"

Nolasco bristled. "The task force had been disbanded."

"Did you run his DNA to determine if it matched the DNA left behind at any of the crime scenes?"

"DNA analysis back then wasn't what it is now, and the killer, it was determined, wore a condom, making DNA scarce."

"Is that a no?"

"Check the file, Crosswhite. Like I said, the killings stopped, the task force disbanded, and I moved to active homicides."

"The task force disbanded but the files were never closed. As the lead investigator it remained your investigation. Yours and Floyd Hattie's."

"Hattie retired."

"Then yours."

"And now it's yours. What's your point?"

"Just trying to find out if you ever ran down Levi Bishop, and if there were any murdered young women with markings that resembled angel's wings carved in their shoulder near where he relocated."

Nolasco's eyes quickly roamed the room. No doubt he looked for boxes containing his task force's investigation. They had not yet been brought up from the vault. "I would have received an alert if that had been the case. The angel's wings evidence was never released to the public. How do you know about it?" Nolasco asked.

"You had a leak."

He looked like he'd taken a punch. "The fuck we did."

"A reporter knew about the angel's wings. Someone had to have told her."

"The same reporter who wrote those articles about the drug task force?"

Unable to secure hard evidence to prove Moss Gunderson or Marcella Weber were on the Last Line's payroll, Tracy had gone instead to Anita Childress, and the *Times* had run a series of articles on Tracy's search for, and discovery of, Lisa Childress living in Escondido. But to tell that story, the paper also had to tell of Lisa's sudden disappearance shortly after leaving her home in the middle of the night to meet a source who claimed to have information on the drug task force. The source had been found shot in the head. Childress had vanished.

Tracy suspected Nolasco or Hattie had been the leak, since it had been their egos on the line. "Why would you ask if Lisa Childress was the source of the leaked information? Her articles never mentioned the Angel of Death cases."

"Because she was the *P-I*'s investigative reporter. She showed up at press briefings we held about the Route 99 killings. And the daughter came to you with a theory her mother was killed because of one of her investigations—the *Times* certainly intimated that to have been the case in the series of articles they wrote casting this department and your fellow officers in such a piss-poor light."

Many of Seattle's PD had supported Tracy and Del's talking to the media, but there had also been the expected blowback. "Did you tell Lisa Childress about the angel's wings carved in the victims' shoulders?"

Nolasco laughed as if he found her question so ludicrous as to be comical. "Tell me why that is important, or relevant to catching the killer now?"

He also didn't answer her question.

"The file indicates the killer first targeted prostitutes and drug addicts, then turned to suburban women not in the sex trade. What was your theory for the sudden shift? It definitely put the killer at greater risk of being caught."

"We concluded his initial victims were victims of opportunity, marginalized women on the fringe. Then he sought greater attention and killed women who would get more mainstream media coverage to taunt us."

It wasn't a bad theory. From her work on the Cowboy Task Force, Tracy had learned serial killers were narcissists who thought they were smarter than everyone else and would never be caught. The Cowboy, Nabil Kotar, had told Tracy he saw himself as an actor starring in the lead role of a serial killer movie.

Nolasco looked at his watch. "Anything else?"

"That's it for now."

He got up and turned for the door, then stopped and turned back. "Do you have any leads?"

So, he was interested. "I have some things I'm going to do to get started."

"Such as?"

"Thought I'd set up another tip line, use social media, and bribe Mike Melton to maybe do some DNA work, among other things."

Nolasco said, "Weber will use your notoriety as evidence she's serious about finding the killer. She'll be throwing your ass on the bonfire, and you'll get burned when you don't find the killer."

Tracy suspected that ass on fire had once been Nolasco's, and she knew how it felt to be in that position. It was the closest thing to empathy Tracy had ever heard from him. "That bonfire is already lit," she said.

"How so?"

"Weber said the *Times* is running a series on the anniversary of the last killings—the last one was twenty-five years ago—and the articles won't be positive."

Nolasco made his chewing-nails face again. "Did you have anything to do with those articles?"

So like him to be paranoid about her stabbing him in the back. "Nothing."

"We ran down more than two thousand tips, processed some three hundred fingerprints, and seriously interviewed dozens of suspects."

"We can get an officer to monitor the tip line I set up, compare any tips with the tips you received, and try to find a thread, or at least run down anything with potential," Tracy said.

"Moss was the lead control officer," Nolasco said, leaving unsaid that Tracy shouldn't expect much in the way of support.

She'd already figured that, and she figured Moss, who Faz and Del both said was lazy, wouldn't have coordinated the tips. "Who was Augustus Cesare?" Tracy asked.

"Augie? He was Moss's lackey. Moss had me pull him from patrol. Said Cesare helped him track evidence in another case and knew computers, one of the first in our section who did. He kept a color-coded spreadsheet of the tips, determined if any overlapped, and named the task force detective assigned to follow up."

"I'll see if I can find the spreadsheet."

"He put it on a disk. Have TESU convert it to a format you can use." Nolasco referenced the Technical and Electronic Support Unit, which was part of the Violent Crimes Section's Intel Unit, also located on the seventh floor. "Let's also get a young officer to monitor the tip line and work with the original spreadsheet. Someone also computer savvy. They can do all kinds of things now we couldn't do back then."

Was she mistaken, or did Nolasco damn near sound helpful?

"I'd like to also start a Facebook page to work in concert with the tip line. I'll have the page made up with the names and photographs of the victims, their personal histories, and the dates and locations they were last seen. Maybe someone will recall seeing or remember something about one of them."

"That was nearly thirty years ago," Nolasco said. "It's a long shot."

"We found Lisa Childress." A woman had recognized Childress's Facebook picture, and her tip led Tracy to Escondido. "All we need is one tip on one victim to get us started."

"Childress was a reporter for a prominent newspaper. These women were prostitutes."

"Not all of them."

Nolasco let out a burst of air and fingered his mustache. "Do what you want, but focus on his later killings."

Tracy would talk with Melton and have him run Levi Bishop's DNA against what little DNA had been found at the one crime scene Faz had documented in the HITS questionnaire. Tracy knew the lab was under the gun, but she also knew Melton's weakness—sandwiches from Salumi, the famed Italian deli in Pioneer Square, especially now that his family had mandated he diet to lower his cholesterol and blood pressure.

"I'm also going to make an appointment to talk to an FBI profiler who Kins and I consulted in the Cowboy case and get her take on the killings, the suspects, what was and wasn't done."

"Profilers are bullshit, Crosswhite. They're one step above the psychics and their Ouija boards. Don't put too much faith in that crap," Nolasco said.

She didn't, but what did they have to lose at this point?

"I'm going to ask her if she has any insight into why the killer switched his victims to middle-class women, and why he ultimately stopped killing."

"He stopped because he's dead or incarcerated for some other crime," Nolasco said.

Tracy had the same thought, but closure for the families would only come from knowing that was true. "Thought I'd also look up where McDonnel has lived the last thirty years and determine whether there have been any unexplained killings of young women in those areas. Maybe pay him a visit and see if it rattles his cage."

Nolasco stared at her. Tracy could almost see the gears shifting. She knew Nolasco's type well enough to know he hated the thought of her solving the killings without him receiving any of the credit. "Keep me posted on getting the tip line and the Facebook page set up. If you get any blowback, tell them to talk to me. And let me know when you meet with Bishop or McDonnel . . . and the FBI profiler. I'll go with you."

"No need. I know you're busy. I can handle it."

"Look, Weber ordered me to work with you. I don't like the arrangement any more than you do, but I'm following orders and trying to make the best of the situation. Maybe we can bring some closure to this thing."

Tracy had always likened Nolasco to a reptile—thin, cold blooded, and scaly—but maybe he had an ounce of human decency. Maybe he *was* thinking about someone other than himself for a change—closure for the victims' families. "I'll let you know when I get it set up."

"Frankly, I think this is nothing more than a publicity stunt and a colossal waste of my time and resources without any likely benefit. But maybe I can get it off my back."

And just as quickly, the reptilian scales emerged from beneath the collar of his shirt.

CHAPTER 4

October 1994
Seattle, Washington

Johnny Nolasco trailed Floyd Hattie, Police Chief Sandy Clarridge, and Stephen Martinez, assistant chief of criminal investigations, into the press briefing room. Both Clarridge and Martinez wore the department's French-blue short-sleeve shirts. Nolasco and Hattie, dressed in sports coats and ties, took up positions behind the podium, their backs against the backdrop bearing the Seattle Police Department logo. Nolasco stared at the throng of reporters, microphones, and television cameras for what would be a public flogging, though he doubted anything could be worse than the tongue-lashing he and Hattie had just privately received.

The Route 99 serial killer had just murdered his tenth victim, but unlike his previous nine, Mary Ellen Schmid had been a married lawyer working in the civil division of the Seattle city attorney's office and living in an upper- to middle-class suburb. Schmid's car had been disabled in a downtown Seattle parking lot. A security guard found her body inside. She, too, had been marked with angel's wings on her left shoulder.

"Before we get started," Clarridge said to the sea of reporters, two to three times more than had attended the press briefings for the prior nine victims, "I want the public to know the Seattle Police Department has provided all available resources to the task force that has the sole purpose of catching the person responsible for these killings."

That wasn't exactly true, but Nolasco wasn't about to debate it, and he refrained from making a face, or looking at Hattie, who no doubt had the same thought. The task force had not been established until after the killer's fourth victim, when the angel's wings could no longer be ignored. Nolasco had asked to head the investigation, believing it would enhance his resume and further fast-track his ascension through the Seattle PD. He had designs on an administrative job, possibly chief of police and, depending on how things went, a political career. But Nolasco's task force had been limited in the number of officers he could utilize. Nobody would admit it, and certainly not Clarridge, but those nine women hadn't justified the department's full resources, not to mention the expense.

Nolasco was the more convenient scapegoat.

"I will let Johnny Nolasco, the task force's lead detective, discuss specifics," Clarridge said, his cue for Nolasco to step forward and absorb the first lash. But the initial question was directed to Clarridge.

"Chief Clarridge, given the differences between this victim and the other nine, including the location of this killing, what leads you to believe it is the same killer? And is your appearance at this press briefing indicative of those differences?" The questions on everyone's mind had come from a female investigative reporter for the *Seattle Post-Intelligencer.*

"The nature of the victim has not and will not dictate the resources we are devoting to finding the killer," Clarridge said. "We formed this task force more than a year ago, and we have held regular press briefings."

"But this is the first press briefing you've attended," the reporter said.

Childress. The reporter's name is . . . Lisa Childress. An odd duck, Nolasco recalled, *but not afraid to ask tough questions.*

"Not true," Clarridge said. "I held a press briefing to announce the formation of the task force and the department's devotion of resources with the sole intent of finding the killer. That intent hasn't changed."

Clarridge, who flushed when angry and had a drinker's nose, glowed a splotchy red. He signaled again, with a bit more urgency, for Nolasco to step to the podium. Nolasco dutifully did so.

"Detective, are you certain this killing was by the same person who killed the other nine victims, given the differences in the victim and the location of this killing?" Childress asked.

"We are," Nolasco said. "I am not at liberty to discuss specifics, but I can assure you the killer is the same person who killed the other nine victims."

"Is that because of the nature of the killings—strangulation? Or is there something else linking all the victims?"

"The cause of death is one consideration. Again, I'm not at liberty to discuss evidence at any of the crime scenes or the task force's investigation."

"So it's evidence at the crime scene? DNA?" Childress asked.

"Again, I won't comment on specifics," Nolasco said, internally chastising himself for his sloppy answer.

"Why has this task force been unable to catch this killer?" another reporter asked.

"The killer doesn't want to be caught," Nolasco said. "These are not crimes of passion or anger. Serial killers have no relation to their victims, which is precisely why they choose them, and why they are so difficult to catch."

"Do you have enough resources?" Childress asked.

Nolasco hadn't had enough, not until that morning. Clarridge had approved several additional detectives and forensic experts to join the team. "Absolutely," he said. "The department only has so many bodies to direct to one investigation, but resources have not been an issue."

"What do you have to say to the families of the nine victims who have waited for closure?" a television reporter for KRIX Channel 8 said.

Nolasco saw this as a moment to take a stand for his team. He would not fall on his sword to save the brass's collective asses. "We're doing everything we can to find this individual. My task force, these detectives, are working tirelessly around the clock. We have not and never will forget any victim—the daughters, spouses, and sisters of the surviving family members. It's what sets us apart, why we volunteered for this difficult job. We empathize not only with the families' pain of having lost a loved one, but their pain of being in limbo. We will continue to move forward and, as Chief Clarridge said, to devote as many resources as possible to solving these crimes."

"How confident are you that you will catch this individual?" the television reporter asked.

"All I can say—" Nolasco started, but Clarridge cut him off.

"This task force will find the killer," Clarridge said, cashing a check on Nolasco's bank account. Then he doubled down. "Count on it."

CHAPTER 5

Wednesday, July 8, Present Day
Seattle, Washington

Tracy sought and received Chief Weber's permission to work directly with the Public Affairs Office, where she spent the rest of her day setting up the social media page for the thirteen victims. She forwarded photographs of the victims, short biographies, and the dates and locations where the women's bodies had been discovered to her contact and requested the page also include a tip line. She called the detective who had manned the Lisa Childress tip line and confirmed she was available to monitor this one. Tracy would have Nolasco clear the assignment with the detective's sergeant. The page would be up and running in a matter of hours.

Next, she contacted the victims' families, those she could reach, to inform them that the investigation would again be actively pursued and told them of the Facebook page. She got a variety of responses—from tears of joy and thanks to skepticism and hostility.

Then, she ran down Dwight McDonnel's current address—a rented home in White Center, a suburb twenty minutes south of downtown

Seattle and associated with a high crime rate. McDonnel had also lived in Ballard, Wedgwood, and two neighborhoods north of Seattle. She checked to determine if there had been any unsolved murders of young women in those areas during the dates McDonnel lived there. She did not find any.

She then turned her attention to Levi Bishop, who had returned to Washington from Twin Falls, Idaho, where he had moved after his parole for a domestic violence conviction. Tracy called the Twin Falls Police Department and spoke to the detective sergeant of the Criminal Investigation Unit under the Operations Division. The sergeant told her the department had a short list of unsolved murders dating back one hundred years, checked the time frame Tracy provided, and said there were no unsolved murders of young women. He said he'd check with other departments nearby and report back.

Deciding it best not to leave a stone unturned, she also looked up the third living and not incarcerated suspect, Alex Bright. Bright had moved to Pierce County, Georgia, for work, but he, too, had moved back to Washington State, living just outside Spokane. Tracy contacted the Blackshear Police Department and the Office of the Sheriff in Pierce County and again provided details. They, too, did not have any recent unsolved murders of young women. Tracy wondered if Bright had relatives in the area. If so, he could have traveled home from Georgia, killed another victim while visiting, then departed. She wouldn't rule him out just yet.

All three men were now in their midfifties to early sixties. Other reasons killers stopped were medical conditions, injuries, and old age. She made a note to check the suspects' medical records.

Finally, Tracy set up an interview for the next morning with Amanda Santos, the FBI agent and profiler she and Kins used in the Cowboy investigation. She emailed Nolasco with the time and location of that meeting, figuring he wouldn't attend since he thought profilers were "bullshit," and she also provided him a summary of what she had accomplished.

He responded with one word. "Okay."

Tracy was about to shut down her computer for the day and head home when her desk phone rang. An inside call. She figured it was Nolasco.

"I've arranged for a press release to go out this evening stating you have reopened the Route 99 investigation," Chief Weber said. "I've also arranged for a press conference tomorrow morning. I want you to be there."

Tracy's gut told her this was the wrong move. "I'd recommend against a press conference, Chief Weber, all due respect."

"I want the public to know it is our intent to find the killer and bring closure to the victims' families."

No, Weber's intent was to capitalize on Tracy being a three-time Medal of Valor recipient and on her recently publicized cold case successes. Tracy hated the publicity, especially for Weber's intended purpose. She believed the focus should be on the victims and their families, whom she had already called. She knew Weber wouldn't be persuaded by that argument, so she tried something much more practical and worrisome.

"I'm concerned that if the killer is still alive," she said, "and not incarcerated or incapacitated for some reason, he might view a press conference as a challenge by SPD and resume his killing. Captain Nolasco believes he changed his victims to middle-class women to increase publicity."

"That cat's out of the bag as soon as the *Times* runs its first article," Weber said, dismissing Tracy's concerns without thought and confirming Tracy's suspicions.

"The *Times* running articles is not the same as SPD broadcasting it is reopening its investigation. Why not just advise the press that the investigation remains active, and we're doing everything we can to find the killer and bring closure to the families?"

"The press briefing announcement is already up on the blotter."

Tracy pulled up the SPD's public blotter on her computer and only needed to read the headline to confirm her worst fears.

Cold Case Detective Tracy Crosswhite to Hunt for Route 99 Serial Killer

She quickly scanned the article. Not only did the headline and the first few sentences omit any mention of Nolasco, they read like Tracy would clean up his task force's mess.

This would not go over well, which, Tracy suspected, was also Weber's intent.

"Chief, do not make this personal."

"I don't do personal. This is strictly police business. What's done is done." Weber sounded like a Roman official washing her hands after issuing a death sentence. Reasoning with her was a waste of breath.

Tracy disconnected and called Nolasco's desk phone, eyeing the time in the corner of her computer. Nolasco answered on the third ring. "Crosswhite," he said.

"Did the chief get ahold of you?"

"No. Why?"

"You need to call her—"

"Hold on. Another call."

"No, Captain, don't—"

But Nolasco had placed Tracy on hold. She hung up and quickly left her office, hurrying down the hallway, dodging people to get to Nolasco's interior office. She knocked once and pushed the door open. Nolasco had his desk phone to his ear, his coloring already flushed and the look in his eyes fierce.

"Yes. I'll be there. Ten a.m." Nolasco hung up the phone.

"I told her it was a mistake, the police blotter, the press conference. I told her it was a mistake."

"What blotter?"

Tracy winced. But Nolasco would see the announcement eventually. Better now when she had the chance to explain she had nothing to do with it. "Weber had an announcement put up on SPD's police blotter."

Nolasco hit the keys on his keyboard and his eyes shifted left to right, reading. He pursed his lips so tight his mustache covered them. Then he swore under his breath.

"I had nothing to do with this. I tried to call you—"

"To rub it in?"

"To get you to talk sense into Weber. Forget for a minute what it says about me. It reads like a challenge to the killer."

"The killer is dead, Crosswhite," Nolasco said. "Dead or incarcerated. This isn't about feeding his ego. It's about feeding yours."

"What? I tried to stop her."

"Bullshit. I know all about your and Weber's relationship. So do a lot of other people here."

"What are you talking about?"

"How Weber comes down to your office to genuflect before the great Tracy Crosswhite; you don't think I know you butter her bread by solving cases and helping her get funding from the city, and she feeds your ego with medals?"

The *Times* had run articles on Tracy's uncovering of the illegal activities of the drug task force, but Tracy had no evidence, beyond the word of a former drug dealer, to prove Marcella Weber had her hands in the pot of confiscated money, and the *Times* wasn't about to print speculation and innuendo. No one within the department, save for Faz and Del, knew Tracy had confronted Weber and tanked their relationship.

But Tracy wasn't about to justify herself to a man who listened to reason even less than Weber did.

Nolasco gave Tracy a painful, ugly smile. "Let me tell you something, Crosswhite. This is all fine. Really. You know why? Because you won't find the killer, not after all these years. And notoriety isn't what you think. Not this kind. The higher you sit, the farther the fall, and the more painful the landing. And when you do fall, I'm going to be there to tell you, Weber, and everyone else: 'I told you so.'"

—

Tracy left work and drove home to Redmond, east across Lake Washington. The nine-hundred-square-foot farmhouse to which Tracy and Dan had originally moved had been everything she had loved about growing up in her tiny hometown of Cedar Grove. The warm and cozy house, isolated on five acres, had felt far removed from her office. She and Dan had tried to make their remodel feel just as warm. They burned wood in the river-rock fireplace insert at night and sat with blankets on comfortable furniture reading books to Daniella, sharing a glass of wine or port, and, on occasion, making love on the sheepskin rug with the fire glowing behind the glass.

Tracy needed that place tonight, but first she needed a long run through the foothills to work off her desire to again knee Nolasco in the balls, as she had done during combat training at the police academy.

She stepped through the front door and dropped her keys in the glass bowl on the pony wall. The sound of the keys in the bowl set off the inevitable and expected alarm—Rex and Sherlock barking—and Tracy picked up Roger, her cat, just as their two Rhodesian-mastiffs barreled around the corner, leaving muddy footprints on the tile floor. Rex jumped up when he reached Tracy, putting his dirty paws on her white blouse and jeans. Roger shot from her hold, leaving scratch marks on the insides of Tracy's forearms.

"Down. Down." She kneed Rex to keep him from further jumping.

Both dogs were wet, and Sherlock took the moment to shake water all over Tracy and the room. Tracy gripped them by their collars and quickly ushered them to an open door leading to the backyard, nearly colliding with Therese coming from the opposite direction and calling for both dogs.

"I'm really sorry, Mrs. O. I thought this door was closed. I took off their sensors to the dog door to give them both a bath. They were full of dirt from their afternoon run with Mr. O'Leary."

The property also provided access to running trails in the surrounding foothills. So much for Tracy's stress-release run. The cozy cottage image had also evaporated.

"I'll get the floor cleaned up," Therese said, then she noticed the mud prints on Tracy's clothes. "I'm sorry, Mrs. O."

"Don't worry about it," Tracy said. "Giving these two a bath is a thankless job. I appreciate you doing it." Tracy's mind shifted to her daughter. "Where's Daniella?"

"Mr. O took her with him to the shower. She was dirtier than the two dogs. Why don't you get changed? I'll keep the dogs locked outside until they dry, and get things cleaned up," Therese said.

Tracy thanked her, removed her flats, and climbed the stairs to the master bedroom. She didn't want to run without Dan. He was her Prozac, a calming influence in her life. She heard water running in the bathroom shower and Dan singing "How much is that doggy in the window," complete with barking, which caused Daniella to laugh uproariously, as Therese liked to say. Tracy quietly opened the bathroom door and watched her husband and daughter behind the fogged shower glass. Dan had his back to the door, holding Daniella.

After a moment, Daniella spotted Tracy. Her eyes widened and she held out her arms and kicked her legs. "Momma. Momma."

Dan turned and smiled. "Who is it? Mommy? Mommy's here!"

Tracy walked forward.

"You want to dry her off," Dan said from behind the glass and held out Daniella.

Tracy shook her head, tears clouding her vision. She unbuttoned her blouse.

"Everything okay?" Dan asked.

Tracy smiled. To hell with her clothes. They needed to be rinsed before washing anyway. She climbed into the shower fully dressed and felt, for the first time all day, like she belonged.

———

Tracy and Dan dressed in casual clothes, and they ate dinner in the backyard beneath the "Gazebo Dan Built," which was what Dan called the outdoor living area he and a friend had erected earlier in the summer. The name was a play on the New York Yankees' original stadium, which was called "The House That Babe Ruth Built." Dan barbecued hamburgers, and Tracy made French fries and strawberry milkshakes. Tracy's father had been a strawberry-milkshake man, and she'd also jumped on that bandwagon. Strawberries tasted sweeter to her than chocolate.

Dan respected her wishes and didn't bring up the subject of work throughout dinner. They talked about his run, and he filled in Tracy on Therese's report of Daniella's first few days at a day care in Redmond.

"Seems our Little Miss Strawberry Face over there is not the best sharer. She apparently smacked a little boy who took her crayon."

"Taking her crayon isn't sharing. It's third-degree robbery. I'd say she was standing up for herself," Tracy said, smiling.

"Sounds like something a cop would say," Dan said. "Honestly? I was pleased also. I'm hoping it's a harbinger of how she'll respond when she's dating, and some boy gets fresh."

"Oh God. I don't want to even think about that. How was the non-sharing resolved?"

"According to Therese, a juice box and Goldfish solve the world's problems. But we do need to teach her social skills besides pummeling boys," Dan said. "You want bedtime duty or cleanup?"

"Having cleaned up once, I'll take bedtime duty."

Daniella went down easily, no doubt tired after her big day at day care. When Tracy came downstairs, Dan was seated in the living room with two small glasses of port wine. "Wine and milkshakes. I feel my stomach curdling already," Tracy said.

"This is that port from Portugal we had the other night at that restaurant. I found it at the local liquor store."

Tracy sipped her port. It wasn't a strawberry milkshake, but it was sweet. "Sorry about the tears earlier."

"What's going on?"

"I guess it's just lingering anger from being unable to get all those who were on the Last Line's payroll."

"I assume you mean Chief Weber."

"The chief called me into her office first thing this morning—never a good sign. She wants me to solve the Route 99 serial killings."

"Those killings must be twenty-five years old," Dan said.

"Nearly thirty since the first," Tracy said.

"Didn't you tell me Johnny Nolasco ran that task force?"

"I did—when I was investigating the Lisa Childress disappearance. The killings were one of four investigative pieces she worked at the time of her disappearance."

"So why does Weber think you can do what Nolasco couldn't?"

"I'm not sure she thinks I can, but she needs the publicity of the PD going after another big case to strengthen her argument to get city council funding, and I'm relevant because of my recent cases." Tracy sipped her port. "I tried to talk her out of publicly reopening the investigation. When I couldn't, I shifted strategy and asked that she assign Faz to work with me. He worked the task force as a young detective. She got me help, but it isn't Faz."

About to sip his port, Dan lowered his glass. "Don't tell me."

"She assigned Nolasco."

"That's bullshit, Tracy. She's just trying to make your life so miserable you'll quit."

"And doing a good job of it. If I succeed, Nolasco will take the credit. We know that. If I fail, the failure will fall squarely on my shoulders. He won't have my back. He said as much this afternoon. But that's not what I'm most worried about. What I'm most worried about is Weber poking a stick at a sleeping dog."

"What do you mean?"

"When I hunted the Cowboy, I learned a lot about these psychopaths. They have huge egos. With each murder they get more emboldened and don't believe they'll be caught. The Route 99 Killer went dormant years ago, but before he did, he changed his victims from sex workers on the strip to four middle-class women living in the suburbs. Nolasco believes he was challenging them by upping the ante."

"And you think it's better to let a sleeping dog lie."

"No, I think it's better to not let the sleeping dog know you're there. Weber is using me and my reputation to help secure funding, but I'm worried this killer could see SPD's reopening of the investigation as a challenge to kill again."

"You told her this?"

"And Nolasco. Neither conversation went well."

Dan set down his port. "Okay. Let's not play the 'what if' game. You don't know if the killer is even still alive. If he's alive, and he hasn't killed in twenty-five years, it could mean something else intervened, maybe prison, or some form of counseling or medication. The odds, after so many years, are he isn't going to kill again, aren't they?"

"Odds exist because people bet. And in this case, if we bet and lose, we're talking about someone's life."

"What are you going to do?"

"I don't have much choice. If I fail to follow orders again, I'll be dismissed, and no doubt someone else will take up the investigation. Not to pat myself on the back, but if anyone is going to catch this guy, I want to be that person."

"So, you're going to do it."

Tracy nodded. "If he's out there, Dan, I'm going to nail his ass. Not to show up Nolasco, or to make Weber look good to the city council, or to feed my incredibly large ego . . ." She smiled but the humor faded. "I'm going to nail his ass for all those young women he murdered, and to bring closure to their families. He's going in either a coffin or a prison cell. His choice, if and when the time comes."

"Well . . . at least we know from which side of the gene pool Daniella gets her anger-management issues," Dan said.

CHAPTER 6

Thursday, July 9, Present Day
Seattle, Washington

The following morning, Tracy entered the conference room beside the press briefing room. Weber and Nolasco were present, though neither said much to her or to each other. Shortly after Tracy entered the room, Seattle's newly elected mayor, Charles Garcia, entered. A Latino Republican, Garcia did not see eye to eye with several council members' politics and the push to defund the police. Garcia grew up in a rough Seattle neighborhood and attended the University of Washington on a football scholarship, playing on the offensive line during the university's heyday. He graduated with a degree in business and ran a successful company before his plunge into politics. He had promised to decrease crime in downtown Seattle, especially violent crimes and property crimes that had driven many businesses out of King County. He also sought to hire and train more officers, particularly officers of color, and to get more of those officers out on the street. His presence at the press conference highlighted the importance of the upcoming budget battle pitting him and Weber against the city council.

Weber turned on her personality when Garcia entered. Following introductions and a general discussion of the morning's events, she concluded with "After the mayor speaks, I will stress the significance of our renewed efforts to find the Route 99 Killer and resolve cold cases in general, then turn the podium over to the two of you. Any questions?"

Tracy questioned why Weber was potentially baiting a serial killer, but she swallowed those words.

Local media packed the pressroom, not surprising given the presence of both the mayor and chief of police, but also because the briefing came on the heels of Tracy's recent and heavily publicized successes. Garcia took the podium first. A big man, he looked like he could strap on pads and still hit someone. Then he walked. Or rather, he limped, from a balky knee and back.

"Thank you all for coming out today," Garcia said to the media. He reiterated his campaign pledge to reduce violent crime and the backlog of rape cold cases, and return business to downtown Seattle. "Seattle law enforcement is committed to bring justice to victims of violent crime, to punish those responsible, and to bring closure to families," he said, then mentioned restoring Seattle as the Pacific Northwest's Emerald City.

Garcia stepped back and Weber, in full-dress uniform, stepped forward and thanked the mayor. "The Seattle Police Department under my command has pledged to reduce crime and to resolve cold cases. With the latter in mind, this year I appointed Detective Tracy Crosswhite to the SPD Cold Case Unit."

That statement was not true. Tracy had been reassigned to the Cold Case Unit by Nolasco upon returning from a PTSD medical leave after hunting a killer in Cedar Grove. Nolasco had filled Tracy's position on the Violent Crime Section's A Team with another female detective. Cold Cases, technically within the Violent Crimes Section, had been Tracy's only option.

"Detective Crosswhite's distinguished career includes three Medals of Valor. She also has experience apprehending serial killers, including the killer known as the Cowboy. Since taking over the Cold Case Unit under the direction of her captain, Johnny Nolasco, Detective Crosswhite has resolved more than twenty cases, including the abduction and murder of fourteen young women by two sadistic serial killers in North Seattle that also resulted in the rescue of three women."

Not surprisingly, Weber made no mention of Lisa Childress or the illegal acts of the Last Line drug task force. Beside her, Nolasco cleared his throat. Tracy could smell his aftershave and sense his displeasure. Both made her queasy.

"Today, I am pleased to announce Detective Crosswhite, under my auspices, will undertake to resolve the thirteen Route 99 serial killings perpetrated between 1993 and 1995." Weber turned from the podium. "Captain Nolasco."

As the chief turned, a voice called out. "Chief Weber?" Tracy recognized Greg Bartholomew's nasal whine. The *Seattle Times'* police and courthouse reporter heaved himself from his chair and tugged at his well-worn blue sports coat. "Is the assignment of Detective Crosswhite to the Route 99 killings in anticipation of the *Seattle Times'* series of articles documenting those murders and the Seattle Police Department's failure to find the killer?"

Weber had clearly anticipated the question. Bartholomew had a history of negativity and a reputation for throwing gasoline on any fire.

"The series of articles to which you make reference was certainly a motivating factor in our decision to reopen the investigation, but SPD's primary motivation is to bring closure to the families of those thirteen victims, not to appease the media," Weber said.

"Is there new evidence to justify reopening those cases?" a female voice called out. Tracy recognized the voice, but it was out of place and unexpected. She was shocked to see Anita Childress standing at the back of the room.

"I'll let Captain Nolasco and Detective Crosswhite answer those questions," Weber said.

In other words, she'd put Nolasco and Tracy before the firing squad to dodge their bullets.

Weber gave Tracy and Nolasco a no-mistake-about-it glare to get to the dais.

Nolasco stepped to the microphone. "We are not at liberty to discuss specific evidence," he said in answer to Childress's question. "With advances in forensic sciences, this was the right time to reopen our investigation."

"There hasn't been a killing in twenty-five years," Bartholomew said. "Is this a case about closure for the families or about SPD rectifying a failed investigation?"

"SPD has nothing to rectify," Nolasco said. Tracy, well familiar with Nolasco's moods, could hear anger leaking into his tone.

Bartholomew poured more gas onto the flames. "You were the lead detective on the task force that failed to catch the killer, Captain Nolasco. Do you perceive this renewed effort as a resolution for the victims or for yourself?"

The muscles in Nolasco's jaw undulated. Chewing nails.

Before Nolasco could spit them out, Tracy stepped forward. Nolasco gave her a sideways glance, like looking at a dog he wasn't sure he could trust. "Every serial killer is difficult to catch. They do not desire to be caught, and they make great efforts to leave behind no evidence that would lead to their apprehension."

"But you successfully caught the Cowboy, Detective Crosswhite. What was the difference?" Anita Childress had just lobbed Tracy a softball. Ordinarily, Tracy would have been grateful to catch it, but with Nolasco already suspicious, Childress's presence at the conference, and her question, did not help.

"Timing and luck," she said, to deflect any perceived praise that could reflect badly on Nolasco. "I had the backing of my captain and my department and a dedicated team. We also caught the Cowboy years after the Route 99 serial killings, which allowed us to utilize advancements in the forensic sciences. If I may—" Tracy signaled to the detective who created the Facebook page, and those behind Tracy stepped aside. The detective put up photographs of the thirteen victims and gave SPD a plug for its robust social media presence used to generate tips.

Tracy's deflection worked. Subsequent questions focused on the missing women and the current investigation. Tracy was glad she had spent time with the individual files. By calling specific victims by name, it gave a personal touch to the long-dormant case.

Then Bartholomew fired another flaming arrow. "What do you say to the argument that SPD's motivation to find the killer relates to the fact that his last four victims were middle-class women living in Seattle suburbs?"

Knowing she'd get this question, Tracy had prepared. "I'd say the statement ignores the fact that every one of these women is marginalized simply because of her gender. The large percentage of murders, unrelated to gang violence, are young women killed by spouses, boyfriends, or someone they knew well. What this investigation says is SPD has not forgotten *any* of these thirteen women, regardless of their race, their profession, their age, or their socioeconomic status. It is our intent to find justice for each and every one of them."

She hoped her response put the question to bed once and for all.

Mayor Garcia stepped forward. Nolasco and Tracy stepped back. Garcia thanked those attending for coming and ended the press conference. Tracy looked down at Anita Childress and gave her a signal to hang around. She went back into the conference room to briefly discuss the morning's events. Garcia emphasized he wanted the killer found, and Weber guaranteed Tracy and Nolasco would do so. Nolasco did not acknowledge Tracy for coming to his aid before he departed, and she didn't expect that he would.

After the room had cleared, Tracy walked back to the pressroom to meet Anita Childress, but another woman intercepted her.

"Detective? I'm Angela Waylon. My daughter was Cathy."

Tracy had spent time with the file. Cathy Waylon had become addicted to painkillers. Her parents spent thousands on rehabilitation, but Cathy had eventually left home and walked the track.

"I'm sorry for your loss, Mrs. Waylon."

"My husband is sick with cancer. I'd like him to pass knowing that his little girl is finally at rest."

Tracy felt her heart breaking. "I'm going to do everything I can to give you that opportunity, Mrs. Waylon."

"Back in the nineties, the task force seemed to forget my daughter and the others like her. They seemed only interested in the last four victims. Can you tell me my Cathy won't be forgotten?"

"I promise I won't forget."

Angela Waylon nodded, but she left looking anything but certain.

Tracy approached Anita Childress. The two women did not embrace in a public setting. "I overheard," Childress said. "I can't imagine working under that kind of pressure."

"Not pressure. Motivation," Tracy said. "I didn't expect to see you here."

Childress smiled. "It's tougher to re-create a history than either my mother or I thought," she said. "I love my mother, but we found we had little in common, save for our mutual desire to remember the past. I could. She couldn't. We decided it was more important for me to look forward."

"Are you okay with that?" Tracy asked.

Childress shrugged. "I was treading water down there, so I came back here, talked to Bill Jorgensen, and got my job back. I see you're looking into another of my mother's investigative files."

"In a way I guess I am," Tracy said. "How is she? How's her memory?"

Childress shook her head. "She doesn't remember much, and my attempts to get her to do so just upset her. It was like talking about a person she had never met. This is better. I call her a couple times a week and I'll visit, but not to discuss the past."

"Unlikely then she remembers anything about this file?"

"Very unlikely," Childress said. "What is it you're interested in?"

"A task force member leaked information to your mother about the killer's method of killing."

"Angel's wings on the victims' shoulders," Childress said.

"And potential suspects. I'd like to find that leak and determine that person's motivation." Something else occurred to Tracy. Anita Childress had written the series of articles on the Last Line drug task force and Lisa Childress's investigation and subsequent disappearance. "Are you writing the articles about the task force?"

Childress frowned. "Bill thought having the daughter of the investigative reporter who originally covered the case would sell newspapers," she said, meaning her editor. "My mother came at the investigation from an angle no one else did."

"You're not going to release news of the angel's wings carved into each victim's shoulder; are you?"

"It was discussed, Tracy."

"Anita—"

"But I convinced Bill the information was clearly given to my mother in confidence, otherwise she would have made it public knowledge twenty-five years ago. If it was given in confidence, we need to honor that agreement. I also told him we have an obligation to the general public, that the release of details could make apprehending the person responsible even more difficult."

"I appreciate it," Tracy said.

"Any new insights into the killer?" Childress asked. "Off the record."

Tracy smiled. She didn't always see Anita as a reporter, but Anita had inherited her mother's curiosity. "Not yet, but you'll be the first to know." Her common refrain. Tracy checked her watch. She and Nolasco had a meeting with FBI profiler Amanda Santos. "Do me a favor?" she asked.

"Name it."

"If you think of anything, learn of anything, let me know?"

"To the extent I can, I will," Childress said. "And you'll do the same."

"To the extent I can."

CHAPTER 7

Tracy had set up the meeting with Amanda Santos, but she had not told Nolasco anything more about the FBI profiler. Nolasco, like Kins, had expressed skepticism Santos, or any profiler, would provide useful information to help them find the killer. She suspected Nolasco—twice divorced, and a rutting pig perpetually on the hunt for his next date—would change his tune when he met the tall, good-looking Santos.

As they exited Police Headquarters on foot, Nolasco, who had said nothing in the elevator, paused to light a cigarette. Tracy didn't know he smoked.

He exhaled and said, "Interesting the daughter of the woman you found happens to show up at a press conference on the subject of a soon-to-be-released series of articles."

Tracy hated passive-aggressive bullshit. "You have something you want to say?"

"You fed her information on the drug task force. I'm just saying it seems a big coincidence."

"You think I'm providing her with inside information?"

"Just think it's interesting," he said.

"If I wanted to take shots at you, Captain, I could have done it at the press conference. I don't need to do it behind your back."

Nolasco scoffed like he didn't believe her. Tracy didn't care what he believed.

Ten minutes later they entered the FBI's offices on Third Avenue. The furnishings had not changed since Tracy's last visit with her then partner, Kinsington Rowe. The lobby still had all the charm of a federal office building—utilitarian furniture, gray carpeting, and off-white walls displaying black-and-white prints. Like stepping back into the 1950s. If Tracy had trouble sleeping, this was the place she'd choose to take a nap.

Santos entered the reception area in blue jeans and a white blouse and still looked like a runway model.

Like Santos, Tracy wore flats, but they both stood nearly eye to eye with the six-foot Nolasco, who, upon seeing Santos, puffed out his chest like a banty rooster and rose to every inch of his height.

"Detective Crosswhite." Santos offered her hand. "It's good to see you. You've been in the papers a fair amount these past months."

Tracy greeted Santos and deflected the attention, which Nolasco would not take well. She introduced him as her captain.

"Thank you for agreeing to work with us," Nolasco said in his best "I'm in charge" voice. "I assume Detective Crosswhite sent over the files for your consideration?"

"The files were already in our system," Santos said. "Apparently, we were asked to review the victims' files back in '95 and ran them through VICAP"—the FBI's Violent Crime Apprehension Program, which was a nationwide data information center. "I also studied them a couple years ago for a presentation at the FBI's national training conference in Cleveland, and I refreshed my recollection yesterday afternoon and this morning."

"Anything of interest?" Tracy asked.

"Come on back to the conference room and we can talk. Can I offer you a cup of coffee?"

They stopped for coffee in a small kitchenette before entering a well-lit but windowless conference room on the building's west side. The table was clear except for a laptop computer plugged into a center console station. "I don't get asked to look into serial killings often anymore," Santos said.

Tracy had done her homework. Santos had written and presented an article at the FBI's training conference that attempted to explain why the number of serial killers—by definition a person who kills two or more victims in separate events—had surged in the 1980s but had seemingly dropped each year since. In 1989, the FBI estimated two hundred separate serial killers were active in the United States. In 2019, just two had been documented. Santos attributed the decline to advances in forensic technology, specifically the ability to analyze very small and mixed DNA samples, and other improvements that made it possible to track and find offenders before they killed again.

"We're getting better at catching murderers," Nolasco said.

"That's also a theory, but not accepted by all," Santos said diplomatically.

"To what is the decline attributed?" Tracy asked, attempting to deflect so Santos and Nolasco didn't get off on the wrong foot.

"I believe it is a combination of factors. As I said, improvements in forensic sciences. And people are less vulnerable than in the past, especially young women. They don't hitchhike as much, and they don't stop to help motorists seemingly stranded along the side of a road. Ted Bundy lured women to his car by telling them it wouldn't start, and he needed a hand. We now call 911 to get a stranded motorist help." She held up her cell phone. "The cell phone also gives us the means of immediately reaching out in emergency situations and documenting things with videos and photographs. If a person is abducted, police can track cell phones and use geo records to reconstruct the movement of both victims and suspects. Cameras are everywhere now. They make getting away with a crime much more difficult. Another theory suggests psychiatric intervention can identify and help troubled children and prevent them from growing up to be killers. Easy access to pornography also provides an outlet to satiate sexual impulses." She looked to Nolasco. "Maybe I'm jaded, but I also believe the decline, if accurate, is due to the detection of killers before they can kill again, the imposition of longer prison sentences for those convicted, and a reduction in parole that keeps killers off the streets longer."

"Which is what I believe happened here," Nolasco said.

"Possible, but I wouldn't be so sure of it," Santos said.

Tracy stifled a smile.

"What makes you say that?" Nolasco said, his voice pleasant, his demeanor not so much. The muscles in his jaw twitched. One of his tells. He didn't like being corrected or contradicted, especially by women in front of women.

"You have an organized killer. A disorganized killer is much more impulsive and haphazard. Disorganized killers make mistakes, leave fingerprints, fail to keep from being seen, and are more likely to be incarcerated. Organized killers consider murder an art they try to perfect. The files indicate your killer left behind very little evidence, an indication he did not kill on impulse or out of anger. He was methodical. He didn't want to be caught."

"Is that why you think he stopped?" Nolasco asked. "He feared getting caught?"

"It's possible your killer pushed the boundaries as far as he cared to, then backed away."

"Can they do that?" Nolasco asked. "Stop? I thought they killed to satisfy an urge."

"The organized killers aren't necessarily killing on impulse or to satisfy an urge. It's often for some other reason."

"Such as practice?" Tracy said, recalling her and Kins's conversation with Santos when hunting the Cowboy.

"The fact that your killer went from killing prostitutes to middle-class housewives is telling," Santos said.

"He was taunting us," Nolasco said. "The task force. He was trying to make us look bad, incompetent. Embarrass us."

"I don't think it was about you at all, Captain. If it had been personal, the killer would have sent you messages, mocked your investigation, professed to be too smart to be caught. I didn't find a scrap of evidence to support that was the case."

Nolasco had let his ego get in the way of his investigation. It wasn't completely surprising since he let his ego get in the way of everything else. He'd even tried to take credit for capturing the Cowboy.

"Do you think he could have been practicing on the early victims to see if he could get away with it?" Tracy asked.

"I think it's plausible, but not necessarily to 'see if he could get away with it.' I think he practiced to prepare to kill the women he intended to kill."

For a moment the gravity of what Santos said silenced the room. Then Tracy said, "So then we might want to focus on his last four victims, who they were, what they did, what they might have had in common?"

"Let's start with the carving your killer embedded on each of his kills," Santos said.

Santos typed on the computer keyboard. The television screen mounted on the wall illuminated, which is why the room had no windows, to protect classified or sensitive information. Santos put up a photograph of a carving on the left shoulder of one victim. "This is the first victim. Notice the carving is crude. You can see jagged edges where the skin pulled." Santos put up another picture. "This is the ninth victim. Notice the difference in the cut. The lines are straight, perfected. The killer used a sharp blade, possibly a scalpel or X-Acto knife."

"Could he have medical training?" Nolasco asked.

"Possibly," Santos said. "He could just as likely be an artist, or he simply decided to use a sharper blade so his intent was clear."

"The markings don't tell us *anything* about the killer?" Nolasco said. "In your opinion."

"I know 'Angel of Death' has been your task force's interpretation of the wings, but angel's wings, throughout history, have represented many things other than death—purity, strength, perfection, and tranquility, for instance." Santos displayed a female in a long white dress with white wings extended behind her back.

"The killer sees himself as pure or perfect and he's what, killing these women because they are not, or have not been?" Tracy asked.

"But the last four kills were not prostitutes," Nolasco said. "They were wives, mothers with reputable jobs."

"That doesn't mean the killer considered the women to be pure," Santos said. "But let me go back to the angel's wings theory. Angel's wings can also represent a person's guardian angel, an angel each of us can call on for help." The screen changed to a male angel who looked more like a Roman centurion with curly bronze hair, a breastplate, leather skirt, and sandals.

"Angels have also been considered God's messengers, capable of traveling swiftly across far distances to deliver justice." An angel in hurried flight appeared on the screen.

Tracy thought of the suspect, Alex Bright, possibly flying back and forth from Georgia to Seattle to kill. She wondered if Nolasco had checked to determine if Bright could account for his whereabouts the days of the final killings.

Santos put up another picture. "In Judaic traditions, the Angel of Justice was the angel Raguel, whose name means 'friend of God.'"

"This one doesn't look as angelic," Tracy said. "And the gender is more ambiguous than the previous depictions. He . . . or she . . . has a harsher appearance."

Beneath the drawing was a note.

> *In the Old Testament an angel represented retribu-*
> *tion—the Angel of Justice's role is to bring the wicked and*
> *the sinners to justice for their crimes.*

And part of the prayer to summon Raguel.

> *Please bring specific types of injustice to my attention,*
> *in situations where God wants me*
> *to help expose the truth*
> *and bring change for the better.*

"Justice can be harsh," Santos said.

"You're saying this person could be a religious nut," Nolasco said.

"I'm saying if the carvings, which look similar to those wings I found online depicting Raguel, are intended to represent wings of justice, as opposed to death, then your killer could have been killing to expose a truth, perhaps an injustice."

"By killing and disfiguring women?" Nolasco shook his head, as if to show he was not drinking the Kool-Aid being served.

"Then why did he stop?" Tracy said.

"That's an interesting question. I don't believe your killer is dead or incarcerated for another crime. I believe he either delivered the message he intended to deliver and received whatever response he sought, or he concluded, for some reason, that his message would not be received by his further killing."

"What's the point of him delivering a message if we never know what his message means?" Nolasco asked.

"Again, the message isn't personal to your task force or to you."

"The killer's message wasn't intended for the police?" Tracy said.

"I don't believe it was," Santos said. "He also could have stopped for other reasons." She reiterated that killers stopped because of old age, injuries, and marriages that fulfilled sexual fantasies and impulses. "It's also more difficult to sneak out at night to pick up a prostitute when you're married, and you can't bring the women home to kill, and disposing of the body becomes more problematic."

"This isn't about sexual gratification then?" Tracy asked.

"I don't think it is," Santos said.

"Anything else that leads you to believe the killer was sending a message?"

"He didn't dump the last four victims in the garbage, or a river, or a lake, or try to bury them in the mountains," Santos said.

Tracy had been told that a reason why Seattle had many serial killers was because there were so many different ways to dispose of a body—dense mountains, rivers, lakes, marshes, Puget Sound. True or false, the explanation remained chilling.

"He wants people to know who the 'victims' are and how they died," Tracy said.

"That speaks much more to someone sending a message," Santos said.

Santos had told Tracy the same thing about the Cowboy, and she had been spot-on accurate. She was telling Tracy and Nolasco the task force's focus on the killer, rather than his victims, had been a mistake.

"But you can't tell us the message this guy intended," Nolasco said, sounding sullen and insolent. "So maybe he's just batshit crazy."

Santos shook her head and spoke calmly. "I think he's very sane, and by sane, I mean he definitely knows right from wrong. Look, Captain, I sense your skepticism. I could give you some psychobabble bullshit about why someone chooses to kill being based on biological, social, and environmental factors, but that's not going to help you. And frankly, it's why profilers have such a bad rap. We try too hard to figure out *why* these guys kill when there is no universal truth. I'm giving you my best analysis based on the evidence in the files." Santos paused. "There is something else to consider," she said, sounding hesitant. She looked to Tracy. "You've been in the news quite a bit recently. If the killer doesn't believe his message was delivered twenty-five years ago, and whatever caused him to stop killing isn't some physical infirmity or incarceration, I think there is a chance he could use your reputation to deliver whatever message he intended to expose whatever injustice he perceives."

"You're saying he could kill again because I'm now involved?" Tracy asked, feeling alarmed.

Santos nodded. "I'm saying he could see you as a herald, a person who can deliver the message he tried but failed to deliver."

CHAPTER 8

January 17, 1995
Seattle, Washington

From Vic Fazzio's seat in the task force conference room, Johnny Nolasco looked like he hadn't slept in days, and Fazzio would know. Nolasco dragged his body as he entered, sat at the table, then tilted back his head to apply drops of Visine to bloodshot eyes. It might temporarily get the red out, but it did nothing to reduce the size or the color of the dark bags beneath those eyes. Nolasco's bags were as prominent as Faz's uncle Ernesto's, and Ernesto's bags were so large Faz referred to them as steamer trunks. Nolasco also reeked of cigarette smoke, and his hair looked to be thinning.

Moss Gunderson and Keith Ellis, two of the more experienced detectives on the task force, were seated at the table looking grim. They had responded, along with a cavalcade of police and fire vehicles, to a report of a woman found floating among the aquatic plants in a pond in the Washington Park Arboretum of the Montlake District. Middle-class and upper-middle-class homes surrounded the Arboretum, including Broadmoor, one of Seattle's wealthiest enclaves.

Gunderson advised that Regina Harris was the Route 99 Killer's eleventh victim. Like his other ten victims, Harris had been strangled. Stuart Funk, of the King County Medical Examiner's Office, would confirm that once he'd completed an autopsy.

"Unmistakable," Gunderson said in response to Nolasco's question whether angel's wings had been carved in Harris's back just below her left shoulder. That piece of evidence was known only to those within the task force room and their Violent Crimes captain.

But news of the death and the possibility Harris was the serial killer's latest victim quickly hit the media stream. Local news stations, more critical of SPD and the task force with each unsolved killing, had interrupted regular programming to bring Seattle residents the most recent unsettling news.

Faz likened the media criticism to a game of dominoes, with Nolasco at the end of the line. At the most recent news briefing, Nolasco had been thrown to the wolves after being stripped naked and having a bloody steak strapped to his testicles.

Nolasco looked like he'd aged ten years since the killer claimed his tenth victim, Mary Ellen Schmid. Schmid and Regina Harris had been middle-class spouses and mothers. Nothing grabbed the attention of the mainstream media or the public more than a brutal murder in one of their seemingly protected enclaves.

The pressure on Nolasco didn't increase one-tenth but tenfold, and each day he looked a little worse for it. He picked up a Styrofoam cup of black coffee and sipped at the rim. His movements looked mechanical, robotic. After a beat, Nolasco considered Moss, who stood as tall as Faz, but with a personality like a blinking billboard—an annoyance always on display. "Tell me what we know," Nolasco said in his tired voice.

"Victim is married with two children. Works for the City of Seattle on city contracts. Member of the PTA for her children's public school. Runs early every morning before she heads to work. Husband takes the kids to school. A nanny picks them up and brings them home. Husband left home after the wife left for her run."

"What does the husband do?" Nolasco asked.

"Works as a building superintendent for a Pacific Northwest construction company building an addition at Seattle Children's Hospital."

"When did he notice the wife went missing?"

"When he arrived home just before six p.m., relieved the nanny, and called the wife's office trying to locate her. Call went to voice mail. He figured she was in a meeting, waited until after getting the kids to bed to call again, without luck. He called the wife's assistant at her home to find out if there was a late meeting or emergency. Assistant said the wife never came into the office. That's when the bells went off. Husband called the police. Responding officers took a statement and learned the wife ran every morning in the Arboretum. Husband occasionally ran with her and said she had two primary routes. Officers walked both routes with the husband but, given the darkness, did not find the wife. They were preparing to go back out this morning with dogs when an early morning jogger called in, said he thought he saw a body floating in the plants in a pond in the Arboretum."

Nolasco again sipped his coffee, and Faz saw a tremor before Nolasco set the cup down. "Nobody noticed she didn't come back from her jog?" Nolasco asked.

"Husband took the kids to school *after* the wife left the house and *before* she got home. Wife usually, but not always, relieves the nanny after work. Nanny doesn't understand or speak English too well but seemed to confirm this."

"Wife's car in the driveway?"

"She parked on the street."

"Wasn't that a giveaway something was wrong?"

"She didn't drive to work. She's an environmentalist, apparently. Caught the bus on Twenty-Third Avenue downtown every morning."

"Twenty-Fourth Avenue," Keith Ellis corrected. "It becomes Twenty-Third Avenue."

Nolasco shot him a look like *who cares?*

Moss shrugged.

"The jogger check out?" Nolasco asked.

"He does," Moss said. "He jogs the same route every other morning. The off mornings he lifts weights in his basement. His wife confirmed he was home in the basement the prior morning, the day Harris went missing, and witnesses confirm he went to work in the SoDo district. He's an attorney. All kinds of alibis at a law firm."

"No pun intended," Ellis said.

Nolasco shot him another look. To Moss, he said, "You confirmed the angel's wings?"

"As I said, unmistakable. Carved in the same location as the others, just above the shoulder blade. As you can imagine, a crowd assembled in the Arboretum. We put up a screen and had uniforms get the names and contact information of every spectator, in case the killer had come back to watch."

"That pretty much cleared out the spectators," Ellis said.

"Any connection between Regina Harris and . . ." Nolasco sighed. "The tenth victim?"

"Mary Ellen Schmid," Hattie said.

"Any connection?" Nolasco asked.

"Maybe," Moss said.

Nolasco's head picked up, though his eyes remained flat. They'd all become distrusting of the evidence and reluctant to hope. They never thought the killings would get this far or reach the mainstream. Undercover female police officers had walked the Aurora track, and the task force believed it was just a matter of time before they caught the killer. They had a handful of suspects. Two, Dwight McDonnel and Levi Bishop, had each been picked up for solicitation, but the task force got no further. The killings had stopped. At least for a short while. When they resumed, the killer had changed his choice of victims. Had the killer reasoned the task force sting operation along the strip made killing another prostitute too risky? Or did the killer just want to up the ante and cause panic in the middle-class neighborhoods and feed his ego?

Whatever the reason, Mary Ellen Schmid's murder had thrown the task force's profile of the killer out the window.

"Different neighborhoods. Different grammar schools and high schools. Both attended UW," Moss said of Schmid and Harris. "What they also have in common is the City of Seattle. Schmid worked in the attorney general's civil division, Harris in the office of city contracts."

Nolasco took an extended inhale, then audibly exhaled. "Any ideas?" He looked around the table. When no one said anything, he snapped, "No one has any ideas?" His gaze found each task force member, including Faz. "Let me make this clear. If I get transferred out of homicide, this entire task force will go with me. This isn't the Navy. I don't intend to go down with the ship out of some sense of duty or loyalty. So, somebody get an idea and throw it out for us to consider."

"Current or former city employee who worked in either department," Ellis said.

"Disgruntled businessman denied a city contract and has a beef with the bidding system and how the contractors are chosen," Faz said.

"Someone who doesn't like lawyers. A litigant who lost a house or some piece of property in some city-initiated action. Eminent domain or something," Moss said.

"How then do the first nine victims fit?" Nolasco said. No one answered.

Faz said what was on all their minds. "If we focus only on the tenth and eleventh victims, it will cause a shitstorm. The media will kick us in the balls, say we're discounting the other nine victims, and that's the reason the killer has made it this far."

"That's why nothing leaves this room. What's said in this room stays in this room." Nolasco tapped his index finger on the table. "No one is to speak to the press except me or Floyd. Faz, I want you to interview the families of Schmid and Harris. See if you can find any other connecting thread. Maybe they knew one another. Then get your ass out to the Arboretum before the sun comes up tomorrow morning."

"Should be easy enough for a vampire," Gunderson said.

"Knock that shit off, Moss. I'm in no mood for bullshit," Nolasco said, his voice sharp. "Faz, talk to anyone and everyone—joggers, landscapers, gardeners, dog walkers, mothers with baby strollers. Anyone and everyone. You got that?"

"I got it."

"Ask if anyone recalls seeing Harris jogging the other day . . . or any day for that matter. Ask if they recall seeing anyone who didn't look like he belonged, who they had never seen before. If anyone does recall someone, get a sketch artist out there.

"Moss, you and Ellis talk to everyone at each victim's place of work. Find out if they know of any disgruntled employees who either woman might have rejected or had a feud with. Find out if any businessmen lost a license, or a bid, or made any threatening statements." Nolasco directed other detectives to explore the possible UW link.

Nolasco turned to Augustus Cesare. "Anything new on the tip line?"

"It's blowing up," Cesare said. The young patrol officer was in his twenties and good with computers. He had prepared a spreadsheet to track the tips and look for connecting threads between the victims. Given the last name, Faz had pegged Cesare as a fellow *paisan*, but his name was spelled differently and apparently of Spanish origin.

"Mostly the crazies and those seeking attention," Moss said.

Cesare had developed a system. Red tips were the most promising and went to Moss for follow-up. Yellow tips were to be run down by task force and homicide detectives, and green tips were pursued by available detectives from Property Crimes, Narcotics, or Fraud. Every significant finding was reported back to Cesare to be input, and then Moss decided if the tip required further review. All written reports were preserved in the murder book. Cesare would sort the spreadsheet to find commonalities in themes, dates, suspect descriptions, and crazies.

But the tips often missed the victimology and focused on the suspects. That was about to change given the nature of the more recent victims.

"Every tip is being run down," Moss said. "If the tip is deemed credible, I'll take over the questioning and put anything I learn in the murder book for internal distribution."

"The mayor wants the FBI to look at the files and run the victims through VICAP, see if they might find any connection with other cases," Nolasco said. "Make it happen. Get them what they need."

Moss looked to Cesare. Moss wasn't just a blowhard; he was lazy. Seemed to Faz that Cesare did all the real work.

"What about a profiler?" Moss said. "I'm told the FBI has one on staff here in Seattle. Might help."

"Maybe. If we get any solid suspects. I don't want to go down the hocus-pocus and voodoo trails and waste more time," Nolasco said. "A profiler will tell us the killer had a poor childhood and abusive parents, skinned cats in his teens, and gets off on the violence, that he killed prostitutes because he doesn't value human life any more than the pets he slaughtered. Blah blah blah. Tell us something we don't know."

"He might be able to tell us why this guy switched from prostitutes to middle-class women," Gunderson said.

Nolasco slapped the table and raised his voice. "He's raising the damn stakes is why. He's baiting us. He's emboldened by our inability to catch him. He thinks we're all dumbshits and, at present, so do the mayor, the chief, and the captain. I'd like to prove them wrong, preferably before this asshole kills again. I don't want us wasting time going down rabbit holes. I want solid police work. And I want leads. If we don't start getting something solid to run with, I've been assured by Clarridge, who was assured by the mayor, that if the mayor goes down for this, he will take the chief with him, and the chief will take all of us. So if you prefer not to find yourself transferred back to patrol, I'd suggest we all get to work and make this happen."

CHAPTER 9

Tracy and Nolasco departed the FBI office back onto Seattle streets and resumed their game of silence, like two schoolyard kids mad at one another. Tracy didn't care. She was focused on what Santos had just said, that the killer could use Tracy's reputation to deliver his message. That more young women might die, not because of SPD reopening the investigation, but because of her involvement.

Nolasco took out a pack of cigarettes from an inside pocket of his blazer, shook out a cigarette, and lit up.

"I didn't know you smoked," Tracy said.

"Neither did I," Nolasco said without elaboration.

"Santos thinks we should focus on the victims, rather than the killer."

"Santos doesn't know what the hell she's talking about, as I predicted."

Tracy wasn't surprised by his comment, but it remained frustrating. "She's reviewed the files. She's given us an angle to explore that the task force didn't have back then."

Nolasco stopped. His eyes narrowed. "What's that supposed to mean? You don't think we considered the victims? This must be a real joy for you, Crosswhite, having Santos rip apart my task force."

"She didn't rip apart your task force."

"We considered the victims. We looked for connecting threads. All we found was the first nine were prostitutes who worked the strip. The latter four worked for or had worked with the City of Seattle. Nothing beyond that."

"So let's go through the files again—"

"Because the great Tracy Crosswhite is going to find something experienced detectives working 24-7 couldn't?"

"Weber wants a fresh pair of eyes, that's all."

"You really get off on the publicity; don't you? The medals. Standing before the media. But be careful what you wish for. Celebrity isn't everything it's cracked up to be."

"Do you think I take any joy in the possibility some sick son of a bitch might kill again because of my reputation? I didn't ask to reopen these cases. I was ordered to do so by Weber."

"The same person who comes down to your office for closed-door meetings."

Tracy shook her head. "I'm done with this conversation." She started up the hill.

"I'm still your superior officer, Crosswhite."

Tracy turned back and saluted. "You're my captain. You're far from my superior." She spun on her heels and left. She'd pursue the investigation, with or without Nolasco and his fragile ego. She was tired of walking that tightrope—be a good enough detective so others would forget her gender but not so good as to show up her male superiors? Screw them.

She walked up Seneca, turned right on Fifth Avenue, and walked past the Seattle Public Library. She had her head down and nearly walked into someone coming from the opposite direction.

"Whoa. Where are you going in such a hurry?" Faz said. Del stood beside him.

"Back to the office." She checked the time on her phone. "Where are you going?"

"Bartell's for my blood-pressure medication."

"He's lying," Del said. "He's buying hemorrhoid cream."

Faz shook his head. "Don't listen to him. Everything okay?"

"You have high blood pressure?"

"In this job? Are you joking?"

"Have you studied the man's diet?" Del asked. He used to weigh more than Faz, who now tipped the scales at 250 pounds, but Del lost the excess weight when he started dating a King County prosecutor and had kept it off.

"What's eating you?" Faz asked Tracy.

"Nolasco. What else?"

"I heard you two were working the Route 99 investigation together. I don't envy you, Tracy."

"Nor do I," Del said.

"I don't envy me either. Weber's setting me up so if the killer takes the reopening of these files as a challenge and kills again, I'll be there to blame."

"Saw the press conference. It was like 1995 all over again."

"What do you mean?"

Faz checked his watch. "You had lunch?"

"No."

"We're going to get a bite to eat at Tulio after I get my meds."

Faz and Del had what Tracy called an Italian sixth sense, capable of flushing out Italian food from almost anywhere. In this instance, Tulio was just across the street. "What about reservations?"

"Ouch," Del said.

"Your lack of faith hurts me," Faz said. "Let me get my meds first. Come on. Walk with us."

Faz picked up his prescription at the Bartell Drugs on Fourth, then they made their way back to Tulio. The maître d' greeted Faz and Del like relatives. "How you doing, Marco? Can you squeeze us in?" Faz asked.

"You're kidding, right? For a *paisan*?"

Faz gave Tracy an *I told you so* look. "Someplace outside?" Faz said. "Hate to waste this beautiful weather."

Marco grabbed three menus and led them to a table on the patio behind the wrought-iron railing.

"Glass of red wine or maybe a bottle?"

"Can't," Del said. "We're working."

Marco handed them menus, then departed. Faz left his menu on his plate.

"You want to talk first or look over the menu?" Tracy said.

"Nothing to look over. Linguini and clams," he said.

"He's only getting the clams because Antonio said they help regulate blood pressure," Del said, referencing Faz's son, who owned an Italian restaurant, Fazzio's, in Fremont.

Tracy set aside her menu. "You said watching the press conference this morning was like 1995 all over again. Why?"

Faz sipped his water and set the glass down. "We were all on edge, Tracy, especially Nolasco. The politicians and brass were really busting our balls. You have to remember this was in the middle of Ridgway's spree, so all these young women were going missing on Aurora and on the south end on the Pacific Coast Highway. The politicians were taking a lot of heat from the media, the advocacy groups, and the victims' families. They accused us of being dismissive because the women weren't exactly Mary Poppins."

"When's the last time a politician accepted blame for anything?" Del said.

"Never," Faz agreed. The waiter came by with bread, olive oil, and balsamic vinegar. Faz shook salt and pepper over the bowl before dipping his bread.

"When's the last time you had a physical?" Tracy said.

"Every year on my birthday, why?"

"Doctor say anything about salt and high blood pressure?"

"No. Why?"

"No reason."

Del shook his head.

"You were saying about the politicians?" Tracy said.

"They were taking heat. Then the victims change and become middle-class housewives living in middle-class neighborhoods."

"And the shit really hits the fan," Del interjected.

"The politicians turned up the heat on the brass," Faz said. "Clarridge's nose looked like Rudolph's half the time. And he let our task force know he wasn't happy. Anyway, you know about how shit—"

"Runs downhill," Tracy said, repeating another Fazism, as the A Team called them.

"Nolasco was at the bottom of the hill holding a pail that would never catch all that shit. The guy was a lot like you."

Tracy felt like she'd been slapped. "Nolasco and me alike?"

"Now *you* stepped in it," Del said to Faz.

"Don't give me that look. Let me explain," Faz said.

"I think you better," Del said. "She might have to revoke your godfather status for insanity."

"Hang on. Hang on. Don't take my head off until I finish. I meant, Nolasco was a rising star, like you. He was solving cases, receiving medals, and moving up the chain of command more quickly than his age warranted. I think he took this task force position because he thought it would add a big feather in his cap and advance his career."

"What do you mean?"

"He didn't intend captain to be his final stop, Tracy. He was thinking politics. Chief of police. Moving up. This task force pretty much tanked those dreams."

"That and his home life was blowing up because he was never home. Wife left him for a personal trainer," Del said. "Nolasco started smoking like a chimney, losing weight, and losing hair. The guy was a mess."

"He had bags under his eyes so big you could have filled them with clothes for a two-week vacation," Faz said.

Tracy thought of the cigarette Nolasco lit up outside the FBI offices. "Have you known Nolasco to smoke? I don't mean back then. I mean recently."

"No. He gave it up years ago, why?"

"He's smoking again."

Faz and Del both shook their heads. "Wouldn't be surprised if it's like PTSD, you know? He's picking up the bad habits he had back then."

"What exactly are you telling me?"

"I'm telling you it was a bad time around the police department. We didn't catch the Green River Killer until years later, and we never caught the Route 99 Killer," Faz said.

"Between the two, some seventy-five women, maybe more, were murdered, and their families never got closure," Del said.

"You're both saying I should cut Nolasco some slack."

"That's between the two of you. I'm just letting you know what it was like, so you can imagine how he feels to go back again," Faz said. "Gives me the shivers just thinking about it."

"How much did you focus on the victims as opposed to suspects?"

Faz dipped his bread in the oil and vinegar and took another bite, then sipped his water. "We ran down the victims and the suspects pretty good, Tracy. Me? I thought it was McDonnel. He liked to pick up the ladies along the strip. We spoke to a couple who knew him. Said he was into rough sex, but he never strangled them. I don't know."

"Seemed the closer you got, the farther you got, as I remember you telling me," Del said.

"We thought we had this guy dialed in on the Aurora strip. Next thing we know he's killing housewives," Faz said.

She told him about Amanda Santos's analysis.

"The first nine were what, then, practice?" Faz asked.

"I don't buy that," Del said. "Never have."

Tracy grabbed a piece of bread and joined Faz in the oil and vinegar. Del refrained, watching his carbs. "Santos thinks his real targets were the final four victims," she said. "She thinks he was sending a message."

"What kind of a message?" Faz said.

"She didn't buy the Angel of Death reference. She believed the wings were intended to be the Angel of Justice."

"What's the difference?" Del asked.

"The Angel of Justice's purpose is to bring justice to the wicked and to the sinners."

"And these women were sinners?" Faz said.

"She doesn't know, which is why I asked how much time you spent on the victims."

"If he was sending a message, why'd he quit killing?" Del asked.

She told them what else Santos had said and also about her own notoriety possibly reawakening the killer.

"It's a terrible thing, what happened, but I couldn't help but think the same thing watching the press conference this morning, that some things are better left alone," Faz said.

"Felt the same way," Del said.

"Unfortunately we're beyond that," Tracy said. "And the families of the victims deserve closure."

"Hey, I hear you," Faz said.

"But at what expense?" Del asked.

"Your task force also had a leak. You know anything about that?"

"I remember you saying something like that a few months back; we were having a drink in the Columbia Tower. Never heard anything about it before then. My first guess would be Moss," Faz said. "He always liked to run his mouth, be a big shot. The center of attention. If I had to choose anyone, I'd pick him."

"I can't see what Moss would have got out of it," Del said. "And Moss didn't do anything unless he could get something out of it, like Last Line money."

The waiter appeared and took their orders and their menus. After he'd stepped away, Faz said, "I got to admit, Tracy. I was more than a little surprised to find out you were working with Nolasco."

"'Shocked' would be the word," Del said.

"He wasn't my first choice, Faz. You were my first choice. Weber paired me with Nolasco," Tracy said.

"She knows your history and she's screwing you because you and Del went public with the task force story." Faz shook his head like shaking a bad thought. "Sorry to say, but I'm glad Weber didn't choose me. That's a time period I'd just as soon forget."

"I don't have that luxury. At the moment the past is my present. Where would you go if you were me?"

"Melton," Del and Faz both said without hesitation.

"If I remember correctly, we had DNA from one of the victims," Faz said.

"You filled out a HITS sheet on the fourth victim and noted DNA."

Faz pointed to his temple. "Got a memory like an elephant. With the advances in forensics now, you might get lucky."

"You have any other advice?"

Faz thought for a moment. "We turned over every stone, seemingly anyway. Maybe we missed something. Or maybe you do something outside the box, something not on the detective checklist."

"Think like a serial killer," Del said. "Sick and depraved."

"Are you calling me sick and depraved, Del?" she asked, smiling.

"Hey, you're hanging around with me and Faz; so, who knows?"

CHAPTER 10

Friday, July 10, Present Day
Monroe, Washington

Tracy spent the night considering what Faz and Del had said, about thinking outside the box and doing something not on the detective's traditional checklist. Something to make her think like a serial killer. *Sick and depraved.*

Her final analysis had come down to one question: What did she have to lose?

The task force had done everything by the book and come up empty. And she didn't have any other bright ideas, other than creating the social media platform and consulting Santos—a long shot, as Nolasco had so eagerly pointed out.

Maybe.

Finding Lisa Childress had also been a long shot, but that long shot had paid off.

And she had science on her side this time. Tracy would consult Melton and determine whether advances in forensics would allow them to do now what they couldn't twenty-five years ago, assuming they had

DNA to run. If Melton could get a DNA profile of the killer, it could be the break they sought, even if CODIS didn't spit out a match. They'd have something to compare to known suspects.

Match, track, confirm, confront, arrest.

Besides, what Tracy currently had in mind would keep her out of the office and away from Nolasco for a few hours. That alone was well worth taking this unlikely shot.

She left the house early for the roughly forty-minute drive to the Monroe Correctional Complex. MCC, like all prisons and jails, did not allow visitors to bring in cell phones, keys, pens or pencils, or anything else that could be used as a weapon. Tracy entered the prison and secured her Glock handgun, phone, and other articles in a locker in the lobby. She signed the necessary paperwork and stepped through metal detectors. A Department of Corrections officer took her through a series of gates to the Special Offender, Maximum Security Unit that housed, among others, mentally ill offenders. The level of noise—men shouting incoherently and talking at a high decibel—reverberated as if inside a metal drum. The officer led Tracy into a private room with a table and two chairs bolted to the floor.

"You sure you don't want me to sit in on this one, Detective?" the DOC officer asked. "This guy is loony tunes."

Tracy nearly laughed. The officer had no idea how accurate his comment was. "I think he'll be more inclined to talk if he perceives no one is eavesdropping on our conversation."

"I'll be right outside the door." He took a step, then turned back. "You got him; didn't you? You talked him out of that motel room and brought him in."

Tracy nodded.

"That was a nice piece of work. Ballsy. Sorry. Gutsy."

"Nice of you to remember."

The officer shook his head. "Wish that were true but . . . actually he still talks about you."

"He does?" That was unnerving.

"Something about a movie he's going to make. Said you'll be a consultant to make sure Hollywood gets all the police work accurate."

Nabil Kotar's sordid upbringing had doomed him to mental illness, killing, and a solitary jail cell for the rest of his life. She had no sympathy for a man who'd hog-tied young women and watched them strangle themselves, but others also shared the blame.

"I'll go get him," the DOC officer said.

Minutes later, Kotar, aka the Cowboy, shuffled into the room in prison-issued khaki slacks, white socks, and flip-flops. He held a thick stack of documents in his cuffed hands, clutching it against his white T-shirt like a holy relic. In 2015, Kotar had been found mentally competent to stand trial and convicted of the murder of five adult dancers. He had been given the death sentence, commuted to five successive life sentences when the Washington State Supreme Court abolished the death penalty in 2018, ruling it unconstitutional as applied. In prison, psychiatrists had found Kotar to be mentally ill and had him moved to the Special Offender Unit at Monroe.

"Detective," Kotar said with a radiant smile. "I didn't expect to ever see you here. Wow. This is a surprise. I wish you had let me know ahead of time. I have a lot to tell you."

Tracy hadn't seen Kotar since his conviction and sentencing. He had been an avid weightlifter when he worked as the Pink Palace strip club's floor manager in Seattle, but he looked to have lost much of his bulk. The serpent tattoo on his right bicep no longer stretched the fabric of his shirtsleeve or looked nearly as menacing as it once had. It looked more like a garden snake with fangs. Tracy had suspected Kotar to be a steroid abuser, drugs not exactly difficult to obtain in prison if you had the proper connections.

"I didn't know I was coming until the last minute, Nabil. You've lost weight and cut your hair." His hair was now a tight buzz cut along the sides with two inches on top.

"You like it?"

"It looks professional," she said.

"I'm watching what I eat and I'm not lifting heavy weights anymore. I took to heart what you said to me when we talked."

Tracy had no idea what Kotar was referring to. "What in particular?"

Kotar sat in a chair across from her and put the documents on the table. He looked up at the DOC officer with distrust.

"Officer, can you give us some privacy?" Tracy said.

"I'll be right outside."

Kotar watched until the officer left the room. He lowered his voice to a whisper. "You can't be too careful. I've heard horror stories about people stealing manuscripts and screenplays and pawning them off as their own."

Tracy motioned to the stack of papers. "Is that what you have there?"

Kotar put his hand atop the pages. "I've been working on a book and a screenplay about the two of us . . . *The Cop and the Cowboy Killer*. That's just a working title. Hollywood has people to take care of those things. Remember you asked me who I thought would play me in the movie?"

"You said Rami Malek." Tracy recalled the conversation.

"Right." He beamed. "But I figure he probably priced himself out of the running after winning the Academy Award as Freddie Mercury in *Bohemian Rhapsody*."

Kotar was an enigma. He could act like an adult when he worked at the Pink Palace, but when Tracy caught up to him in the motel room on Aurora Avenue where he had bound another dancer, Kotar had been watching a Looney Tunes cartoon and become childlike. The psychiatrist who evaluated him to stand trial said Kotar's mental development had been stunted in his formative years. His mother had been a stripper and a prostitute, and she would sit him in front of the television to watch cartoons while she entertained men. If Kotar didn't behave, she'd beat him with a cord and tie him to a chair, a pattern that continued until one of her customers 'hog-tied and strangled her. The man was never found. Kotar now seemed to be stuck in his youth.

"You might be right," Tracy said, a thought dawning. "You lost weight and cut your hair to look like Rami Malek."

"Who better to play the role of the Cowboy?" Kotar said. "I look like him, don't I?" He inched forward, like he was about to climb across the table. "Remember what I told you as we left the motel room that evening?"

"You said you were born to play the role."

Kotar looked amazed Tracy had remembered. "That's right. That's what I said. And I think you should play the detective."

"I think consultant is a better role for me."

Kotar stopped, as if remembering something else. "You said you were thinking about quitting being a detective and going back to teach. Chemistry, right?"

"You have a good memory too," Tracy said.

"I said, 'You quit and the assholes win.'" He tapped the top page. "It's all here in the manuscript. I wrote it all down. I'm so glad you convinced me to walk out of that motel room so I could tell my story. I put in the first line we talked about. You remember?"

"I don't."

"'The Cowboy had time to kill,'" Kotar said. "It's a double entendre."

Tracy let him savor that thought. After a moment she said, "I actually came out here on business, Nabil."

"Business?"

"That's right. I'm looking for some help."

"Okay," he said, his tone and his body posture becoming tentative.

"Back in the midnineties, Seattle had a serial killer called the Route 99 Killer. He killed nine prostitutes in motel rooms, then killed four other women. Then he stopped."

"Never been caught?"

"No."

"When did he stop?"

"Back in 1995."

"Did they have a task force?"

"They did."

"You weren't on it, though."

"That was before my time. These are cold cases I'm working. I'm trying to catch the guy who did it. Wondering if maybe you had insight into the killer or why he killed those women."

Kotar's eyes narrowed. Tracy could see the paranoia set in. "How could I help?"

"You never told me why you killed those women, Nabil."

Kotar looked wounded. Then he spoke in rushed sentences. "I didn't kill them. They killed themselves."

Amanda Santos said Kotar had fashioned the elaborate choking mechanism to absolve himself of any crime. But Tracy had never directly asked Kotar.

"What do you mean, Nabil?"

Kotar gathered his manuscript. "Why are you doing this? This was a good meeting. I wanted to get your approval of my manuscript."

"I have to do this, Nabil. It's my job." Tracy got an idea and hoped it would keep him from leaving. "Think of this as another scene in *The Cowboy and the Cop*."

Kotar stopped moving and looked up at her.

"The cop comes to the Cowboy in prison and asks for his help catching an—" Tracy caught herself before she could say *another serial killer*. "A killer."

Kotar paused. He looked to be giving her idea some thought. "That could be good," he said, though he did not sound convinced.

"Absolutely," she said. "Maybe it's a whole new movie. A sequel. Redemption. People love stories about redemption, Nabil."

"'Redemption'?" Kotar said, as if trying out the word for the first time.

"The Cowboy can't change what was done, but he can change the future."

Kotar's eyes glittered, a hint of a smile forming at the edges of his lips. He said the words slowly, softly. "'The Cowboy can't change what was done, but he can change the future.'"

"I can see the cop character consulting with the Cowboy on her other cold cases as well. Maybe this isn't a movie, Nabil."

"No?"

"Maybe it's a series. Series are popular now with all the streaming services out there. People like to watch series in their homes."

"It could continue for years," he said, getting excited again. "I could write each episode."

She waited. Kotar lowered his gaze to the table, chewing on his lower lip. He looked up at Tracy as if expecting a question. She didn't ask one. "What did you ask me?" he said.

"Why did those women kill themselves?" she asked, careful in her phraseology.

"Because they had to die."

"Why did they have to die?"

"So the police would find the man who killed my mother."

"Your mother? So the police would search for the man who killed your mother?"

"He tied her up so if she moved, the cord around her throat would strangle her."

"You watched him do it?"

Kotar nodded. "I didn't want to tell you I wasn't really the Cowboy. He was."

"It's just background, Nabil. It's what makes your character the Cowboy. What do they call that in acting?"

"My motivation."

"It was part of your motivation."

"It didn't work. They never caught the man who killed my mother. They didn't care because she was a prostitute," he said, his tone something close to, but not quite, anger. "I wanted people to pay attention to my mother's murder. I wanted them to find the connection to the others who killed themselves so they would search for the man responsible for killing her."

So he had re-created the killing mechanism.

The corrections officer in the doorway turned his head and looked at Tracy. She gave him a nod everything was all right.

"You tied them up just like he tied up your mother because you thought the police would figure out that your mother was killed the same way, and they would then search for the man responsible, thinking he killed the other women."

"Isn't that what you're doing? Trying to find the man responsible for killing those women."

"I'm trying, Nabil."

Amanda Santos had told Tracy to focus not on the suspects but on the last four victims—the middle-class women. Kotar was saying the same thing—focus on the victims to find the killer.

"Can I ask you a question?" Kotar said. "Were they all killed the same way?"

"They were all strangled."

Kotar sat back. "He's angry."

"At the women?"

"Maybe. Or maybe he's angry at someone else and killing the women is his way of getting back at that person."

"Getting back at that person how?"

"I don't know. Maybe that person killed someone—like the man who killed my mother. And he wants you to find him."

Tracy gave this some thought, uncertain if there was anything of substance to it or, like the manuscript, it was just the ramblings of a demented mind. "Let me ask you this. Why might the person who killed these women leave a mark in the same place on each of their bodies?"

"What kind of mark?" Kotar asked.

"A scar," she said, not wanting to be too specific.

Kotar gave it some thought, his gaze fixed on the tabletop. Then he lifted his gaze to Tracy and smiled. "It's a sign. A message."

She thought of Santos. "What kind of sign?"

"That they were all killed by the same person." He shrugged.

"You're saying it's a message for the police?"

"Maybe. But maybe it's also some sort of message to the person he's really mad at." It sounded plausible, rational, if not exactly very specific. Then Kotar added in an animated voice, "'Ba-dee, ba-dee, ba-dee. That's all, folks!'"

He was crazy, but maybe crazy like a fox.

Tracy wondered if she was even more crazy for considering what he had to say.

CHAPTER 11

O n her drive back into downtown Seattle, Tracy stopped at Salumi and bought sandwiches, then drove to the Washington State Patrol Crime Lab. The sandwiches were a blatant bribe, though she didn't look at them entirely in that way. She enjoyed Mike Melton's company. During her two-year stint working the various CSI departments in the Park 90/5 building, Tracy visited Melton's office frequently at the lunch hour, when Melton was inclined to pick up his guitar and rehearse for an upcoming gig. He played in a band with three other scientists called "The Fourensics." They played mostly country-western covers. Tracy and others ate lunch listening to songs by Garth Brooks, John Denver, and Tim McGraw, but also Steely Dan, the Doobie Brothers, Journey, Fleetwood Mac, and Pablo Cruise. Melton had once told Tracy, "Music soothes the savage beast," and said he believed his playing calmed the CSI detectives who spent too much of their time dealing with horrific crime scenes. Other detectives also took in the impromptu concerts, and Tracy called in sandwiches to give Melton maximum time to entertain. They became friends. Melton had said more than once Tracy was his seventh daughter.

Park 90/5 was a block-long, squat, cement structure in an industrial area south of downtown. As Tracy walked the halls, she instinctively listened for Melton's guitar and soothing baritone voice, but today the halls were silent.

She slowed her approach as she neared Melton's office door, surprised to find it closed. As director, he had cultivated an open-door policy to promote collaboration and to increase interaction among the detectives, which he believed was essential to team chemistry and morale.

Tracy knocked, heard a soft "Come in," and tentatively pushed open the office door. Melton reclined in his chair, his socked feet propped on the corner of his desk, hands folded in his lap. He had the groggy look of someone awakened from a nap.

"Did I catch you at a bad time?" she asked, holding back a knowing smile.

Melton grinned like a child caught with his hand in the cookie jar. "The great Tracy Crosswhite graces my doorway." He pointed at the white bag in her hand. "And lo! She bears gifts. Do tell. A dish fit for the gods?"

"Maybe not the gods, but certainly kings."

"Flattery, my dear, will get you everywhere. Salumi?"

"I know. It's not on the diet."

"Neither am I."

"You quit?"

"I met my goals." He swept his arms over his body. "Twenty-five pounds."

"I was going to say you look like half the man I once knew."

"According to my doctor I am the perfect weight for my height, my cholesterol doth not darken my arteries, and my blood pressure doth not near the threshold of hypertension."

"You're very William Shakespeare-ish today."

"Indeed. Last night the missus and I took in my grandson's performance in *Romeo and Juliet*."

"Which grandson?" Melton had a dozen or more grandchildren.
"George."
"Little Georgie? He's a kid."
"*Was* a kid. He's now eighteen, a senior in high school, and the lead in *Romeo and Juliet*." Melton sighed. "I remember the day he was born."
"We're getting old."
"'Tis inevitable, I'm afraid, though you, fair lady, are but a child."
"A child with a child."
"How is the little one?"
"Running me ragged. I wish I could nap like you."
"*Au contraire.* I was not napping. I was meditating."
"*Meditating?* Okay, who are you, and what did you do with Mike Melton?"
Melton smiled. "Meditating fifteen to twenty minutes a day lowers blood pressure. I do not want to take drugs." He put his feet on the floor and sat forward. "What did you bring me this time that is sure to clog my arteries and make me put on weight?"
"You could at least say you're happy to see me," Tracy said.
"I'm always happy to see you, and anyone else who brings me Salumi. What are my choices?"
"The Grindhouse or the Porchetta?"
"Ah, a difficult choice. Hot sopressata salami, mortadella, and cheese, or the classic slow-roasted pork with onions and pickled green peppers. What is a man to do?"
"We could split them and each take half."
"You are wiser than Solomon," Melton said.
Tracy unwrapped the sandwiches, handing Melton napkins and one of the wrappings to place on his desk. Melton took a bite of his sandwich and another moment to savor the taste. "So let me guess. These are a bribe to get me to rerun what DNA we have for the Route 99 serial killer."
"I'm offended." Tracy feigned being indignant. "And impressed. Can it be done? Is there enough?"

"Can be done. Will it be done? Not so certain."

"Because you're still struggling with the thousands of rape kits the legislature mandated be analyzed?"

"That, and because I pulled our file after I watched your news conference, and we didn't get a hit when we last ran the DNA."

"But that was twenty-five years ago."

"No. That was a few years ago. Two or three."

"Who requested . . ." The answer dawned on her. "Nolasco?"

"He had us run the DNA for a suspect," Melton said.

"Levi Bishop," she said.

"Wouldn't know," Melton said.

"But you didn't get a hit."

"You wouldn't be here if we had."

Nolasco still hunted the killer. The task force's failure must have eaten ulcers in his stomach lining, as Faz had intimated.

Melton said, "You get me a suspect's DNA, and I'll run it for you free of charge and compare it to the sample obtained at the one crime scene. Until then, I can't do much more for you."

Tracy was discouraged, but she knew Melton was right.

"Got another question."

"I knew the silence wouldn't last."

"Why would he only have sex with one victim?"

"Was it only one?"

"He could have used a condom. Hard to be definitive given the women's line of work, but assuming he had used a condom on his first three victims, why not use one on his fourth victim? Why leave behind DNA?"

"That is out of my expertise, I'm afraid. And cutting into lunch."

Tracy smiled and unwrapped her sandwich, but the questions seemed worth pondering.

CHAPTER 12

Tracy returned to Police Headquarters in the early afternoon. After dumping her belongings in her office, she took the elevator to the fourth floor and made her way to the Human Resources Department. Within that department, a detective unit performed background checks on entry-level police candidates to determine if they were fit for police duty. The detectives confirmed and verified information the candidate put in his or her Personal History Information Packet, including the candidate's criminal record, traffic record, past employment, financial credit history, and drug history. Detectives on the verge of retirement often took HR positions. They were easy pay, and the detectives remained available to discuss active investigations and help resolve any criminal trials in which they had been involved before they stepped down.

According to Tracy's digging, she'd find Augustus Cesare in one of the background detective positions. When the task force had disbanded, Cesare had returned to patrol. Though he'd eventually passed the detective exam, he'd never reached Violent Crimes, which was unusual, but not unheard of. Tracy wondered if something happened to derail his progression—such as being jammed up by a bullshit complaint or over-stepping a warrant. His current job indicated his impending retirement.

Tracy entered the HR Department, which was quiet as a dentist's reception area, and weaved her way through cubicles looking for the nameplate "Augustus Cesare." She spotted it atop a cubicle at the back of the room. As she stepped closer, a full head of gray hair came into view. Cesare spoke on his desk phone. Tracy kept her distance, a buffer so as not to intrude on his conversation. On his desk was a collage of photographs of two young girls through the years, which made her think of Daniella and how quickly time passed. Cesare spoke quietly and looked to be taking notes. After less than a minute, he muttered, "Thanks for your time," and hung up. He turned to face his computer and caught sight of Tracy.

"Detective Cesare," Tracy said. "I'm—"

"Tracy Crosswhite." Cesare flashed a thin smile beneath a silver goatee that matched the color of his hair. "I know who you are."

"Was hoping for a minute of your time. Can you spare one?"

Cesare adjusted his oversized silver glasses. "In this position? I can spare more than one. I assume this has to do with your cold case investigation?"

"It does," Tracy said.

"Saw the press conference. Don't envy you."

"You're the second person to tell me that."

"Vic Fazzio?"

"You've spoken to him?"

"No. But I know you worked together in Violent Crimes."

"Why don't *you* envy me?"

Cesare shrugged his thick shoulders beneath a light-blue dress shirt. He wore a colorful yellow tie. Many of the older detectives, Faz and Del included, were old-school, buttoned up in slacks, sports coats, and, occasionally, ties. "Because we gave the investigation everything we had. It was a sad day when the task force got shut down without any resolution."

"Is there someplace we can talk?"

Cesare stood. A shade under six feet with a ruddy complexion, he looked Tracy in the eye. He led her from the cubicles to an interior, windowless conference room, flicked on fluorescent lights, and closed the door. They sat on opposite sides of the table. Cesare had a thick build, perhaps that of a man who at one time lifted weights, which was common among officers. The muscles had slipped with age and disuse and had now become a spare tire.

"What can I help you with?"

"Just wanted to ask a few questions about the task force," Tracy said.

"I'll tell you what I know, though I wasn't intimately involved. Nolasco would be a better source."

If they had a working relationship, perhaps. "How did you come to work on it? Seems unusual for someone so young and inexperienced. How old were you? Twenty-five?"

"Twenty-six," Cesare said. "And yeah, it was unusual, but Moss Gunderson and I had a history, so . . ."

"What kind of history?" Tracy asked.

"I worked a case with him when I worked patrol—first responding officer to a murder. I found some information he needed and basically became his gofer on the case. Moss needed help. I offered him a reprieve from having to do many of the mundane tasks that come up in every investigation." Cesare shrugged. "I either impressed him or just made his life easier. When the task force formed and Moss became lead control officer, I saw an opportunity that suited my skills, called him up, and offered my help. He convinced the powers that be that I could be an asset."

"What skills?"

"I was good with computers when not many were. I had taken night classes at a technical school to improve my skills. Moss knew from the case we worked together that I also had good organizational skills and paid attention to detail."

"So Moss convinced Nolasco to bring you on board?"

"He did. I know Moss's retired now, so I can't get him in any trouble, but I soon learned that if Moss could get out of doing the work and still get credit for it, he didn't hesitate."

"Why were you so eager to work the task force?"

Cesare shrugged. "I saw it as a way to advance my career."

"But you never worked Violent Crimes." Tracy found that incongruous with his prior answer.

"Never did."

"Why not?"

"I guess I got my fill of violent crimes working that case," Cesare said. "Decided it wasn't for me. I got married shortly after the task force disbanded, and had two daughters. I didn't want to bring that stuff home with me. I wanted something not so emotionally taxing and more structured. Working in Violent Crimes takes a lot out of a person physically and mentally. I'm not telling you something you don't already know, I'm sure."

He wasn't. "Got to ask you a question about the task force."

"Shoot."

"First, tell me about your job, what you did?"

"Pretty simple. I manned the tip line and coded the information as it came in. I suggested to Nolasco we use a color code for the tips—red, yellow, and green." Cesare confirmed what Nolasco had told Tracy. "Tips would be run down and reassessed, and I'd update the spreadsheet if a second interview was deemed warranted."

"Who made that decision?"

"Moss. At least he was the guy I answered to. My job was also to sort the spreadsheet looking for commonalities and any connecting threads between the tips and the interviews."

"Did you find any?"

"Some, but after all these years . . ." Cesare held up his palms.

"Tell me what you do remember."

"The first victims walked the Aurora strip. I focused on johns and pimps. Had a couple suspects who seemed viable, but then the killer changed his victims and everything we thought we had learned was off the table. We had to start fresh. The tips changed also."

"How?"

"The women weren't prostitutes, so the tips were more about things like demographics—where the victims lived, what schools they had attended, whether they had any past boyfriends in common or common enemies."

"Did you find anything that tied those last four victims together?"

"Their employment," Cesare said. "I remember they each worked for or with the city. What they did, I don't recall. My memory is good but not that good."

"Anything come of that connection?"

Cesare smiled. "You're asking the wrong guy. As I said, I was just the computer nerd who put it all together in a spreadsheet for Moss and the team."

"You passed the information on to Moss?"

"And logged it into the computer program I had created," Cesare said. "So each task force member had the information. If they ever bothered to search for it."

"I should check whether Moss remembers anything."

"Good luck," Cesare said. "Like I said, it was a long time ago."

Maybe, but Moss had an ability to remember things that could impact him. He remembered well Lisa Childress's disappearance, thinking it related to Childress's investigation into the Last Line drug payouts, of which he had been a payee.

"What did you do with the information when the task force disbanded?"

"Copied it onto a disk and gave it to Moss to put in storage with everything else." So Nolasco's memory had been accurate.

Tracy thought of Amanda Santos and Nabil Kotar. Two different sides of the same coin perhaps, but both told her to focus on the victims. She'd have TESU convert the disk to a format she could use, then review the material specifically looking for a connection between the final four victims.

"I got a question," Cesare said. "It's been what? Twenty-five years. Why are you jumping back into this investigation now? Something new come up?"

Tracy couldn't stifle a laugh. "'Pushed' might be a better word. No, nothing new on the investigation, but the *Times* is preparing to run a series of articles on the twenty-five-year anniversary of the last killing, and the brass has sources indicating the series isn't going to be flattering. The chief wants a preemptive strike to let the public know we haven't given up."

"Seems like a tall order given the task force's failure."

"You might be right there." Shifting gears, Tracy asked, "Did you ever hear the killer referred to as anything but the Route 99 serial killer?"

"Like the Angel of Death?"

"What did you know about that?"

"The killer carved angel's wings in his victims' shoulders."

"Who did you hear it from?"

"Moss would be my guess, but . . . maybe Nolasco. I don't really recall. Why is that important?"

"I don't know if it is," Tracy said. "But the task force had a leak."

Cesare stared at Tracy for a moment. Then he said, "You think I might have leaked information?"

"Did you?"

Cesare shook his head. "It wasn't me, Detective. I was on the periphery. What would I have gained from leaking information?"

"Any idea who might have?"

"No."

Tracy stood. "Thanks for your time. If you think of anything, let me know."

"No worries. I have plenty of time now. Not a lot of candidate applications with everything happening in the news about defunding the police and holding officers legally liable. Who would want this job?"

"When's retirement?"

"Not soon enough."

"You and your wife have plans?" Tracy often wondered what she would do with herself if she retired. She worried she'd go stir-crazy. Dan had suggested retirement when everyone suddenly wanted an officer's head, but police work was in her blood. She'd contemplated quitting, but every morning she kept getting up and coming back.

"We're divorced now, but I'd like to get away," Cesare said. "Finally live life in peace."

"Sounds nice."

"Good luck," Cesare said. "I think the investigation damn near drove Nolasco crazy. I hope it doesn't do the same to you."

—

Tracy returned to her office and got her first glimpse of crazy. It looked more like a storage room. She counted twenty-five boxes stacked five high along her far wall, each marked with the Route 99 case number. She sighed just thinking about the amount of time it would take her to go through those boxes and read all those documents. Weeks at a minimum. Maybe months. She wished she had an Augustus Cesare to perform her drudgery.

She decided to find the disk Nolasco and Cesare had mentioned and have TESU convert it into a usable format. She removed the lid of the first box and searched through its contents, using the opportunity to generally familiarize herself with the materials, but she did not find a disk. She searched the second box. Then the third and fourth. An hour later, she'd removed the lid on the final box. She had found several floppy disks, each clearly labeled as the copied computer files of task force members. She did not find one labeled with the name Augustus Cesare, or that indicated it contained the tip line information he had described.

She called Cesare, but he didn't answer his desk phone, which prompted Tracy to check her watch. It was after five. A man on the verge of retirement was not going to work a minute past five. She didn't blame him.

She recognized the three knuckle raps on her office door and wished she, too, had left the office a minute earlier.

"Come in," she said reluctantly.

Johnny Nolasco stepped in and took a long look at the stacked boxes. "That should keep you busy."

Tracy didn't respond.

"I left you a couple messages," Nolasco said.

Tracy glanced at her phone. "I just got in a few minutes ago."

"Where have you been?"

"Why didn't you tell me you asked Mike Melton to rerun the DNA he had from one of the crime scenes and try to match it to Levi Bishop?"

Nolasco didn't immediately answer, clearly measuring his response. Finally, he said, "There was no reason for me to tell you; you had no involvement with the case until two days ago. It's another dead end. Now you can concentrate on going through all those boxes."

"But you knew the killer wasn't Levi Bishop, or someone else incarcerated for another crime."

"It might not be the killer's DNA," Nolasco said.

"Then why ask Melton to run it?"

"Why not? What did I have to lose? Maybe we get lucky, get a hit, find the killer. Solve those thirteen murders."

They were talking in circles. "At the moment I have another suggested route to take," Tracy said.

"I'm all ears."

"I talked to Augustus Cesare, and he confirmed what you told me about copying all the leads that came in over the tip line, which included any connections, onto a disk. He said he gave the disk to Moss Gunderson to be filed in storage."

"And?"

"And the disk isn't in any of those boxes." She gestured to her side wall.

"You've been through them?"

"Looking for the disk, yes. Santos said to focus on the last four victims." Tracy didn't add that Nabil Kotar, aka the Cowboy, had said something similar. "I'd like to determine what tips might have come in about the final four victims, determine if they could be related in any way."

"They weren't."

"They all worked for or with the City of Seattle," she said, repeating what Cesare told her.

"And I had that very question explored to see if there was more to it. There wasn't."

"Explored by whom?"

Nolasco paused. "Moss Gunderson and Keith Ellis."

"And now the disk Cesare says he gave to Gunderson is missing? I find that curious."

"It's been years. The disk could have simply been misplaced. Not everything is a dark conspiracy."

"How could the disk have been misplaced? Who's been looking at those files?"

Nolasco offered no response, which meant she had a point.

"I'd like to talk to Gunderson about it," she said.

"Be my guest."

Tracy needed Nolasco to get Gunderson to speak with her and decided to play to the man's enormous ego. "I need your help." Her request seemed to knock him back on his heels. "Moss and I don't exactly get along, given my investigation into the Last Line and his involvement. He won't talk to me. But I'm betting he'll talk to you."

"Why is that?"

"You were his superior officer. His captain. He'll still see you that way. And you were around when all this was going down with the Last Line. You might have some leverage over Moss."

"I don't."

"But he might think you do, which is just as good, but listen, if you don't . . . just forget about it."

"What?"

"Nothing. I'm probably overplaying my hand. Moss is retired. I doubt he'd talk to you either."

Nolasco gave her a blank stare, but she could tell the wheels in his head were spinning. "You know where to find him?"

"Moss? I know exactly where he'll be tomorrow morning." Moss had a standing golf date every Saturday morning with three men who collectively called themselves "the Mailmen" because they played in rain, sleet, or snow.

"Set something up."

Men. They were so predictable.

CHAPTER 13

January 27, 1996
Seattle, Washington

Nolasco stepped into the restaurant and considered the few people seated at the tables and in the booths along the wall. A waitress greeted him and told him to sit anywhere. He chose a booth at the back and sat facing the door. The waitress brought him a glass of water and two menus. Nolasco looked over the menu and realized the restaurant was vegan. A cursory glance didn't reveal anything appealing. He set the menu down, took a deep breath, and tried the relaxation breathing techniques his counselor had given him.

They didn't work.

He pulled the prescription bottle from his coat pocket, shook out one of the small lorazepam tablets his doctor had prescribed, and slipped it under his tongue. The pill's effects would take a few minutes. In the meantime, his mind churned over his most recent fight with his wife, though they had become so frequent they had begun to blend together. She wasn't happy with the long hours he'd been working and said if she had wanted to be a single parent, she could have found a sperm donor and not gone through all the other crap, namely having sex with him.

Nolasco was putting in sixty to eighty hours a week. The overtime pay helped to get out from under some expenses, like his wife's car lease, but the hours were taking a toll on her, him, and their marriage.

The latest fight erupted when he suggested she sell the Volvo so they could ditch the monthly lease payment. Nolasco wanted to buy a used car. She told him it would be over her dead body. She wasn't about to drive her kids to school in some beater. Most of the cars in the parking lot of their private grammar school on North Capitol Hill were Mercedes and BMWs. The Volvo, his wife said, was already not in that league, making it sound like she was schlepping the kids in a Pinto. But the argument wasn't about the car. The car was just an excuse to fight. If she wasn't complaining about the car, she complained about their two-thousand-square-foot home. Most of the other parents with children at the school lived in stately homes with spacious yards.

Nolasco had purchased his home before they married. The Realtor had told him it was a teardown, but on a great lot. He did much of the cosmetic remodeling himself, painting the interior and exterior, stripping and refinishing the hardwood floors, replacing countertops in the kitchen and bathrooms with marble, and modernizing the light fixtures.

The house had not been an issue until his wife enrolled their children in the same private school she had attended. Nolasco had lobbied for public school, but the district was reassigning children at random, and the school to which their eldest child had been assigned was not up to his wife's standards. *Not a chance in hell,* she had said.

Between the private school, the lease on the car, the mortgage, and the private trainer his wife paid twice a week at her local gym, they were having trouble making ends meet, not that his wife paid any attention to money. Except how to spend it.

Nolasco also suspected the personal trainer was more than just a trainer. Each time he suggested his wife knew the workouts and no longer needed the trainer, she acted as if he'd suggested she get rid of her parents. Nolasco was so busy at work, he didn't have time to determine if his wife was doing deep-knee lunges on top of her trainer. He didn't have time to crap in peace.

The bell above the restaurant door chimed. Nolasco's potential contact walked in, looking as spacey as she had looked at the press conferences, until she opened her mouth and asked those precise questions that cut through most of the rehearsed bullshit he'd been told to say.

His task force had not caught the Route 99 Killer. They had no solid suspects and little in the way of clues about where to go after the third and fourth killings of middle-class women.

Lisa Childress looked around the restaurant as if expecting someone else. She saw him and walked to his table carrying a handbag. Nolasco didn't stand. This wasn't a date. "Thank you for coming," he said.

She sat across from him.

Nolasco handed her a menu. "I assume you're vegan?" he said.

She had been looking up at the hanging light above the table, then lowered her gaze. "Why would you assume that?"

"This is a vegan restaurant. You suggested we meet here."

"It is?" She looked around. "I've never been here."

"Why did you suggest it?"

"I noticed it on my drive home from work."

The waitress returned to the table and asked if she could get them started with drinks.

"I'll have a Heineken," Nolasco said He motioned to Childress.

"Coke," she said. "No ice."

After the waitress departed, Nolasco said, "You must have been surprised to get my call."

"Why?"

"Do police officers call you often?"

"No. I usually have to call them."

She said it matter-of-factly, rather bland. Nolasco didn't know if Childress was being deliberately obtuse, but he didn't think so. It was just her demeanor. "I'll cut to the chase," he said, but the waitress reappeared with their drinks and asked if they needed more time to order. Nolasco said, "Do you want anything to eat?"

Childress checked her watch, then said no.

Nolasco handed the waitress back the menus and she departed. "As I said, I'll cut to the chase, but I'd like this conversation to be off the record."

Childress drank her Coke, nearly half the glass.

"Do we have a deal?"

She sat back against the green vinyl seat. Nolasco half expected her to belch. "Off the record?" she said.

"That's right. I want this to be a private conversation just between the two of us."

"Okay."

He assumed she had agreed. "I think we might be able to help each other."

"Help each other?" she said.

"The recent killings have thrust the investigation into the public spotlight. The pressure is mounting for us to find a suspect. We're working on several leads." It was a bluff.

"How does that help me?" She said it without any animosity.

"I'm willing to give you the names of five suspects, names we have not yet made public, with the caveat that you don't run the information in the newspaper until we have narrowed the list to a solid suspect and I give you the okay."

"Won't the information come out when you have a solid suspect?"

"Not necessarily. We'd want to confirm it, but I would ensure you knew before any other reporter. It would be exclusive. You would run the story before any other media outlet, print or television."

Childress finished her Coke. "What do you want from me?"

"You're an investigative reporter. I know you've been digging on this file."

"And others," she said, matter-of-fact.

"What I'm asking is, should you come up with information on any of the five suspects whose names I provide you that might link a victim to a suspect, you will advise me of what you've learned."

Again, she didn't immediately answer. Then she said, "Can I run this agreement by my editor?"

"No." Nolasco shook his head and wondered if Childress had been listening to the part about the conversation being off the record. "And no one can know I am your source of information."

"Until I write the story."

"Not ever."

"And all you want from me is information I might learn in my investigation?"

"That's all."

"What makes you think I can uncover more information than your task force?"

Nolasco could only hope Childress had better success. "We're limited by certain rules and regulations when it comes to suspects. Trying to get phone taps or to tail the suspects has been met with some resistance by the judiciary and because of budgetary concerns. We're under intense pressure to find the killer, but we're facing roadblocks in our efforts to obtain sufficient evidence to properly vet each suspect. I know you have ways of getting information that I can't. I'm not suggesting you do anything illegal or put your life in danger, just let me know if you discover anything suspicious that we should look into further. If you find something, we'll take it from there. And you'll get your story."

"I'd have the story anyway."

"Not if we haven't released any of the suspects' names, or the piece of evidence that links each of the killings together."

Childress looked to be digesting what Nolasco had said, though it was hard to tell. Her gaze never stayed in one location or on one thing for long.

"Do we have a deal?" he asked.

Childress rubbed her forehead as if the Coke had given her a brain freeze, then extended her hand across the table. "Deal," she said.

Nolasco nodded to her large handbag. "No tape recordings, but you're going to want to take notes."

CHAPTER 14

Saturday, July 11, Present Day
Bellevue, Washington

Tracy met Nolasco in the Glendale Country Club parking lot in Bellevue early on a glorious Saturday morning. She didn't like giving up weekends, but Moss played so early Tracy would be home before Dan and Daniella got their day started.

The sun had just climbed above the trees lining the course and delineating the fairways, the sky an inviting light blue with stratus clouds streaked red, orange, and yellow. Native Washingtonians considered July, at least after the Fourth, to be the start of summer. Tourists fell in love with the Emerald City during summer visits, promptly moved, then second-guessed their decision when the wet winter arrived and carried well into spring. Unfortunately, the rain had no longer stalled the most recent migration fueling Seattle's decade-long run as the fastest-growing big city in America.

"Moss did all right for himself." Nolasco blew out cigarette smoke while looking over the lush fairways and picturesque greens. They descended a concrete staircase to the breezeway between the pro shop and the locker rooms.

"Moss had some help," Tracy said.

"The Last Line?"

"Bet on it," Tracy said.

"But you can't prove it."

"Not in a court of law."

"How do you know he'll show this morning?"

"He golfs every Saturday morning at this hour with three other men—rain, sleet, or snow."

"How do you know that?"

"The last time I needed to speak with him he made me ride passenger in his golf cart."

Nolasco chuckled. "Beautiful day, but I ain't riding in his golf cart. And he isn't going to like having his golf game disrupted."

"Which makes the day all the more beautiful," Tracy said.

Tracy and Nolasco didn't have long to wait. Within minutes, Moss stepped from the locker room in his colorful golf clothes and started barking at others grabbing pushcarts or climbing into golf carts. He looked like a neon, Norwegian version of Del and Faz, a big man who carried his height and girth with confidence. He glanced at Nolasco and Tracy, but their presence didn't immediately register, like snow falling in May. It took him a moment to process what was out of order. When he did, he lost the smile.

"Moss," Nolasco said.

Moss glanced at Tracy but spoke to Nolasco. "What brings you here, Johnny?"

"Need a word."

"About?"

"You want to do this here, out in the open?"

Moss looked suddenly concerned. He glanced at the men and women coming and going—some were giving him side-glances—and decided he didn't. "There's a conference room in the back of the locker room. You can follow me. Crosswhite will have to go around."

"We'll all go around," Nolasco said.

Moss hesitated, perhaps weighing the fact that he no longer had to take commands from anyone against the possibility Tracy and Nolasco had additional information to put his butt in jail. He decided to be a good boy.

"Hey, Stan," he said to an elderly man getting into a golf cart. "I'm going to be tied up a bit."

"You afraid of losing money this morning, Moss? Chickening out?"

"I have some police business to attend to. I'll catch up. Keep your phone on so I can text and find out what hole you're on."

Then he led Tracy and Nolasco through doors to the restaurant but turned down a hall with photographs of past club presidents and plaques identifying yearly champions. At the end of the hall, he stepped into a conference room of round tables with windows looking over the pool and the golf course. He closed the door on the other side of the room, presumably leading to the men's locker room, pulled out a chair, and sat.

"What's this about?" Moss asked. He was nervous. He put on a good show, but Tracy could see in his somber expression that Moss thought they had come to confront him about the money he'd taken from the Last Line. She wondered if it had been worth it. He had to live in fear that someday, someone would talk, and he'd find himself in handcuffs and maybe wearing a much blander wardrobe than at present, though again, statutes of limitation made that unlikely. Tracy didn't think it was Moss's conscience that bothered him. He had rationalized his crime, as Chief Weber had done. He was looking out for himself. Tracy had no doubt he'd sell out someone else to save his own butt.

"The Route 99 serial killer," Nolasco said.

Moss initially looked confused, then relieved. He exhaled. "You find the killer?"

"We're working on it."

"That was twenty-five years ago, Johnny."

"Twenty-seven from the date of the first murder," Tracy said.

Moss spoke to Nolasco. "The killer's likely dead or in prison."

"That's what we're trying to find out," Tracy said. She wouldn't be ignored. "You were the lead control officer."

Moss finally acknowledged her. "Yeah, I was."

"You followed up on tips deemed worthy and kept track of the evidence?"

"Again. Yeah."

"Don't be like that, Moss," Nolasco said, surprising Tracy. "We're not here to rattle your cage. We're here trying to find answers."

Moss sighed and pursed his lips. Then he gave a brief and curt nod.

"Did you find anything in common between the victims?" Tracy asked.

"Which set?" Moss said. He looked to Nolasco. "The prostitutes or the PTA moms?"

"The PTA moms," Tracy said.

Moss broke eye contact. "Only thing that jumped out at me, at least what I can remember from so long ago, was the women all worked for the city, though in different departments. You remember, Johnny. We tried to determine if maybe the killer held a grudge against the city—had a permit turned down, was evicted from a home or apartment. But I don't remember anything coming out of it. Do you?" Moss asked Nolasco.

Tracy wondered why Moss had broken eye contact, then looked to Nolasco for assurance.

Nolasco shook his head.

"I don't remember anything else," Moss said.

She had a sense that wasn't true. "You focused on the killer," Tracy said. "Whether he held a grudge. Did you focus on the women?"

"We *were* focused on the women," Moss said, sounding defensive.

"I mean did you determine whether the women had something else in common."

"Such as?"

"I don't know," Tracy said. "I wasn't part of the task force."

"Bingo," Moss said. "So don't question what you know nothing about." Again, he sounded defensive. Tracy had experienced something similar when she accused Moss of taking money in the Last Line investigation. He got defensive, told her she didn't know what she was talking about, then lashed out. Guilt. What could he be guilty about in this case?

"Anything come in over the tip line about any of the women—a connecting thread you could pull between two or more of them?"

"Beyond working for the city?" Again, he looked to Nolasco. "A couple went to the UW, but that isn't unusual up here. At least not back then. Everyone who lived here went to the UW."

"Same sorority? Same classes? Same apartment building? Same boyfriend?" Tracy asked.

"I don't remember anything like that," Moss said. "And you're ignoring the other nine women. They certainly didn't join the same sorority."

Tracy wasn't ignoring those victims. She was accepting Santos's opinion that the first nine women had been the killer perfecting his craft and maybe sharpening his nerve. The last four had been about sending a message. "I spoke with Augustus Cesare," Tracy said.

"How's old Augie doing?" Gunderson said. The shortened name sounded like a typical Moss put-down.

"He said when the task force shut down he put his work—the tips and any connecting threads—on a computer disk and gave it to you."

"First, that was my work, not his. Augie was just a grunt I brought in to free me up. Second, I don't recall a disk, but if he says he did it, then the disk would be in the file boxes with everything else."

"It isn't," Tracy said.

Moss looked between Tracy and Nolasco, as if expecting something more. When neither said anything further, he shook his head. "Don't know what to tell you."

"Did you take it?" Tracy asked.

"What is this shit?" Moss shook his head and looked to Nolasco. "What is this bullshit, Johnny?"

But Nolasco wasn't offering any help. "Just answer the question, Moss, and you'll meet your friends on the fourth tee box."

Gunderson looked at Tracy as if looking at dog shit on the bottom on his shoe. "No. I didn't take the disk. I don't even remember a disk. If Cesare created one, I would have boxed it up with everything else, and it would be in storage. So maybe you didn't look hard enough, or maybe Cesare is mistaken and he didn't prepare a disk. Maybe he printed out the material and it's in a box but on reams of paper."

Tracy doubted that had been the case, given Cesare's statement he had only worked the task force because he was proficient with computers at a time when not a lot of SPD's officers had been. Certainly not Moss. Still, she wondered why Moss remained defensive.

"Did you have any conversations with the media?"

"While working the task force? No. None. Johnny was the only one."

"You knew Lisa Childress?"

"Knew of her. Didn't know her."

"You never talked with her about the investigation?"

"Why would I?"

"Is that a no?" Tracy asked.

"Yes, it's a no. Why do you ask?"

"The task force had a leak," Nolasco said.

Moss looked to Nolasco. "Did we?"

"It appears someone told Childress about the angel's wings on the victims' left shoulder."

"It wasn't me. Never talked to a reporter in my life."

"Except maybe to cut a deal," Tracy said.

"Excuse me?" Moss's brow furrowed and his gaze narrowed.

"Childress was also investigating the Last Line drug task force. If she had evidence you took drug money . . . I don't know. Maybe you tried to keep your name out of the paper by bargaining with information you were privy to, working on the Route 99 serial killer task force."

"Are you for real?" He looked to Nolasco as if to say, *you should know better.* "I don't know anything about any money from the Last Line. And if I did, why would Childress make such an agreement with me?"

She wouldn't have, Tracy knew. The Lisa Childress she'd come to know through Anita would have seen such a deal as a breach of her ethical duty as an investigative reporter. She just wanted to gauge Moss's reaction to the accusation, see if she could probe the cracks in his armor. He looked and sounded like a guilty man.

Moss stood. Angry. "We're done here; aren't we?" He looked to Nolasco. "I expect this shit from her, but you . . . This is disappointing, Johnny. This is beneath you." He pushed back and knocked over his chair, then flung the door open and stormed into the locker room.

"You got a way with people, Crosswhite," Nolasco said.

"Why is he so defensive?" Tracy asked.

"Because he doesn't like you, and he really doesn't like you accusing him. Do you have anything to indicate Moss took the disk or was the source of the leak?"

"Nothing except I believe Cesare when he said he made a disk and gave it to Moss. And now it isn't there. And Moss is a blowhard. Always has been, according to Del and Faz. I could see him trying to work a reporter if she had information on him taking drug money."

"So nothing solid then," Nolasco said.

"Nothing solid," Tracy said.

"And I gave up my Saturday morning for this. I think we're done being a burr in the man's ass." Nolasco stepped past her and back out the door they had entered. They were done, but Tracy still didn't have an answer to her question.

Why was Moss so defensive?

CHAPTER 15

February 28, 1996
Seattle, Washington

Nolasco stubbed another cigarette into his ashtray already filled with half a dozen butts as he continued to review documents. This early in the morning, he wasn't worried about the newly established smoking policy. He wasn't going down seven floors to smoke outside in the blistering cold. With the door to his task force office closed and most of SPD gone but for the graveyard shift, he wasn't bothering anybody.

He could have taken the materials to his sparsely furnished apartment, but that would have only depressed him. Things had progressed from bad to worse with his wife. They could no longer stand being in the same home together or tolerate one another for the sake of their grade school daughters. His kids, no doubt sensing the tension, had become rebellious and sullen. Nolasco had suggested a family counselor. His wife said it was just typical preteen years, and what did Nolasco care since he was barely home anyway, leaving her to be the disciplinarian.

They had separated. He'd moved out and let his wife remain in his house, the one he had bought and remodeled. He didn't want his daughters to be uprooted from familiar surroundings and possibly have to change schools. In return, they blamed him for the separation and impending divorce, the long hours he spent at work. No doubt their mother had put that thought in their ears. He didn't tell them about their mother's affair, which he had confirmed. He didn't think it fair to them.

The wheels were also coming off at work, one lug nut at a time, and his once-promising career wobbled more with each passing day. His rapid rise through the detective ranks had not just stalled, it had crashed. People no longer spoke about him in terms of how high he might ascend within the SPD, or about all he had accomplished at a young age. They only spoke of what he had not accomplished. He had not arrested the killer. And it was looking less and less likely, barring some unforeseeable break of luck—a witness who happened to stumble onto something or see someone; a piece of DNA they could match; a fingerprint; a concerned neighbor who noticed something unusual. Something. Anything.

It had been six months since the killer's thirteenth victim, Debbie Langford, a housewife living on Beacon Hill. The twelfth murder, Christina Griffin, had been the month prior, in July 1995, and with each succeeding death, the hysteria in middle-class suburbia increased, as did the pressure on SPD—Nolasco specifically—to catch the man responsible. There had been talk of replacing him as head of the task force, but that stalled because no one knew the case as well as Nolasco, and it would take anyone outside the task force weeks, if not months, to catch up. The brass had brought in the FBI and, in so doing, made it clear Nolasco was to give them everything they needed—to lick their boots to a high-gloss shine if asked.

Then the killings stopped.

Six months.

Nolasco ran his hands through his hair and examined his desk calendar, which revealed several more fallen strands. His hair felt brittle to the touch. He probed the cowlick atop his head and could feel where his hair had noticeably thinned. It wasn't genetics. Both his grandfathers had died with full heads of hair, and Nolasco usually had to have the barber thin his hair when he got it cut. Not anymore.

He slid open his desk drawer and removed the bottle of lorazepam. He didn't want to take the pills for his anxiety and stress. One of the side effects was drowsiness. He was already tired. Dog tired. And likely depressed. He'd been self-medicating with a stiff Scotch at night and recognized the drink was becoming more than a habit. He didn't want to shitcan what was left of his career by becoming an alcoholic, especially since it looked more and more like he was about to be a single father of two. The doctor told him the medication would help shut down his mind long enough to sleep at night, and he was sticking to routine.

Someone knocked on his door. Nolasco replaced the bottle and quickly closed his desk drawer, then tossed the ashtray and butts into the garbage can beneath his desk.

"Yeah," he said.

Moss Gunderson pushed open the door, filling the doorway with his large frame. He winced, an indication he smelled the smoke. "Saw the light on beneath the door. You're still at it, huh?"

"Still at it."

"They going to shut us down?" Moss asked.

"Don't know. Until I do . . ." Nolasco shrugged. There had been talk of shutting down or at least reducing the size of the task force.

"What's on your hand?" Moss asked.

Nolasco looked at the outside of his right palm, black from using it to erase the whiteboard on which he'd been listing the suspects, the dates the victims had been killed, and confirming whether each of the five suspects had been in the state of Washington or had possibly returned from out of state. He hoped to find some thread that would lead them down the yellow brick road to the killer's front door. Instead, he learned two of the five had been incarcerated at the time of the last two killings, and a third had moved out of state.

He wasn't getting closer to the killer. He was getting farther away.

"What's up? Why are you here so early?" Nolasco asked.

"Ellis and I are the on-call team this week. We're on our way to pick up a pool car. We got a call of a missing person."

"Why are they sending you two? Why not another team?"

"Sergeant said task force members are returning to their detective units. That's why I asked if we were getting shut down."

"No one has said anything to me," Nolasco said, angry. He was being isolated. "What type of a missing persons case?"

"A wife. The husband called last night. Said she's been missing since leaving the house at two yesterday morning."

"Why'd he wait so long to call? Do they think he killed her?"

"That's what Keith and I hope to find out. It's always the husband or a boyfriend; isn't it?"

"Not always," Nolasco said, stating the painfully obvious.

"But that's not why I'm here." Moss paused. Something clearly on his mind.

"What is it?"

"The woman who went missing is Lisa Childress, the investigative reporter for the *Post-Intelligencer* who's been covering the Route 99 killings."

The name hit Nolasco like a dart. Childress had called him just a few days ago and left him a cryptic message. Cryptic to him. Probably not to her. She said she was looking into something that would tie everything together but didn't explain further. He'd tried to call her back, without success.

Gunderson looked to be measuring Nolasco's response. "Like I said, thought you might want to know."

"Anybody have eyes on her or know where she went at that hour of the morning?" Nolasco asked.

"Husband says she went to meet a source for a story she was investigating."

Shit.

Another bolt sheared off the wheel, Nolasco's career about to crash. If Childress left the house at two in the morning, could she have gone to Aurora to walk the track, bait a killer? Or had she reached out to one of the five suspects? She wouldn't be that stupid; would she? Nolasco didn't tell her to do that. He was just hoping she'd come up with some angle the task force hadn't thought of, maybe find a witness they hadn't interviewed or a piece of evidence that led somewhere.

Could she have been so careless? Could she have done something like that?

Everything ties together.

"Did the husband know her source, or the story she was working on?" Nolasco asked Moss.

"Responding officer asked. Husband says she never told him those things. He did say it was not unusual for her to be working multiple stories. Again, that's something Keith and I will seek to verify, try to determine if he's lying. We'll also have a conversation with her editor at the *P-I*, see if he knows what she was working on."

"Keep me posted," Nolasco said.

"Will do." Moss turned for the door, then turned back. "You all right? You look pale."

"Too many late nights and early mornings, and shitty food," Nolasco said.

"I hear you. You don't think Childress could have gotten too close to the Route 99 Killer, do you?"

"Why would I think that?" Nolasco said and realized he sounded defensive.

"She was covering it for the paper."

"I have no idea."

Moss turned for the door but again turned back. "One other thing. You hear about the murder down in the industrial district yesterday morning?"

That triggered Nolasco's pulse. His adrenaline kicked in. "Another woman?"

"No. No, nothing related to our guy. This was a man. They found him shot in his car behind a trucking company. The superintendent called it in when he arrived at five a.m. The guy's car was blocking the trucks."

"They have any suspects?"

"Don't know. I'm not handling it. Just heard about it. Interesting though."

"Why is that?"

"The guy who got shot. Name's David Slocum. He was the harbormaster over at the Diamond Marina in Lake Union. We fished two bodies out of there not long ago."

Nolasco shook his head, uncertain why Moss was telling him this. "That supposed to mean something to me?"

"Nah," Moss said. "Just wondering if you'd heard about it."

"I've been pretty busy, Moss. I'm up to my eyeballs here." *And possibly soon to be working alone.*

"Yeah, I know. You think maybe our guy is done?"

"Voluntarily? No. Definitely not. For the moment everything is still a go. The brass is treating this as an open investigation, and I will also, until I'm told otherwise."

"I better run," Moss said. He rapped his knuckles on the door.

"Moss?" Nolasco said. "Anything interesting come in over the tip line recently?"

"Nothing new," he said.

After Moss had closed his office door, Nolasco opened his desk drawer, popped the lid on the prescription bottle and shook a small tablet into the palm of his hand, then placed it beneath his tongue. While he waited for the lorazepam to kick in, he pulled another cigarette from the pack. When he went to light it, his hand shook. He needed his other hand to hold the flame still. He inhaled, then stood and paced. He thought about how he might explain it if they found Lisa Childress's body with angel's wings carved just below her left shoulder.

CHAPTER 16

Sunday, July 12, Present Day
Redmond, Washington

Tracy sat in the backyard sipping a cup of coffee and listening to the baby monitor for signs Daniella had awakened. Dan lay in bed, no doubt in that dream state. Tracy would bring him the Sunday newspaper and coffee when she went back upstairs. She was enjoying the morning, the peace, and the sunshine warm on her face.

She opened the paper to the metro section and groaned. So much for a peaceful Sunday. The *Times* had run the first of the series of articles on the Route 99 Killer and his victims. Reading it made her queasy. She could only imagine what it would do to Nolasco.

Her personal cell phone rang on the table. Speak of the devil.

"Meet me in the lobby of Police Headquarters ASAP," Nolasco said.

"You read the article?"

"I didn't bother to read past the headline. Meet me."

"What's up?"

"I'll tell you when you get here."

"You're already there?"

"Catching up. Got a call. You'll want to be there."

"Be where?" she asked, but Nolasco had already hung up. Dan was going to get his newspaper and his coffee early.

—

Tracy reached Police Headquarters but Nolasco, already in the lobby fingering an unlit cigarette, didn't wait for her to enter. He pushed open the glass door and stepped out onto the sidewalk, walking past her. "We need to hurry."

Tracy rushed to catch up as Nolasco hurried down the sidewalk, hands cupped in front of his mouth to light the cigarette.

"Where are we going?" she asked.

"King County Jail." He blew out a stream of smoke.

"Okay. Why?"

"Because they're booking Dwight McDonnel, and I told the arresting officer I want to talk to him before he makes a call and lawyers up."

"Dwight McDonnel, the Route 99 suspect?"

"One and the same. He's got a bulldog for an attorney, at least he did. If he tells McDonnel to shut up, we won't get a word out of him. I don't want to take the time to have him brought over to Police Headquarters and talk to him in an interrogation room. We might get further if we surprise him at the jail and he feels the weight of confinement."

"What did they pick him up for?"

Nolasco glanced at her from the corner of his eye. "Apparently he tried to strangle a prostitute in an Aurora Avenue motel."

—

Fifteen minutes later, Tracy and Nolasco waited inside a windowless interrogation room of the King County Jail. They were told McDonnel would be processed, held overnight, and have a first hearing in the jail courtroom in the morning.

"If he gets convicted or pleads, we can get a DNA sample," Tracy said.

"I know," Nolasco said.

"You consider the timing—the twenty-five-year anniversary of the killings? You think he could have done this on purpose?" Tracy asked.

"No idea, but yeah, the timing is suspicious."

Feet shuffled outside the room, and they looked to the door. A corrections officer ushered in McDonnel, though Tracy would not have recognized him from the photographs in the Route 99 files. The man in those photos had been young, with chiseled features, dark hair with sideburns, and well built. McDonnel was no longer a young man. Now fifty-eight years old, age and gravity had taken over. His paunch pushed out his scrub shirt above the drawstring of his pants. His once-sharp facial features sagged like candle wax in the hot sun. His dark hair had turned white, the sideburns shaved. He wore glasses. When he saw Nolasco, he groaned audibly. Then he closed his eyes and shook his head, uttering an expletive.

"Good to see you too, Dwight. Though you've looked better. You look like you got in a fight with a wildcat."

Medical tape wrapped McDonnel's right wrist, and he had a scratch beneath his left eye, which looked watery behind his glasses. He shuffled forward in flip-flops, his wrists cuffed together and to a bellyband around his waist.

McDonnel uttered a string of profanities. In between, Tracy deciphered what he said. "Bitch bit me and tried to take my eye out. I'm filing a criminal complaint and a civil suit."

"A civil suit?" Nolasco said. "Good call. I'm sure you could go after her savings account, 401(k), pension plan."

The corrections officer pushed on McDonnel's shoulder to make him sit. McDonnel turned his body and looked away, like a sullen kid expecting a reprimand. Tracy and Nolasco remained standing, an inter-rogation technique to gain higher status than the suspect.

"As for a criminal complaint, she says it was self-defense." Nolasco had briefly spoken on the phone to the sergeant of the two responding uniformed officers.

"Bullshit."

"Says you tried to strangle her, Dwight."

"More bullshit."

"Yeah? Well, if the emergency-room doctor finds bruising around her throat, it will prove who's the bullshitter, so no need to quibble. You want to tell me what happened?"

"I don't have to talk to you. My lawyer told me that."

"You give him a call already? Sounds like the first move of a guilty man, Dwight."

"He's dead. Had a heart attack a decade ago."

"Can't say I'm heartbroken. Always thought he was a prick. Leaves you in a bit of a bind though."

"I have a right to a public defender."

Nolasco smiled. "Words spoken by many men just before they were convicted."

McDonnel let out a burst of air, perhaps the gravity of the situation hitting him.

Nolasco took a seat across the table. Tracy mimicked him. "You want to tell me what happened before I go talk to her and get her story?" Nolasco said. McDonnel still wouldn't look at them. After a long minute, Nolasco gave a sharp rap of his knuckles on the table and said to Tracy, "Okay, Detective, let's go talk to the victim. I'm betting she has a lot more to say. Officer, take him back to his cell."

"I didn't do it," McDonnel said quietly, still avoiding eye contact.

"She says you did," Nolasco said. "And as I said, examination will likely prove that much."

"I meant, I'm not your guy, Detective." He turned and addressed Nolasco. "I know why you're here, and I'm not your guy."

"It's captain now, Dwight. And why am I here?"

McDonnel shook his head. "Because of what she's saying—that I strangled her. It's how the Route 99 guy killed his victims, back when you were the detective. It was in the paper back then. Everybody knew he strangled them. I'm not your guy."

"About the paper, Dwight, anything significant about today's date?"

"No idea what you're talking about."

"I'm talking about you strangling her, Dwight."

"Like I said, it was consensual."

"You were just having fun then?" Nolasco said.

"I paid for rough sex. She said it was all good. We negotiated up front. Then it wasn't."

"Apparently one of you was seriously mistaken about the definition of rough sex. Did you specifically say strangulation?"

McDonnel didn't respond.

"You two discuss anything other than strangulation?"

"Like what?"

"I don't know. I clearly don't know the definition of rough sex. Educate me, Dwight."

"We didn't discuss details. I said rough sex. She said it would cost more. I paid."

"Where have you been, Dwight?"

"When?"

"Where have you been all these years? What have you been up to?"

McDonnel again swore under his breath. "Seriously? We're going to start this again? The same place as the last time you asked—working as a mechanic . . . until I hurt my back a year or so ago. Since then, I've been laid up at home."

"Remind me. Where did you work?"

Tracy mentally pulled up McDonnel's suspect file. "Ford dealership in Shoreline. They put me through their mechanic's program. Worked there twenty-five years. You can ask. I'll give you their number."

"You married, Dwight?" Nolasco asked.

"Was."

"Divorced?"

"Yep."

"How long ago you get divorced?"

"Year or two. Why, are you looking for date prospects?"

"How long were you married?"

McDonnel shook his head. Tracy thought he'd refuse to answer, but he kept on talking. "About twenty-five years."

"You don't know for sure?"

"We lived together before she got pregnant."

"You're a father, then? Son? Daughter?"

"Two daughters."

"I know divorce can be tough and lonely. Am I right?"

"We did it amicably."

"That's good. Saves a lot of money that otherwise just goes to the attorneys. Kind of like criminal defense lawyers. They get paid win or lose, though they don't really lose. You do. Why don't you be smart here, Dwight?"

"What do you want from me?"

"Just tell the truth. You tell the truth and I'll let the judge know you cooperated."

"I told you the truth. There's nothing else to tell. I paid for rough sex. Then she assaulted me."

"Okay . . ." Nolasco stood. So did Tracy. "You do know that we'll get your DNA," Nolasco said. "I walk out this door, Dwight, all deals walk with me. I won't come back."

"I'm not your guy," McDonnel said.

They left the room without another word from McDonnel and found the responding officers who had arrested McDonnel and brought him to the jail. "Where's the woman?" Nolasco asked.

"She's receiving medical treatment at Harborview. My partner is taking a statement."

"How badly was she hurt?"

"He beat her up pretty good after she bit him. They took X-rays for facial fractures, but given the look of her, he definitely broke her nose."

Tracy and Nolasco walked the few short blocks up James Street to the Harborview Medical Center's emergency room and spoke to the officer in the lobby. He told them the woman, Yvonne Clarke, was in a recovery room.

As they made their way down the linoleum floor toward Clarke's room, Tracy was concerned Nolasco's straightforward, take-no-prisoners interrogation style was not the best approach for questioning a woman who'd just been through an ordeal. "Captain," Tracy said before they stepped inside the room. "Maybe it would be best if you let me take the lead. I can talk to her woman to woman."

"I can interview a woman, Crosswhite."

"I don't doubt it, Captain. It's just, she's likely to be fragile and maybe a little distrusting of the legal system, given her line of work."

"Fine," Nolasco said. "You want to talk to her . . ." He gestured to the door. "Be my guest."

Yvonne Clarke sat upright in bed, a tray on a rolling cart angled across her lap. Her eyes were swollen red puffs that would soon turn black and blue. A bandage covered her nose, and more bandages ran beneath her nose from one cheek to the other. She looked at Tracy and Nolasco with angry, distrusting eyes.

"Ms. Clarke. I'm Detective Crosswhite. This is Captain Nolasco. We'd like to ask you a few questions about what happened."

"Look what he did to my face," Clarke said, the words slightly garbled from a swollen lip. As Clarke spoke, Tracy noticed she was missing teeth. Given Clarke's age, late forties, emaciated condition, missing teeth, and the brown color of those teeth that remained, she was likely a meth addict. "How am I supposed to make a living looking like this?"

"I'm sorry," Tracy said. "I know you must be in considerable pain, and we won't take up much of your time so you can get some rest. We'll come back another time to get a longer statement, but we wanted to speak with you while everything is still fresh in your mind."

"Oh, I won't forget. You can bet on it."

"Why don't you tell us how you met Mr. McDonnel."

"Is that his name—McDonnel?"

"What name did he give you?"

"Said I could call him Mickey, like the mouse."

"Where did you meet him?"

"On Aurora. He pulled up in a truck. Said he was looking for a good time. When I was satisfied he wasn't a cop or a weirdo, I gave him the name of the motel and a room number."

"You didn't get in the truck."

"No. No. No. You get in the truck, and he can take you anywhere. Kill you and dump your body. I know the motel and the motel knows me."

"McDonnel met you at the motel room then?"

"He did."

Tracy would get those details later. "What exactly did he say?"

"Just like I told you. He was looking for a good time. I told him what a good time would cost. He said fine."

"No negotiation?"

"I don't negotiate. The price is what it is."

"Okay. Did he get any more specific about what he meant by a good time?"

"Nope," she said shaking her head.

"What about at the motel room? Was he any more specific?"

"Nope. Just got down to it."

"Did the subject of rough sex come up?"

"If it had, I would not have agreed, and we wouldn't be here."

"You aren't into that?"

"Is this his definition of rough sex?" She pointed to her face. "Then the answer is 'definitely not.'"

"So he never brought up the subject."

"Never did."

"Why don't you tell me what happened when you got to the motel room?"

"He got to it, like I said. Didn't waste no time. Next thing I know he puts his hands around my neck and starts squeezing and saying things like 'You like that? You like how that feels?'"

"What did you do?"

"What I know how to do. I raked my fingernails across his face and caught his eye. When he quit squeezing, I bit his hand. That's when he went crazy. Started punching and slapping me and yelling things. If the people next door hadn't called the security guard, he might have killed me."

"Did McDonnel say anything else?"

"Yes, he did," Clarke said, sounding and looking bold but not continuing.

Tracy asked, "What did he say?"

"He said he'd killed bitches like me before and had no problem killing another."

Tracy glanced at Nolasco, who was doing a good job of keeping a poker face, but she could tell by his intense stare he wanted to bolt out the door to the phone to get a search warrant.

"Did he say anything else?"

"I don't know. At some point I think I blacked out or stopped listening."

"Did he say when he'd killed other women?" Nolasco asked.

"I don't know. I don't think so."

"But he did say he'd killed other women?" Nolasco persisted.

Clarke waffled. "I can't say for sure. He might have. He might have said, 'I strangled bitches and I'm going to strangle you.'"

"Do you recall those words?" Tracy tried to slow the conversation.

"It was something like that. Killed or strangled," but Clarke already sounded less sure.

"Did he say he did anything else about those women he killed?" Nolasco said.

"Like what?"

"Anything?"

"I don't think so."

Nolasco turned for the door. Tracy thanked Clarke and said she'd have an officer get an address so Tracy could come back and get a recorded statement. Nolasco questioned the officer in the hallway.

"What did you recover from McDonnel?"

"Wallet, keys, a watch."

"Anything sharp? A knife? An X-Acto blade? Scalpel? Razor blades?"

"No, nothing like that. No weapons."

Nolasco turned to Tracy. "Call Faz. He knows this file. Ask him to come in. I'll approve his overtime. Have him put together a search warrant for McDonnel's car and house, and a swab for a DNA sample. We're going back to the jail."

—

They waited in the same windowless room. A different correctional officer escorted McDonnel inside.

"I told you, Detective. I'm not your guy."

Nolasco looked like someone hooked to electrodes, expecting to get shocked but not sure when and struggling to hold himself still. "Had an interesting conversation with Yvonne Clarke, Dwight."

"Who?"

"The woman you tried to strangle."

"I told you it was consensual."

"She begs to differ."

"My word against hers."

"Maybe. The doctor's examination will clearly show the bruising on her throat."

"Again, consensual."

"Uh-huh. And her testimony that you told her you would kill her, and that you had killed other women."

"I didn't say I killed anyone."

"Strangled then," Nolasco said.

McDonnel licked his lips, doing his best to remain calm. His Adam's apple bobbed as if a fish had just hit the hook at the end of a line in his stomach. "I don't . . . I don't know what—"

"Yeah, you do know what she's talking about, Dwight. You know exactly what she's talking about. And so do I. In fact, I'm going to get a warrant for your home, your car, and for your person. I'm going to get your DNA also, Dwight. And I'm going to match it to those other murders, the thirteen women."

McDonnel looked like he was chewing his cheeks. "I was just trying to scare her, for what she did."

"You can tell that to the judge, Dwight. But don't expect any sympathy."

"I'm not your guy, Detective," McDonnel said in a burst. "I was just angry. My back hurts and the doctors won't give me any more pills. I can't work. My wife left me. My daughters want nothing to do with me."

"Were you angry when you killed those other women, Dwight?" Nolasco said.

McDonnel shut his eyes and blew out a breath. Nolasco waited.

"I think I want a lawyer," McDonnel said.

CHAPTER 17

Late morning, back at Police Headquarters, things moved quickly. Nolasco commandeered a conference room on the seventh floor and he, Tracy, and Faz spoke on the speakerphone in the center of the table with the on-call homicide prosecutor, trying to put the finishing touches on a broad search warrant.

"I've included his cell phone," Faz said. "The geo records will tell us where he's been."

"What's that got to do with the sex worker he beat up?" the young female prosecutor asked.

Nolasco leaned forward like he was about to go through the box and yell in the woman's face. "She's giving an affidavit that McDonnel threatened her. She'll state he told her he'd kill her like he'd killed other women. McDonnel was a suspect in the Route 99 serial killings twenty-five years ago. Those women were also strangled."

"Will state or did state?" the prosecutor asked.

"Will. But she made the statement to me and Detective Crosswhite. We're going to get a written statement, but I don't want to wait."

"And is Detective Crosswhite—"

"I'm here, and what Captain Nolasco told you is accurate."

"Twenty-five years is a long time ago, Captain—"

"Are you serious?" Nolasco barked. "We're trying to solve thirteen cold cases. We finally get a break, and you want to debate this?"

"I'm just telling you the kind of questions we can expect from the on-call judge."

"And we can tell the on-call judge that families have waited decades to get some closure, some resolution," Tracy said. "We're obligated to pursue this lead."

"Did you confront McDonnel with what Clarke said?"

Nolasco grimaced but kept his composure. "Yes, I . . . we confronted him," he said.

"And—"

"And he said what he said twenty-five years ago. He wants a lawyer."

"He didn't confess, then."

"Do you know any serial killers who confess?" Nolasco said.

"Gary Ridgway—"

"Confessed only after we had his DNA conclusively proving he was the Green River Killer," Nolasco said. "That's what we're asking for here. I want this guy's DNA to compare with DNA left at one of the crime scenes."

"And he didn't deny strangling Yvonne Clarke," Tracy added. "He said he was 'angry.'"

"Didn't deny but also didn't confess."

"This debate is unnecessary," Tracy said, tired of arguing with the young prosecutor. "The bar is low to collect DNA and cell phone records, and an admission he strangled her is sufficient to establish probable cause that evidence *may be found*, justifying a warrant to search. It's also sufficient to establish his identity for comparison to other cases—not just the Route 99 Killer cases."

The prosecutor was quiet. Tracy got the sense the woman, duly chastised, was taking notes. Then the young woman said, "Why search his car and home?"

Nolasco threw up his hands in frustration.

Tracy kept her voice calm. She wanted to correct the prosecutor, but not embarrass her. "The Route 99 Killer cut his victims in a specific manner and in a specific location. We want to determine if McDonnel brought a knife or other sharp instrument with him or had access to them."

"Every home has a knife," the prosecutor said.

"Not the kind this guy used. To make the precision cuts he made, he had to use something like a scalpel or an X-Acto blade."

"Did he cut this woman—Yvonne Clarke?"

"He didn't have time. She raked his eyes and bit his hand and screamed before he could kill her."

"And his car? Why his car?"

Nolasco looked like he was going to come unglued. "I'm coming over to your office and we're going to put this together with any supporting declaration you need. Then we'll send the warrant over to the on-call judge. I'll be there in five minutes."

He had no sooner disconnected than the phone on the table rang. Tracy answered. The receptionist told them he had Chief Weber on the phone for Captain Nolasco. Nolasco waved at Tracy indicating he wanted her to tell Weber he'd already left the room. Tracy told the receptionist to wait a moment and put the call on hold.

Nolasco said, "Faz and I will go over and make sure we get a warrant and that it includes a swab to get McDonnel's DNA. You talk to Weber."

After both men had left the conference room, Tracy took a deep breath, hit the button, and told the receptionist to put Weber through.

"Captain Nolasco?"

"Captain is not here, Chief. He's working with the prosecutor to put together a search warrant."

"My office," Weber said and disconnected.

Tracy swore under her breath. She hadn't expected Weber to be in on a Sunday afternoon, but news traveled fast in the department, bad and good. She left the conference room and took the elevator to the eighth floor. Minutes later, with no need to announce herself since the assistant wasn't working on a Sunday, Tracy entered Weber's office. Weber stood by the round table and chairs dressed in blue jeans, flats, and a white shirt. The Sunday *Times* lay faceup on the table, displaying the headline of the article about the anniversary of the murders. She had the television tuned to a local news station. "I heard we picked up a suspect in the strangulation of a prostitute."

"Dwight McDonnel. He was a suspect in the Route 99 killings but was never picked up for a crime."

"So we don't have his DNA," Weber said.

"Not yet, but if we get a swab, we can compare it to what was collected at one of the victims' crime scenes."

"What did McDonnel say?"

"He says he isn't our guy. He says he paid the woman, Yvonne Clarke, for rough sex. That it was consensual."

"Did he strangle her?" Weber asked.

"She says he did, and he doesn't deny it. We haven't yet spoken to the emergency room doctor, but Clarke does have bruising on her throat consistent with what she says."

"What else did she have to say?"

"She fought back, raked her nails over McDonnel's face, and bit his hand. She said McDonnel lost it and began beating her and telling her he was going to kill her like he'd killed the other women. That he would strangle her."

Weber's eyes shifted to the newspaper. The chief was no doubt thinking what this could mean, to solve these thirteen murders the same day the newspaper ran the first in a series of articles critical of her department. She returned her gaze to Tracy. "Is she credible?"

Tracy paused and took a breath. "Ordinarily, I'd see a prosecutor punching all types of holes in her credibility. Based on her appearance, her teeth, I'd say she's a meth addict. But I can't see why she would make up something like this—something that specific."

"Did you confront McDonnel with what this woman had to say?"

"As I said, he doesn't deny saying it. He said he was angry, that he wanted to scare her. Then he said he wanted a lawyer."

"Sounds like bullshit. Sounds like he's our guy."

"It's too premature to make any conclusions. Captain Nolasco and Vic Fazzio are working with the on-call homicide prosecutor to put together a search warrant for McDonnel's car, home, and cell phone, and to obtain a DNA swab."

"His first appearance will be tomorrow morning in the jail courtroom," Weber said. "Let the prosecuting attorney's office know what we suspect and tell them to push to have McDonnel charged at his second appearance, and to oppose any bail when he's arraigned so he's held at least until we get the DNA back."

A person arrested was usually arraigned within two weeks. "Keep me posted," the chief added. "I'd like to have the paper run a different kind of article. And soon."

Tracy returned to her office and pulled up the file the task force had put together for Dwight McDonnel. The night McDonnel had been picked up for cruising the Aurora strip, the task force had set up a traffic-stop checkpoint for vehicles with any man traveling alone. McDonnel claimed he was heading to the supermarket to get groceries. The police photographed his truck and ran his driver's license. Women who walked the strip recognized McDonnel. They said he came by the track maybe once a month or every couple of weeks. They didn't report any problems with him, though one woman had said he put his hands around her throat during intercourse but removed them when she slapped his arms. After the checkpoint, police put McDonnel under surveillance, but he had never returned. Which could be why middle-class women became his target.

Nolasco called and said the judge had signed off on the search warrant. "I'm having Faz coordinate towing McDonnel's truck to the impound and put in a request to have a CSI team detail it. Faz will stay with the truck. I'm sending another detective to the jail to get a swab sample. Get ahold of Melton. Let him know what's going on. Ask him to rush processing McDonnel's DNA and the comparison to what's on file. I'll call the CSI sergeant and get a team sent to McDonnel's home in White Center. When you're done, meet me there." Nolasco provided the address. "And I want to keep this quiet for as long as possible."

"That's a problem," Tracy said. She grabbed her things and moved for the door. "Weber already knew about the arrest and that McDonnel tried to strangle Clarke."

"How did she know?"

"I don't know, and I didn't ask. I assume patrol or the first responders. She asked me if McDonnel could be our guy."

"What did you tell her?"

"I told her it was premature to know for certain, that you were putting together a search warrant for his house, car, and his DNA. But she's anxious to shove that article that ran this morning up the *Times*' collective asses."

"Aren't we all," Nolasco said.

—

Tracy, Nolasco, and the CSI team worked well into the night searching the one-story rambler McDonnel rented in White Center. The home was no more than fifteen hundred square feet, but with a considerable backyard enclosed by a wooden fence, portions of which were rotted and falling over. Nolasco had cadaver dogs brought to the site, but they did not alert to bodies beneath the brown lawn or the house. The detectives went through every nook and cranny of the home, found a 9-millimeter handgun and several knives, but nothing that appeared to fit the description of the knife the medical examiner had said the Route

99 Killer likely used. They inventoried everything and would take the knives to the crime lab for further processing, testing, and comparison to the cuts made on the victims.

Neighbors came out of their homes like moths to a flame. They described McDonnel as a quiet man who kept mostly to himself, especially after his wife and two adult daughters moved out of the house. Tracy asked if they'd ever witnessed McDonnel bringing home women, but no one had any such information. Those who knew McDonnel confirmed he had gone on disability for a bad back. They said he walked in the mornings.

About an hour into the search, Tracy looked down the block. Word had spread. Several cars and a news van and reporters waited in the summer light, which wouldn't fade until close to ten p.m. Greg Bartholomew was among them. As was Anita Childress.

Tracy found Nolasco in the backyard. "We have a news van down the street and reporters. Including Bartholomew."

"How the hell did they find out?"

"I don't know. Neighbors likely called in asking what was happening, and they picked up the call would be my guess. I'm assuming we don't want to say anything about anything."

"Tell patrol to make sure the cameras and reporters stay back. We're almost done here anyway."

"Anything?"

"Nothing specific."

Tracy returned out front and instructed two patrol officers to keep reporters as far back from the house as possible. She then stepped aside and made a call. Down the block, Anita Childress reached for her cell phone, looked at caller ID, and moved away from the others.

"Tracy."

"What's everyone doing here, Anita? What's the attraction?"

"You picked up and booked Dwight McDonnel for soliciting and assault and battery. McDonnel was one of the suspects in the Route 99 killings."

"But only you knew that."

"There's you."

"Meaning what?"

"Weber held a press conference stating you were reopening the Route 99 killings. If you're here, the reporters are just putting two and two together. Is there anything you can tell me?"

"Not at this time. No."

"I understand McDonnel's first appearance is tomorrow in the jail courtroom."

"You'll have to get that from the court, Anita."

"And the search of his house?"

"Can't respond at present."

"Jorgensen expedited the first article in the series."

"I'm aware. And I appreciate you letting me know."

"You have any comment at all?"

"None. I'll stay in touch."

Tracy disconnected and blew out a breath. She looked down the street at the cars and the news van, then back to the house where Nolasco stood on the porch, his head tilted back, blowing smoke into the air. A cigarette dangled from his fingers. He ran his other hand through his hair, examined it, then looked to be rubbing off loose strands. She was beginning to more fully understand the amount of pressure Nolasco had been under.

—

Late at night, Tracy stepped quietly into her house, going so far as to remove her shoes before closing the front door. It didn't help. The alarm system alerted. The barks, however, were muffled. Tracy had called earlier to tell Dan she would be working late, and she asked him to lock the dogs in the room at the back of the house with the dog door, so they wouldn't wake Daniella.

Tracy made her way down the hallway to the back of the house, the floors illuminated by LED lights in their socket covers. She opened the door, speaking gently and softly to her two big boys who were always happy to see her. The dogs pranced and bounced, their tails whipsawing and banging off the hall walls. Unconditional love.

"Hey, guys," she whispered as she rubbed their heads and coats. "You two are the best alarm system in the world. Yes, you are. Nobody is coming into this house with you two home."

Tracy never discouraged the dogs from barking when someone came to the door, and if anyone ever asked if her dogs bite, her standard response was "All dogs bite." She figured you didn't install an alarm system and then tell people it was turned off at night.

She and the dogs made their way upstairs. She peeked into Daniella's room—the yellow wallpaper with zoo animals softly aglow from the merry-go-round lamp on her dresser. Tracy entered, kissed Daniella's fingers, and gently touched her daughter's temple, which was sweaty. She retreated and made her way down the hall to the master bedroom.

Dan was sitting up in bed, reading on his Kindle.

"I wasn't sure you were still awake," she said.

"Got caught up in a good book. I'll pay for it in the morning. How was the search?"

"Nothing obvious. We were hoping to find something to tie him more closely to the killings, but I don't think we're going to find anything."

"I thought you said he confessed?"

"Not to the killings. But we'll know soon enough. We got a warrant to get a DNA sample while he's in custody. If his DNA is a match with the DNA at the one crime scene, it won't matter what he admits or denies."

"How are you holding up?"

"Funny you should ask that question. I was just this evening thinking the same thing about Nolasco."

"Really?" Dan asked, his tone not hiding his skepticism.

"He's smoking like a chimney and losing his hair. I've never known him to smoke, but Faz says he smoked when the task force was active, lost weight, his hair thinned, and he essentially had his career derailed by his failure to catch the killer."

Dan smiled. "You almost sound like you feel sorry for him, Ms. Crosswhite."

"I don't know about 'sorry' but I can certainly empathize with him. The Cowboy Task Force took a lot out of all of us."

"How long before you can match the DNA?"

"I asked Mike Melton to push it down at the lab, but it will be a few days, maybe a week."

"And until then?"

"McDonnel will be held in jail for his first two hearings, then arraigned, probably the following Monday. I'm expecting a crowd. Word got out. The media showed up at McDonnel's home tonight."

"Any idea who is the leak?"

"Not certain there was one. I spoke to Anita Childress, and she said my presence at the scene, in light of the news conference that I would pursue the Route 99 Killer, was telling. But Weber benefits most if McDonnel turns out to be our guy."

"You think it's this guy . . . What did you say his name was?"

"Dwight McDonnel. And I don't know. He wouldn't be the first serial killer to quit for a long period of time, then start again. McDonnel also said he's recently divorced. Could be the changes in his life are driving him to kill again. That's also not unprecedented. Could also be it's the anniversary of the murders. What I find unusual is for McDonnel to tell Clarke he killed others. Serial killers don't get caught because they don't talk about their kills."

"Maybe he thought he'd kill her too. She'd take his word to her grave."

"Maybe."

ONE LAST KILL   149

"I read the paper," he said. "If it is this guy, they may throw you a ticker-tape parade downtown."

"Not if I can help it. I'll deflect credit to Nolasco. His ego took a beating the first time. I don't think he could stomach my receiving the credit. If you think things between us are bad now . . ."

"Can you keep McDonnel in jail until the DNA analysis comes back?"

"He'll stay in jail until his arraignment. After that, it's not likely, according to Cerrabone," Tracy said, referring to Rick Cerrabone, a senior prosecutor she consulted often and had called before leaving work. "McDonnel has never been convicted of a crime and, at the moment, he has no connection to any of the Route 99 murders. We can't simply tell the judge we're waiting for a DNA test that may tie him to the other deaths."

"Can you put a tail on him, make sure he doesn't take off?"

"Nolasco and I have already talked about that. The department is hurting for funding and for officers. Staffing is at a thirty-year low and crime has escalated."

"So now you wait."

"Now we wait."

"Want to do anything while you're waiting?"

Tracy smiled. "Reading a good book, huh?"

Dan grinned as if caught. "I just picked up the Kindle as an excuse to still be awake."

"Since when do we need an excuse?"

"Hey, I don't want you to think I'm one of those guys who isn't genuinely interested in your day and just waited up to have sex."

"As long as you're one of those guys who's genuinely interested in waiting up to have sex with his wife, I'll cut you some slack."

"Then guilty as charged, Detective."

"Do you wish to post bond?"

"No, ma'am. I prefer to move forward with my sentencing."

CHAPTER 18

Monday, July 27, Present Day
Seattle, Washington

J ust about two weeks later, Tracy arrived for Dwight McDonnel's
arraignment and bail hearing in the arraignment courtroom, E1201
on the twelfth floor of the King County Courthouse. The pews were
uncharacteristically full. Families offering moral support and suit-clad
attorneys—if the accused could afford their own counsel—sat in the
nicked and scarred bench pews waiting for the roll call to begin. This
morning they were joined by local media.

McDonnel had made his first and second appearances in the jail
courtroom, at which point prosecutors had charged him with solicitation, and assault and battery, and held him over. No mention was made
of a connection to the Route 99 killings, but that was now a poorly kept
secret, especially with Tracy involved. It explained the media's presence.

Bill Jorgensen had used McDonnel's arraignment to move up the
next article in the series.

Anita Childress had let Tracy know ahead of time, but it didn't change the fact that the article had painted bull's-eyes on the foreheads of Tracy and Nolasco.

Inside the courtroom, the judge and the attorneys performed their jobs behind a plexiglass wall, their voices amplified by microphones and speakers. A correctional officer staffed a door to let counsel in and out as the bailiff called their clients' case numbers. The accused were brought over a catwalk from the jail to a holding cell and ushered into the courtroom.

Tracy recognized Greg Bartholomew seated at the far end of the first pew. He turned and considered her with a *so it's true* look, as did Anita Childress and other reporters Tracy either recognized or deduced from the notepads and pens in hand. Camera operators shouldering video equipment prepared to film through the plexiglass wall. This kind of attention only occurred for the more notorious arraignments.

Tracy found a spot near one of two arched windows providing bright morning light. Minutes later, Johnny Nolasco walked in the door dressed in a sports coat and tie. He paused to consider the crowd, spotted Tracy in the back, and made his way over. He smelled of fresh cigarette smoke and chewed a piece of mint gum.

He swore and said, "What a circus."

"Thinking the same thing." They waited in silence as the court worked through several cases on the docket. Defendants being arraigned, mostly men, entered behind the plexiglass wearing red jail scrubs, some with belly chains and handcuffs and accompanied by armed correctional officers. A young prosecutor stood below the bench with a stack of files, some of which that prosecutor probably hadn't seen before this morning. Nolasco had tried to convince Rick Cerrabone to handle McDonnel's arraignment, but he had declined, saying the only charges before the judge were for solicitation and assault and battery. Tracy agreed with Cerrabone. Having a senior prosecutor from the Most Dangerous Offender Project handle the arraignment would only add fuel to what was already a growing fire.

After half an hour, the prosecutor at the judge's bench shuffled her files and called the next matter on the docket—Dwight Thomas McDonnel. The reporters collectively sat up. The camera operators filmed. McDonnel entered the courtroom wearing the red prison scrubs and a belly chain. His right wrist remained bandaged, and the scratches on his face seemed more prominent beneath a shiny film, likely Vaseline. No attorney stood from the pews to enter the door.

"Public defender," Nolasco said.

The assembled crowd seemed to give McDonnel pause. His chest rose and fell, and he shook his head before the correctional officer turned him toward the bench and the judge. His public defender, a short Asian woman, stepped to his side, and McDonnel bent to listen to her. He nodded just once before straightening.

After the court clerk read the charges, McDonnel pled not guilty. The issue of bail was resolved almost as quickly. McDonnel and his counsel would contact a bail bondsman, and bail would be posted in the court registry. The judge set a pretrial date three weeks out and confirmed McDonnel understood that a failure to appear would result in a forfeiture of bail and he would be taken into custody. McDonnel said he understood and left without reconsidering the crowd.

As soon as McDonnel left the courtroom, Nolasco said, "Let's go," but there would be no escaping the reporters. Bartholomew and others caught them outside the courtroom. "Dwight McDonnel was a suspect in the Route 99 killings, was he not?" Bartholomew said.

"We had a number of suspects in those murders," Nolasco said, not stopping his progress toward the elevators.

"But McDonnel was one of them, wasn't he?"

"I can't comment on whether anyone was or was not a suspect."

"You undertook a search of McDonnel's home and his car following his arrest. What were you looking for?" Bartholomew persisted.

"Evidence tying him to the case for which he was just arraigned," Nolasco said.

"The beating of a prostitute?" Bartholomew said with disbelief. "Why would that necessitate a search warrant?"

It wouldn't, Tracy thought but didn't say.

Nolasco didn't answer, just made his way toward the elevators.

"The warrant also sought McDonnel's DNA," Bartholomew said. "Is there crime scene DNA that could be used to link him to the Route 99 killings?"

Nolasco lowered his gaze from the old-fashioned numbers that resembled a clock above each elevator. "I understand you all have a job to do. As do I. I cannot comment on any individual or evidence at this time. When I can comment, I will."

"Are you worried about McDonnel being granted bail?" Bartholomew asked.

"That was within the purview of the judge who granted it," Nolasco said. "I had no control over it."

"So you don't currently plan to arrest Dwight McDonnel for any of the Route 99 killings?"

"Again, I can't comment on any persons, evidence, or circumstances."

Bartholomew turned to Tracy. "Detective Crosswhite, have you uncovered evidence that SPD's task force failed to discover twenty-five years ago?"

"No comment."

Bartholomew spoke as the elevator arrived. "You're no stranger to solving cold cases. What is it you did that the task force team didn't do?"

Tracy didn't look, but she could almost feel the heat emanating from Nolasco's body.

"The victim, Yvonne Clarke, claims McDonnel tried to strangle her and told her he had strangled others," Bartholomew said. "She said you spoke to her?"

"We spoke to the victim at the hospital," Nolasco said. "We cannot comment on what was discussed."

"But whatever was discussed was sufficient to seek a warrant to search McDonnel's house and obtain a DNA swab. That would seem to corroborate what Yvonne Clarke said, that McDonnel strangled her and said he had strangled other women."

People stepped off the elevator before Nolasco and Tracy could step inside. The reporters did not follow. Inside the elevator, Nolasco audibly sighed. "When we get back to HQ, I want you to go through what we took from McDonnel's home. Look for anything and everything. Maybe your *fresh eyes* will spot something I can't."

"That was Weber's quote, not mine."

"See how long Melton thinks it will be before we find out if there is a DNA match."

They stepped from the elevator to the first floor. Nolasco briskly crossed to the exit. Tracy followed but once outside she turned right in the direction of headquarters. Nolasco turned in the opposite direction. She didn't ask him where he was going.

Minutes later, after a quick breakfast stop, Tracy stepped into her office and put her belongings away. She dropped a white bag containing a jalapeño bagel with cream cheese on her desk and picked up the phone. She called CSI and asked to speak to the sergeant to find out if they had processed any of the knives taken from McDonnel's home for comparison with the carvings.

As the two spoke, Tracy flipped through the mail in her in-box. She came to a dark-orange, five-by-eight-inch envelope. It had been mailed to the attention of Tracy Crosswhite with five forever stamps, and postmarked July 24. She felt something hard and square inside the envelope that her brain immediately processed and identified.

"I'll call you back," she said to the CSI sergeant. "Something has come up."

She set the envelope on her desk, then opened her desk drawers, but didn't find what she needed. She picked up the envelope by a corner and slid it into a desk drawer, locking it. She left the office and hurried to the A Team's four cubicles. Faz sat at his desk, talking on his telephone. Del also. Kins was not at his desk, nor was his new partner. Del gave Tracy a nod and a *good-to-see-you* smile.

Tracy gave Faz a gesture that she wanted to speak to him.

"Vera, let me call you back in a minute. Tracy just stepped into my cubicle looking like an addict in need of a fix. Yeah. I will. Okay." Faz hung up the phone. "Vera says hello and 'Don't do drugs.'"

"'An addict'?" Tracy said. "Seriously, Faz?"

"But you do need something."

"I need N-DEX gloves."

"Told you. I know that look."

"Do you have your go bag handy?"

"What do you need gloves for?"

"I want to shoot up some heroin."

Faz opened his locker beside his desk, retrieved his and Del's go bag, and handed her a box of gloves.

"Come with me," she said.

Back inside her office she slipped on the gloves and removed the envelope from the desk drawer, again holding it by an edge.

"What is it?" Faz asked.

She took an envelope opener and inserted it under the flap, cutting the top open, in case the person who mailed the envelope left fingerprints. She would also have the glue of the flap tested in case the person licked it with their tongue.

She turned the envelope upside down, shaking a computer disk onto her desk. On the label someone had written:

Tip Line Route 99 Task Force

Augustus Cesare

CHAPTER 19

Tracy slipped the envelope and the disk into an evidence bag and used a black permanent marker to identify the contents. Before she had TESU convert the disk into a usable format, she'd have SPD's Latent Print Unit check the disk and envelope for fingerprints and, if they found any, have those prints run through AFIS, then send the envelope to Park 90/5 to be checked for possible DNA.

First, though, she and Faz took the elevator to the HR Department. They found Augustus Cesare on his computer. He looked up as Tracy and Faz approached, then stood.

"Faz," he said with a smile.

"Augie, how are you?" Faz said.

"You're still the only one who calls me that without it sounding disparaging."

"What can I say? I'm one of a kind," Faz said.

"What's up?" Cesare asked.

"Is this the disk you told me about?" Tracy said. "The one on which you copied all the tips and your work attempting to connect threads."

Cesare considered the contents of the evidence bag. "Yeah, that's it."

"That's not a duplicate?"

"No. That's definitely my handwriting. Why is it in an evidence bag?"

"Because it just showed up on my desk."

"What do you mean, 'just showed up'?"

"It wasn't in any of the storage boxes."

"It was mailed?" he said, looking at the envelope. "By who?"

"That's what I'm going to try to find out. You're certain this is the disk you gave to Moss?"

"As certain as I can be after twenty-five years."

"Could you have given it to Nolasco or Floyd Hattie?"

"I didn't have much interaction with either of them, other than the task force meetings. My interaction was with Moss."

"Can you think of any reason why someone would not have put the disk in the storage files?"

Cesare shook his head. He frowned. "No. Like I said, it's just the tip line calls and my work trying to find any connecting threads."

"A better question might be why send you the disk now, after all these years?" Faz asked. "Especially given the recent arrest of McDonnel."

Tracy didn't know, but she, too, thought the timing interesting.

"Heard he said he had strangled prostitutes." SPD was like a fishbowl. "Is it true?" Cesare asked.

"Don't know yet," Tracy said.

"What are you going to do with the disk?" Cesare asked.

"Have it and the envelope run for fingerprints, then DNA."

"Why?"

"I don't know," she said. She wondered if maybe Cesare's intimation was correct. Her job was to find the killer. What good would it do to determine that someone had kept the disk? Was she making a personal decision because of her dislike of Moss Gunderson, whom she suspected? Even if she determined Moss had sent the disk, what would that tell her?

Maybe nothing. Then again, she couldn't dismiss her gut feeling that it meant something.

Tracy thanked Cesare, and she and Faz departed. "What do you think I should do?" she asked Faz in the hallway.

"Me, I'd want to know who kept the disk and why," Faz said. "Especially if it was that blowhard Moss. But I'm Italian. I'm a vindictive son of a bitch."

"It has to be Moss; doesn't it?" Tracy said.

"Run it over to the Latent Print Unit and have them dust it for fingerprints, then you wait for hell to freeze over before you can get a DNA analysis. If it's Moss, you'll have some leverage to find out why he kept the disk."

Faz was right. A twenty-five-year-old disk would not be treated as high priority at the crime lab, no matter how many Salumi sandwiches Tracy bought Melton.

Tracy dropped the disk at the fingerprint unit.

Twenty minutes later, she pulled into the Park 90/5 complex and went inside to Melton's office. Melton shook his head before she opened her mouth. "I know what you're going to ask. They sent over McDonnel's DNA this morning. I can't get to it today, Tracy, and likely not for several weeks. Someone must have bitched about us putting the Route 99 DNA atop the pile, because I got a stink email from the prosecuting attorney and the attorney general's office about the lab prioritizing the rape cases."

"Who would have bitched?"

"Someone who wants the rape kits done. All I can tell you is what they'll tell me. The Route 99 cases are decades old. There isn't exactly a rush to get the DNA analyzed."

Tracy didn't push it. She knew DNA testing, like so many other things, had become political, and Melton would do her a favor, if he could.

"I understand."

"Don't do that. You look and sound like my daughters when they were trying to guilt me into changing my mind about something."

Tracy left Melton's office and called Nolasco. "I just left Park 90/5. Melton received McDonnel's DNA swab but says he can't do us a favor and run it. Someone bitched about us jumping the line. It could take weeks, maybe months before they get to McDonnel."

"Did Melton say that?"

"He didn't have to," Tracy said.

Nolasco issued a string of profanities. "I can make some calls."

"What about getting a private lab certified for this kind of forensic testing? We can have them run McDonnel's DNA and compare it to the DNA in the semen evidence for the fourth Aurora victim Faz tagged in the HITS form."

"Outside labs cost money," Nolasco said, "and the lab needs to be approved. The three that I know of are already busy processing the rape kits."

As captain of Violent Crimes, Nolasco had control over the budget for his section and a line item for "professional services" that included evidence testing. But Tracy also knew he'd been over budget the past two years because of the city council cutbacks, and he'd had his ass chewed for it.

"Let me see what I can do," he said. "At the moment I can't even get authorization to have a patrol car sit on McDonnel's house. We're that thin."

"If Weber wants us to solve these cases, this is the only way to get it done."

"You're preaching to the choir, Crosswhite."

Frustration crept into Nolasco's tone, and Tracy decided to back off and not say anything more.

"Where are you now?" he asked.

"On my way back in from Park 90/5."

"Let me know when you arrive. We'll both talk to Weber, since she's taken a liking to you."

Tracy bit her tongue. Weber liked Tracy the way the public liked O. J. Simpson.

Half an hour later, Tracy and Nolasco again sat in the anteroom outside Weber's office.

"Bartholomew called for a quote about Dwight McDonnel," Tracy said. "They're going forward with an article that McDonnel was a suspect in the killings."

"What did you tell him?"

"Said I couldn't comment."

The assistant's desk phone rang. She answered it, then looked to Nolasco and Tracy. "The chief will see you."

Tracy followed Nolasco into the office. Weber, seated behind her desk, refrained from greetings, getting right to the point. "How sure are you this guy McDonnel is the Route 99 Killer?"

"That's why we're here," Nolasco said.

"According to Bennett Lee, we're getting phone calls from the victims' family members wanting answers" she said, referencing the public information officer. "How the hell did the media find out about the search warrant for McDonnel's home and his DNA?"

"We don't know," Nolasco said.

"Either someone leaked it or they're just following logic," Tracy said.

"Meaning?"

"The press conference announced the reopening of the investigation and my involvement."

"If there is a leak, plug it. Now."

Tracy wanted to tell Weber this wouldn't be happening if she had listened to Tracy and not held the press conference or issued the press statement about reopening the serial killer investigation, but she didn't think that would get them very far. What she needed now was to have Weber expedite the DNA testing.

"Someone also leaked information twenty-five years ago that McDonnel was a suspect and that the killer branded his victims with angel's wings."

Weber looked to Nolasco. "Is this true?"

"Apparently," Nolasco said, giving Tracy a sharp-looking rebuke.

"How do you know about it?" Weber asked.

"The daughter of the reporter had her mother's investigative files. The angel's wings, along with McDonnel's name and the names of other suspects, were in her file on the Route 99 Killer."

Weber looked back to Nolasco. "You didn't know this?"

"That we had a leak? No." Nolasco closed his eyes. A habit for sure, but also a tell. Was he hiding something?

He looked to again be chewing nails.

"The point is," Tracy said, "the longer we have to wait to get McDonnel's DNA tested, the more phone calls Lee is going to receive asking what we're doing and why it's taking so long. The reporters are going to again imply that SPD doesn't care."

"Don't lay that on my doorstep," Weber said.

"I'm not laying it on your doorstep, but the media has and will continue to do so. Word is the *Times* will try to tie McDonnel to the killings and ask what we're doing to prove he is or isn't. I just came from the crime lab and was told they can't move McDonnel's DNA analysis up the line to be tested."

"Your solution?" Weber asked.

"Authorize funds to have the testing performed by a certified forensic lab. We can have the results back end of the week, before the paper runs its next big Sunday feature talking about our incompetence."

Nolasco looked from Tracy to Weber. The chief knew she was being played. She also knew she didn't have much choice. She didn't want to fight with the legislature and other politicians and look insensitive to the hundreds of raped women, but she also didn't want to take another shot to the chin in the media.

"You know a lab?" she asked Tracy.

Nolasco and Tracy left the chief's office, keeping their poker faces and not saying a word until they were in the stairwell heading back down to the seventh floor.

"Thought you were throwing me under a bus, Crosswhite."

"No, just trying to create some urgency so Weber would authorize funds."

"You have a lab in mind?" Nolasco asked.

"I'll get on it as soon as I'm back to my desk," Tracy said. She turned for her office.

"Crosswhite?"

Nolasco had that chewing-nails look again. Then he said, "Nice work back there."

It was as close to a thank-you as she was ever going to get.

CHAPTER 20

August 16, 1996
Seattle, Washington

M oss?"
Gunderson looked up from his desk cubicle. Augustus Cesare stood beside it. He raised his hand. "Hail, Cesare."

Cesare noticeably cringed. It was just too easy.

He handed Moss a computer disk.

"What is it?"

"All the tips I catalogued and the connecting threads I found between them. We are shutting down the investigation, right?"

The Route 99 Killer had not killed in a year.

"Not the investigation, just the task force," Moss said. "We announce that we're shutting down the investigation and the public will have a shit fit. I don't envy Nolasco. This investigation will stay with him like the chain around Jacob Marley's waist."

"Jacob Marley?"

"Come on, Augie. The ghost in *A Christmas Carol.*"

Cesare shook his head.

Moss took the disk. "I'll see it gets to storage."

"What are you going to do now," Cesare asked, "with the task force ending?"

"Me? Returning to Homicide. Top of the food chain, my friend."

"Are you going to need any help? Maybe a fifth-wheel position or something?"

"They give those positions to guys on their way out, Augie," Moss said, passing the buck. "One step to retirement. But I'll keep my eyes and ears open for you, and if I hear of anything, I'll put in a good word."

"I appreciate that, Moss."

"Anything else?" Moss asked when Cesare didn't immediately leave. "I got a lot on my plate here."

"No. Nothing else. Just been good working with you again."

"Yeah," Moss said, and deduced Cesare was looking for a compliment. "You done good, Augie. Not our fault we didn't catch the guy. Let's hope he's rotting in a hole somewhere or locked up in a prison cell getting gang banged."

"Definitely." Cesare smiled. "And you're welcome."

"For what?"

"What?" Cesare lost his smile.

Gunderson laughed. "I'm just yanking your chain, Augie. Get the hell out of here."

After Cesare left, Moss opened his drawer for an interoffice envelope to send the disk to storage with the Route 99 serial killer files. He was about to slide the disk into the envelope, then decided he'd better at least take a look at the contents, not that he was in any position to fix any mistakes, or even recognize them, though he doubted Cesare had made any. Still, if the shit ever hit the fan, he'd be the guy covered in feces.

He inserted the disk and heard the computer whir and hum. He followed the prompts, pressing buttons until he was looking at a log of thousands of phone calls. He hit the arrow on his keyboard and scrolled through them, slowly at first, then more quickly, and finally rapidly to the end.

He noticed a second tab at the bottom of the page and clicked on it, deducing it to be Cesare's attempt to find connecting threads between the killings and information learned from the calls. Moss skipped the first nine victims. The connecting thread was obvious. Prostitutes. Aurora motels. Prostitutes never brought their johns to the motel lobbies. They rented the rooms for the night or the week. So no witnesses.

He went to the tenth victim, Mary Ellen Schmid, and read Cesare's notes. Then he read the notes for Regina Harris, the eleventh victim. A note from Cesare caught his attention. He scrolled to the twelfth victim, which had a similar note. He pressed the arrows, moving to the thirteenth victim, quickly reading each line, and seeing the notation yet again.

"Holy shit," he muttered.

"You want to grab lunch?" Keith Ellis said.

Moss jumped and uttered a profanity.

"Shit, why are you so jumpy? You watching porn on your computer again?"

"What the hell?" Moss said. "You can't use a damn phone?"

Ellis laughed. "You're as white as a Klansman in uniform."

Moss felt himself perspiring. "Funny."

"Seriously. You don't look good."

"I'm fine. I took some aspirin on an empty stomach, and it made me nauseated."

"Then you better eat," Ellis said.

"Yeah. I'll meet you downstairs in the lobby. I have to take a leak."

Ellis left. Moss looked back at his computer monitor and went through the threads again. Each thread connected. Each certainly required further investigation. He took a deep breath and blew it out.

Sitting back. The task force was over. They were told to shut it down and turn in any material related to the investigation. Going after this kind of lead . . . nothing but trouble. Especially for Moss. Besides, the killer hadn't killed in a year. The percentages were he was either dead or incarcerated, and those percentages increased each day. Probably received a life sentence. Probably never again see the light of day.

And hopefully, neither would the disk.

CHAPTER 21

Friday, July 31, Present Day
Seattle, Washington

Tracy arrived at the office earlier than usual and hoped to also leave early to get a start on the weekend. She'd been working nonstop for nine days straight. The Sunday forecast was heavenly, midseventies. She and Dan planned to get outdoors early and hike with Daniella up the Poo Poo Point Trail. They'd enjoy the weather and each other's company, and have a late lunch.

She had spent much of the past three days going through the boxes of materials from the task force. To say it had been tedious was an understatement. She'd focused primarily on the binders for each of the final four victims, as Amanda Santos had suggested. She reread the facts about the women, their backgrounds, and their education. She reviewed the interviews of their coworkers, friends, and family. She picked up the thread of the four women working for or with the City of Seattle: Mary Ellen Schmid, in the city attorney's civil division; Regina Harris, office of city contracts; Christina Griffin, the city's minority contracting program; and Debbie Langford, who worked with city hall as a lobbyist.

It seemed a foregone conclusion the killer had some beef with the City of Seattle, but beyond that much, the interviews did not reveal anything more substantial.

She put her belongings in her desk drawer, hit the space bar on her computer keyboard, and entered her password. As the computer monitor displayed her email messages, she recognized some from the family members of the victims. Once they knew Tracy was involved in the investigation, and McDonnel had been arrested, they felt a renewed sense of hope. They asked that she do everything possible, talk to this person and that person, look into this and that. Follow up with him or her. Unfortunately, this type of involvement could be both a blessing and a curse, as Tracy had learned during the Cowboy investigation. The public's desire to help led to an onslaught of tips, fractured evidence, hypotheses, and hundreds of interviews. The resulting mound of information to be culled and studied could be overwhelming.

No way had Moss Gunderson had the patience or the empathy to perform that job. He had delegated the responsibility to Augustus Cesare, which reminded Tracy of the computer disk. She picked up the phone and called Sherri Belle at SPD's fingerprint unit.

"Was going to call you," Belle said. "I was able to run the envelope and the disk in the tank last night, and I think it's rather interesting."

"You found multiple prints?" Tracy surmised.

"I found multiple prints on the envelope," Bell said, "but not a single print on the disk."

"None?"

"Not a one. I find that curious."

"So do I."

"Thought you might. I ran the envelope prints for you and got nothing in the local or national systems."

Meaning the automated fingerprint identification system did not contain the prints of anyone who had touched the envelope. The prints likely belonged to persons handling the envelope at the post office, though Tracy knew from another investigation that most postal workers wore gloves to keep their hands from drying out. The prints were also not likely left from the person who had mailed the envelope. Someone smart enough not to leave their prints on the disk, or who had gone so far as to wipe the disk clean, had likely worn gloves when handling the envelope. Someone wanted Tracy to have the disk but didn't want her to know their identity.

"You want me to send it over to the crime lab?"

Knowing how busy Melton was, Tracy realized that trying to get someone to pull DNA from the envelope glue would take months. She also knew that someone careful enough not to leave a fingerprint on the disk was unlikely to have licked the envelope seal. In the past, information that someone wore gloves to avoid leaving their print or their DNA on a piece of evidence would lead to the logical conclusion the person had some type of law enforcement training. Now, with the dozens of CSI and other police-based television shows airing each night, everyone had been educated.

"Send the envelope to the crime lab but walk the disk over to TESU. I'll call and tell them to expect it and ask them to convert the disk to a readable format."

"Will do."

Tracy called TESU and explained what she needed and followed up the discussion with an email and the required form. Disconnecting, she called the crime lab and alerted a detective in the DNA lab of the envelope being sent over, then hung up and was about to follow up with an email and the required form when her computer pinged. Her gaze shifted to an email from the private lab to which she had sent Dwight McDonnel's DNA for analysis and comparison to the DNA obtained from the fourth victim.

Her pulse quickened. Goose bumps ran along her arms.

She opened the email and read, then reached for the desk phone, but it rang before she lifted the receiver.

"Are you reading this email?" Nolasco asked.

"Just now," she said, rereading it.

"Come to my office."

Minutes later, Tracy and Nolasco were again outside Chief Weber's inner sanctum. Nolasco held several pages, the attachment to the email from the lab. He declined to sit. He paced the carpeting like an expectant father, something noticed by and seemingly unnerving to Weber's assistant, who kept glancing up at him as he passed her desk. When the phone rang she practically leapt for the receiver. Nolasco wasted no time getting into Weber's office.

"McDonnel is our guy." He held out the pages to Weber. "The forensic DNA testing from the outside lab just came in. McDonnel is a match for the DNA we collected from the fourth victim." He sounded winded, as if exercising and trying to catch his breath. Adrenaline. The guy was going to have a heart attack from all the cigarettes and the stress.

Weber listened to him while reading the documents. "This says the DNA is mixed—more than one person. Who's the second person?"

Tracy knew from Melton's tutelage—he loved to show off—that the continuing improvement and development of DNA testing now allowed the lab to collect and to analyze smaller and smaller samples, and to differentiate between mixed genetic materials from two or more persons. In those cases, DNA profiling could be determined using a technique called "fragment analysis," which allowed for the identification of individual genetic profiles of multiple criminal offenders. It was particularly effective in identifying the perpetrators of gang rapes.

"The particular victim from whom this DNA sample was collected was a prostitute," Nolasco said with measured calmness, but he couldn't hide the rawness in his voice. He sounded like a man hoarse from yelling at an athletic event. "It would not be uncommon to find a mixed DNA sample since she likely had intercourse more than once that evening. Regardless, the lab left no doubt this was a positive match. McDonnel is our guy. I want to pick him up today."

"We can hold a press conference this afternoon before the weekend articles come out," Weber mused.

But to Tracy it sounded like a smoke detector alerting. A warning of an impending fire. "Why rush?" she said, trying to clear the smoke and slow the fire. "Why not pick up McDonnel, confront him with this information, and see if it compels him to confess to the killings? If he knows about the angel's wings, we know we have our guy. No doubt."

"More so than DNA evidence?" Nolasco said, looking and sounding disbelieving.

Weber shook her head. "I want to hold the press conference before the weekend's article is published. Bring McDonnel in and do what you need to do."

As Tracy and Nolasco left Weber's office, Nolasco held up the DNA report. "What the hell was that? We have proof positive right here."

Tracy hurried to keep up. "I'm just saying let's talk with McDonnel and get a confession before we parade him before the crowd seeking to crucify him."

Nolasco pushed through a door to the interior stairwell, his descending footsteps and his voice echoing. "I've waited twenty-five years to look this guy in the face and tell him I got him. Now I can."

Tracy wanted to tell Nolasco not to make the case personal, as Santos had said, that this was about the victims and their families, not him, but she knew from Faz that she was decades too late. "What's a few more hours?" Tracy said.

"A few too many. You want to interview him? We can do it after we arrest him and before the press conference. If he confesses, fine. If he doesn't, we still have him."

Tracy and Nolasco spent the next hour getting their ducks in a row. They put McDonnel's house under surveillance, then called the SWAT commander and asked him to prepare his team to breach the house.

They told him of the recent search in which they had found and taken a Glock handgun and knives from McDonnel's home but, given the nature of his crimes, that he should still be considered dangerous. They pulled up a GPS image of his White Center home and noted the access and egress points, as well as the major cross streets they would have to cover, in case McDonnel became a rabbit and tried to run.

"When do you want to do this?" the commander asked.

"As soon as you're ready," Nolasco said.

An hour later, Tracy and Nolasco arrived at the staging ground in a strip mall parking lot a few blocks from McDonnel's home to go over last-minute details with the SWAT sergeant. Those shopping at the stores stared with curiosity and trepidation at the black van and the officers in their full military gear. The patrol unit sitting on McDonnel's house said his truck had remained parked in the driveway since they'd arrived. There had been no sign of any activity inside the house or in the yard. McDonnel had not been sighted all morning. Several newspapers remained unretrieved in his driveway.

Tracy wondered if the uncollected newspapers were evidence McDonnel had anticipated what the DNA would reveal and had already left town. He could have strategically parked the truck in the driveway to make people think he was home, then taken a car service to almost anywhere, possibly received help from friends or family, maybe manufactured a fake passport and boarded a plane to a country not subject to United States treaty laws. They could have already lost him. She had no idea what that might do to Nolasco, who chain-smoked in the parking lot and looked more tightly stretched than a Speedo on a sumo wrestler—another Fazism.

After final instructions, the SWAT commander confirmed he and his team were ready to proceed, and Nolasco gave the order to breach the home. They drove to the house and the SWAT van bounced over the curb onto the brown lawn, and then the team exploded from the rear van doors. Tracy and Nolasco parked behind the truck. Patrol cars were positioned at both ends of the street and at the rear of the house.

One SWAT team member held a heavy ram, swinging it just once. The front door burst inward. It sounded like it had splintered into a hundred pieces. The team members snaked through the door in a choreographed and well-rehearsed line developed from hours of training. Tracy and Nolasco remained outside. Nolasco held a walkie-talkie to allow them to listen to the SWAT team clearing each room.

After just a few minutes, the commander announced the house clear. Nolasco looked to Tracy with uncertainty. He tossed his cigarette into the street gutter and moved toward the fractured front door, entering the house and the living areas. The commander met them in the kitchen near a door leading to a descending staircase. "We found him in the basement," he said.

Nolasco went down the stairs quickly, but Tracy considered the SWAT commander's expression and the tone of his voice. She'd been recruited by the SWAT team for her shooting skills, and she had done these types of breaches enough to know that while the team wasn't all cowboys, the members possessed a certain machismo and took pride in bringing down criminals. She detected no joy or pride in the commander's expression or his tone to indicate they had captured a man who had evaded arrest for decades and was responsible for thirteen killings.

She descended the nicked and scarred stairs to a room of dull yellow light from a single, bare bulb. The smell hit her first, prompting a visceral reaction that only came from an intimate acquaintance with decomposing bodies.

Nolasco stood in the middle of the basement staring at Dwight McDonnel, who hung from a rope wrapped around an overhead beam. At his feet was an upended wooden step stool.

Nolasco would not get his chance to look the son of a bitch in the eye and tell him he caught him.

McDonnel had evaded Nolasco's wrath one final time.

CHAPTER 22

Nolasco stepped outside Dwight McDonnel's home looking like a hunter who had shot a prized elk but had been denied the trophy rack.

"Coward," Nolasco said, anger and frustration creeping into his voice as he pulled the pack of cigarettes from his pocket. "He knew I had him. He knew I was going to take him down."

Not lost on Tracy was Nolasco's use of the singular pronoun "I" instead of the plural "we." Not that she was about to bring that up. "You think he hung himself?"

He shot her a sharp look. "As opposed to what?"

She shrugged, sensing Nolasco was in no mood for other theories. "How long do you estimate he'd been dead?"

"Four to five days, based on the dates of the newspapers in his driveway. Not long after he was released on bail would be my guess."

Tracy had come to the same estimate, though not necessarily the same conclusion that McDonnel killed himself to avoid prosecution. Again, not that she was going to say anything now. She'd let Nolasco fume for a while. He had a right.

"He had media camped outside his home and knocking on his door, according to the neighbors. They said they hadn't seen him, not even on his regular walks. You let Weber know?" she asked.

Nolasco had. "She's setting up a press conference for this afternoon."

"Still seems premature, Captain. Especially now."

Nolasco shot her another look, cigarette dangling from his lips and a BIC lighter in hand. "He committed suicide, Crosswhite. He isn't going to confess, and he didn't leave a note saying *I did it*. He knew it was just a matter of time once we had his DNA."

"Seems prudent to wait until the scene is processed and the ME has a chance to at least look at the body."

"Processed for what? We just did a search and seizure of the house and his truck a few weeks ago. There's nothing to find. We always suspected McDonnel. We just never had anything serious to confront him with. His DNA confirms he strangled at least one of those prostitutes, and we have his statements to the more recent victim . . ."

"Yvonne Clarke."

"Right. So in a sense, he did confess."

"What beef did he have with the other victims?"

Nolasco opened his mouth to speak, then caught himself, as if uncertain. "Why did he have to have any? He wasn't about to come back to the strip once he knew we were watching it. So, he changed tactics and went someplace else to satisfy his sick urges. Why do you have a problem with this?"

"Serial killers are narcissists. They think they're smarter than everyone, even when it looks like they've been caught. Remember the Cowboy? He didn't think he'd get caught even when he was in that motel room with the entire department in the parking lot aiming rifles at him. He saw it as an opportunity for greater fame."

"You're going to throw the Cowboy in my face?"

"Forget the Cowboy. What about Bundy? He served as his own counsel, jumped out of a courtroom building, boarded a bus to Florida, and killed again. Even when caught he thought he could outsmart everyone."

"So?"

"So, why would McDonnel kill himself? It doesn't fit the profile."

"I told you the profiles are worthless." Nolasco lit his cigarette. "It's guesswork. There is no unifying profile. McDonnel killed himself because he's a coward and didn't want to face the music. Or maybe this was his way of saying he'd never be caught for what he did."

"He could have run. He could have taken off."

"Where is he going to go?"

"Tell me your first thought when you saw the newspapers in the driveway?"

"Don't do this, Crosswhite." He stepped away.

Tracy followed. "What was your first thought, Captain? Did you think he was dead, that he'd killed himself? Or did you think he'd got away, that he was on the run?"

Nolasco turned back, pointing at her. "You just can't stand it, can you?"

"What?" The change in his tone, now more accusatory than upset, confused her.

"You can't stand the fact we got McDonnel and you can't take the credit for it. The great Tracy Crosswhite didn't solve the case."

His comment dumbfounded her. Every time she gave him credit for one human characteristic, he reverted to being the cold reptile she had come to despise. "Answer my question, Captain. Did you think a man who had eluded capture for decades had suddenly given up and killed himself?"

"He knew it was just a matter of time when we got his DNA."

"Why? You never released the information that you had DNA evidence from a crime scene. I went through the boxes of materials and Lisa Childress's handwritten notes. Nowhere was it ever reported that you had potential DNA of the suspect. How would McDonnel have known you could match his DNA with DNA from a crime scene?"

"I told him in the jail. I told him we'd get his DNA and it would just be a matter of time. So he knew, or assumed, we had DNA from the one time he got careless and screwed his victim. Or maybe it's just like you said—he thought he was omnipotent and couldn't be caught. Nobody knows, Crosswhite. They spent hours interviewing these psychopaths, and you know what they learned?"

She did. She'd read the report prepared by an SPD detective who had interviewed Ted Bundy during the department's chase to find the Green River Killer. No unifying reason explained why they killed. No common thread was found in their upbringing.

"Santos said this guy was delivering a message—" Tracy started.

"I told you, Santos is one step above the psychics. It's all hocus-pocus, bullshit. They don't have a book on these guys because no book exists."

"Fine." She felt herself becoming combative but kept her voice calm so as not to escalate the situation. "I was only suggesting we wait until after the autopsy. I thought it might be prudent."

"Yeah, well, you're not the one being vilified in the press, Crosswhite. You're not the one they crucified twenty-five years ago, the person who had his career and marriage derailed. I was fully invested in this case, and I lost everything," Nolasco said in what Tracy perceived as a rare moment of vulnerability.

"I'm sorry," she said. "Faz told me what happened."

Nolasco caught himself. He made a face like he immediately regretted what he'd said. Then he shook his head. "I don't need Faz to tell you or anyone else anything. I'm a big boy, and I'll take the beating without complaint."

"It wasn't personal, Captain. It still isn't."

"Who are you to tell me it wasn't personal? You don't know. You weren't here. They made it personal. The press. The brass. The victims' families. They all scapegoated me." He pointed at the neighbors watching the show. "Well, this is my chance to tell them all to screw themselves. Weber has called a press conference for four p.m. You can be there or not be there. That's your choice." He took two steps, then turned back. "No. You know what? It isn't your choice. I'm ordering you to be there. For once you can take a back seat. See how it feels."

Nolasco took another drag on his cigarette, then flicked the still-burning butt onto the driveway as he reentered the house.

Tracy did her best to avoid Nolasco for the remainder of the day. At three o'clock she checked in with the CSI sergeant and the medical examiner's personnel who were finishing. The CSI sergeant said there was no sign of a struggle inside the house. The ME said nothing on McDonnel's body indicated his preliminary opinion, that McDonnel hanged himself, was wrong.

Tracy got a ride back to Police Headquarters in a patrol car. No way was she riding back with Nolasco.

Back in her office, someone knocked on her closed door.

"Come in," she said.

Faz entered with Del and Cesare. "Is it true?" Faz asked. "Is McDonnel our guy?"

She had not called them. She doubted Nolasco had. "It looks like it," Tracy said. "McDonnel's DNA is a match for the DNA recovered at your crime scene."

"No shit," Faz said.

"I heard McDonnel is dead," Cesare said. "That he didn't confess."

"He's dead. CSI is still processing the scene. Preliminary analysis is he hung himself."

"After all these years, my God." Faz let out a breath. "Well, I'm glad for Johnny. That's a hell of a monkey to carry on your back all these years."

"Apparently," Tracy said.

"You don't sound happy," Del said.

"I'm glad it's over," Tracy said, but she could tell Del and Faz weren't buying it. They knew her too well. "Weber has called an afternoon press conference to start in—" Tracy considered her watch. "Less than fifteen minutes."

"We know. She wants us there also," Cesare said.

"Then I'll see you there," Tracy said. "I have to call Dan and let him know I'm going to be late."

After Faz, Del, and Cesare left, Tracy picked up the phone and called the FBI's office in Seattle. She asked to speak to Amanda Santos. The receptionist said Santos wasn't in but invited Tracy to leave a message. Tracy did.

Ten minutes after four o'clock, Mayor Garcia led a group from SPD that included Chief Weber, Nolasco, Tracy, Faz, Del, and Cesare into the pressroom. Reporters filled the chairs behind the victims' family members in the first rows. Several advocates from the Victim Support Team were also present. Tracy counted half a dozen TV cameras and more than a dozen reporters, Anita Childress as well as Greg Bartholomew among them. A cluster of microphones had been attached to the podium.

Garcia greeted the assembled and said, "Today I am pleased to announce the hunt for the Route 99 serial killer has come to an end. The Seattle Police Department, under the leadership of Police Chief Marcella Weber, has confirmed that a Washington State crime lab has matched a DNA sample obtained from Dwight Thomas McDonnel by use of a warrant, following his recent arrest for the attempted strangulation of Yvonne Clarke, with DNA recovered from one of the Route 99 serial killer's victims. It is with tremendous respect and humility that we address the family members of the killer's thirteen victims, some of whom are present here today. We wish to tell you that the long hunt for the person responsible for the death of your loved ones is over. We hope this is the first step in finding closure. Chief Weber?"

Weber stepped to the podium and discussed the raid on McDonnel's home, which revealed he took his own life following his recent arrest and release on bail. "A CSI team is processing Mr. McDonnel's home and treating it as a crime scene, though we have no indication Mr. McDonnel's death was by anything other than his own hand. I don't want to repeat what Mayor Garcia has already said." She looked down at those seated in the first row. "I wish only to say to the family members of the thirteen victims that the Seattle Police Department never gave up trying to locate the killer of your loved ones. The Seattle Police Department investigates every crime without consideration to the victim's occupation, socioeconomic status, or race. The solving of this case proves if you commit a crime in Seattle, we will catch you. And we will bring you to justice. The credit for this work should largely go to a dedicated Cold Case Unit run by veteran Violent Crimes detective Tracy Crosswhite." Weber turned to Tracy. "Detective Crosswhite."

Tracy felt like she'd had the rug pulled out from under her feet and knew Weber's acknowledgment had been purposeful. She didn't know what, exactly, Weber was playing at, but she was playing. Was she trying to drive a further wedge between Tracy and Nolasco, make it even more unbearable for Tracy to work in his department, and ultimately get her to quit? Tracy had fully expected Weber to recognize Nolasco and the remaining members of his task force.

From the corner of her eye, Tracy could see Nolasco's body posture stiffen and his jaw clench. She didn't dare look in his direction.

Though uncertain what she would say, she was not about to let Weber win this round. Tracy stepped to the podium. "First, let me clear something up. While I appreciate Chief Weber's acknowledgment, I played a very small part in the resolution of this case. The capture of the Route 99 serial killer was due to the ceaseless efforts of Violent Crimes captain Johnny Nolasco and the task force he led, which included Violent Crimes detectives Vic Fazzio, Del Castigliano, and Officer Augustus Cesare, who are here today. It was Captain Nolasco's task force that first identified Dwight McDonnel as a suspect in the killings and that continued to pursue that lead."

"But it was only upon the reopening of the investigation and your involvement that McDonnel was identified," Bartholomew interrupted.

"Wrong," Tracy said. "Captain Nolasco put a system in place ensuring he would be notified if Dwight McDonnel was ever arrested for a crime. His persistence paid off when Mr. McDonnel was arrested for assault and battery of a woman in a motel room on Aurora Avenue. Upon McDonnel's arrest, Captain Nolasco interviewed him and the victim, and he put together the search warrant for McDonnel's DNA. It was Captain Nolasco and his task force that obtained the evidence needed to put this matter to rest." Tracy stepped back. "Captain Nolasco."

Nolasco looked as uncertain as Tracy had felt moments earlier. Tracy had given him his moment to shine. She stepped back from the podium to stand alongside Faz.

"Nice move," Faz said out of the side of his mouth. "Nolasco won't thank you, but the alternative if you had taken the credit would have been much worse."

"Don't I know it," Tracy whispered.

"So how come you're not happy?" Faz said.

Tracy noticed some on the stage looking over at them.

"I'm happy," she said, further quieting her voice and turning her head. "But I still have questions."

Faz turned his head sharply. Too sharply. Weber and Garcia took notice. Faz recovered and turned toward the podium.

After the press conference ended, Tracy quickly left the pressroom to avoid the reporters. She checked her voice mail and found a message from Amanda Santos. Tracy had avoided the press, but there was no avoiding Faz and Del, who waited by her car in the parking structure.

"Spill. What did you mean you still have questions?" Faz said.

"McDonnel is dead. We have no confession," she said.

"Don't need one. You have DNA," Del said.

"Which showed two different sources. Once being McDonnel, the other unknown."

"Come on, Tracy, what are the chances there's been some kind of mistake?" Faz said. "McDonnel was a suspect. Just a few weeks ago, he's picked up for trying to strangle another prostitute. Why would he shoot off his mouth and say he'd killed others if he didn't?"

"You're right," Tracy said. "The chances are less than minuscule. So why not wait until the ME finished processing McDonnel's body? Weber rushed the press conference to beat the articles the *Times* intended to run. What's a few more days when we're talking decades?"

"She makes sense," Del said.

"The families of those victims have been waiting long enough," Faz said.

"Come on, Faz, you know as well as I do that press conference had nothing to do with bringing closure to the victims' families and everything to do with heading off the press's criticism of the department at a time when funding is critical. This was about Weber's budget."

"Maybe so . . . But so what? They got their man and they beat up the *Times*. Why not both?"

"I wouldn't have done it that way."

"You weren't in those meetings," Faz said. "You don't know how it was."

She'd heard it before. "When's the last time a serial killer killed himself?"

"What does that have to do with anything?"

"I'm just saying some things don't sit well with me. I think we should have resolved those things before holding the press conference."

"Is that all?" Faz asked.

"Meaning what?"

"You sure this doesn't have to do with your personal animosity toward Nolasco?"

"You were just in the press conference. I gave him one hundred percent of the credit."

"For solving an investigation you're worried isn't solved and could come back to bite us all in the ass," Faz said.

"He's right," Del said. "It could bite everyone in the ass, but it will take the biggest chunk from Nolasco's ass if it does."

She shook her head, wounded. "You two know me better than that."

Faz raised his palms. "Look, I'm sorry. I apologize. That was a cheap shot."

"Do you remember the Cowboy Task Force?" Tracy asked. "Nolasco jumped the gun on that investigation and said the killer was David Bankston because everything pointed in his direction, but he was wrong."

"The circumstances aren't the same, Tracy," Faz said. "This time we have DNA."

"I know, Faz. And I'm hoping you're right. I'm hoping Nolasco is right. But I have a feeling about this. I don't know why, but I can't deny it."

Faz was silent for a moment. Then he said, "This one time, I hope your intuition is wrong."

"So do I," Tracy said.

Amanda Santos's message to Tracy said to call her. Tracy decided it would be better to see her in person and walked to the FBI's office.

"I watched the press conference," Santos said, entering the reception area. "I assume that's why you called, to let me know you had identified the killer."

"Actually, I have a question for you."

"Okay. Come on back."

They went to the same conference room as before. Neither sat. "In your research, how likely is it a serial killer will commit suicide rather than face a criminal trial?" Tracy asked.

Santos smiled as if she had anticipated the question. "A study was done on that very question about a dozen years ago. The percentage is low."

"How low?"

"Don't quote me on it, but less than ten percent. Closer to five percent."

"It's unlikely."

"According to the study. But suicide is not unheard of. When a serial killer finds himself in an environment that will not allow him to seek the kind of pleasure he craves—"

"Like police custody?"

"Like police custody. And he's facing a life sentence without parole, or the death penalty, it is not unthinkable he would take his own life. The few I'm aware of who committed suicide did so after conviction and while in custody. Most hung themselves."

Tracy thanked Santos for indulging her and left the building feeling a bit more at ease. She resolved not to let the matter interfere with her weekend and her time with Dan and Daniella.

She was good at making resolutions.

She wasn't always good at carrying them through.

CHAPTER 23

Monday, August 3, Present Day
Seattle, Washington

Tracy shut off her work phone over the weekend and placed it in her desk drawer so it didn't interfere with family time. Shutting off the phone was easy. Shutting off her thoughts, not so much. Despite Amanda Santos's assurance some serial killers took their own lives, Tracy continued to have doubts. Or maybe it was just the lack of certainty that bothered her. She told herself that even if McDonnel had lived, he might not have confessed. He'd had the chance in custody but steadfastly refused.

As she grew older, Tracy realized everybody struggled with something, even those who looked sure and confident. Her *something* was needing to be certain. Needing things to be buttoned up and put to bed without loose strings. It was likely a product of her sister's death and the twenty years Tracy had spent compulsively searching for Sarah's killer, needing to know what had happened.

It became her obsession. She recognized it and she'd sought counseling. She'd had to learn how to lock her work in a box so it would not dictate her personal time. Not let it keep her from enjoying life. Reuniting with Dan, the birth of Daniella, creating a family of their own, had helped. She no longer wanted to think about work 24-7. She didn't want to bring her work home with her.

She spent Saturday and Sunday with Dan and Daniella, as planned. Monday morning, she refused to turn on her work phone until she arrived at the office. Her counselor said it gave her control over her work instead of her work having control over her.

As she entered the seventh floor, she felt an energy in the detective division that came with the resolution of a big case. A buzz filled the air. Everyone seemed charged, their movements and conversation more animated. Victories were to be celebrated. Success put pep in everyone's step, as her mother liked to say.

Tracy considered the boxes of documents against the far wall of her office. She'd call storage and have them returned to the vault; she marked each of the thirteen cold case files as closed. She checked her voice messages. She had several calls from reporters wanting to talk to her about the investigation, including Anita Childress. Tracy felt like she owed the young woman a return call. The rest she'd send to Nolasco.

"Tracy," Childress said.

"Hey, Anita. I got your message but I took the weekend off and was out of cell range. What can I do for you?"

"I just wanted to ask a few questions for an article I was working on this morning, but I spoke to your captain. We ran an article yesterday morning in place of the feature pieces I put together about McDonnel's capture." Tracy had taken a look at the Sunday paper and did see the article atop the metro section.

"Should have run it on the front page," Tracy said.

"I lobbied Bill for the placement but lost that battle."

At least Nolasco would be happy. Childress's article quoted Tracy at the press conference highlighting Nolasco and his task force. The article was accompanied by two photographs, one of Nolasco from twenty-five years ago at one of the crime scenes, and one taken recently at McDonnel's home. Nolasco was surprisingly humble, giving credit to those members of his task force as well as to the advances in the forensic sciences that made it possible to identify McDonnel's DNA. Childress had also spoken with Melton and got a quick synopsis of fragmented DNA analysis. Tracy knew Melton didn't talk to the press, especially not on his weekends, unless ordered to do so. She figured that order had come from Weber.

"Melton is probably a better source than I am," Tracy said, not meaning to rush Childress, but now in work mode. She'd pulled up her emails and scrolled through them as she and Childress talked. When Childress went silent, Tracy asked, "Something else, Anita?"

"I was just thinking about my mom."

"What about her?"

"Still some things that I haven't resolved."

"Such as?"

"Who attacked her the night she lost her memory and went missing."

The question surprised Tracy. So did Childress's doubt. "Had to be someone on the Last Line task force. My bet would be Rick Tombs," Tracy said referring to the deceased veteran narcotics sergeant who had run the illicit task force and kickback scheme.

"I know we came to that conclusion, but we never really proved it," Childress said.

"I'm not sure we can prove it, Anita. Not definitively. Sometimes we just have to lock those things in a box, so we can move on with our lives. You got your mother back. That was a small miracle. Take solace in that."

"I am. It's just . . . I got a woman back who I know to be my mother. Unfortunately, she doesn't have much emotional attachment to the past or to me."

"Make a brighter future, Anita," Tracy said, hoping the young woman was fortunate, as Tracy had been, to find comfort in her work and in another person, to start a family of her own.

They said good-bye and Tracy hung up. She'd received a message from Stuart Funk while on the phone with Childress. She called him back.

"Toxicology isn't back yet, but blood work indicates McDonnel was intoxicated. No bruising or injuries to indicate this was anything other than a suicide."

Tracy thanked him. Maybe it was as Nolasco had said; McDonnel was the killer but did not intend to spend a day in jail or give Nolasco the satisfaction of apprehending him. Or maybe McDonnel couldn't take the media's intense scrutiny, the inability to go anywhere without being hounded.

Tracy went back to scanning her emails, finding one from Andrei Vilkotski of TESU. He had converted the disk into a usable format and provided it in several attachments. He told her that, per her instructions, he had sent back the disk. Tracy picked up an interdepartmental package from TESU from her in-box. With the case now resolved, the killer dead, and the victims cold cases, all the Salumi sandwiches in the world wouldn't persuade Melton to prioritize trying to collect DNA from the disk's mailing envelope, if it even had DNA on it.

Tracy set the envelope down and opened the first attachment Vilkotski had sent her on her computer. She scrolled through an Excel spreadsheet with cells identifying each call, the date the tip was received, the name of the caller, if provided, the substance of the call, and the task force member to which the call had been assigned for follow-up.

She searched for those calls coded red and noted an asterisk beside several, probably to indicate some type of further priority. She looked to the column that identified the person tasked with following through. Moss Gunderson. Curious, she scrolled to the next asterisk. In many, though not in every instance in which an asterisk accompanied a tip, Gunderson had been tasked with performing the follow-through.

"Not your problem any longer," she said and went to shut down the Excel application, but her hand just wouldn't move the mouse to the X in the upper right-hand corner of her screen. "Screw it. In for a penny, in for a pound," she said and pulled up the call log. She picked up her desk phone and called a number beside a red asterisk. The call rang once before a computerized voice indicated the number was no longer in service.

She called a second number, got a live person, but was told the person who had called in and left the tip was dead, and the person who answered the phone had no idea why the now deceased person had called.

Tracy called a third number with an asterisk and asked to speak to the person whose name was in the cell on her spreadsheet.

"Speaking," he said. "If this is a solicitation, please put me on your do-not-call list."

"It's not a solicitation. My name is Tracy Crosswhite. I'm a detective with the Seattle Police Department." Silence. As usual. "I was hoping to ask you about a call you made to the Seattle Police Department in reference to the murder of—"

"Mary Ellen Schmid," the man said.

"You remember the call?"

"Mary Ellen was my sister-in-law," the man said. "She was married to my younger brother, Bill. So, yeah, I remember everything like it was yesterday."

"Were you at the press conference on Friday?"

"Me? No. I know Bill was asked to attend. He called and told me they'd identified Mary Ellen's killer, but he opted not to go."

"Did he tell you why?"

The man sighed into the phone. "Bill's remarried. He has a new family and a new life. It took a lot of time to get past what had happened."

Tracy understood well. "Those are painful memories I don't wish on anyone. Bill once told me not a day goes by without him thinking of Mary Ellen. But he met a woman and he remarried, and things are better for him and his two kids. I think having it come back up now, after all these years, is like ripping off a bandage from an open wound. He told me he and their two kids would go to Mary Ellen's grave, spend a quiet moment there, and put her to rest."

"I understand," Tracy said. She'd done much the same thing when she resolved her sister's murder.

"No, I don't think you do, Detective," the man said. "People say they understand, but until you go through something like that . . ."

Tracy didn't tell him her own story. "Do you remember why you called the tip line?"

"Not specifically. I know at one time I had a wild theory, but . . . You solved the case. You identified the killer. That's good enough for me."

"Just out of curiosity, though, what was your wild theory?"

"Well, not really a theory. Just a bit of information. The detectives came to Bill asking all the questions."

"You were there?"

"My wife and I moved in with Bill for a few months to help with the kids, getting them to school, grocery shopping, those kinds of things. Emotional support, you know? The detectives were looking for something to connect the killings. Something to tie them together. They asked Bill about Mary Ellen's background, where she had worked, where she went to school, former boyfriends. Neighbors. They were very thorough. I remembered something after they left that Bill hadn't told them. The detectives had given us business cards with a tip line to handle all the calls they were getting. So I called it in on the tip line."

"And what was it that you remembered?"

"Mary Ellen had at one time worked for Mayor Edwards as a 'special assistant' after she went to law school and before she worked at the city attorney's office."

Tracy's pulse quickened, though she was uncertain why. "Did you get a call back from a detective?"

"I don't know. I can't really remember the details. I barely remember making the call."

"Does the name Moss Gunderson ring any bells?"

"Moss what?"

"Moss Gunderson."

"Is that a detective who worked on the case?"

"You don't recognize that name?"

"Like I said. It was a long time ago. No. I don't."

Tracy wrote down the man's name, thanked him, and hung up.

She scrolled through the Excel spreadsheet with a bit more urgency, looking for the next asterisk and reading the summary of the phone call. Her eyes stopped on one asterisk in particular. The caller had provided information on Regina Harris, the Route 99 Killer's eleventh victim. The notes indicated Harris, too, had at one time worked as a "special assistant" in the mayor's office. Tracy's gaze panned across the spreadsheet's cells to the detective tasked to follow up on the call. Moss Gunderson.

Another memory nudged her brain. She opened her desk drawer and pulled out Lisa Childress's files, finding her investigation of corruption in Mayor Edwards's administration. Edwards had been accused of all kinds of graft but never charged. The FBI had investigated some of the city's business dealings when Edwards had been in power, contracts awarded to Edwards's friends or, some said, to Edwards's financial supporters. But Tracy was interested in something else. Edwards had also been a notorious womanizer, particularly fond of young women. Again, however, nothing had ever stuck beyond the rumors and innuendo. He had retired from office unscathed and was still revered by some and feared by others in Seattle.

She flipped through Lisa Childress's notes.

On one of those pages Childress had written:

Credible source.

Pissed off.

Girlfriends.

Willing to talk.

Tracy wondered who the person might have been—a jilted lover? Maybe one of those special assistants? Childress had written a news article regarding women rumored to be or to have at one time been the mayor's girlfriends, though Edwards had been married with children. Could the credible source have been someone Childress spoke with?

Tracy found the article and reread it, confirming that these "girlfriends" had started their careers in one of nearly 150 much-coveted mayoral special assistant jobs created by Edwards. Two rumored girlfriends became legislative aides, another a political advisor, and a third, a woman Edwards had helped to secure the position of city attorney, had gone on to win a seat in the United States Senate.

Tracy went to the boxes of documents in her office, removing tops and fingering through the file tabs until she found the tabs for Christina Griffin and Debbie Langford. She scanned through the files one at a time. Christina Griffin, the twelfth victim, had run the city's minority contracting program. Debbie Langford, the thirteenth victim, had been a lobbyist. Both Langford and Griffin had at one time also worked in one of Edwards's coveted special assistant positions.

Tracy hurried back to her desk, her mind spinning. She went down the Excel spreadsheet on her computer for tips marked with an asterisk, this time with more deliberation, and found one beside the name Debbie Langford, and another beside Christina Griffin's name. Both tips had also been assigned to Moss Gunderson.

Tracy had thought Lisa Childress's four investigative files represented four separate investigations, but what if they didn't?

What if the four investigations were all somehow related?

Tracy's investigation into the Last Line had revealed that in addition to Moss Gunderson and Marcella Weber, Mayor Edwards had also
received kickbacks from the drug busts and drug sales. Tracy's contact,
Henderson Jones, who had known Weber growing up in Rainier Valley,
said Weber and Edwards had both taken kickbacks. When Tracy asked
for proof, Jones had said Edwards was so crooked he couldn't put on a
straight-legged pair of jeans.

Hardly evidence to get a conviction, but information nonetheless.

Edwards also had a connecting thread to the subject of another
of Childress's investigative files, Seattle city councilman Peter Rivers.
Rivers, a highly popular, liberal councilman, had declared his intent
to run for mayor and vowed to expose Edwards's corruption and graft.
Shortly after Rivers had made his intent known, he became the subject
of lawsuits brought by men who claimed they had sex with Rivers in his
apartment while underage. Rivers, who was married to his husband, initially fought back and accused Edwards of running a smear campaign.
He said his accusers had been encouraged to file the complaints, and
the complaints had been leaked to the press. Still, one accuser filing a
lawsuit could be a scam. Even two could be a coincidence. Three or
four, however, would be perceived by the public as a pattern of behavior.
Rivers pulled his candidacy and shortly thereafter retired from public
life. Edwards had been reelected.

Four investigative files. The Last Line. Peter Rivers. The Route 99
killings. Graft and corruption inside the mayor's office.

One connecting thread. Edwards.

Could Lisa Childress have seen this same thread? Is that why she
was investigating all four cases as one—because they weren't four separate cases; they were all somehow related to Edwards?

Tracy looked back to the spreadsheet, to the one name that came up in the follow-through cell for each asterisk tip. Moss Gunderson.

She picked up the phone and called Augustus Cesare. When he answered, she asked if he'd be at his desk for a few minutes.

"Where am I going to go?"

She grabbed the disk and took the interior stairwell down to the HR Department. Cesare was waiting for her. She put the disk on his desk.

"Did you ever follow up on any of the tips that came in?"

"Some of the crazy shit. You know, the mystics and the wannabe detectives. Moss gave me autonomy to further cull through the bullshit before I passed on the tip to whoever was designated. Why?"

"Did Moss ever ask you to follow up on a tip for him?" Tracy knew how lazy Moss could be. Cesare didn't immediately answer. An admission of guilt? "Did he?"

"Look, Moss did a lot for me and for my career. If it wasn't for him, I might still be walking a beat. He stuck his neck out for me and got me working investigations. I owed him. Okay? I don't want to get the guy in any trouble."

She tried a different tack. "Moss is retired. The case is decades old. I'm just trying to put it to bed."

"It doesn't sound like it. It sounds like you're going after Moss."

"He's retired, Cesare. How could I go after him? I just want to know if you followed up on some of the calls. You did, didn't you?"

"Yeah. I did," he said reluctantly. "I made an initial pass, and those I deemed important I brought to Moss's attention."

"How? Did you mark the calls in any way?"

"I put an asterisk by the call. It was an indication to Moss to follow up with the person. Nolasco had made it clear he wanted everything followed up."

"Did you ever follow through with Moss? Ask him if he called the tips you marked with an asterisk."

"I don't remember, Tracy. I have a vague recollection of Moss telling me the tips didn't lead anywhere, or maybe were a dead end. Listen, why are we going through this? We have McDonnel. We have his DNA match. He's our guy."

"Yeah," she said. "We have his DNA match." But somehow a case that couldn't be solved in decades seemed just a little too easy to resolve in the few weeks since it had been handed to her.

CHAPTER 24

Monday, August 3, Present Day
Bellevue, Washington

Tracy had been to Moss's home with Del while investigating Lisa Childress's disappearance. They'd tried to get Moss to talk about the Last Line drug task force. Moss told them he was no "rat" and to go pound sand. Since they had no leverage, they had no choice but to walk away.

Moss lived in Northeast Bellevue in a beautiful house just above Lake Sammamish. This time, Tracy drove to the house alone. She couldn't very well ask Nolasco to go with her, or even Faz for that matter, not without admitting she continued to investigate the Route 99 cases, an investigation that was supposed to be buttoned up and the boxes on their way back to storage. She had no desire to get Faz in any trouble, the way Del had got in trouble pursuing the drug task force with her.

She wasn't afraid to confront Moss alone. He was, as Faz said, a big blowhard. Tracy had dealt with his kind throughout her career.

She parked the pool car in the circular drive and approached the dark-green clapboard home with black trim nestled between trees and shrubbery. The house wasn't much to look at from the street, but it descended down two levels to the lake, with plate-glass windows offering a panoramic view.

Tracy rang the doorbell and heard footsteps. Moss's wife, Frieda, answered the door. She was petite, blonde, and much younger than Moss. She wore a blue visor and a cute golf outfit. Tracy reintroduced herself.

"I remember. You're that detective who came before," Frieda said. "Moss didn't tell me he was expecting visitors."

"I was in the area and thought I'd drop by to discuss an old case. I was hoping he wasn't on the golf course." Tracy knew he wasn't. She'd called the golf shop, told them she was a guest of Moss Gunderson, and asked for his tee time. He'd played earlier in the day.

"He already played eighteen," Frieda said. "And no doubt had a couple of drinks with his lunch. He's sleeping it off in the backyard on a lounge."

"You look like you're on your way out the door," Tracy said, noting Frieda's golf attire.

"I have a lesson. I like to get there and hit a few balls to loosen up."

"Listen, don't let me hold you up. I can find my way to the backyard. I noticed some steps along the side of the house."

"That will get you there." Frieda stepped onto the front landing and closed the door behind her. "Would you mind telling Moss I'm headed over to the club?"

"Happy to." Tracy smiled at the thought of waking him.

She descended the steep wooden staircase to the backyard. Moss lay in a lounge chair, fast asleep. Snoring. Tracy carefully undid the gate latch and stepped inside. Maybe sneaking up on a former police officer was a good way to get shot, but she doubted Moss hid a gun in his hideous golf shorts, which were black with neon-colored golf balls. He had a golf cap propped on his head, the bill covering his eyes.

Tracy pulled up a chair and sat. When Moss didn't wake, she decided to have some fun. She called out, "Fore right."

Moss nearly fell from the lounge chair, his cap tumbling from his head. His concern quickly became confusion. Likely the alcohol contributed. When he had recovered, he groaned and swore at her. Then he said, "What the hell are you doing here?"

"Frieda told me to remind you she has a golf lesson this afternoon."

Gunderson sat up, still unnerved but trying to regain some composure. "What do you want?" He sounded groggy.

"Want to talk to you about your Route 99 investigation."

"What for? Saw the press conference. Weber invited me to stand on the podium and receive a participation award. I declined. Watched it on TV though. You really kissed Nolasco's ass. You two make up?"

"His investigation. His credit. Found something interesting when I was getting the files ready for storage."

"Yeah, what's that?"

She held up Augustus Cesare's disk. "This. You might not be able to read the writing without your glasses, but it says 'Tip Line Route 99 Task Force Augustus Cesare.'"

"What game are you playing at, Crosswhite?"

"Why would you think I was playing at anything, Moss? Didn't you tell me you placed the disk in storage?"

Moss paused. Then he said, "You said you couldn't find it."

"Maybe I wasn't looking hard enough. Anyway, now I have it. I learned something interesting reviewing it."

Moss didn't respond.

"I learned that Cesare put an asterisk beside the tips he thought should be followed up and listed the detective given that responsibility."

"Congratulations."

"He put your name by several of those tips."

"And . . ."

"And I called a couple of them. They don't have any recollection of speaking to you. Don't even know your name, which, you'll admit isn't easy to forget. You know, 'a rolling stone gathers no . . .'" She imitated a Moss refrain.

"That was twenty-five years ago, Crosswhite. I doubt those people could even remember what they had for breakfast, let alone who they talked with. Why are you bothering me with this?"

"So you did talk to them?"

Moss studied her. She could see the wheels turning. If he said he followed up, then how could he have missed such an obvious connection? If he said he didn't follow up, then he was guilty of malfeasance, at best, or a deliberate obfuscation of evidence that might have meant something, likely because he feared Mayor Edwards. Edwards no doubt knew Gunderson had taken drug money. Weber also. That was Edwards's best political skill and why he'd remained in office so long. Blackmail.

Moss tried to act nonplussed. "If that's what the disk says, I suppose it would be the best source of information."

"So then you know."

"Know what?"

"The connecting thread between the killer's tenth, eleventh, twelfth, and thirteenth victims."

"They all worked for the City of Seattle. So what? We ran that down and it went nowhere."

"I believe you, Moss. I believe you ran it down, and you learned that all four of those women had, at one time, worked in a special assistant position to Mayor Edwards."

Moss didn't respond.

"Which means you deliberately didn't pursue that line of inquiry. Why not, Moss? Here was the connecting thread the task force had been looking for, and you didn't tell anyone Cesare had found it. Why not?"

Moss smiled, but it was tentative and unsure. An attempt to bluff. "What do you care, Crosswhite? You found your killer. The case is over. You got another fifteen minutes of fame."

"Just curious, Moss. Curious why you would withhold this information. Maybe it was because Mayor Edwards knew you were dirty, that you took money from the drug task force, and you feared he would expose you if you confronted him."

"Sounds like rank speculation to me, Crosswhite. How exactly are you going to prove it?"

She held up the disk. "I know you didn't send me this disk. And I know you didn't put it into storage, though the log indicates it was part of the box of documents you submitted. The question is, who had it, and why did they send it to me? And what else do they know about this case, Moss?"

"The case is over, Crosswhite."

"Maybe. But maybe it could have been over earlier. Maybe, if you'd done your job and brought this to the attention of the task force, maybe confronted Edwards, you could have saved a life. But you didn't. You chose to bury it and save your career."

"Again, rank speculation. But for the sake of argument, and I do love a good argument, let's say you're right. Let's say Cesare sent me the information and, let's say, for argument's sake, I followed through with Edwards. Tell me how that would have led the task force to Dwight McDonnel?"

"Exactly," Tracy said.

Moss's eyes narrowed. He tilted his head. Then he laughed. "Are you saying you don't think McDonnel is the killer?" He laughed louder. "Oh man. How I wish I could be a fly on the wall when you try to convince Weber and Nolasco the guy just scapegoated as the killer, the guy paraded before the victims' families, the guy who forced the *Seattle Times* to eat crow, isn't the guy. Now that is a news conference I would attend, Crosswhite."

Moss was right, of course. Neither Nolasco nor Weber would ever accept McDonnel was not the killer and, at the moment, Tracy couldn't prove he wasn't. She was just trying to pull together all the loose ends.

"It's just me and you, Moss. Nobody else here. No tape recorder. Nothing to document what gets said. Did you follow up on the tip that these women all worked as special assistants to Mayor Edwards?"

Moss smiled his shit-eating grin. "You know what? I'm going to tell you the truth, because a part of me hopes you go forward with this. Nothing would please me more than to see you get your ass handed to you." Tracy waited. "Yeah, Cesare sent me the tips. And again, let's say for argument's sake I called and learned of the connection. And let's say I did follow the lead, and Mayor Edwards did tell me that if I pursued it, he'd burn me. If you can somehow, some way use that information to implicate me in the subsequent deaths of any of those women, well, you go right ahead. I'm retired. They can't touch me. You, on the other hand, remain a servant of the public. In fact, some might call you famous. They can do all kinds of things to your career, and they can make your private life miserable. So you go right ahead and pursue this." Moss picked up the cap from his lap. "Now if you don't mind, I would like to get back to my nap, because I have a feeling I'm going to dream a beautiful dream of retribution." He put the cap back over his eyes, but not low enough to hide the broad smile on his face.

Tracy was tempted to implant the bill of that cap in his teeth.

CHAPTER 25

Tuesday, August 4, Present Day
Redmond, Washington

Tracy awoke to a loud boom that shook the house and rattled the windows. Rex's and Sherlock's accompanying barking was almost as loud and certainly as disturbing. Daniella cried out from her bedroom crib, and both Tracy and Dan shot out of bed as if the home were under mortar attack. On her way past the hallway window, Tracy saw a purple fork of lightning descend from a dark sky, followed by a second fork, then a third, but no rain.

Daniella stood in her crib, holding the railing, tears streaking her cheeks. Tracy picked her up and consoled her. "You're okay. You're okay, baby." Dan was in the other room trying to calm the dogs, but when another boom rolled over the rooftop like a bass drum announcing a Broadway production, the dogs erupted again, further scaring Daniella.

Tracy cradled Daniella to her chest as Dan came into the room.

"Thunderstorm," he said. "Weather over a hundred degrees multiple days in June. What's next? Locusts in August? Tornados in September?"

Just as Tracy thought nothing could get worse, her cell phone rang on her nightstand in the bedroom.

"Who could that be?" Dan asked.

"No idea," Tracy said. She might as well have said: *but it can't be good.*

The sound of a cell phone buzzing in the early hours of the morning still caused a visceral reaction from the years she'd served on the on-call detective team working Violent Crimes. She handed Daniella to Dan. "Take her. If this is spam, I'm about to go nuclear."

She hurried back into the bedroom. Her work phone. Caller ID indicated Faz. That brought a completely different visceral reaction. Her initial thought was something was wrong with Vera. But just as quickly as the thought came, so, too, came a second thought. Why would Faz be calling Tracy's work cell phone?

"Faz," Tracy answered. "Is everything okay?"

"Tracy, I'm sorry to wake you."

"You didn't wake me. We're having thunder and lightning, which triggered the dogs, which triggered Daniella."

"We're having it here also."

"Where are you? Sounds like you're outside."

"I am. I just stepped out of a home on Queen Anne. Del and I are the on-call team this week. We got a problem, Tracy." She could hear the urgency in Faz's voice, the eerie creaking of his words that was as disturbing as the thunder.

"What is it?"

"Unfortunately, you might have been right about it being prudent to wait before we broadcast the news about McDonnel being the Route 99 Killer."

"Oh shit, Faz. What happened?"

Faz went into work mode, a place that veteran homicide detectives could access to handle the sick and depraved things they too often experienced. He turned off being human and focused on the facts, like

Sergeant Joe Friday on the old *Dragnet* show. "Sixty-year-old grand-mother. Widowed. Strangled in her home. She has the angel's wings carved on her left shoulder."

—

Tracy flashed ID to get past the uniformed officer blocking traffic and drove the narrow streets made narrower by the patrol and pool cars parked on both sides that led to the A-framed brick house in the Queen Anne neighborhood. The home looked to be original from when the neighborhood was first built. Small front and side yards with driveways separated the tightly packed homes.

The house was lit by the flashing lights of police cars. The blue-and-gray CSI and medical examiner's vans had squeezed into spaces in front of the house. Neighbors looking confused and concerned watched from covered porches and lawns. Some ventured to the sidewalk. Patrol officers talked with several. This type of police presence in the upscale neighborhood was rare.

Faz and Del met Tracy on the front step beneath a narrow porch. "Shit, Tracy, we don't know what to think. We were both hoping your intuition was wrong about this."

"Who found the woman, Faz?"

"A granddaughter has been living with her while working the sum-mer for a company downtown. She got home late Monday from a weekend event and found the grandmother lying on the floor in the living room," he said.

"Kid is pretty shaken up. Her mother and father came quickly. They're all out back," Del said.

"You get in contact with Nolasco?" Tracy asked.

"He's on his way," Faz said. "Said there had to be some kind of mistake."

"What do you think?"

Faz nodded over his shoulder to the front door. "Take a look for yourself."

Del handed Tracy N-DEX gloves and booties from his go bag, and she slipped them on. They stepped inside the home. A living room was to the right of a staircase ascending to the upper floor. The woman lay on an oval-shaped throw rug near a couch and a coffee table that faced a flat-screen television in the corner of the room. The ME's office was preparing to transport the body downtown. Stuart Funk had come personally.

"Hey, Stuart," Tracy said softly.

"Tracy," Funk said. He looked like he'd just gotten out of bed. Then again, he always looked like he'd just gotten out of bed.

"What can you tell me?"

"Same mark on the left shoulder just above the shoulder blade," Funk said in a voice barely above a whisper. "Looks like angel's wings."

"Any chance this is a copycat?"

Funk shrugged. "I'll need to look microscopically when we transport the body downtown, but my initial impression is it's the same guy. The cut is precise, a sharp blade, minimal tearing of the skin. Again, let me look at it microscopically and compare it with the others."

"Mind if I have a look?"

Funk spoke to the medical attendants, and they carefully turned the woman over to reveal her bloodied shoulder. Funk was right. It looked just like the ME's photographs of the other thirteen victims.

Tracy returned to Faz and Del, and they stepped outside onto the porch.

"What do you know about the woman?" she asked.

"Not much yet," Faz said.

"What the hell is going on, Tracy?" Del asked.

"What's her name?" Tracy asked.

"Bonnie Parker," Del said.

Tracy couldn't recall if she'd read the name in Lisa Childress's article in the investigative file. "Did she work for the City of Seattle?"

"She was retired is all we know at this point," Del said.

"Before she retired."

"Don't know," Faz said. "The son is out back consoling his daughter. We can ask him."

Tracy turned to go back inside but noticed an approaching pool car. Its front wheels bounced over the curb onto the sidewalk and came to a stop on grass near a small maple tree. Johnny Nolasco pushed from the car and hurried up the concrete walk and steps, his eyes wide and in search of answers.

"Angel's wings carved in her left shoulder," Faz said before Nolasco got a word out.

Nolasco swore under his breath. His body sagged as if he'd been handed a huge anvil. In a sense, he had been. He exhaled a frustrated sigh.

"Funk is in there now, but he got a good look, and I asked to see it," Tracy said. "Wings are of the same design and cut with a sharp blade and with precision. Funk says he'll know more when he can view it microscopically."

"Not likely a copycat?" Nolasco said.

"Not unless we have a leak we don't know about," Tracy said. "As far as I know, the only persons outside of the task force who knew about the angel's wings were Lisa and Anita Childress."

Nolasco swore again. "This can't be. It can't be the same guy."

Tracy remained silent.

Nolasco exhaled his frustration. "I guess you called this one. This guy took the reopening of these cases as a challenge and came out of hiding."

"The timing certainly implies he saw the press conference and is letting us know we didn't get him. And this time, it does seem personal."

"The DNA was conclusive," Nolasco said, his voice a controlled fury. "Conclusive. Melton confirmed it. McDonnel is our guy."

"The DNA was mixed. The second source was not identified, not in the CODIS—"

"I know that," Nolasco snapped. He took another deep breath. "What then? This guy just happened to have sex with the same woman on the same night as McDonnel, a suspect in our investigation?"

"I think he did," Tracy said. "But it didn't *just* happen. The odds it was happenstance would be astronomical. Which only leaves the alternative. He did it purposefully."

"Why would he do that?"

"I don't know. Maybe to throw the task force off his scent," Tracy said. "But to do what he did, he had to know McDonnel was a suspect."

"The task force had a leak," Faz said.

"So do we," Tracy said.

Nolasco followed her gaze to Greg Bartholomew, who waited on the sidewalk across the street.

"That's all we need right now is that arsonist," Faz said.

"If he sees the two of you, he'll know what this is about," Faz said.

"We'll have a wildfire on our hands," Del said.

"He sees us," Tracy said. "We're the reason he's here. Captain, there's something I need to talk to you about."

"Can it wait?"

"No. It could be directly relevant."

"I'll go talk to the family," Del said, and he stepped inside the home again.

Tracy told Nolasco and Faz about the tip line disk mailed to her attention, which Augustus Cesare authenticated as the disk he had given to Moss Gunderson. She told them about the connection she found between the killer's final four victims having worked as special assistants in Mayor Edwards's administration. She told them about her conversation with Gunderson in which he all but admitted he had not questioned then mayor Edwards about the connection.

"Why would Moss not question him?" Nolasco said.

"I think it's because either Edwards threatened to burn him or Moss anticipated getting burned. Edwards had moles everywhere. He likely knew who took the drug money."

"When did you find out about the disk?"

"Just a few days ago."

"You didn't tell me? You let me make an ass of myself at that press conference."

"I didn't get the files until after the press conference." Tracy wanted to say she had warned both Nolasco and Weber about the press conference being premature, but that wouldn't help present matters. "What's done is done. We need to find out if this woman ever held a special assistant position. And we need to determine the source of the leak."

"You think it could be Moss?" Faz asked.

"The leak? Yeah I do," Tracy said. "For one thing he hates my guts, and this doesn't paint any of us in a favorable light."

Nolasco looked to Faz. "Anyone here who would know where the woman worked?"

"Like I mentioned, the son is out back consoling his daughter," Faz said. "She found the grandmother."

"Find out if his mother ever worked for the city, if she ever held one of those positions. What did you call them?" Nolasco said to Tracy.

"Special assistants," Tracy said. Faz walked inside the house. "Captain," Tracy said.

"I know we need to talk," Nolasco said. "But not here. Follow me."

Tracy descended the steps with Nolasco. As they did, Bartholomew called out, "Detective? Captain Nolasco? Can you comment on what has happened?"

Tracy and Nolasco ignored him.

"Is your presence here related to the Route 99 Killer? Did you make a mistake naming McDonnel?"

Tracy got into her car and followed Nolasco several blocks, coming to a church parking lot. He stopped and got out of the car. Tracy met him at the hood, which he leaned against before lighting and smoking a cigarette. She waited.

"I'm going to tell you something in confidence," Nolasco said, puffing on his cigarette. When he held it, his hand shook. "The kind of confidence partners keep while working a case together. Can you commit to it?"

"Yeah, I can commit to it."

"I have your word?"

Tracy was more than curious. "You have my word," she said.

Nolasco blew out smoke and what sounded like a great deal of tension. "I was Lisa Childress's source."

Nolasco said it so quickly, Tracy almost didn't have time to react. "You told her about the angel's wings?"

"And the suspects the task force was pursuing."

"Why?"

"Because we weren't getting anywhere, and she was good. Odd, but very good at her job. I hoped that by giving her certain information, in confidence, she might uncover something we had not. I thought she might find something on one of the suspects we hadn't, past training in a medical profession. Something."

Tracy leaned back against the car's hood.

"Then, when Childress disappeared, I thought maybe she'd done something stupid," Nolasco continued. "Gone undercover. Met the killer. I didn't know. She was just gone, so I thought the worst. Then they found her car and they found blood, but they didn't find her. I didn't know what had happened to her. Not until you found her."

"You didn't say anything to anyone?"

"What was I going to say? I had no idea whether her disappearance had to do with the Route 99 case."

"But you suspected it. You thought it."

"Her disappearance didn't fit the pattern of the killings, Crosswhite. The killer left the bodies for us to find. He wanted us to find them. He marked them, for Christ's sake."

"You should have said something to someone."

"Hindsight is twenty-twenty."

"So is common decency."

Nolasco looked away, a tacit admission he knew Tracy to be correct.

"You let Childress just disappear and didn't tell anyone what might have happened to her."

"Look," he said, becoming angry. "I told you; her disappearance didn't fit with the other killings, and then . . . the killings stopped. The killer stopped."

"So you just stepped away."

"I didn't step away. I stayed involved in the investigation as to what happened to her. I learned about the Last Line, about the kickbacks and the payoffs. I tried to find out if her disappearance was somehow related."

"Then you know about Edwards, about his taking a payoff as well."

"Suspected. Never proven," Nolasco said. "But what was I going to do about it? Who was I going to tell?"

"A prosecutor. Someone from the Justice Department," Tracy said.

"I didn't have any solid evidence to make a charge stick. Neither did you."

They sat in silence. The air was humid, and Tracy perspired beneath her corduroy jacket. She hated to admit it, but Nolasco was right.

"Where do we go from here?" Nolasco finally said.

Tracy gave it thought. "Lisa Childress wasn't investigating four separate stories. She believed they were all linked together. I'm sure of it. The Last Line. Corruption in Edwards's administration. Councilman Rivers accused of having sex with underage teens just as his mayoral campaign was taking off. And the Route 99 Killer. Each of his last four—possibly now five—victims worked as a special assistant in Edwards's administration. Childress might have been investigating Edwards for corruption, but she was also investigating his connection to those other three cases."

"What are you saying? You think Edwards is our killer?"

"No. No, I don't. I'm thinking about what Santos told us—"

"Santos—"

"Hang on and just listen. Santos said the killer was sending a message to someone. So, too, did Nabil Kotar."

"The Cowboy?" Nolasco asked, his voice incredulous.

"I went to the Monroe maximum security facility and spoke to him, asked him about the killings, if they meant anything. He said much the same thing Santos said. He said the killer was sending someone a message by marking the victims. I think the person the killer intended to get the message was Edwards. I think the common thread is Edwards. Something Edwards did caused this man to murder the women who worked for him and leave them as bread crumbs for us to follow."

"You mean me. Bread crumbs for me to follow."

"Moss withheld the information. You couldn't have followed," she said.

Nolasco fumed. His nostrils flared. After several long seconds, he said, "Why not just tell us what Edwards did, whatever he did?"

"The killer is angry. He wants Edwards to pay. He wants Edwards to live with the knowledge that he's the reason these women died."

"You think Edwards knew about the connection and didn't say anything?"

"He had to, Captain. He had to know."

"But he didn't say anything?" Nolasco repeated. Tracy, too, was finding that hard to accept. "Do you think the killer could be a woman? Jealous rage?" he asked.

"No. The prostitutes don't fit."

"Why not, if the killer used them to practice?"

"To overpower a person in that way . . . Seems it had to be a man, but okay, we don't rule out a woman."

Nolasco let out another sigh. "We can't very well confront Edwards with what we have."

"Why not?"

"It's innuendo and speculation. The FBI and the Justice Department went after Edwards with everything they had, multiple times, and never got anything to stick. He insulated himself with dozens of layers, didn't use email, and only used his phone sparingly. He generally did everything by a handshake. They couldn't even prove he took kickbacks. What makes you think Edwards even knew the killer intended the killings as some type of message?"

Tracy's cell phone rang. "Faz." She put Faz on speakerphone.

"You're right," Faz said. "About the victim. According to the son, his mom worked for the City of Seattle as the director of the Department of Construction and Inspections. As soon as the office opens, I'll make a call and find out if she also worked as one of Edwards's special assistants. Son didn't know."

"Nobody is to talk to the press," Nolasco said.

"Absolutely," Faz said.

Tracy thanked him and disconnected the call. "So it isn't four messages he's sent," Tracy said. "It's five."

CHAPTER 26

Tuesday, August 4, Present Day
Seattle, Washington

When Tracy arrived at Police Headquarters, it was like entering after the press conference to announce McDonnel was the Route 99 serial killer. Bad news spread as fast as good news, but like a serious case of the flu. The rumor spreading was the Queen Anne murder *might* be related to the Route 99 Killer. If so, Dwight McDonnel was not the killer. Like the flu, nobody would admit to having started the rumor, which caused everyone to be on edge and guarded.

The phones in Tracy's office rang nonstop, but the only call she answered was the one she could not ignore. Weber summoned her and Nolasco to her office. She did not sound happy.

Everyone in the department, especially the brass who appeared at the recent press conference, was about to have egg all over their faces, and that included Weber and Nolasco. Tracy couldn't help but think that had been the killer's intent.

As Tracy and Nolasco took the interior stairwell to the eighth floor, Tracy said, "Faz called again. Bonnie Parker worked as a special assistant in Edwards's administration."

"Shit," Nolasco said.

"We can't tell Weber about Edwards. About the possible connection."

"Why not?" Nolasco said, slightly winded as he shuffled up the steps.

"Because we have to assume Edwards is also holding the Last Line money over Weber's head. Any suspicion we share with her is sure to be shared with Edwards. I want to interview him before he figures out what we know."

Nolasco stopped his ascent, eyes wide in surprise. Footsteps descended from above, echoing. They waited until a detective passed them on the staircase and exited one floor below. "What do you mean Edwards is holding Last Line money over Weber's head?" Nolasco said, a little too loud. "You're saying she took dirty money too?"

Tracy spoke in a soft voice. "In my search to find Lisa Childress, I spoke to a man who used to deal drugs in Rainier Valley when Weber was a young girl living there. He said she knew the dealers. When the Last Line started pinching them, the dealers suspected someone with intimate knowledge of the valley was providing the task force with inside information about where drugs deals were being made."

"Why would Weber do that?"

"It's a long story, but her father worked in the department, and his partner set him up on a drug bust, accused him of taking some of the confiscated money before it was counted. It was bullshit, but Weber's father took the fall and was discharged. He worked private security until he got a bullet in the back that left him paralyzed. Weber never forgot what happened to him. Taking kickbacks from the Last Line was her way of getting the money she believed the department owed her father."

"You can confirm this?"

"Not in a court," she said shaking her head. "If I could, Weber wouldn't still be here. And Moss might be in jail, though the statute of limitations would protect him."

"But you confronted her."

"I did."

"That's how you got your job back, how Del was reinstated after Weber suspended you both."

"That's how."

"Which means the allegation was accurate."

Tracy nodded.

Nolasco squinted as if fighting an impending headache. "That's why you went to the newspaper with those stories about corruption, because you didn't have the evidence to take them down in court?"

Tracy explained how she had consulted Cerrabone, and he advised she didn't have enough evidence to stick, and that the statute of limitations would protect them from criminal prosecution.

Nolasco almost smiled, but he caught himself. "So you and Weber really don't get along."

"Let's just say we're both working under a highly volatile truce."

He nodded as if he understood. "Okay. What do we tell her then if we don't mention the possible Edwards connection?"

Tracy had given this some thought on the drive in to headquarters. "We tell her we don't know anything with certainty, but we're investigating, and we will get to the bottom of it. We don't mention any suspicion of a connection to Edwards."

"That's not going to satisfy her."

"She doesn't have a choice. She jumped the gun on the news conference and got sprayed with skunk stink. She won't want to get sprayed again."

"'Sprayed with skunk stink'?"

"A Fazism."

Nolasco gave a small growl, clearing his throat. He didn't like it, but he also realized Tracy was right, which he might have liked even less.

Tracy and Nolasco once again waited outside Chief Weber's office. Once again, the captain did not sit. He'd tried for a moment, but his leg jackhammered like his foot was trying to bust through the floor. He paced. The fingers of his right hand, the one that now held the seemingly always-present cigarette, quivered for a nicotine fix.

The receptionist hung up the phone and told Tracy and Nolasco to go in. When they stepped through the door, Weber's stare looked sharp enough to cut diamonds. She spoke in a clipped tone, as if measuring her words and struggling to hold back a flurry of expletives that wouldn't do anyone any good.

"I just hung up the phone with the mayor," she said, letting Tracy and Nolasco know the shit was already tumbling downhill. "Do you want to tell me what the hell is going on? The phone is ringing off the hook, and I'm being told Dwight McDonnel might not be the Route 99 Killer."

"I'm not certain what's going on," Nolasco said, sticking to the script.

"You're not certain? What about you?" Weber shifted her diamond-cutting gaze to Tracy. "Do you know what's going on?"

"Not with certainty," Tracy said, trying not to sound insolent, which only got Weber's goat all the more.

"Well, somebody in this room better get some certainty, because I just stood in front of the families of those victims last Friday and told them the killer of their loved ones had been identified. Were you wrong?"

The shit pail tumbled farther down the hill.

"McDonnel's DNA was a positive match with DNA left at one of the Route 99 serial killer crime scenes. No doubt about it. No mistake," Nolasco said. "We reconfirmed with Mike Melton this morning."

"Then why am I hearing about a murder on Queen Anne that may be related to the Route 99 killings?"

"The woman murdered this morning was strangled, like the others," Nolasco said. "About the same age as the four prior victims would have been, had they lived. She also had angel's wings carved in her left shoulder, just below the shoulder blade. The ME is going to look microscopically and confirm whether it matches the others."

Weber swore, turned, and paced the carpeted room, shaking her head. "Copycat?"

"Not sure how they would have known about the markings," Nolasco said.

"You said there was a leak," Weber said to Tracy.

"I said someone had told Lisa Childress, the reporter. I have no information that fact was disseminated to anyone else, or to the general public."

"We stood at a press conference and told the world we had our guy," Weber said.

"The killer might be playing games with us," Tracy said.

Weber grabbed hold of the lifeline. "What kind of games?"

"The killer, if this most recent killing is legit, might have been upset we held the press conference and told everyone we'd caught him. This most recent killing could be intended as a message that we haven't."

Weber pointed to Nolasco. "He just told me the DNA was solid."

"It is solid. But he also told you the DNA was fragmented. That there existed two different DNA profiles."

"What are you saying? That the killer killed a prostitute McDonnel had sex with? How the hell could he do that? What are the odds?"

"Too high to have been coincidence."

Weber gave Tracy a wide-eyed stare. "You're saying he did it on purpose?"

"That would be the logical conclusion," she said. "The killer knew McDonnel was a suspect, and this was an opportunity to deflect any potential attention in McDonnel's direction."

"How could he have known McDonnel was a suspect?" When neither Nolasco nor Tracy immediately answered, Weber deduced the ramifications herself. "Are you intimating the killer might have been someone within the police department?"

"Anything is possible," Tracy said. "The Golden State Killer was a former police officer. Lisa Childress's notes identified five suspects, including McDonnel, so someone leaked McDonnel's name," Tracy said.

"It was your task force," Weber said to Nolasco. "Do you have any idea who might have been the leak?"

"I warned every team member that nothing was to leave the task force room," Nolasco said.

Weber said, "What do you suggest I do about all the phone calls I'm receiving asking me to confirm or deny this latest killing relates to the Route 99 killings?"

"Ignore them," Tracy said.

"I can't very well ignore the mayor."

"If you can't ignore them, tell them your detectives are taking all steps to properly investigate the most recent murder, and a statement will be made at a later date, after we have more information. So far, the press hasn't mentioned the angel's wings. Let's assume they don't know about them," Tracy said.

"Until when?"

"Until we have more information?" Tracy said.

"And how are you going to get more information?"

Tracy looked to Nolasco. "We'll start with the fragmented DNA sample."

Tracy and Nolasco returned to the Park 90/5 complex. This time, they called on the drive over, so Melton expected them and was prepared for their questions.

"What happened, Mike?" Tracy slumped into one of the two chairs across from Melton's desk and felt for the first time that morning that she could relax and speak plainly. "Did we make a mistake?"

"No mistake," Melton said matter-of-factly. "I've gone over the findings. We determined the allele profile of the thirteen core STRs for both the sample retrieved at the crime scene and the suspect's sample. They matched with Dwight McDonnel. No ambiguity."

When it came to DNA evidence, Tracy was like a person who relied on Google for information. She knew just enough to be dangerous. Her time working CSI had included working in the Latent Print Unit and the DNA Unit. She knew a DNA sequence was like a fingerprint, and for two fingerprints to match, there needed to be a certain number of matching "points" between the fingerprint collected at the crime scene and the print obtained from a suspect, or a fingerprint already in the FBI's Integrated Automated Fingerprint Identification System. Criminal courts generally accepted eight to twelve points of similarity as a match. She knew DNA profile matching, on its most basic level, involved attempting to match the DNA markers obtained at a crime scene with markers for DNA samples previously entered into the combined DNA Index, or CODIS, system.

"We just came from a crime scene that makes it highly unlikely Dwight McDonnel is the Route 99 Killer," Nolasco said.

"I've heard. Bad news travels fast."

"Any thoughts?" Nolasco asked.

"Likely the same ones you're having and the reason you are here," Melton said. "The killer had to be the second DNA sample in the fragmented sample we obtained from the victim."

"Which you've run for me before and did not find a match in the CODIS software," Nolasco said.

"No *direct* match," Melton said.

"What do you mean, 'no *direct* match'?" Tracy asked.

"I mean, the last DNA analysis run was for a direct match, not a partial match."

"Educate me, Mike. What would a partial match show? A maybe?" Tracy asked.

"Not a maybe. A relation."

"A family member?" Tracy said. She'd read about the rapid advances in DNA technology and how they'd been used to build family trees that eventually led to relations of the killer.

"The CODIS software we now have can be set to search at different stringency levels: high, medium, and low. High-stringency searches require the two DNA samples to match exactly. Moderate- and low-stringency levels allow for the identification of partial matches— meaning we can identify familial relationships due to the inherited nature of DNA and the fact that family members have more genetic similarities than nonrelated individuals."

At times, Melton could not help but sound like a scientist. "But I understood CODIS was not designed for familial matches," Tracy said.

"It isn't, but jurisdictions, including this one, have obtained separate software and genetic algorithms to specifically identify family relationships. It's a technique called FDS, and it greatly reduces false positives."

"I thought there was a move to ban the use of familial DNA by law enforcement, arguments that it was racist profiling," Nolasco said.

"The use of CODIS set at high stringency levels does not code for any known genetic traits or observable characteristics such as race, gender, or health," Melton said. "Medium- and low-level searches do. The controversy you're referring to is Washington House Bill 2485, which sought to ban medium- and low-level searches, but which has not passed."

"Because of the controversy?" Tracy said.

"There will always be controversy," Melton said. "But the controversy to which you're referring relates to law enforcement's use of biological data held by a genealogy website like GEDmatch. Law enforcement creates a fake profile, uploads the unknown DNA gathered at a crime scene, and an expert in genetic genealogy takes months to build a family tree of distant ancestors and, from the genetic data, a profile of the suspect—hair and eye coloring, for instance. You, meaning *you* detectives, then spend months tracking down relatives to narrow the list of suspects. Probably the most infamous case was the 2018 arrest of Joseph DeAngelo, aka the Golden State Killer, who was subsequently convicted of more than a dozen murders, rapes, and a hundred robberies across California. Here in Washington, investigators have used it to make breakthroughs in several unsolved murder cases, including the Tacoma Police Department's arrest and conviction of the person responsible for the 1986 rape and murder of a twelve-year-old girl outside her home."

"You sound like you know a lot about it," Tracy said.

"Yours truly testified before the Washington State Legislature. I argued *we*, meaning law enforcement, can use the DNA to make society a safer place and possibly deter people from committing crimes. We can also use it to resolve cold cases and exonerate the wrongfully convicted."

"And the opposition?"

"Argued it's a violation of the Fourth and/or Fourteenth Amendments. A 'genetic stop and frisk,' if you will."

Melton explained that opponents argued police, in their search for an unknown criminal, could gather information on hundreds of innocent family members who did not provide their DNA to a genealogical site, and thus the search violated their right against unreasonable searches and seizures. "As for the Fourteenth Amendment, which guarantees equal protection under the law, opponents argue the DNA search targets people of color because a high percentage of the samples in the CODIS system are from people of color. They also argue it subjects those relatives to being investigated and harassed by the police."

"So are we SOL?" Tracy asked.

"No. You asked for an explanation, and I gave it, but nothing prevents us from running the fragmented sample in the Combined DNA Index System at a low stringency level to look for a close relative like a parent, child, or sibling. Maybe we get lucky."

Tracy looked to Nolasco. "Seems unlikely but more hopeful than anything we currently have."

"Pessimism, my dear lady, never won any battle," Melton said. "Dwight Eisenhower. The police used a low-level search in Arizona after they lost all hope of ever solving the murder of a thirty-one-year-old woman in her home. The unknown DNA was entered on low stringency and partially matched to a fifty-four-year-old man convicted of child molestation and serving forty years in prison. Police learned the convicted man's brother had been living in the same area as the murder and, years earlier, had a DUI arrest and had given a blood sample. A high-stringency DNA analysis matched him as the murderer."

"How long will it take to run a medium- or low-stringency search?" Nolasco asked.

"I know the brass is breathing down your necks. But we already have the DNA. We just need to run it. You could have an answer by the end of the day."

"Thanks, Mike," Nolasco said. "We both appreciate it."

Tracy did a double take. Had Nolasco just made a statement for both of them? Unity?

"And just so we're clear," Melton said, looking and sounding serious. "This has nothing to do with you bringing me, or in this instance, not bringing me, a Salumi sandwich, though I will say such gestures certainly don't hurt."

Tracy and Nolasco left the Park 90/5 complex and drove to the *Seattle Times* building in an area undergoing rapid redevelopment. Tracy wanted to speak to Anita Childress about her mother's investigative files. She called from the car and told the reporter they needed a moment of her time.

They met Childress in the third-floor conference room where a few months earlier Tracy had met Anita to discuss her mother Lisa's missing person case. Childress's editor, Bill Jorgensen, approached like a magnet pulled to metal. Reporters had a sixth sense for news, and Jorgensen smelled a story.

"Getting word you guys made a mistake, that McDonnel is not the Route 99 Killer," Jorgensen said. "How does something like that happen in today's day and age with the advances made in forensic sciences?"

"Sorry, Bill," Tracy said, deflecting the question. "But we won't confirm or deny McDonnel is or is not the Route 99 Killer."

Jorgensen had enough experience to know he wasn't going to get an answer to his questions, but that didn't mean he wouldn't try. "Friday, the mayor and the chief of police said McDonnel was the killer. If you're telling me you won't confirm or deny it, it's a denial, isn't it?"

Tracy was giving Jorgensen something because she couldn't give him the story he wanted. Not yet.

"The fact that you're here is also indicative a mistake was made," Jorgensen said.

"Or we're just tying up some loose ends," Tracy said. "If you want to run that story, without any evidence or quotes to substantiate it, that's your prerogative. If you want to wait . . ."

Jorgensen knew they'd reached a stalemate. "Do me a favor?" he said, because he had to, not because Tracy would. "When you obtain more definitive information and *conclude* your investigation, let Anita know? Because I have a series of articles waiting to be run about the failed investigation, and a story about the present investigation also failing would fit nicely. If you have something to tell me I'm wrong, I'll listen. Otherwise . . ."

Jorgensen was issuing a tit for tat. Tracy respected him for it, but she could sense Nolasco tensing and quickly said, "Anita will be the first to know, Bill."

Jorgensen left the conference room.

Tracy turned to Childress. "We need to know if anyone other than you and I has seen your mother's investigative files."

"Jorgensen," Childress said. "When I first went to him and told him I wanted to find my mother, we pulled the files and found her spiral notebooks. And, I guess my father, back when my mother disappeared."

"Do you know for certain your father saw those files?"

"No. Not really. Not unless he saw the file at home."

"Anyone other than you and Bill who had access to your mother's files?"

"I'm not aware of anyone else, Tracy, but I also don't know who he would have told or why."

"You ever get a sense, Anita, that your mother's files weren't four separate files but were all related?" Tracy was testing the waters, wondering if Anita had determined the link between what was now five victims who had worked on Edwards's staff.

Childress shifted her attention between Tracy and Nolasco. "Not all of them, but I did wonder about the Last Line and Peter Rivers's investigation. Do you think there's some relationship between Edwards and the serial killer?"

"I'm just trying to fit together a lot of pieces from a long time ago," Tracy said. "Your mother never mentioned anything to you, a memory that came back to her?"

"No, nothing."

—

Tracy and Nolasco returned to Police Headquarters, but not to the seventh floor. They stepped off the elevator on the fourth floor and went immediately to the HR Department, finding Cesare.

"I expected I'd hear from you. Word's going around that a murder on Queen Anne was the work of the Route 99 Killer."

"Who did you hear that from?" Nolasco asked.

"It's all over headquarters, Captain. People are saying McDonnel isn't the guy. That the press conference on Friday jumped the gun."

Tracy wanted to get down to the reason they'd come back to Cesare. "Who did you share the information on the tip sheet with, other than Moss?"

Cesare looked to Nolasco. "Every member of the task force got a copy of the tip sheet. We divided the responsibility of follow-through among the team, after the calls were initially culled and color coded."

"What do you mean 'initially culled'?" Tracy said. "I thought you told me you culled the calls?"

"I didn't man the tip line. That was done by a patrol officer. He weeded out the crazies and forwarded me the ones he deemed most viable, and I made calls to determine if the tip was worthy of follow-up by a task force member."

"You remember that officer's name?" Tracy asked.

Cesare looked to Nolasco. "Henry K. England. Used to say the 'K' stood for King. You know, King Henry . . . England."

"And the last time you spoke to England?"

Cesare scoffed. "Twenty-five years ago. I understood he didn't go back to patrol, that he moved away, but don't quote me on it."

A lot of Seattle officers left the area upon completion of their service. A number of factors forced that move, including the rising cost of living, not to mention they'd spent much of their adult life putting Seattle's criminals behind bars. Many police officers wanted a fresh start, in a place where they didn't have to be concerned about walking into a bar or a restaurant and having someone recognize them.

But there was something else interesting about Henry K. England leaving the department and the area.

The Route 99 killings had also come to an end in Seattle.

CHAPTER 27

Nolasco returned to his office. He told Tracy he had a fire burning in another homicide case that needed his attention. Tracy hunkered down in her office with Henry K. England's personnel records. England had left SPD effective January 1, 1996, not long after the Route 99 Killer stopped killing. England had been just twenty-eight. He'd served seven years on the force. Further research revealed England married around the same time and had moved to Ellensburg, which was roughly a two-hour drive, without traffic, east of the Cascade mountains. Tracy did a Triple I background check on England—a fingerprint search of the FBI's Interstate Identification Index's criminal records. She did not get a hit. She also ran England through the National Crime Information Center. That, too, came up negative. She pulled up the Department of Licensing's records and retrieved England's license and his records, and she noted the vehicle registered in his name, a Ford F-250 truck. She and Nolasco would check with the Department of Transportation about cameras between Ellensburg and Seattle, and, if they deemed it necessary, they'd have someone check specified cameras to determine if England drove his truck into Seattle over the weekend.

She made a call to the Ellensburg Police Department to let them know of her intent to speak to England and told a captain she'd stop by his department when they arrived in town. She asked if they had any unsolved murders of young women. He said they did not. He confirmed an address and told her England lived with his wife on a hay farm outside of town. He also said England did not have a record.

Tracy called Nolasco and said she thought the circumstances, England marrying and moving away, warranted a drive. Nolasco agreed and said they'd both go. Tracy called back the Ellensburg captain and asked if he'd have one of his men do a drive-by to ensure England was home, so they didn't make a wasted trip.

"No need," he said. "July and August is harvesting season for timothy hay. England will be at it sunup to sundown."

Ellensburg, located on the Yakama River in Kittitas Valley, was mostly agricultural, and had once predominantly grown wheat. As with most agricultural regions, wineries and microbreweries had moved into the area to grow grapes and hops. It was also an outdoorsman's paradise, with fly-fishing on the Yakima River close by, hunting grounds, hiking, and camping. Tracy had dreaded the prospect of a two-hour drive in the car with Nolasco—both directions—but he spent much of his time on the phone playing catch-up on his other cases and putting out small fires. When he was off the phone, she filled the time explaining what she'd learned about England. They stopped at the Ellensburg police station as a courtesy and let the chief know they were in town.

England lived outside of town at the end of a long dirt-and-gravel road that cut through large fields, some of which looked to have been recently mowed, the clippings piled in long lines extending the lengths of the fields.

"What do they grow out here?" Nolasco asked.

"Hay," Tracy said. "Timothy hay, to be precise."

Nolasco shook his head. "How the hell do you know that, Crosswhite?"

She smiled, thinking of how she might jerk his chain, then settled for the truth. "Ellensburg Police Department said England married the daughter of a family who've farmed hay up here for decades."

"My dad used to take me and my brothers fly-fishing up here," Nolasco said. "All over this area. We fished the Yakima, camped, swam in the mountain lakes."

Tracy didn't think of Nolasco as having things in common with the way she'd been raised in the North Cascades. She'd always thought they were oil and vinegar, which was why they didn't get along.

They took an exit and minutes later turned off a paved road, tires crunching gravel on a road stretching between white horse fencing and leading to a two-story, well-kept farmhouse. It looked like something built in the 1800s, with a tin roof extending over a porch complete with two rocking chairs and a porch swing. Farther to the left of the house was a metal garage with two large rolling doors, both bays open. Inside one bay was a large tractor. The other bay was empty.

Tracy parked on the asphalt drive, and she and Nolasco approached the house. A collie, partially hidden behind a rocking chair, sat up and barked. The bark wasn't mean. The dog had likely been startled from a good slumber and was expressing displeasure.

Tracy talked to the dog in a soothing voice and calmly climbed four steps to the screen door. She noticed Nolasco had stopped at the bottom of the steps and did not look eager to greet the dog. He lit a cigarette. The door behind the screen was open, probably to generate a draft with the outside temperature, mideighties.

Tracy rapped her knuckles three times on the screen door, generating more barking from the dog, this time a call to alert the owners they had company. A woman came down the hall, barefoot in blue-jeans shorts and a T-shirt. Judging from her appearance, Tracy estimated the woman to be mid to late fifties. England's wife, not a daughter.

"Can I help you?" She unlatched the screen door and pushed it partially open.

Tracy raised her detective's badge and introduced herself and Johnny Nolasco, who remained at the foot of the stairs. "We're looking for Henry England."

"That's my husband. I'm Katlyn England. What is this about?" She didn't appear overly concerned. She stepped out of the house onto the porch, letting the screen door slap closed.

"We're investigating a case your husband worked on when he was with the Seattle Police Department and hoped to ask him a few questions."

"That had to be almost twenty-five years ago," Katlyn said.

"It was," Tracy said. "I take it you weren't married then?" She was fishing.

Katlyn shook her head. "We had just met. We got married after he left the force and we moved up here. My father needed help with the farm, and Henry was looking to get out of police work."

The timeline fit with the Route 99 Killer's final victim.

"Is Henry home?" Tracy asked.

"Harvest season. He won't be in until after the sun goes down. Up here we take that saying about making hay while the sun shines to heart." She finished with a not fully at ease smile and slid her hands in the pockets of her cutoff jeans.

Tracy returned the smile. "Can we talk to him? Is there a way you might contact him?"

"I can drive you out in the truck to the field where he's working. I don't imagine you'll want to drive your car out in the fields."

"He's close by then?" Tracy asked.

"He isn't far," the woman said. "Let me get some shoes and the truck keys. I'll be out in a minute. Casey needs to get some exercise anyway."

Minutes later, Tracy jumped in the front seat of a Ford F-250 diesel truck. Nolasco climbed in the back seat, looking ill at ease with Casey the collie sticking his head in the window slider from the truck bed.

"Don't mind Casey," Katlyn England said. "He just wants to be part of the conversation."

England drove down a dirt road extending along the side of the house into a field of tall, green grass. Hot air whipped in the truck's open windows and brought the smell of fresh-cut grass. The fields had been cut in a checkerboard pattern, some squares harvested, others not yet. In the harvested fields were more of the long lines of clippings, as well as large circular-shaped hay bales. They crisscrossed a field to one with a large green-and-yellow tractor pulling a larger machine over the row of piled hay.

"That's Henry," England said. "Driving the baler."

"I imagine it's a lot of work when it's harvesting season," Nolasco said. "Did Henry work all weekend too?"

"Not this past Sunday," she said. "Henry loves to fly-fish. It's his passion. He took Sunday off and spent all day on the river."

"The Yakima?" Nolasco asked. "I used to fish it as a kid with my dad. Where did he go?"

"Up near Cle Elum. He has his spots."

"Do you fish also?" Nolasco raised his voice to be heard over the wind coming through the open windows.

"I do, but not this past Sunday. I visited a sister for a few days. She's sick and going through chemo."

"I'm sorry about your sister. So does Henry fish with a buddy, or is it time he likes to get away?" Nolasco asked.

Katlyn glanced in the rearview mirror. "Sometimes with friends. But sometimes coordinating schedules can be more work than the fishing. Henry likes his time alone too. So do I."

"I can appreciate it," Nolasco said. "I like to get away also. It's peaceful. He went by himself this weekend then?"

This time her glance in the rearview mirror seemed more deliberate; perhaps she recognized Nolasco's questions were more specific than just casual conversation.

"He did. Left early and didn't get home until after the sun went down. That's what he said anyway."

"Did Henry bring home any trout, or is it all catch and release?" Nolasco asked.

"Catch and release," she said.

Katlyn drove alongside the tractor hauling the baler that Tracy deduced made the circular hay bales she saw in the field. Henry England had a look on his face that was a mix of curiosity and confusion. He shut down the tractor, and it spit a puff of black diesel smoke from the stack. He pushed open the cab door and stepped down, looking like a country-western singer in a mesh baseball hat, black T-shirt flecked with pieces of grass, well-worn jeans, and square-toed boots. "What's up?" he said in a volume indicating it had been loud inside the cab.

"You have visitors from your days working at the police department," Katlyn said.

England clearly didn't recognize Tracy, but he looked past her to Nolasco. "Johnny Nolasco," he said.

Nolasco put out a hand. "How are you doing?"

"Fine," England said. "What brings you all the way out here?"

"Hoping to ask you some questions about one of our cases," Nolasco said. "One you worked the tip line for us."

"The Route 99 serial killer."

"That's the one," Nolasco said. "You remember it?"

"Only serial killer case I ever worked. Only task force I ever worked, though not really."

"What do you mean?" Tracy asked.

"I just filtered through all the tips that came in over the tip line to try to weed out the crazies." He looked to Nolasco. "You ran that task force. Didn't you?"

Katlyn said, "I think that's my cue to take Casey for his walk. I don't care much for police talk. No offense."

"None taken," Tracy said.

"Come on, Casey." Katlyn and the dog walked down the field, Katlyn pulling a cell phone from her back pocket.

Henry England said, "That was a long time ago. Twenty-five years?"

"That's about right," Nolasco said. "Curious about how you filtered through all the calls?"

"Something new come up?"

"We've reopened the investigation and are going back over some old ground in case we missed something," Nolasco said.

"Just listened to the tips," England said. "If it sounded promising, for any reason, I'd call the person back—if they left a number, many didn't. My job was to try to determine what they had to say and whether it was worth passing up the chain."

"What was the chain, if you remember?" Nolasco asked.

"I sent calls along to Cesare. Augustus Cesare. That's a name you don't forget. That was the end of the road for me."

"How did you determine if the tip should be passed along?"

England scratched at the back of his neck. "It was a gut thing. I just asked the person questions to find out if they had something specific or were just speculating. A lot of speculating. We got people claiming they were psychics, and others who were just crazy. We got people who fancied themselves as detectives, but who didn't have anything substantial to say. I erred on the side of caution and sent along probably more than I should have, but I didn't want someone to come back and say I missed something important."

"Did you get a copy of the digital version of Cesare's tip line?"

"Not that I recall. No reason for me to get it."

"Have any interaction with him or any of the other members of the task force?"

"None other than 'here are the calls I weeded out, and here are the ones I think should be followed up.' Can I ask what this is about? The task force was disbanded because the killer stopped killing. Why is this an issue now? He isn't back in business, is he?"

Tracy couldn't tell if England's question was legitimate or intended to throw them off his scent. Many serial killers were very bright and very good at obfuscation. "I work cold cases," she said. "I'm trying to solve the thirteen murders, bring some closure to the victims' families."

"Like I said, I really wasn't a member of the task force," England said. "I just worked the tip line. Nothing beyond that."

"Any tip come in that caught your attention more than any others?" Tracy asked.

"Not that I can remember from way back then."

"You didn't sit in on any task force meetings either, did you?" Nolasco said.

"No."

"You ever hear the killer referred to as anything other than the Route 99 Killer?"

This time a scowl and shake of the head. "Nothing I can recall."

Nolasco looked to Tracy. They asked another fifteen minutes of questions, until it was clear England didn't have much to add.

"Why didn't you just call?" England asked.

"Figured you'd be hard to get, working a farm," Nolasco said. "I used to come up here often as a kid with my dad. Wife says you like to fish the Yakima?"

"Some of the best fly-fishing in the state," England said. "Hard to get away though. Always something to be done on a farm."

"That's what I hear. Love to give the Yakima a run again, but it's been decades. When's the best time of year to go?" Nolasco asked, and Tracy wondered if his question had a purpose or if he was just being friendly.

England paused. He looked to be considering the question. "You can really fish it year-round," he said.

"I understood they elevated the river this time of year for irriga-tion," Nolasco said, and Tracy got the sense the question was intended to convey to England he should not bullshit, that the man asking questions might know more than England realized.

England looked concerned. "They do," he said. "But you can still fish if you know where to go. I just went Sunday, in fact."

"No kidding. Where'd you go? Maybe I'll give a try?"

England laughed. Nerves. What was he hiding? "I got my spots, you know. Unless you know the river it really wouldn't help for me to describe them."

"Your wife said you fished up north near Cle Elum."

"There she goes, giving away all my secrets." England laughed again, though it looked to be with discomfort.

"Anyplace you'd recommend?"

"Just here and there," England said. "Just got to walk the river, find out where the water is running too fast, and look for the pockets shaded by overhanging bushes and trees along the banks. If you fly-fish, you know it changes daily."

"No secret honey holes?"

"No self-respecting fisherman gives away his honey holes. Otherwise, you're surrounded by more fishermen than fish."

Nolasco smiled. "Well, if you're ever willing to share . . ."

England gave a pained smile, then checked his phone. "I really should get back to it," he said. "Up here we like to make hay while the sun shines."

"Literally," Tracy said.

"Thanks for your time during this busy season," Nolasco added.

England turned toward where his wife and Casey had walked off, put two fingers between his teeth, and whistled. The collie and Katlyn made their way back.

Katlyn dropped Tracy and Nolasco back at their car. They thanked her for the ride.

Back in their pool car, Nolasco said, "Fishing on the Yakima is year-round, but the best months are February to June. In July they raise the water levels to allow the farmers to irrigate their fields. Any experienced fly-fisherman knows that. You don't catch fish when they raise the river. It's running too fast."

"You think he's lying about his whereabouts Sunday?"

"About fishing on Sunday? Not necessarily. About catching fish? Probably."

"Don't all fishermen exaggerate?"

"The only thing England said about fishing I agree with is the Yakima is one of the best rivers in the state. I think we should check the Department of Transportation and have someone look at traffic cameras up here for Sunday, see if they spot England's vehicle. See if he drove farther than Cle Elum, maybe all the way into Seattle. Let's also run his background a bit deeper, determine where he went to school, where he worked, try to determine if he had any connection to the victims, or any reason to have a beef with the departments they worked in. He's about the same age."

"Or any connection to Edwards?" Tracy said.

"Might as well."

As they descended the pass after crossing over the mountains, Tracy got a call on her cell phone from Mike Melton. "Where are you at?" Melton asked.

"North Bend. Driving back into Seattle."

"Stop by Park 90/5. I have something for you."

"You got a hit?"

"In baseball lexicon, this might be a home run. But I'll let you and Captain Nolasco decide."

Tracy disconnected and looked across the car to Nolasco. "I'm not sure if that's good news or bad," she said.

"Good news if we're batting," Nolasco said. "Bad news if we're the pitcher."

CHAPTER 28

Tracy and Nolasco drove straight to Park 90/5 but hit late-after-noon traffic and didn't arrive until after five thirty. Melton had waited for them. Tracy smelled microwave popcorn throughout the hallways, and it still had a déjà vu effect, though it had been years since she worked there.

"Sorry to keep you waiting, Mike," Tracy said as she and Nolasco entered Melton's office. He sat strumming his guitar.

"No worries. I'll be here late." He turned and set his guitar on a stand to the side of his desk, as if they had all the time in the world. In a sense, they did. They'd waited twenty-five years. If this was a moment of truth, it must have been what the detective chasing Gary Ridgway felt when they finally had his DNA from a discarded piece of gum and learned he was responsible for the deaths of dozens.

Melton opened a file on his desk pad and calmly handed Nolasco a document. Tracy read it over Nolasco's shoulder. Melton said, "Got a partial hit for the fragmented sample."

Nolasco said, "Jonathan Michael Edwards."

Tracy read just as Melton said the name. She asked what was also clearly on Nolasco's mind. "Any relationship to former mayor Edwards?" She asked with both anticipation and some trepidation.

"His son," Melton said.

"Home run," Nolasco said, though also without enthusiasm. Then added, "Shit."

"Jonathan Edwards was picked up thirty years ago on a DUI and had his blood drawn. His DNA is in the CODIS system."

Nolasco lowered the document and rubbed at the back of his head. Tracy had been right about the case having a connection to the former mayor, but not in her wildest imagination did she envision this scenario. "You're saying Jonathan Michael Edwards is a genetic relation to the Route 99 serial killer?"

"The fragmented sample is definitely a familial match. A half brother."

"I need a computer." Tracy walked around Melton's desk to his computer.

"If you're going to Google Mayor Edwards and look up his family, I've already done it. He has three children. Two daughters and one son, Jonathan. He does not acknowledge any other children. At least not publicly."

"Could there be something wrong in the testing?" Nolasco said, cautious now after what had happened earlier.

"Science doesn't lie," Melton said. "And there's nothing wrong with the testing."

"You're sure," Tracy said, then corrected herself. "I'm sorry, Mike. You can imagine."

"I can. Full siblings share between 1,613 and 3,488 centimorgans of DNA. Half siblings share between 1,160 and 2,436. The centimorgans in this instance were 2,156. I'm not saying anything, so I don't take your questions personally. The science is saying he's a brother or half brother."

"A son Edwards has never acknowledged," Tracy said. Nolasco and Melton both looked at her. "We all know Edwards was a notorious womanizer. Maybe still is. Santos said the first nine victims were discarded and concluded they were practice. The last four, and now five victims, Santos said the killer was sending a message, that the angel's wings were a message justice was coming. The message was to Edwards. Each of the five women worked as a special assistant on his staff and likely had a relationship with him. A half son, never acknowledged, holding a grudge. The markings don't represent the Angel of Death. They represent what Santos postulated. The Angel of Justice."

"That's one hell of a grudge," Melton said.

Nolasco looked unprepared for the information. He held up the sheet of paper. "What the hell do we do with this?"

"We get a warrant for Mayor Edwards's DNA," Tracy said. "It's like Mike said. We don't prove or disprove anything. We let the science prove the DNA is his son, and when it does, we confront him."

"You don't just walk up to the former mayor's house and ask him for a DNA sample," Nolasco said. "Especially not Edwards. From what I hear he still has his hands in half the shit that goes on in this city."

"Exactly," Tracy said. "So better to ask forgiveness than permission. We tell him we'll keep this quiet as much as we can, if he cooperates. If he doesn't, he'll end up on the front page of the *Times*."

"Edwards will never agree. And no judge is going to grant a warrant without something more substantial. And if you're right about Weber being on the Last Line's pay sheet and Edwards knowing about it, you and I will be walking a breadline tomorrow."

"It's DNA. How much more substantial can we get?"

"You know what I mean."

Tracy did. "Let's talk with the son," she said. "Let's talk with Jonathan."

"It will get back to his father."

"Exactly," she said. "Let's put a little pressure on Edwards, let him know what we have. Maybe he'll do the right thing. Maybe he'll tell us."

"Not if he's already received the killer's message loud and clear, he won't," Nolasco said. "How is it going to look if we accuse the mayor of knowing the killer's identity back then but keeping it quiet and letting him continue to kill? He's never going to admit to that. Never."

Nolasco had a point, but Tracy thought there might be another way to go. "He doesn't have to admit it. We can go about this in a way that gives him an out, that allows him to say he never got the message, that this is a complete surprise to him. He just has to tell us the mother and we'll take it from there."

"And if he still won't?"

"Then we leverage the information. We tell him either he does the right thing, or the gloves come off. We let the media take whatever shots they care to take. If he won't do it out of a sense of morals or ethics, maybe he does it out of narcissistic self-preservation and saves his image."

Nolasco took a breath and exhaled. "I should run this higher up the flagpole."

"You know you can't. You just said Edwards still has a grip on much of what goes on in the city, meaning he still has his moles. The higher up you run it, the more you increase the likelihood Edwards learns what we have and gets his lawyers lined up to protect him. The best time to do this is now, when we can be certain he doesn't know what we know."

—

Michael Edwards lived on Mercer Island, an enclave in the southern portion of Lake Washington between Bellevue and South Seattle connected by the I-90 floating bridge. The island was home to one of Washington's most expensive housing markets, with lakefront lots.

Home prices had escalated on the island, as they had escalated just about everywhere in King County.

Tracy convinced Nolasco not to call Edwards, not to give the former mayor the chance to manufacture a story or to tell them he was too busy to speak to them, which would allow him time to get his moles working. If he already knew the connection between the five women, he would know why they wanted to talk to him, and he would get his legal team involved. They'd tell him to keep his mouth shut. Edwards, who Faz once described as slicker than snot on a doorknob, would be difficult enough to pin down without giving him a chance to think through what he might say and how he might say it. The former mayor had been infamous for holding press conferences to get free television time and seemingly answered every question without answering a single one.

Edwards lived at the end of a narrow, steep road cut into the hillside off West Mercer Way. His multistoried stucco home dropped down to the shores of Lake Washington. Nolasco parked to the far left of a three-car garage, and he and Tracy approached a door beneath a protected, fifteen-foot portico that bespoke wealth.

The doorbell brought the deep bark of multiple dogs, followed by a man's voice instructing them to hush and commanding them to sit. When the door pulled open, Tracy took note of two Chesapeake Bay retrievers dutifully sitting at Michael Edwards's side. Chesapeake Bay retrievers were known for being stubborn. She hoped the choice of dogs did not emulate the owner.

The former mayor's appearance took Tracy by surprise. Though he was rumored to still have power and influence in Seattle, he had largely stayed out of the public eye since retiring from political office after a failed gubernatorial campaign. Tracy remembered Edwards as a tall, vibrant man with a head of dark hair, a radiant smile, and piercing blue eyes. He had inherited a sharp wit from his father, who had also been mayor. Stories of graft and corruption had also swirled around his father's administration.

The man who answered the door did so with a cane, hunched over as if in chronic back pain. His hair was snow white and his skin flecked with age spots and sagging in the all-too-common areas—his jowls and beneath the eyes. He adjusted black-framed glasses as if having trouble seeing. His eyes looked cloudy.

"Mayor Edwards." Nolasco held up his badge and identification.

Although Edwards's smile did not have the voltage it once had, it remained radiant nonetheless. "Put that away. I know who you are from the recent press conference, and I remember when you were running your task force, Captain Nolasco." Nothing wrong with the man's memory or his vision. Edwards looked to Tracy. "And you're the famed detective Tracy Crosswhite, solver of cold cases. Congratulations to you both. I'm impressed by your doggedness. You must feel a profound sense of accomplishment and relief."

Tracy wasn't certain to what Edwards referred, but she assumed he referred to the press conference announcing they had identified Dwight McDonnel as the killer.

"Thank you," Nolasco said. "A little of both, certainly."

"To what do I owe this *unexpected* late-afternoon surprise?" Edwards said. Tracy caught the intended bite in his words.

"Wonder if we can have a moment of your time, Mayor?" Nolasco said.

"No more 'mayor' required, Captain. I'm retired. This time for good. What's this about?"

"The investigation. We're putting to bed a few loose ends."

Edwards eyed them, his smile fading, letting them both know he wasn't buying their pretext. "And you think I can help."

"We think you might," Nolasco said.

Like most narcissists, Edwards seemed convinced he was smarter than everyone else as he pulled open the door. "Well then, come on in. I'm not one to turn away a public servant who thinks I might be of assistance." He hobbled back a few paces and closed the door behind them. "I just poured myself an old-fashioned. I don't suppose I can offer either of you a drink."

"We're on duty, but thank you," Nolasco said.

Edwards led Tracy and Nolasco to a descending staircase, the dogs at his side. "I'm on grandpa duty this afternoon," he said over his shoulder. He looked back to Tracy. "Could I trouble you to hold my drink? This damn cane and these stairs don't go well together."

"What did you do?" Tracy asked, noticing an Ace bandage around Edwards's knee.

"Knee replacement. It was time. Hurt it playing college basketball, and it has troubled me ever since. Got to the point I could no longer walk the golf course, which was my regular exercise, and the reason I've put on weight."

Not exactly third-world problems, Tracy thought but didn't say.

"Doctor says a couple more weeks of rehab, and I'll be as good as new. When you get to be my age, the question is not if a body part is going to fail, but when."

He hobbled down the stairs using the handrail to ease his steps on his rehabilitated knee. "Have some of the grandkids in the backyard. Me and Marilynn are keeping an eye on them this evening. Don't be hurt if she isn't happy to see you. She'll think I'm shirking my grandpa duties. It's a common complaint when you were away from home as much as I was in my career."

"You're not still working?" Tracy asked.

She understood Edwards had been on the board of several firms, including the large construction firm he had once run as CEO. He resigned when he became mayor to prevent an appearance of impropriety, though the firm still managed to get certain lucrative business contracts with the city, including the renovation of the SeaTac airport.

"I do a bit of consulting, help people get projects through the bureaucracy that is today's city hall, but for the most part I'm done. My son runs the firm. He's a workaholic like his old man." Edwards flashed another brilliant smile. "I don't know how the current mayor does it. I would go crazy dealing with all those personalities and the roadblocks now. In my day we got things done." Often with a thick layer of crisp bills lining Edwards's billfold, if you believed his detractors. "Today everything is a quagmire."

They followed Edwards and his dogs into a room with a bar, poker table, and a leather movie-style sofa facing a mammoth screen. A young boy, maybe ten, ran into the room wearing a bathing suit and pulled a Coke from a refrigerator under the sink.

"Did you ask Nanna if you could have a Coke this close to dinner?" Edwards asked.

The boy responded with a knowing grin—a spoiled kid used to getting his way. He would again in this instance. He snapped open the pull tab before his grandfather had time to reach him, took a sip, then ran back out the open sliding glass doors.

They stepped onto a covered concrete patio with an outdoor kitchen and living area. Across a patch of lawn, a pool with a slide was being put to good use by a handful of Edwards's grandchildren. The lawn sloped to a pier with a boathouse protecting a large speedboat and two Jet Skis, all raised above the choppy waters of Lake Washington. A black wrought-iron fence enclosed the yard and the pool.

Edwards caught Tracy admiring the view. "We put the fence in when the grandchildren were born," he said, the wind off the lake ruffling his hair.

Two younger boys, who looked to be five or six, ran around the yard with large squirt guns despite the cooling temperatures and the breeze. A woman who looked to be Edwards's age noticed them but went back to supervising. The fact that she didn't acknowledge them was perhaps indicative of a woman who had likely spent her life being introduced and feigning interest, but who no longer cared to play that game.

"We're sorry to keep you from them," Tracy said.

"We get them several times a week. For kids, this is like Disneyland. Do you remember when you could run around in a bathing suit squirting someone with water in these temperatures? I get cold just watching them."

Tracy didn't grow up on a lake, but her family had hiked, and she recalled swimming in lakes with her sister, Sarah, that their parents wouldn't dip a toe in.

Edwards motioned to a table and chairs on the covered porch. The dogs lay down in a patch of sun on the lawn. "It's why we bought this place and all the toys, to entice the grandkids. I'm making up for lost time. It's one of the hazards of political office. You get little downtime. You have to make sacrifices." He pulled up the sleeves of a blue cashmere sweater, revealing several gold bracelets. "So, Detectives, how can a humble, former public servant help you?"

"We're investigating a murder over on Queen Anne this morning," Nolasco said.

"Read about it and saw it on the news. Tragic."

"The woman's name was Bonnie Parker," Nolasco said. "She retired from being the director of the Department of Construction and Inspections for the City of Seattle."

Edwards sipped his cocktail, as if the name meant nothing to him.

Nolasco continued. "We're concerned because this woman, Bonnie Parker, seems to fit a pattern similar to four of the Route 99 Killer's thirteen victims."

"A pattern?" Edwards said.

Tracy looked for any tells the information meant more to Edwards than he was revealing.

"All five of the women either worked, or in Parker's case had worked, in a City of Seattle office."

"I remember reading or hearing something about that back in the day."

Not true, Tracy thought but didn't say.

"There's more," Tracy said, as she and Nolasco had scripted. "All five of the women got their start working as special assistants in your administration."

If the news alarmed Edwards, he covered it well. "I created the special assistant position to give interested young people a chance to serve their city and get a taste for politics," he said with pride.

"Did you know any of these five women?" Tracy asked.

Edwards smiled. "We created many of those positions. I couldn't possibly know all of the people who filled them."

"Any of them?" Tracy asked, pushing him now. "Specifically, any of the five?"

Edwards locked his gaze with hers. "You have names, photographs?"

Tracy provided Edwards with the names and showed him photographs on her phone. With each victim he shook his head. "The names don't ring a bell, nor do their photographs. I'm not surprised. That was a long time ago. And my memory isn't what it once was," Edwards said, firing off his first excuse. "But let me ask you something. Are you telling me this most recent murder is somehow related to the Route 99 killings?"

"That's what we're investigating," Nolasco said.

"The connection of this fifth victim to a position in your administration and her later elevation to a city department seems an unlikely coincidence," Tracy said.

"Meaning what, Detective?" Edwards asked.

"Meaning one or two of the victims working as special assistants might be a fluke, or happenstance. All five, however, is a pattern we can't ignore, as I'm sure you appreciate."

"It seems like it is something worth exploring," Edwards agreed. He turned his gaze to Nolasco. "Why, if I might ask, didn't you explore this pattern back when you had the task force? Seems like it might have been significant."

Indeed, Tracy thought, *but either Moss Gunderson had buried the information, or he'd pursued it and Edwards had threatened to bury him.*

"That's something else we're looking into," Nolasco said.

"Seems like shoddy police work if you ask me, Captain. You ran that task force; didn't you?"

"I did."

"Then let me ask you both this question. Are you intimating Dwight McDonnel was not the Route 99 Killer, after your superiors held a press conference Friday with families of the victims stating the killings had been resolved?"

Nolasco looked to be chewing his bottom lip.

"That's where it gets interesting, Mayor." Tracy stepped in to deflect the blows the mayor was delivering and start delivering some of their own. Good cop. Bad cop. She had no problem being the bad cop in this instance. "You see, Dwight McDonnel's DNA is a certain match for DNA found at one of the Route 99 killings."

"Again, I recall that information from the press conference. But if it's a certain match, then why are you here interrupting my evening with my grandchildren?"

"Are you familiar with 'fragmented DNA,' sir?" Tracy asked.

"I'm not."

"With the advances in technology, forensic scientists are able to analyze smaller and smaller DNA samples, and to differentiate between mixed DNA, such as in the case of a gang rape."

"Okay."

"Mr. McDonnel's DNA was fragmented DNA. The crime lab detected his DNA had mixed with the DNA of a second person."

Edwards sipped his drink, then shook his head as if to say, *And . . .*

"And we've been able to identify this second person. That is, the second DNA found is a partial match to a relative of the killer."

"A partial match. How can you have a partial match?"

"The advances in the forensic DNA include advances in the use of certain software to identify DNA that, although not a direct match to the crime scene DNA, is a genetic match, a family member. A brother, for instance. We had the crime lab run the DNA using this software, and we got a hit for a person whose DNA was in the CODIS system. Someone arrested many years ago for driving under the influence, and who provided a blood sample."

Edwards looked between Nolasco and Tracy. Tracy did not notice any change in his appearance or demeanor. He didn't pale. He didn't look nervous. His hands didn't flinch and weren't clutching the table. When she didn't continue, Edwards said, "Who is this person?"

"The hit was to DNA provided thirty years ago by your son, Jonathan Michael Edwards."

Now Edwards paled. Whatever he might have anticipated, even prepared for, it was not this.

"The crime lab is certain the DNA obtained from the victim at the Route 99 serial killing is a half brother of Jonathan Michael Edwards, which, to an investigator, makes the fact that each of these five women also worked in your administration much more than a coincidence. An investigator has to assume the killer chose these women for a reason related to their positions. Wouldn't you agree?"

Edwards was too well heeled to cave. He sipped his drink to buy time and gather himself, but he was no longer a young man, or even middle-aged. He was old, and old men couldn't hide certain things they once could. Time could be cruel in this regard, like tremors in the hand or the voice, or the way the Adam's apple got in the way of swallowing.

"What exactly are you implying, Detective Crosswhite?"

"I'm not implying anything. It's science, sir," she said, stealing a line from Mike Melton. "I'm asking you directly why the DNA would indicate Jonathan has a half brother when every news article I've read about you and your family indicates you have just one son and two daughters."

Edwards put down his glass. "I . . ." He cleared his throat. "I don't know, Detective. Clearly there has been a mistake."

"No mistake. The crime lab confirmed it. 'Science doesn't lie,'" she said, stealing another Melton line. "A blood relative. A half brother."

"But the people interpreting the results could be mistaken."

"Mayor Edwards, it is late, and it looks like your wife could use your help with your grandchildren, so I'm going to cut to the chase here and ask you to do the right thing. The moral thing. The ethical thing. I know you have another son. I want to know his name and the name of his mother. And before you tell me you don't know what I am talking about, let me make this perfectly clear. We are here because we are willing to give you the benefit of the doubt that you didn't know of the connection of the other four women to your administration when these killings occurred. But you know now. If you tell us what we want to know, we will do everything we can to keep your name out of the newspaper. But if you refuse, then all bets are off, and we will tell the media everything and let the public come to their own conclusion."

Edwards smiled, not as if amused but as if rising to Tracy's challenge. He kept his voice soft. "Are you threatening me, Detective?"

"Call it whatever you want."

"How dare you. How dare you come to my house and in the presence of my wife make such an accusation."

"You invited us in. You said it was your civic duty to help public servants. And your wife is not here. More important, you didn't answer my question. Let me ask it again, and this time let me preface it by saying fourteen women are dead, Mr. Edwards, and it is possible more could die because, as you confirmed, you created many of those special assistant positions. We would like to prevent that. We'd like to catch this person before he kills again, and we believe you can identify him. Now, having said that, I ask again, are you aware of another son with any other woman?"

Edwards stared, his eyes once again the piercing blue that had cut through his political opponents like a sharp knife. "Detective Crosswhite, I think you've let all those medals you've won go to your head. I think you have forgotten your place."

"I know my place very well, sir. I am a servant for the people of King County, Washington, tasked with solving fourteen murders and maybe saving lives in the process. I think it is you who've forgotten your place. Or maybe you never knew it."

Edwards's gaze turned ugly, as did the tone of his voice. "I will destroy you, Detective. You will be out on the street before you get back to your car."

"That's your prerogative, Mr. Edwards. But as I made clear to you, I will go to a prosecutor, and he will go to a judge, and we will seek a warrant to get your DNA to confirm the forensic lab's findings."

"You think you will get that subpoena? Have at it."

"And I am duty bound, sir, to let the people of the State of Washington know a serial killer might still be out there killing, and to protect the public by letting the other women who worked as special assistants in your administration know their lives might be in danger. And when we're asked why we no longer believe Dwight McDonnel was the Route 99 Killer, we'll have to explain, as I just explained to you, what the fragmented DNA proved."

Edwards smiled the same wicked smile his grandson had given him, a man used to getting his way, who believed he would again. "Try me, Detective."

Tracy stood. "I intend to."

"That is what you don't understand, Detective."

"What's that?"

"People like you will never be in a position to make that choice. The decision will be made so far over your head you couldn't see it from the top rung of a ladder. All that will come from your climb is a long, painful fall that will end your career."

"My father used to say something similar about people who exalted themselves," Tracy said. "He used to say the view from the top is never as enlightening as the view at the bottom, but those people arrive in both places, nonetheless."

Tracy and Nolasco showed themselves out, climbing outdoor steps along the side of the house to the driveway. When they reached the top, Nolasco was huffing and puffing.

"I got to hand it to you, Crosswhite. You got guts. I'll give you that. But he's going to get you fired. Maybe both of us."

"I'm not going to get fired and neither are you. If I get fired no one can stop me from going to the press with the connection between Edwards, the five women, and his son. He doesn't want that. We have a volatile truce, just like the truce between me and Weber. They want to get rid of me, but they can't. Their hands are too dirty, and I know now where they buried some of the bodies."

Nolasco laughed.

"What's so funny?" Tracy asked.

"There was a time you could have said the same about me."

"Not anymore, Captain?" she asked.

Nolasco shook his head, smiling. "You're entertaining, Crosswhite. The way I figure it, as long as you're around, they'll beat on you and leave me be."

"Very chivalrous of you, Captain."

"Chivalry no longer exists. The woke crowd considers it sexist. It's all about survival of the fittest now. The better question is where do we go from here?"

"Where we should have gone in the first place."

"Where is that?"

"I'll tell you in the morning in Weber's office."

Nolasco didn't even question her prediction. He also knew Weber's office to be a certainty.

CHAPTER 29

Tracy didn't bother to go back into the office, and Nolasco took his cue from her and also went home. Before they split, he surprised her. "You want to get a drink? Talk over our investigative strategy other than rushing forward into a chipping machine."

Tracy almost laughed, but she knew Nolasco was serious. She also knew it was more their circumstance than any real connection between the two of them. They were both under siege, like two infantry soldiers in a foxhole during a prolonged fight. They could either dislike one another or direct their dislike to a mutual enemy and hope for strength in numbers. Whether that endured if they survived the foxhole remained to be seen.

"I'm going to get home to Dan and my little girl," Tracy said.

Nolasco started off, then turned back. "Crosswhite?"

"Yeah?"

"Thanks for having my back with Edwards."

"Not a problem, Captain."

"I still think you might have got us both fired, but . . ."

"We're not fired," she said.

"You're lucky to have a family to go home to."

"I know," she said. "Have a good night, Captain."

"Sounds like something said just before the *Titanic* hit the iceberg."

Twenty minutes later, on her drive across the 520 bridge to the east side of Lake Washington, Tracy's phone rang. She'd been in a daze. She'd been thinking that going to Mayor Edwards had been like a confessional. They had done what they could to get Edwards to confess his sins, but he had refused and maybe chose the fires of hell just to save his mortal reputation. The phone ringing had been like an alarm.

She recognized the number for headquarters. Weber for certain. Edwards had made good on his threat. She sent the call to her voice mail. Weber could wait. Minutes later the phone rang again. Caller ID indicated the King County Medical Examiner's Office. Tracy answered it.

"Tracy, it's Stuart Funk."

"What did you learn?" she asked without preamble.

"Not a copycat. The cut is too precise, likely made with the same type of blade as the others."

Tracy didn't know what to say, though she had expected the information. It was hard to believe, all these years later, the killer wasn't in prison for another crime. He wasn't dead, and the investigation into his thirteen cold case victims had awakened his desire to kill, to renew his attempt to deliver whatever the message she now knew for certain was intended for Mayor Edwards.

"You still there?" Funk asked.

"Still here. You let Nolasco know?"

"About to call him now."

"Thanks, Stuart."

She disconnected and thought about the latest victim, and possibly others to come. She couldn't allow that.

Minutes later she parked on the gravel drive, stepped from the car, and went inside, dropping her work cell phone and keys into the basket. Therese's high-pitched voice came from the backyard. Tracy followed it outside. Therese had Daniella in a blow-up pool on the lawn, though the pool contained just a couple inches of water. Therese had staked a large umbrella in the ground and positioned the pool beneath the shade. Daniella wore her blue bathing suit, her diaper filled with water. Dan had said she looked like a big blueberry. She had a floppy sun hat strapped beneath her chin as she slapped at the water and giggled, Therese encouraging her.

When she caught sight of Tracy, Daniella crawled to the edge of the pool, calling to her.

Tracy knelt and splashed the water in the pool. "Are you swimming, angel? Are you swimming?"

"She loves it," Therese said. "I can't get her out. She's been in here for an hour."

Tracy played with some of the toys in the pool with Daniella. Then she asked, "Dan's not home yet?"

"Called a couple of minutes ago. Just picking up a few things from the store. Says he wants to barbecue tonight and eat on the veranda."

Tracy looked at the outdoor gazebo. "Veranda, huh? Is that what he's calling it now?"

"Apparently."

"I'm hoping I can convince him to go for a run. I need to burn off some energy and frustration."

"Not a good day?"

Tracy thought of Bonnie Parker and of the granddaughter who had found her. She thought again that she could not allow it to happen to another woman and her family.

"No," she said. "Not a good day."

"Go for your run," Therese said. "You'll feel better. I can play with Little Miss Sunshine here."

Tracy went upstairs to get changed. Dan came home and, after a minute or two, came up the stairs. Tracy was stretching at the foot of their bed. "What's this I hear about a run?"

"You up for it?"

"I am."

Ten minutes later they reached the foothills on a slow jog. Dan was breathing hard, trying to catch his wind. "No matter how many times I do this, it never gets easier."

"It's not supposed to be easy, that's why it's good for you," Tracy said.

"You're a ball of sunshine. Is that dark cloud over your head related to the call from Faz this morning?"

Tracy told him about Bonnie Parker and the angel's wings. She told him Stuart Funk confirmed what she already knew. The Route 99 Killer was back in business.

Dan stopped running. "Wait. I thought he was the guy who hung himself."

"So did we." She explained to Dan what Melton had told them about the fragmented DNA and how he had matched that DNA to a sample in the CODIS system.

"You're shitting me? The mayor's son?"

"It's a partial match, meaning the DNA from the crime scene is a relative of the mayor's son. A half brother. Edwards has only one son and two daughters with his wife."

She told Dan about the connection of the last five victims to Edwards's administration and how she believed Moss Gunderson had ignored the information when the connection was made years ago. Then she told him about her and Nolasco's conversation with Edwards, how they had given him the chance to do the right thing.

Dan shook his head before jogging again, this time faster paced. "What are you going to do?"

"I thought about it on the drive home. I'm going to warn the women who worked for Edwards who are still alive and still live in the area. I don't have a choice. I'm just not sure how to get a list of those women from back then."

"It would be in the city archives," Dan said. "Take it from someone who has sued the city on multiple occasions and fought over documents. The archives will have their employment records, including their Social Security numbers. They're computerized now. You get the names you can, then find the women."

"That might take too long, Dan. I'm thinking I need to reach a larger audience more quickly."

"How are you going to do that?"

"Anita Childress," Tracy said. "I let her know the connection so she can get an article in the paper."

"That will create a shitstorm."

"I won't mention yet what the DNA revealed. We just warn other women who worked as special assistants that there is a connection."

"The brass will know you leaked the information," Dan said.

"What are they going to do, fire me for trying to save lives? They're stuck. Besides, Anita won't reveal her source, and she has her mother's files. She could say she figured out the connection on her own."

"Maybe the woman who had the kid will come forward."

Tracy stopped running. "What?" Dan said.

"Lisa Childress's investigative file includes notes about a 'credible source' being 'pissed off' and 'willing to talk.' Do you think she could have made the connection and found the woman?"

"Based on what you told me about the files she was working on, I'd say it's a possibility. But Childress doesn't remember anything. She can't help you."

"Maybe she already has."

When they arrived home, Dan went upstairs to shower and said he'd get dinner started. Tracy turned on her work cell phone again and went into the home office. She quickly checked her messages and found a stink email from Weber, which she ignored. She called Johnny Nolasco, but the call went immediately to his voice mail. He, too, had turned off his phone.

She sat and used a towel to wipe at perspiration from her run. Maybe it was better Nolasco didn't know what she was about to do. If anyone was going to take the hit, better her than Nolasco, after what he'd already been through. Better he knew nothing about her decision.

She looked up Anita Childress's cell phone number and called her.

When she eventually disconnected, she felt queasy. She would not sleep well. She'd be awake, expecting to get another phone call like the one she'd received from Faz the prior morning.

CHAPTER 30

Wednesday, August 5, Present Day
Seattle, Washington

Tracy had been right about the minimal sleep. She'd tossed and turned the moment she'd shut her eyes, anticipating her phone would ring, the way you anticipate an alarm will go off when you have to awake earlier than normal to catch a plane or for a meeting you can't miss. To make matters worse, Daniella had been fussy much of the night. Tracy suspected her little girl got water in her ears and had developed an earache. She put in eardrops prescribed by Daniella's pediatrician for an earlier earache and brought Daniella into bed with her. Eventually her daughter had settled down, though she tossed and turned and twisted, waking Tracy when she did doze off. She awoke mentally and physically tired. Dan said a few things to her, but they barely registered.

The fog lasted until her cell phone rang, like that alarm going off. It jolted Tracy out of her malaise, and she quickly answered it.

Johnny Nolasco. "Did you see the morning paper?"

"No. Not yet," she said, almost afraid to ask him who had died.

"The *Times* ran an article about the connection between Bonnie Parker and the four other Route 99 victims; that they all at one time worked for the City of Seattle and had started as special assistants in Mayor Edwards's administration. The end of the article noted you were working the cold case killings and encouraged anyone with information to contact you at the Seattle Police Department."

Nolasco did not sound happy. He sounded like a man who had just read his termination letter. "I know about the article," Tracy said without further elaboration.

"You leaked the information?"

"You can deny knowing anything about any of this, Captain," she said without answering his question. "This is on me."

For once, Nolasco remained silent, no doubt realizing what Tracy had done was to protect him.

She continued. "But those 150 women need to know their lives could be in danger if Edwards won't help us determine the killer."

Nolasco didn't argue with her. They agreed to arrive at SPD early and meet in her office to tackle how to quickly find so many former special assistants.

Tracy entered SPD a little after seven, coffee cup in hand, caffeine beginning to kick in. The detective room was subdued, but the article in the paper would give the detectives in the room a jolt. SPD brass, detectives, and officers hated it when an article indicated someone had leaked information. The detectives and officers would withdraw inward and quietly speculate about the origin of the leak. Not this time, though. This time speculation would put a bull's-eye on Tracy's back.

She expected it and was prepared for it.

Tracy set her coffee on her desk and removed Lisa Childress's file on Mayor Edwards from her locked desk drawer. She flipped to Childress's handwritten notes, the ones she kept seeing in her mind throughout the night.

Credible source.

Pissed off.

Girlfriends.

Willing to talk.

This time, however, the notes weren't just scribblings in a reporter's notebook. This time, the words looked to have been written with a purpose. Each letter looked crisper, as if written with intent.

And that got Tracy to thinking. When she had first received Childress's investigative files from Anita, she'd ultimately been focused on the Last Line investigation. She'd read the other files, including the file on Edwards, but not with any real purpose. Now she had a purpose.

She flipped to the newspaper clippings Childress had placed in the file about graft and corruption in Edwards's administration and scanned each until she again found the article mentioning the 150 special assistant positions created by Edwards during his tenure as mayor. Childress quoted Edwards as saying something similar to what he had said when Tracy and Nolasco paid the former mayor a visit. He said the special assistant positions were intended to indoctrinate young people into city government and to inspire them to serve, but the FBI had asserted the special assistants were more than just political interns, that they had been Edwards's stable of girlfriends. Some of these special assistants had accompanied Edwards to dinners, the theater, Benaroya Hall, and political functions more appropriate for his wife to have attended. When questioned, Edwards had said his wife, Marilynn, chose not to attend these social gatherings to stay at home to raise their kids.

Possibly, but likely more of Edwards's bullshit.

The article noted that most of the women had declined to be interviewed, but some had agreed and had been quoted. As Tracy read, she recognized the name Mary Ellen Schmid. Curious, she read on, not recognizing the names until reading Regina Harris. She read farther and found two more names she didn't know, but then a third name she did know, Debbie Langford. She felt a rush of adrenaline, her eyes skimming over the words in the article, then stopping when she saw a fourth name she knew. Christina Griffin. Her gaze swept across the remainder of the article, hunting for the last familiar name, finding it near the end. Bonnie Parker.

"Oh no," she said, sitting back, her mouth dry.

The killer had not switched prey to taunt the task force or the Seattle Police Department. He'd switched prey because he'd learned the names of several of the women who had served as special assistants and with whom Edwards was suspected to have had affairs.

The article had become the Route 99 Killer's kill list.

Someone knocked on her office door.

Tracy startled, then recovered. "Yeah."

Nolasco came into her office, bringing the smell of fresh nicotine, and closed the door behind him.

"How bad is it?" Tracy asked.

"A scale of one to ten? I'd say an eleven." Nolasco chewed a piece of spearmint gum. "Weber is pissed about the leak. She's asking who's responsible, though I think she knows."

"Don't cover for me, Captain."

"I denied being the source of the article."

"I'll own it," Tracy said.

"I told her you weren't the source either."

His unexpected comment caught Tracy off guard. She'd only known Nolasco as her captain, a member of the brass, and, largely, her antagonist. She'd never known him as a partner the way she'd known Kins, Faz, and Del, whom she could count on to have her back.

"Thanks, Captain."

"I knew nothing about it, so technically it wasn't a lie. I just told Weber that Childress isn't going to reveal her sources," Nolasco said. "Besides, Weber knew that much already. Childress apparently called Weber and asked for a comment. She asked if the information had been released to save lives that could possibly be at risk. Weber didn't have any choice but to take that lifeline and tell Childress saving lives was always SPD's first priority."

Anita Childress had played Weber at Tracy's request. Weber likely knew it, but being given the choice between offering a terse "no comment" and making her department look magnanimous wasn't much of a choice. She had accepted the latter.

"You told Childress to call Weber; didn't you?"

"No comment," Tracy said.

Nolasco chuckled. "Weber wants to see you in her office as soon as you get in."

"Figured she would." Tracy had also predicted Weber would want to see her alone. If Weber was going to accuse Tracy of a wrong, without hard evidence, she didn't want anyone else in the room to hear Tracy accuse Weber of giving Edwards a pass because Weber feared he'd burn her for taking the Last Line's drug money.

"Before I go, I found something you need to see. Take a look. I think it's going to reduce the number of women we need to contact."

Tracy showed Nolasco Lisa Childress's file and the article on the special assistant positions. "Look at the names of the women quoted." She could see from the look on his face that as he read farther and saw the familiar five names, he was reaching the same conclusion a step ahead of her explanation.

"Oh my God," Nolasco said.

"I think it's his kill list."

"Santos said the kills were intended to deliver a message," Nolasco said, surprising Tracy by giving Santos's opinion credibility. "Do you think his mother could have been one of these special assistants? Someone who Edwards took advantage of?"

"I don't know, but you remove the five victims and that leaves nine names in the article." She flipped back to Lisa Childress's notes, the ones that suddenly had more meaning than they'd had the day before. "One of them might be the 'credible source' who was 'pissed off' and 'willing to talk.'"

Tracy's desk phone rang. She looked at caller ID. "Weber," she said.

"I'll get someone started on finding the remaining nine women and determine which ones are still alive and living in the area," Nolasco said. "I think we focus on those still here and most at risk."

—

This time, Tracy didn't have to wait in the anteroom to be summoned into Weber's office. The chief's assistant pointed to the open door and said, "She's waiting for you." The sight and the smell of fresh-cut flowers on the assistant's desk, the juxtaposition of the beauty with the often-ugly business of police work, seemed more pronounced, like finding a blooming flower in a desert.

The morning's edition of the *Seattle Times* was on Weber's desk, the articles beneath the fold faceup. Seeing the story jolted Tracy. Those women had taken those positions with joy. Fresh out of college, they thought they'd secured a foothold in the difficult job market. A way to advance their careers. Instead, the job had subjected them to sexual harassment, and now another man's thirst for vengeance.

"Are you responsible for this?" Weber tapped her finger on the newspaper.

"I thought it might be you," Tracy said, shaking her head. "I thought you might be warning the women their lives could be in danger. To me, that would seem to be a good thing. Am I wrong?"

"Don't bullshit me, Crosswhite. And don't patronize me. I know you and the reporter who wrote this are close from the time you spent finding her mother."

Tracy merely shrugged.

Weber's lips pinched. "Where were you last night?"

"Home," Tracy said.

"You turned your phone off."

"I usually do when I'm off work. Family time. Did you call?"

"Again, don't bullshit me. Mayor Edwards called me at home last night and chewed my ass for half an hour. He said you went to his home and accused him of knowing who the killer is. He said you threatened to get a search warrant for his DNA. What the hell were you thinking?"

"That he might know the killer's identity, and that he is related to the killer."

Weber's eyes widened. "Do you want to explain yourself?"

For the next several minutes, Tracy did, concluding, "The match is for a relative. A son. Melton assures us the science is solid. No doubt. I told Edwards if he cooperated, helped us find the killer, we would intimate he didn't know what was going on, he didn't learn of the connection between the victims and their having worked in the capacity of his special assistants until we learned of it. He refused my offer."

"What makes you think he might have known of the connection all those years ago?" Weber asked.

"Amanda Santos, the FBI profiler, said angel's wings carved in the shoulders of the victims were intended to send a message to someone."

"What kind of message?" Weber asked, her voice no longer confrontational, more inquisitive.

"She doesn't believe the wings represent the Angel of Death, as all of us have presumed. She believes the wings represent the Angel of Justice. One victim isn't a message. Two remains debatable. Three is a pattern. Four is clarity. And if the person intended to receive the message still didn't get it, the fifth murder was a gruesome reminder."

"Of what?"

"According to Santos, the Angel of Justice's role is to bring the wicked to justice for their crimes."

"You said five victims. There were fourteen."

"The last five victims worked as special assistants on Mayor Edwards's staff," Tracy said. "Santos told us to focus on those."

"What about the others?"

"She isn't certain. They could have been the killer's practice, trial runs to perfect his craft."

"Then why carve the wings?"

"Again, we can only presume either it was practice, or perhaps the killer wrongly thought the wings would be broadcast to the public, including the person he intended to reach."

"Edwards told me you were grasping at straws. There were more than 150 of those special assistant positions created throughout his years as mayor, and the chances of him knowing the five women are slim to none."

"He's lying," Tracy said. "Edwards was a womanizer who couldn't keep his pecker in his pants if the fly had been sewn shut."

"What evidence do you have he had a sexual relationship with any of these women?"

"Just his history and his reputation." Before Weber could jump in, Tracy added, "And I don't really care if he did. What I care about is getting him to tell us the identity of the woman he got pregnant and the name of that child, who I believe is the person who killed those women and, more recently, killed Bonnie Parker."

"You're not going to get a warrant to get Edwards's DNA," Weber said in a knowing tone. "He'll argue that *if* the killer is related to Jonathan Michael Edwards, you already have the connection and don't need his DNA."

"It's more than that, Chief. The mayor won't tell us the name of the mother. Without that information, how are we supposed to find the killer before he kills again? Edwards will have more blood on his hands, but you know full well he'll wipe that blood on the back of your shirt and the walls of this department."

"Find another way," she said, though without conviction. She said it like someone who had been trapped in corners much of her life but had learned how to fight her way out. "Leave the mayor out of it."

"I didn't bring the mayor into this. He did it himself."

"If I see his name in the paper intimating that to be the case, with the information attributed to an 'anonymous source,' I won't turn a blind eye again."

"Meaning?"

"My meaning is clear."

Since they were now throwing punches, Tracy countered. "The connection between the victims and the special assistant positions was in the task force's possession, but Moss Gunderson buried it. I think he feared Edwards would burn him for taking Last Line drug money. Bonnie Parker did not have to die. How is it going to look if it gets out the department sat on that information?"

"I could suspend you right now, Crosswhite."

"And I could quit and go to the press with what I know. I'd be sainted."

Weber's jaw undulated. Her eyes narrowed. Tracy didn't like draws, and this didn't feel like a draw, but it certainly didn't feel like a knockout either. This felt like she was ahead on points on every judge's scorecard, but that could change with one good punch.

"Find another way," Weber said again, a punch delivered by a tired fighter without force or impact.

Tracy would.

—

Tracy found Nolasco in his office making phone calls to the remaining nine women in the article in Lisa Childress's investigative file. "I called the first number on the list. The woman moved to Oregon and died two years ago."

"Natural causes?"

"Thought that and pulled up her obituary. Natural causes. I didn't get much further down the list. I got a fire burning in another matter—that murder in the homeless encampment last week," he said. "I'm not sure how much time it's going to take."

"I'll take over," she said, and she reached for the numbers and addresses of the remaining women.

Tracy returned to her office, and for the next two hours she called the numbers of the women left on the list. Of the eight, four had moved out of state. In addition to the deceased Oregon woman, another woman had passed away in Colorado, also from natural causes. Another lived in Florida, and a fourth lived in California. That left four living in Washington State who remained in immediate danger.

Tracy reached two of the women by phone. They hadn't yet seen the article in the morning paper, which did not bode well for her intent to have the information widely disseminated. Tracy confirmed both women had worked in the special assistant's role and went on to positions in city government offices. Both initially denied having affairs with Edwards, but after Tracy directed them to the article, they changed their tunes. Panicked. Each said Edwards had initiated the affair, and that they weren't the only ones to sleep with the former mayor. They had subsequently learned that Edwards's affairs lasted anywhere from one night to more than a year.

Tracy didn't feel entirely sorry for the women. They had known the mayor was married but saw their affairs as a possible way to get ahead.

All of the women were reticent to discuss a period in their lives they had tried to forget and hadn't shared with their spouses, but they were also generally afraid. Tracy sensed they tried to answer her questions while wondering how they would explain to their spouses, and their now-grown children, why their lives might be in danger. Tracy told them she'd send a patrol car to check on them and ask to have officers increase their presence in their neighborhoods, especially at night. She told them they shouldn't be home alone or venture anyplace unaccompanied, which only further unnerved them. Both asked Tracy if they should go someplace else until the person was captured.

"It isn't a bad idea," Tracy said, which led to increased sighs and sniffling.

Tracy informed Nolasco, as well as Faz and Del, the investigating detectives on the Bonnie Parker murder, of her conversations with the two women she had reached living in the state. While she waited to hear back from the other two women in Washington, or from the patrol officers she'd sent to their homes, Tracy reached out to the women living out of state and had the same conversation. She told them she did not believe they were in immediate danger, but again suggested they not go anywhere alone.

As she made the calls, Tracy received email messages and half a dozen phone calls from other women who had read Anita Childress's news article and had worked in Edwards's administration as special assistants. They wanted to know if they were in danger. One had not read the article but said a *Times* reporter had contacted her. Tracy gave each the same admonitions about not being alone in or out of their homes.

—

Early in the afternoon, the receptionist contacted Tracy. "Have another call for you regarding the article that ran in the newspaper this morning," he said. "The woman wouldn't provide a name."

"Okay," Tracy said, assuming the woman didn't want to advertise her affair with Edwards. "Put her through."

After the call clicked over, Tracy introduced herself.

"I have information that relates to the article in the newspaper this morning," the woman said.

"Okay. Why don't we start with your name?"

"I won't do this over the phone."

"Do you want to come to Police Headquarters?" It was her standard response to an anonymous caller who claimed he or she had information vital to a police investigation. Most did not opt for a trip downtown.

"That's not possible either," the woman said. "Have you been to the Kubota Garden?"

"No."

"I'll meet you there in an hour. Come alone." Tracy was hesitant but the caller continued. "You won't be disappointed. I have information on Mayor Edwards no one else does."

"How is that?"

"Again, not over the phone."

"How will I find you?"

"Just enter under the main gate and start walking the paths. I'll find you."

—

Tracy got off the phone and pulled up Kubota Garden on Google Earth, wanting to get a better sense of the twenty-acre Japanese-style garden in Rainier Beach, a roughly fifteen-minute drive from Police Headquarters. She looked for places where someone might hide, of which there were many. The garden was not as well known as the Seattle Arboretum, but it was a public place in a residential neighborhood, and the woman had asked Tracy to meet during daylight hours.

But just in case, Tracy slid her Glock into her shoulder holster and slipped on her lightweight corduroy jacket before she left to get a pool car.

Fifteen minutes later, on a bright day with a high blue sky without a cloud or a breeze, Tracy parked in a dirt-and-gravel parking lot and crossed the lot to a covered information board with a map. She found the gated entrance into the park and wandered the trails, as if without much purpose other than to admire the beauty of the garden. Her senses, however, were on alert. She listened for footsteps, looked for other women strolling alone, and for unnatural colors behind the garden ferns, Japanese maple trees, bamboo stalks, and evergreens. She passed a pond with koi fish, then a stone garden, and came to a red bridge. A sign identified it as Heart Bridge. She stopped halfway across, looking down at the pond's murky water and the surrounding foliage growing around the boulders and stones.

A moment after Tracy had stopped, an elderly woman approached the bridge and made eye contact. Tracy recognized the woman and understood immediately why she couldn't come to Police Headquarters or be seen in a public place, and how she could have information on Mayor Edwards no one else had. She also better understood Lisa Childress's notes.

Credible source.

Pissed off.

Girlfriends.

Willing to talk.

"Mrs. Edwards," Tracy said.

CHAPTER 31

M arilynn Edwards turned toward the bridge railing and looked over the side. "You came to my home last night," she said. "This morning I read the article in the paper about the connection between the five victims and my husband's administration. I'd like to know what you talked to him about. He was very upset when you left and spent much of the evening in his office on the phone."

Marilynn did not look or dress like a politician's trophy wife. She looked like a Northwest grandmother, perfectly common, someone who came to stroll the park's pathways in jeans, tennis shoes, and a light-weight shirt. She carried what looked to be a windbreaker. Something else Tracy quickly picked up on—Marilynn Edwards didn't strike Tracy as particularly concerned or upset, at least not about her husband, as if she'd sought answers to these kinds of questions before, and likely knew the answers, answers she didn't like one bit.

"He didn't tell you?" Tracy said.

"My husband and I don't talk about those things. We never have."

"'Those things'?" Tracy asked.

Marilynn sighed. Tracy sensed it was more exhaustion than frustration. "I'm not naïve, Detective," she said matter-of-factly. "My husband was a cheat. He had multiple affairs. I know it, and he knows I know it. He's a chip off the old block. Takes after his father. When his father was mayor in the 1950s, men having affairs was more common. His father had a longtime girlfriend. A woman who worked for him. My husband learned by osmosis. He idolized his father. He wanted to be just like him. I'm not making excuses for either man. Ultimately, the appendage is theirs to control. They chose not to. Egos. Inflated egos. I'm just telling you how it was. At the end of the day, Michael always came home to me. I learned to live with his flings not because I wanted to, or because I was afraid of divorce. I came from humble means, and I would have gladly returned."

"You stayed with him for your family. For your children," Tracy said.

Marilynn nodded. "You have children."

"A daughter," Tracy said.

"Mothers will do amazing things for their children; won't they? They'll suffer greatly. Affairs and divorce tear families apart and hurt the children, who are often forced to take sides. I wanted my children to love their father and my grandchildren to love their grandfather. It was best for their development. I managed to accomplish that, though I don't love my husband and haven't for many years. We don't share a bed or even a bedroom."

"I'm sorry," Tracy said.

"I want to know if the article is accurate, Detective. Do you believe a connection exists between the serial killer and the women who worked in my husband's administration?"

"I believe it's a possibility we need to explore."

"So do I," she said.

"What do you mean?"

"There's a stone bench just around the corner. Why don't we sit?"

Tracy followed Marilynn to a bench in the reflective garden. Tracy thought it particularly appropriate. She knew women who had ugly divorces, and she knew what it had done to them and to their children. She admired Marilynn Edwards's strength to have endured what she went through for her children.

"This park is a frequent place for engagements and weddings. Coming here renews my belief in love," Marilynn said, in a reflective tone. She glanced at Tracy. "Don't look at me like that, Detective. I'm not seeking your pity. I chose my bed years ago, and I'll sleep in it. I have three wonderful children and eight grandchildren who will keep me busy and run me ragged until they lay me to rest—alone. That's more than my husband can say."

"Your children know about your husband's infidelity."

"Of course. Children don't remain children. They become adults and they're intuitive. They figure things out. They tolerate my husband as I have, but there isn't any love lost between them. Their relationship with their father is superficial, at best. My son doesn't idolize him, and he doesn't want to be like him. He wants to be better. He puts his wife on a pedestal, and he's a wonderful father."

"You raised him well, then."

"I tried."

"What is it you wanted to tell me, Mrs. Edwards?"

"Marilynn," she said. "When my husband was mayor, there were many investigations of his business affairs. The FBI. The Justice Department. His political opponents. Every time he ran for office his opponents called out all the suspected graft and corruption. But nothing ever stuck. My husband had spent years at his father's feet learning how to cheat, and not just with women. He learned well. He never put anything in writing. Did not talk business over the telephone, only in person, and was certain no one ever recorded him or photographed him in private. He also kept a book on just about everyone of any interest in

Seattle. He knew where all the bodies had been buried, how to leverage those people. How to hurt them."

"Peter Rivers," Tracy said.

"The name rings a bell. City councilman running for mayor?"

"That's right."

"I have no doubt Michael's men found young men who claimed they'd performed sexual acts on Mr. Rivers when they were underage."

"Kickbacks from the drug task force, the Last Line?"

"No doubt that money found its way into my husband's pockets. But more valuable to him was the information on who else received those kickbacks, which allowed Michael to invoke an uneasy detente."

"Okay," Tracy said. Uncertain where the discussion was going.

"Those large investigations were too public. Once my husband got wind of them, he could get his legal team prepared. They were never going to get Michael. I learned from those failures."

"Learned from them?"

"I wasn't so accepting of Michael's girlfriends, Detective. I was young and mad as hell. I wanted to get even with Michael for humiliating me in public, for all the times he took those women to public gatherings—dinners, the ballet, the opera. Those should have been mine by marriage."

"You contacted Lisa Childress to talk about your husband's girlfriends."

"She was a woman in a male-dominated profession. An investigative reporter. I thought she might understand. I gave her names and the positions to which these women had been elevated in my husband's administration, favors he'd granted them for keeping his affairs quiet. I even told her about the kickbacks my husband received from the drug money, and I told her Michael likely found those men to accuse Peter Rivers."

"How many names of young women did you give her?"

"I don't know. Perhaps a dozen. I thought the reporter would run with the information, but nothing ever came of it other than a couple of articles. I tried to call the reporter, but the number she gave me rang through to voice mail, then was no longer in service. The newspaper said she no longer worked there and would not provide further information. I thought maybe she'd taken a promotion and moved out of state. Then I read an article about her sudden disappearance. I thought she was dead, and I suspected Michael to be responsible. I had tremendous guilt. I thought I had put her in that position. I thought that until this year when I read about how you found her. About how she was investigating the drug task force at the time she had disappeared. How she had amnesia, likely from a blow to the head, and couldn't remember anything. I still wonder whether my husband could have had anything to do with that reporter's disappearance. Do you know?"

Tracy took a breath. Birds chirped in the branches of the trees overhead, and children laughed. Both seemed out of place given the ugly nature of their conversation. Marilynn Edwards had suffered enough. "No, I don't believe so. I believe the man responsible ran the drug task force and acted on his own."

"But you don't know for certain."

Tracy wasn't going to lie. "Not for certain. He's dead."

"Did you come to my house last night to talk to my husband about whether he had anything to do with the reporter going missing?"

Tracy shook her head. "No. I came to your house, Mrs. Edwards, because we've recently run DNA from one of the Route 99 serial killer's crime scenes. The DNA technician identified two different DNA. The first DNA belonged to Dwight McDonnel."

"I watched the news and read the newspaper. Michael was very interested in the story."

"After the press conference, another woman was killed on Queen Anne—and the killer left clues sufficient to convince us he is the same person who killed the other thirteen victims."

"What did you want from my husband?"

"There was a second DNA sample recovered at the earlier crime scene. The Washington State Crime Lab ran the sample and found a partial match for a DNA profile in the DNA matching system."

"A partial match?"

"Meaning the person in the system is not the killer, but he is related to the killer. A half brother. The DNA sample identified belonged to your son, Jonathan, Mrs. Edwards."

Tracy let that information set in. Marilynn Edwards didn't gasp. Her shoulders didn't collapse. Her eyes didn't widen in shock or surprise. They didn't even become glassy. No tears pooled in her eyes. Instead, her eyes hardened and her face stiffened. No matter who she might have been when she married, the woman seated with Tracy was now one tough lady. As Tracy's mother had liked to say, each time she got hurt, it punched a hole in her paper heart, and when it healed, the scar toughened her. Marilynn Edwards's heart was one big scar.

"We came to ask your husband whether he has another child by another woman and to determine that woman's name. We believe it will help us catch the killer."

"He said he didn't know what you were talking about; didn't he?"

"That's what he said."

She scoffed. "Deflect, divert, deny. As I said, he learned at the feet of a master." Marilynn Edwards took a deep breath, then exhaled. "Bastard," she uttered.

"I'm sorry to be the one to bring this out into the open, Mrs. Edwards."

Marilynn waved off the impact as inconsequential. "I'm just sorry it took this long, took so many lives."

"So am I." Tracy told Marilynn about Amanda Santos's belief the killer intended to send a message with his killings. That he was seeking justice. "We believe the message was intended for your husband, and the latest killing to be an indication the killer has a renewed interest in getting his message heard."

"And my husband chose to save his political ass rather than give you a name," Marilynn said. She thought for a moment. Her look changed to concern. "I gave the reporter the names of those women. I told her they had been Michael's girlfriends. Did I cause their deaths by having their names published in the newspaper?"

Tracy shook her head, though, inadvertently, Marilynn might very well have done so. She wasn't going to pin that burden on anyone but the killer, and maybe Michael Edwards. "No," she said. "This isn't your doing, and it wasn't your husband's doing, though he certainly has information we need. I worry more women are going to die if we don't find out the name of the woman who gave birth to your husband's son and find that person."

Marilynn stood. "Come to the house this evening. Michael is golfing, but he'll be home after he has a few drinks at the club."

"He won't talk to me, Mrs. Edwards. He made that abundantly clear."

"Do you know why the FBI and the Justice Department never got my husband?"

"No."

"They never asked the person who had all the answers, the person who kept scrupulous details of all the deals Michael made, the person who knew about the kickbacks and bribes. I knew where the bodies were buried. I made it my point to know everything. My husband hasn't cheated on me in more than twenty-five years, Detective. Not because he suddenly lost the desire. He fears me. He's afraid of what I know, and even more afraid of whom I'll tell."

CHAPTER 32

That evening, Tracy returned to the Edwards home without telling Nolasco. She didn't want any of the fallout from her refusal to follow Weber's orders to impact her captain. He'd had her back earlier that morning, and she would have his now. They were still partners. She'd continue to treat him as such.

She'd gone back into the office but told Nolasco she'd learned something that could be promising, and that she'd keep him advised. He had enough experience to know when not to ask questions. But he *was* curious. Or maybe he still didn't fully trust Tracy. Their history was deep and not easily forgotten. But Nolasco was also knee-deep in some other case, a problem with a search warrant used to collect critical information. He was working hard with the prosecutor to prevent a criminal from walking free on a technicality.

"We don't have the manpower or the budget to keep patrol cars watching those women's homes," he said.

Like most big-city police departments, SPD had lost police officers at a time when they needed more. Young candidates were rethinking a career in which they could end up in prison if they made a mistake. No amount of money was worth that risk.

The two Chesapeake Bay retrievers barked, but this time Marilynn greeted Tracy at the door. She looked remarkably composed.

"Come on in, Detective. Michael is in his office in back," she said. "Can I get you a glass of water?"

Tracy declined. Marilynn led Tracy past the living room with cathedral glass providing a view of the island paradise Michael Edwards had created for his grandchildren. "Disneyland," he'd called it. But it hadn't been Edwards who built it. He may have earned, or stolen, the money to pay for it, but it had been Marilynn who created the mirage for her children and her grandchildren that her home was akin to the happiest place on earth.

Marilynn stepped into a large office. Michael Edwards stood near windows providing the same picturesque view. He had a glass of liquor in hand. Against the back wall was built-in shelving cluttered with books, framed pictures of Edwards with Seattle and national luminaries, sculptures, and knickknacks from a career in the public eye. In a mirrored alcove were crystal glasses, decanters, and an assortment of booze. A large multicolored abstract painting covered another wall. The area in front of Edwards's desk, a sofa across a glass coffee table facing two comfortable chairs on an oval-shaped rug, reminded Tracy of the Oval Office.

"I'll leave you two alone to talk," Marilynn said, but not before she gave her husband a hard stare. If looks could kill, Tracy would have been measuring Michael Edwards for a coffin.

Edwards turned from the windows and pointed to the sitting area. Tracy sat in one of the chairs. Edwards at the end of the sofa, as far away as he could get. He set his glass down on a coaster on the table between them. Tracy noticed a thin manila file. He looked up at her with resigned disdain. She didn't much care.

"My wife says you have some questions of me?" he said with none of the fire and brimstone he had unleashed the prior visit. "Am I to assume the offer you made yesterday afternoon, giving me an out, is no longer on the table?"

Tracy wanted very much to tell Edwards to pound sand, and she had no reason to again offer the deal. She'd used it hoping to create leverage, unaware Marilynn had enough leverage for the entire Justice Department. But this was not just about Michael Edwards. This was about Marilynn, her children, and her grandchildren she'd worked to protect.

"I want to know the name of the man you fathered."

"I don't know his name."

Tracy paused. She was tempted to call in Marilynn to rap Edwards's knuckles with a wooden ruler.

"That doesn't help me much."

"I don't know his name or if he even exists, but I suspect, from what you told Marilynn, that he does," Edwards said.

"What *can* you tell me?" Tracy asked.

"I can tell you the name of his mother."

"Then let's start there."

Edwards drank from his glass. His hand shook. This was not the poised politician Tracy had previously encountered. This was a frightened old man who had been put in his place. "I was young, in my early twenties. My parents had a maid. She was young, Hispanic, very good looking. Sexy. She had an accent. I learned Spanish in school, and I'd just spent a semester in Barcelona before coming home to graduate and assimilate into the family construction business. I was living at home, which meant I was home on days Rosie came to clean the house. I spoke to her in Spanish and sought her tutelage. We flirted, innocently at first, then more serious. One day she called me, crying. She had been to the doctor and needed to speak to me.'

"She was pregnant," Tracy said

"And Catholic," Edwards said with some disdain.

"She wanted to keep the baby."

"I didn't know where to turn. Eventually, I didn't have a choice. I turned to my father. He was mayor at the time. Before he ran for governor and lost. He was angry. He didn't understand how I had allowed myself to be taken advantage of by this woman."

"An interesting take," Tracy said.

"My father had my career planned. I would succeed him at the construction company, then politics. I'd become mayor, then governor. He told me everything he had worked for on my behalf would be ruined because Rosie had lied and said she was on the pill."

"Again, an interesting take," Tracy said. It was no wonder Edwards didn't learn his lesson. He'd never had to.

"I asked him what to do. He said to get rid of it."

"But she wouldn't," Tracy said.

"She wouldn't." Edwards sighed. His shoulders sagged. "She said she'd raise the child on her own. That didn't satisfy my father. He wasn't about to have terms dictated to him by some uneducated maid. I don't know for certain what he did, but he came into my room one night and told me Rosie had agreed to an abortion. He said the matter was concluded. I never saw or heard from her again."

"So you don't know if she got the abortion?"

Edwards shook his head. "I didn't. Not for certain."

"Or if your father actually paid her to get an abortion or threatened her with deportation or something else?"

"I don't know."

"Were there any other women? Any other children?"

"Other women, yes. Other children, no. I learned from my mistake."

Tracy released a derisive burst of air. "But she paid for your mistake."

Edwards offered no response.

"What was the woman's name?"

"Rosenda Alvarado. We called her Rosie."

"How old was she?"

"Twenty-six or twenty-seven."

"Where was she born?"

"Someplace in Mexico."

"Illegal?"

"Yes."

"You don't even know if Rosenda Alvarado was her real name or one she made up when she came into the country; do you?"

"I don't."

"She had no documentation?"

"She had an ITIN number."

ITIN stood for Individual Taxpayer Identification Number. "Do you have her number?"

He opened the file on the table and handed Tracy a single-page tax document with a nine-digit individual identification number just beneath the name. Rosenda Montemayor Alvarado. "My father didn't want to see his or my political career derailed because he'd hired an undocumented alien who cheated the government out of its taxes. It's why Rosie had the ITIN and paid taxes."

"Did the killer ever contact you—either now, after Bonnie Parker's death, or back twenty-five years ago?"

"Never."

"But you knew the connection; didn't you? You knew these women had all at one time worked as special assistants in your administration. You knew because you had affairs with each of them." Again, Edwards did not answer, but his silence was as profound as any admission of guilt.

Tracy reached into her briefcase and removed a forensic DNA kit. "I'll be collecting your DNA, Mr. Edwards, and checking it against the DNA obtained at the crime scene. This time there will be no mistakes."

Edwards did not dare object.

CHAPTER 33

Tracy left the Edwards home disgusted by the man's audacity, his huge ego that prevented him, even now, from fully understanding the gravitas of what he had done. Edwards didn't respect women; that much was clear. He hadn't respected Rosie, his wife, or the young women he had systematically seduced, who then died for his transgressions. But it was like Marilynn had said. His was learned behavior, and he'd learned from a man just as egocentric and narcissistic. Women became only something else for him to conquer. He hadn't learned love, but he'd learned fear. He'd feared his father. And he feared Marilynn, what she knew. Tracy hoped he now feared her.

Tracy shook the thought. She did not want to waste any more time on the man. She focused instead on what she had learned. It invigorated her. For the first time since Chief Weber had reopened the investigation, Tracy had a direction, a path that might lead to the killer. She hated the thought that Edwards would get away, again. But this was no longer about Michael Edwards. This was about the victims and their families, and about Tracy issuing her own justice and finally putting the killer behind bars.

She called Nolasco from the car and told him what she had learned, providing him with Rosenda Alvarado's name and ITIN number. "It gives us something we can run down, a last known address we can follow."

"I'm on it," Nolasco said. Tracy heard him scratching a pen across paper. "Where are you now?"

"Just leaving Edwards's home and heading back in. With traffic, I could be as long as an hour."

"That will give me time to run this down. Any chance I'm going to get a call from Weber?"

"None," Tracy said.

"You sound certain."

"I am. Weber can't help him now. Someone has more leverage."

Traffic was lighter than Tracy expected, with the heavier flow leaving the Seattle city limits. When she arrived at Police Headquarters, Tracy took the elevator to the seventh floor and hurried through the maze of cubicles to Nolasco's interior office. Being in his office had once made her skin crawl. Not this time. She knocked and stepped inside.

Nolasco glanced at his computer screen and read. "Rosenda Montemayor Alvarado, aka Rosenda Aranda from Montemayor, Mexico, died in 1984 of breast cancer in Tacoma, Washington."

Tracy swore and slumped into one of the two seats across from Nolasco's desk. "Did she have a son?"

"One dependent declared on her income taxes."

"Name?"

Nolasco grinned. "Michael Edward Montemayor."

Tracy almost laughed. "Seriously? She named her son after Edwards?"

"It's official." Nolasco handed Tracy a printout of a birth certificate for a baby boy at Saint Joseph's Hospital in Tacoma. The space to list the father's name had been left blank.

Another thought came to her. "The son would have been in his early teens at the time of his mother's death. Relatives?"

"Apparently not. He was placed in foster care, a ward of the state until he turned eighteen."

"Did you run him?"

"Every which way. No criminal record. No DNA ever provided. No fingerprints. No social media of any kind."

"High school? College?"

"No college I could discern. He graduated from Lincoln High School in Tacoma in 1988."

"Work history?" she asked.

"No Social Security number ever issued to that name. No Tax Identification Number. No credit cards. No license. No wedding certificate. No credit checks. No social media. Nothing. It's as if Michael Edward Montemayor never existed."

"What about the foster care family?"

"Foster parents are deceased. Looks to me like it was more of a business than a family. They had many foster kids. I'm not optimistic about finding any who might have information on Montemayor. I intend to call the school tomorrow and determine if anyone there recalls him. See if they have any yearbooks from that time, and if we can get a photograph. Maybe we can find a teacher or a student who knew him and who can provide us with something to go on."

Tracy wasn't sure what more they could do, not at this hour of the evening. "I'm going to do some work on the computer and see if I get any hits for this guy, though I suspect from what you've learned so far that the name Michael Edward Montemayor has been buried for years."

Tracy went back to her office, called Dan, and told him she'd be home soon but wanted to do a little hunting on the internet. She pulled up an online search engine and tried to find a Lincoln High School yearbook from 1984 through 1988. She was surprised to find one for sale on Amazon and another on eBay, which made her wonder just how big a market existed for used yearbooks. The two sites displayed only the cover, not interior pictures. She looked up alumni sites. Not surprisingly, given Nolasco's lack of luck, she did not find anything on Michael Edward Montemayor. She used search engines and entered his name and high school. Again, she found nothing promising.

As she was about to shut down her computer and head home, Tracy's desk phone rang. She answered it while closing out open screen pages.

"Detective Crosswhite," Tracy answered.

"Detective." A man's voice. He sounded surprised. "It's Bill Kinney. I didn't think I'd reach you. I was going to leave you a message and follow it up with an email."

Kinney was the fifth wheel working with the Violent Crimes Section's A Team. What was once her team. "What can I do for you, Bill?"

"I think the question is what can I do for you."

"Okay, what can you do for me?"

"Captain Nolasco asked me to review Wash-DOT tapes look-ing for a Ford F-250 truck last Sunday afternoon leaving Ellensburg, Washington."

Henry K. England, the former police officer who had manned the Route 99 Killer tip line. "I apologize if I was abrupt. I didn't know Captain Nolasco delegated that job. What did you find out?"

"Picked up his truck on a camera on I-90 near Cle Elum early Sunday morning." Papers shuffled. "At 6:14 a.m." That sounded about right for someone getting up early to fish. "Wasn't difficult after that," Kinney added.

"What wasn't difficult?"

"Tracking him." *Because he parked along the river to fish,* she thought, anticipating what Kinney would say.

"He stayed on I-90 all the way into Seattle."

Tracy's mind kick-started, thinking of all the things she needed to do. She hurried back to Nolasco's office and told him what Kinney had found. Nolasco said they could cover more ground if they split up. He'd drive to Tacoma and try to find a yearbook with a photograph of Montemayor, or someone who knew him. Tracy would drive to Ellensburg and confront England.

She agreed, but she intended to do more than confront England.

She called the Ellensburg Police Department, this time not just as a courtesy. She needed their help. She spoke to the captain she had previously spoken with, which saved her from having to explain the situation. She asked if the Ellensburg Police Department could perform surveillance on England's truck and let her know if it appeared to be on the move toward Seattle.

The captain said it could be done, but they'd have to take a soft approach due to the topography and ease of being noticed. He said he'd send an unmarked car to the access road leading to the hay farm to determine if the truck was parked in the drive. If so, they would do periodic drive-bys to ensure the truck didn't go anywhere. If they sat on the truck, they weren't going to sneak up on anybody.

Tracy also worried about England learning of their interest, but she was more concerned about the women who still lived in Seattle. She didn't want to have another Bonnie Parker.

The captain said she had two choices. "I can give my officers verbal authorization to follow England if he leaves, or you can contact the state patrol to take over pursuit."

Knowing England was more likely to notice Washington State Patrol vehicles, and not wanting to further complicate the matter by involving another law enforcement agency, Tracy asked that the Ellensburg PD stay on England.

He agreed.

They didn't have enough evidence to take England into custody. They had tracked his truck into Seattle, but they couldn't yet pinpoint where he'd gone. More specifically, they couldn't place him on Queen Anne. And the Tacoma high school was closed for the evening, preventing Nolasco from possibly confirming England was Montemayor.

Tracy looked at her watch. She wanted to get to HR. She needed to review England's personnel file before traveling back to Ellensburg.

The details were starting to fit together. England had performed work, at least tangentially, on the task force. He could have known about the suspects the task force had been pursuing, including Dwight McDonnel. He could have followed McDonnel, learned the identity of the woman McDonnel had slept with, then picked up that same woman and killed her, hoping to throw detectives off his trail. He would not have known about fragmented DNA back then because the technology did not yet exist. He would have been banking on McDonnel's DNA already being in the system for another crime. He also would have known from the information coming in over the tip line that the task force realized each of the latter four women killed had worked on Edwards's staff, and probably believed Edwards would soon be exposed. But that never happened, because the message had stopped at Moss Gunderson. Perhaps frustrated, England could have accessed the vault where the stored boxes had been kept and taken the disk on which Cesare had downloaded the information, believing, perhaps, there would be a more opportune time to reveal the information. He married, moved away from Seattle, and stopped killing. Then Weber announced Tracy would pursue the case, and he saw it as a second opportunity. He sent Tracy the disk with renewed hope the evidence would lead to and expose Michael Edwards.

She rode the elevator to the fourth floor and met Augustus Cesare, who had on a lightweight jacket and looked to be leaving for the day.

"No rest for the wicked," Cesare said. "What brings you back?"

"Looking for Henry England's personnel file," she said.

Cesare's eyes narrowed. "What for?"

"I need to determine if he lied on his application about his identity or his background."

"You think England could be the Route 99 Killer?"

"I'm not thinking anything at the moment except to get enough evidence so a judge will have to grant me a warrant for his DNA."

"Why? You have the killer's DNA?"

"Fragmented DNA. We identified Dwight McDonnel's DNA, and Melton made a partial match to someone in the system. A half brother."

"No shit."

"No shit," Tracy said.

"It would be definitive then, if you get England's DNA."

"If he's our guy, and a judge grants me the search warrant." She checked her watch. "I need to call the on-call homicide prosecutor and get an affidavit put together to send up to the Kittitas prosecutor's office. If the judge grants the request, I'll take a drive up there tomorrow morning."

"Why don't you let me run down his application?" Cesare said. "It's what I do. At least for a few more days. I can run down England's application a lot more quickly than you can, and it frees you up to put together the warrant. It would be a fitting end to my career if I helped you wrap up this case. Those killings were as personal to me as they were to everyone else. I'd like to know that when I retire, I can do so without the investigation hanging over my head also."

"You aren't the only one."

They exchanged cell phone numbers, and Tracy went back to the office and called the on-call homicide prosecutor. Together they put together a search warrant supported by Tracy's affidavit to obtain England's DNA when she was in Ellensburg. The prosecutor told her she'd spoken with a prosecutor in Kittitas County who said the chances of the warrant being granted were fifty-fifty. The judge on call was a former public defender, and the prosecutor could see him ruling the evidence, mostly speculative at this point, did not justify such an invasive intrusion of England's privacy.

They'd find out soon enough.

Tracy left the office and had no sooner pulled into her driveway than her phone pinged, indicating an incoming email. The on-call prosecutor. The judge had denied Tracy's request to get a DNA sample from England.

CHAPTER 34

Tracy fumed about the judge denying her warrant. Her anger was irrational, at first. She focused on the judge's politics. She surmised that his having once been a public defender meant he believed all accused were misunderstood, police were evil, and prosecutors cared more about their personal scorecard than the well-being of the accused. She took out her frustration on the on-call prosecutor, who had the displeasure of being in Tracy's direct line of fire. After calming, Tracy realized the judge's declination wasn't the prosecutor's fault; it was hers and Nolasco's. Right now, she had little more than hunches, and a lie by England about his Sunday whereabouts. Yeah, the judge's decision could be explained, but it still stung. It was one of the things she disliked about police work. The bureaucracy, and the rules and regulations, were too often applied inconsistently, depending on the judge's political bent. Tracy saw things differently. She focused on fourteen women murdered. Families' lives forever altered. The judge was more concerned about invading Henry England's personal privacy.

With time to think over the judge's rationale, she agreed. She needed more evidence. She just wasn't sure how she was going to get it.

Seemed to her the judge's ruling was asking her to first prove England was the killer before they could obtain his DNA to prove he was the killer.

When she stepped inside her home, she hadn't completely flushed the ruling. She was short and snippy with Dan. Thankfully, he knew her and understood her displeasure wasn't personal. Tracy apologized more than once for bringing her work home with her, but some nights it was inevitable. Dan also knew this all too well.

On nights like this, her irritation made it difficult to set her thoughts aside so she could sleep. Her mind went over the same question. What additional evidence could they get to convince the judge?

Maybe if England had lied on his police application, it might be enough to tip the scales of justice in their favor. The prosecutor could argue England's lie fit a pattern Tracy and Nolasco were slowly unearthing. She needed to show that England was concealing his past.

She climbed into bed with her Kindle. After twenty minutes, Dan set his Kindle on the nightstand. "Can't keep my eyes open," he said, then leaned across the bed to kiss her good night. She envied him. Within minutes of his head hitting the pillow, he was snoring softly.

After an hour reading the same ten pages and still not comprehending what she'd read, Tracy got out of bed and walked downstairs to the kitchen, filling a glass with water from the fridge dispenser. She contemplated meditating, a practice Dan had recently undertaken, along with yoga and Pilates. His doctor had told him he needed outlets other than running to relieve his stress. His joints remained strong, but he wasn't getting any younger.

Nor was Tracy.

She wasn't as gung ho as Dan about the meditation. Dan didn't ease his way into anything. He jumped, feetfirst, and only if he couldn't dive in. Tracy was more skeptical. She couldn't help it. She worked in a world starkly black and white with little gray. You were either guilty or not guilty. A good person or a bad person. Something worked or it didn't. Dan was a lawyer. His job was to find the gray areas between the black and the white and shade facts to best suit arguments advanced on behalf of his clients.

Tracy considered her reflection in the window. She was hunched over the kitchen counter pouting like a teenager who didn't get her way.

"What could it hurt?" she said to her disgruntled self.

She opened the meditation app on her phone, chose a recorded ten-minute session, then settled on a pillow on the floor, crossing her legs. She hit "Play." The woman's voice spoke over calm music, a minute-long description of the meditation to give Tracy the chance to settle in. The woman encouraged her to shut her eyes or, if it made her uncomfortable, keep them open. "Everyone gets an award just for participating," Tracy said, then chastised herself for being skeptical.

She closed her eyes.

She mistook a ring on her work cell phone as a chime to start the meditation session. When the phone rang a second time Tracy's response was Pavlovian. A late-night call was never good news. She feared hearing the homicide sergeant's voice telling her the Route 99 Killer had claimed another victim.

She hurried into the room and answered her phone.

"Detective Crosswhite? This is Captain Joe Dittmer with the Ellensburg Police Department." Tracy felt a rush of adrenaline. "Looks like your guy, Ergland, is on the move."

"Which direction?" Tracy asked.

"Yours. West. He's coming your way on the interstate." Tracy could hear the excitement in the officer's voice and imagined Dittmer to be young and likely thinking about riding this wave of excitement all the way over the Snoqualmie Pass.

So much for a calming meditation session. That was fine.

Tracy wasn't built that way.

Dittmer provided Tracy with England's exact location on I-90, roughly an hour and twenty minutes from Seattle.

"You don't think he's noticed your tail?"

"He isn't acting like it." Dittmer said England hadn't pulled off any exits and driven back onto the freeway, and he wasn't suddenly changing speeds or lanes.

"Keep me updated if he stops somewhere or if his progress turns in some other direction."

"Roger that," Dittmer said. "Do you want me to pull him over at any point?"

Tracy gave Dittmer's question a moment of thought. It was possible Dittmer could find a scalpel in England's car. If he did, it would be more evidence than even a liberal judge could ignore to justify a warrant to obtain England's DNA. But it was also just as possible England wasn't driving the 107 miles into Seattle, or that he wasn't going after another victim, or that he didn't have a blade with him, in which case pulling him over prematurely would only alert him to being a suspect and being followed, which would put him on guard. Something similar had happened with the Green River Killer. The police had suspected Gary Ridgway for some time. Employees at the car paint shop where he worked were said to refer to him as "Green River Gary." Knowing he was a suspect, Ridgway had replaced the rug in his house, thrown out clothing, and was careful about getting rid of anything that could contain his DNA. It was years before he made a mistake, tossing a piece of chewing gum in the garbage outside his work. The lone remaining task force detective obtained the gum and had the DNA analyzed.

"No," she said. "I'd rather he didn't know he was being followed, but I also don't want him out of your sight. Keep me posted on his progress."

She hung up and called Nolasco at home, waking him, but he popped awake when she gave him the news. They agreed to meet at Police Headquarters downtown. They had time . . . if Seattle was

England's target. Nolasco told her he'd ask the SWAT team sergeant to put his men on standby.

Tracy went upstairs to change. She turned on the light to the walk-in closet, which awoke Dan. "Where are you going? What time is it?" he asked.

"I have to go in," Tracy said. "We may have something developing. The suspect is on the move and might be headed into Seattle. I have the Ellensburg PD tailing him."

"What do you intend to do?"

"If he comes into Seattle and goes to a home, we'll arrest him."

"Just be careful," Dan said, no longer sounding half-asleep. "And please don't do anything rash."

"Me?" she said, keeping her voice light, though she knew Dan was serious.

"Why don't I believe you?" he said.

"Because you're a distrusting person. I won't do anything rash." She kissed him good-bye. "Tomorrow's the morning one of us has to take Daniella to preschool; Therese has an online class."

"Aye, aye."

"Go back to sleep."

"Like that's going to happen. Call me when everything is finished."

The two dogs, asleep in their dog beds, never stirred.

———

Half an hour later, having received frequent updates on England's progress, Tracy arrived in Nolasco's office with a cup of black coffee. The coffee was a habit. She didn't need the caffeine. Her body was amped up and anxious to get going. Nolasco had beaten her into the office. Dressed in blue jeans, tennis shoes, and a green polo shirt, he didn't look like he took time to primp. He might have run a comb through his hair, but not much more. He, too, did not need caffeine. He paced the area behind his desk like a cat on a hot tin roof, forsaking every rule that forbade smoking in the building. He had at least turned on an air filter he kept hidden along the side of his desk.

"How far out is he?" Nolasco asked.

England had driven over the Snoqualmie Pass into North Bend, Snoqualmie, and Issaquah.

"Any indication he suspects he's being followed?"

"'Ellensburg PD doesn't think so,'" she said.

When Dittmer called to report that England's truck had reached the I-90 bridge across Lake Washington, England's destination seemed a foregone conclusion. Tracy and Nolasco hurried to their pool car, and Nolasco drove to the James Street on-ramp, parking off to the side to wait until alerted by Dittmer of England's approach. Nolasco didn't say much, and neither did Tracy, as if afraid any acknowledgment could jinx the situation.

Dittmer called and told Tracy England's truck had exited I-90 and took I-5 north toward downtown. Tracy's adrenaline and anxiety spiked. She had the tingling sensation in her joints that always preceded an arrest. Nolasco gripped the steering wheel so tight his knuckles were white.

Minutes later, Dittmer advised that England approached the James Street on-ramp. Nolasco shifted into drive and eased up the ramp, increasing his speed to the flow of traffic, which, at that early hour of the morning, was light. They had no difficulty spotting England's black Ford F-250 as it passed, but they would need to be careful. Tracy radioed Dittmer and said they would take the tail. She had already reached the acting SPD watch sergeant and the SWAT sergeant and put both on alert.

Again, England gave no sign he knew he was being followed.

"He's exiting," Nolasco said. The black truck descended the Mercer Street exit, then circled underneath the freeway and headed east toward Capitol Hill.

"Where are you going?" Tracy said as she opened her laptop, pulling up the known addresses of the special assistants whose names Lisa Childress had highlighted in the newspaper articles.

"Check the addresses of the women we spoke with," Nolasco said.

"Ahead of you," she said. "I'm not seeing an address on Capitol Hill."

She alerted the East Precinct's acting watch sergeant of England's whereabouts and asked that he put his patrols on standby.

"Somebody not in the article?" Nolasco asked, his tone anxious.

"Maybe," she said. "More than 150 of those special assistant positions were filled during Edwards's time in office, many by young women."

England made a right turn, then a left, heading east on East Aloha Street. Nolasco gave the truck more room, pausing before each turn. They needed to be extra careful now. England would be on alert, and it would not be difficult for him to spot a car following him on residential streets at that early hour. But they also couldn't lose him.

The truck slowed, red brake lights illuminating the night.

"What's he doing?" Tracy asked.

"Shit," Nolasco swore. England made an unexpected right turn on Twelfth Avenue East, going the wrong direction on a one-way street.

"Should we take him now?" Nolasco asked, looking like he was about to lower the window and put the light on the roof.

England could have picked up the tail and become spooked, but Tracy couldn't be certain.

"I say we take him," Nolasco said, about to turn.

"It could also be a test," Tracy said calmly. "Drive past."

Nolasco hit the accelerator, and the car lurched past the traffic sign in the center of the road.

"Take a left."

Nolasco made a left on Thirteenth Avenue East, then a right on East Prospect, driving to where it intersected with Twelfth Avenue East, a dead end at Volunteer Park.

When the black truck didn't arrive at the intersection, Nolasco said, "We might have missed him. Do you think we missed him?"

"Drive down the block," Tracy said, trying to remain calm.

Nolasco cut the car's headlights, turned, and drove slowly down the narrow street. Cars parked on the west side of the one-way street.

"Truck." Tracy pointed. Halfway down the block the truck had parked, now facing the correct direction.

Nolasco pulled into an open curb space at a driveway several cars behind the truck. "Can you see anyone in the cab?"

"No. Nothing." She looked to the homes, searching for lights.

Nolasco had his head on a swivel, turning in all directions and swearing. "Shit. Shit. Shit."

"Turn off the interior dome light," Tracy said.

"What? Why?"

"Just turn it off."

"You're not going in, Crosswhite. Not alone."

"Turn it off. I just want to see if he's in the cab and take a look around. You get SWAT in position, in case we need them."

Nolasco turned off the dome light, and Tracy opened the car door, stepping out. She shut the door quietly and walked down the sidewalk, using the maple and purple-leaf plum trees in the sidewalk as cover. As she neared the bed of the truck, she paused and dropped to a knee, watching. The cab was empty.

She considered the surrounding homes. No lights. If England was being careful, he wouldn't have parked directly in front of his victim's house. Hell, he might not have even parked on the same block. He could be two blocks over in either direction. Now Tracy was swearing under her breath and perspiring beneath her clothes.

She thought she heard what sounded like a gate latch shutting and turned toward a Craftsman bungalow on her right. She proceeded slowly. A light from a window reflected on a concrete driveway along the side of a house. She went down the driveway and came to a wooden gate with a latch. She heard a door open and shut. She lifted the lever on the gate latch and crept into a backyard, silently closing the gate. Again, she listened. Voices. A man and a woman. She climbed two stairs to a porch. The voices were more pronounced. She leaned over the porch railing to look through a window on the left, into the illuminated room. A kitchen. She saw no one. She leaned and looked through the darkened window on the right and saw shadows in the ambient light.

She pulled the radio from her clip. "I have the suspect in sight inside the blue bungalow halfway down the block on the right. Going in."

"Crosswhite, wait for SWAT."

"No time, Captain." She turned off the volume, removed her Glock, and pushed in the back door. She moved quickly through the kitchen to hardwood flooring, crossed a small dining room, then to a living room. Two people on the stair landing, a man with his arms around the woman, pressed up against her.

The woman screamed.

Tracy took aim. "Seattle Police. Freeze."

CHAPTER 35

Henry England sat on the sofa, his elbows on his knees, his forehead resting on folded hands, eyes closed. He looked like a death-row inmate making his last, impassioned plea for mercy. Tracy would not be his executioner, but she also wouldn't be his savior. Near as she could tell, England had joined the idiot club—men and women who threw away a good spouse or took them for granted, like a comfortable chair, for a roll in the hay with someone else. The analogy gave her pause. It added a whole new meaning to the adage: making hay while the sun shines.

England had cleaned up, at least his physical appearance. He'd taken a shower and combed his hair, put on black jeans and a long-sleeve white shirt. He wore loafers instead of boots.

The woman sitting to his right looked equally uncomfortable. England had not had his hands on Bridgit Garza to strangle her, but to caress her. She had not been fighting him off. She was welcoming him with impassioned moans. She did not scream at him, but at seeing Tracy inside her home.

Now, she looked like a guilty teenage girl who'd snuck a boy inside her parents' home only to be busted. Garza wore a terry-cloth bathrobe Tracy had allowed her to retrieve from a hook on the back of a bathroom door. Beneath it, Garza's red teddy covered less skin than most bikinis.

Tracy fought a terrible feeling that things had gone horribly wrong again, and she suspected that Nolasco, who had endured too much disappointment and failure in this one investigation, already knew it with certainty. He smoked on the covered front porch, the smell of nicotine sneaking inside the house. He had talked with the SWAT sergeant and told him he and his team could leave. Up and down the block, lights illuminated windows. Some neighbors ventured out onto their porches or their lawns, wanting to know if they needed to be worried. Garza would have some explaining to do. What she might tell them would be anyone's guess.

"This is why you came into Seattle last Sunday?" Tracy said, continuing to question England.

England looked up at her as if disturbed from prayer. He blew out a breath. "Yeah," he said quietly.

She glanced at Garza. "You'll confirm he was with you?"

Garza looked surprised that the question was directed to her and only briefly looked at Tracy, as if embarrassed to meet her gaze. "Yes. He was here Sunday."

"Your story about fly-fishing was just an excuse to get away then?" Tracy asked England.

England nodded. Nolasco had been right about England's pretense for being away from home sounding fishy, no pun intended, just not about what England had been covering up.

"What was the excuse to leave home tonight?" Tracy asked.

"I didn't need one. My wife went to Yakima to care for her sister for a couple of days."

Which made England an even bigger schmuck, but that was not for Tracy to judge. "Why come so early in the morning?" Tracy asked, though she suspected it had to do with a burning desire to get laid.

"Harvest season," England said.

"And you need to make hay while the sun shines."

England took another deep breath and cleared his throat. "You really thought I could have been the Route 99 Killer? Why?" He looked and sounded disbelieving.

"You're the right age," she said. "And your work as a police officer on the task force would have given you access to certain information."

"And you lied," Nolasco said from the doorway. He'd apparently been listening while he finished a smoke. He flicked the butt down the covered porch and stepped inside, smoke and the smell of nicotine trailing him. "You didn't go fishing Sunday. Not this time of year. Not with the water running high."

"Traffic cameras captured your truck driving into Seattle the day the Route 99 Killer killed his last victim."

"Wow," England said softly. He again lowered his head to his fists. "I can't believe this." Tracy imagined he was contemplating the repercussions of what he had sown. He looked to his right, to Garza, but when he reached out for her hand, she visibly stiffened and inched her body away from his touch. Nothing like police detectives suggesting the man you've been cheating with is a suspect in fourteen murders to throw cold water on sizzling embers. Tracy doubted England and Garza would be seeing much of each other after this night.

"How long has this been going on?"

"About seven months," England said. "We used to work together a long time ago at the police station."

"You were a cop too?" Tracy asked Garza.

"Dispatcher," she said.

"We dated," England said. "I left the force when it didn't work out, met Katlyn, and eventually moved up to Ellensburg and got married. I was coming down to Seattle and we ran into one another and exchanged information. The next time I came down I called to get a drink. I don't know."

Tracy didn't want to hear the details, but she did want to be certain this time. She didn't want anyone second-guessing her, again. "We need to be certain, Mr. England. I'm sure as a former police officer you can understand we can't have any mistakes. We'll do our best to keep your names out of the newspaper."

"No promises," Nolasco said, sounding pissed.

"But we'll try." Tracy looked to Garza. "Given everyone is a bit jumpy because of the murder on Queen Anne, I suspect you'll get some phone calls and knocks on your door from your neighbors, and maybe the press. How you handle those questions is up to you."

"What do you need?" England asked. "My blood?"

His wife might be out for blood, but not Tracy. "Just a swab. I'm assuming you have no objection?"

"No," he said. "But . . ." His voice trailed off, though Tracy knew what England was going to say. He was going to say, *But do we have to tell Katlyn?*

Tracy wasn't looking to break up the man's marriage. England had demonstrated he was more than capable of doing that on his own. But she also wouldn't lie for him. Not a chance. She thought of Michael Edwards's infidelity and the havoc it had wreaked on his wife and his family. She wanted to tell England the repercussions could be long and far reaching.

In some cases, much farther than could possibly be imagined.

But that wasn't her job.

She obtained a DNA swab, then stepped from the room onto the covered porch and descended the steps to where Nolasco inhaled another cigarette. Smoke streamed from his mouth.

"I got a horrible feeling," he said. "Like we got set up and the killer is out there, somewhere, taking another life."

"We did what we could to warn them," Tracy said, meaning the other women. "And this was a viable lead."

"Doesn't feel like it now."

She thought of England sitting with his head against his hands, like a grieving penitent, and she thought of the angel's wings carved in the victims' shoulders. Angel of Justice. "You get the feeling all these people are in some perverted way paying for their transgressions?"

"If by transgressions you mean their sins, that's a hell of a price to extract, but yeah, the thought has crossed my mind," Nolasco said. "Along with the thought that someone is laughing his ass off watching us flail around trying to catch him."

Nolasco flicked the butt of his cigarette in disgust, the burning embers sparking when it hit the sidewalk.

CHAPTER 36

Tracy drove to Police Headquarters rather than return home; she didn't want to wake Dan a second time or have the two dogs scare Daniella. They'd sound the alarm as soon as her car tires crunched gravel. Instead, she sent Dan a text to let him know she was okay and that she had gone into the office and would be home later. She wasn't tired, though she had the lethargic malaise of someone awakened after too few hours of sleep. Thoughts on what she and Nolasco could have missed and where to take the investigation cluttered her mind. Hope faded. She'd felt this way chasing the Cowboy, and she suspected from her frank discussions with Faz that Nolasco had the same feeling all those years ago when one promising lead after the next failed, and he'd been left responsible for thirteen unsolved murders.

Nolasco stopped by Tracy's office to tell her he'd make the drive to Tacoma. She got a sense that, like her, he needed some time alone after the recent letdown. She was relieved, but not because she didn't want to be in the car with him. This time, she didn't want to experience the profound silence born from the shared experience of their failure.

"Someone should remain here just in case we get a call," Nolasco said, without elaborating further. Tracy knew he meant a call telling them their failure had resulted in the death of another woman.

"I phoned ahead. It's summer. It didn't even dawn on me that the school might not be open," Nolasco said.

"Is there anyone at the school?" she asked.

"School is out, but they're having their summer session for incoming freshmen. I spoke to the principal. Two teachers who taught back in the 1980s still work at the school. He'll have the yearbooks pulled and waiting for me, but he got squirrely about the transcript. Let's get a warrant."

"I'll get it and email you a copy," Tracy said.

"Then go over your notes and the file documents. Maybe we can get back on course." He said it without conviction in either his voice or his body posture. His shoulders slumped. He looked defeated. Maybe he, too, was just physically tired and mentally drained. He had a right.

Tracy knew Nolasco would internalize any death as being his fault and something he could have prevented. That was simply part of being a cop. She imagined surgeons dealt with the same thought when patients died unexpectedly on the operating table. They could rationalize the death as out of their control, but it didn't deaden the pain, and it wouldn't for some time.

—

Nolasco waited until the school opened, then sucked down a cigarette and got his nicotine fix, and drove a pool car south on I-5 toward Tacoma.

He glanced in the rearview mirror to check traffic and did a double take. He didn't recognize the bloodshot eyes staring back at him. He leaned forward to see more of his face. His bags had become more pronounced. He'd lost weight and it showed in his gaunt features, his nose and chin narrow, his cheekbones more prominent. Twenty-five years ago, he'd looked up the word "gaunt" when someone used it to describe his appearance while hunting the killer. *Lean and haggard, often because of suffering, hunger, or age.* Back then it had just been suffering. He'd been young.

Not any longer.

"I'm too old for this shit," he said and sat back.

The traffic driving south was light, compared to the northern-lanes commute into Seattle, which looked like a slow-moving parking lot. He hoped it cleared by the time he drove home. He'd contemplated not making the drive to Tacoma, just handling everything by phone and email—Montemayor's transcript, photographs, and any other pertinent information. God knew he needed the time. His work on other files had backed up. But he'd always found it better to keep moving forward and at least feel like a case was progressing, even if he was just running in place. He also knew the school, like most state institutions, would be hypersensitive about releasing information on a former student. They'd want to refer the matter to legal counsel, which would only lead to further delays. Nolasco also wanted to speak in person to the teachers who might have known Montemayor. Speaking to a witness over the phone was not the same. It changed the dynamics. Nolasco wanted to gauge not just what they had to say but how they said it, their body language and their facial expressions. That would often dictate the questions he asked.

His phone pinged. An incoming email. Crosswhite had attached the signed search warrant for Montemayor's school records and any yearbooks or other documents or photographs that depicted him. It was a smart addition. Nolasco might not have thought to do it. Crosswhite might not be his favorite person, but she was a good detective, dogged and determined. She thought outside the box, and she wasn't afraid to take chances to get the job done.

He respected how well she performed her job.

Forty-five minutes later, armed with the warrant for Montemayor's records, Nolasco found the school's main office. He greeted a woman sitting behind a counter and advised her that he had a meeting with the school principal, Lawrence Donaldson. Upon the woman's prompting, Donaldson came out of his office to invite Nolasco back. He looked to be midforties, balding in a horseshoe pattern, overweight, flushed. Though summer, he wore a suit and tie.

"I assume you have a search warrant?" Donaldson said after shaking hands. "We can't do anything without the proper paperwork. The students have more rights than the faculty and the staff." His voice was high pitched, though he wasn't whining. He was just stating facts.

Nolasco said, "If you provide me with your email address, I'll send it to you right now."

Donaldson did, and Nolasco forwarded the warrant.

"Thanks. And I'm sorry if I'm a bit rushed," Donaldson said, pulling on the knot of his tie as if it were strangling him. "We're in summer session, but I have a school board meeting this afternoon for some matters related to next year."

"I'll try not to take any more of your time than necessary," Nolasco said.

Donaldson invited Nolasco to sit in one of the chairs at the round table that contained four yearbooks and a manila file. He opened the first yearbook. "You said the name was Montemayor?"

Nolasco felt his pulse quicken. Despite his best effort to temper his expectations after so many false leads, Nolasco couldn't stop the involuntary impulses triggering the flushed feeling in his chest spreading to his extremities, or the belief that this time things would be different. This time, Montemayor would not escape him.

Donaldson ran a finger down a column of mug shots of freshman students, then across a row. He flipped the page, then went back to the prior page and scanned it a second time. He looked at Nolasco. "It's blank." Donaldson turned the book so Nolasco could see the page. "There's no picture."

Amid the mug shots of smiling students was a square space containing a silhouette above the name Michael Montemayor. Several other silhouettes, male and female, also marked the page and the page across from it.

"What about the other years?"

Donaldson systematically opened the other three yearbooks to the corresponding year Montemayor would have been a sophomore, junior, and senior. Nolasco already suspected he knew what they would determine, and it became easier to predict as each succeeding year showed the same silhouette where the mug shot of Montemayor should have been. He had not even had his senior picture taken.

The lack of any pictures was likely practical and related to Montemayor's circumstances. A mother dead from an aggressive cancer, no father to speak of, no aunts or uncles or relatives, a ward of the state. What was the point of getting his picture taken? Who would have any interest?

No one, except a homicide detective, decades after the fact and seeking to learn the identity of a serial killer.

"Can I see his transcript?" Nolasco asked to cover his frustration.

Donaldson opened the envelope and pulled out the transcript, handing it to Nolasco. Montemayor had been a poor student. Most of his grades were Cs and Ds. "He didn't exactly light the school on fire," Nolasco said. He set it aside. "You said two teachers might remember Montemayor?"

Donaldson led Nolasco to a second-story classroom with newspapers hanging on the walls, along with photographs and clippings of articles. An attractive woman who looked to be mid to late fifties was going through a stack of materials at her desk.

Donaldson said, "Ms. Evers, this is the detective I told you about who is trying to track down information on a student enrolled here between 1984 and 1988."

Evers greeted Nolasco and answered his questions. She told him she had started at the school in 1986. "Larry gave me the student's name. Michael Edward Montemayor? I'm sorry. I don't recall him," she said. "I have a good memory, but that name is just not ringing any bells. I was teaching freshman English and composition when I started, so I could have missed him. I was just looking through our archives for the corresponding years to see if I had him on staff, but I'm not finding his name. Do you have a photograph?"

"No. I'm sorry, I don't," Nolasco said.

"He didn't sit for any of his portraits in the yearbooks," Donaldson explained.

"It's possible there's a picture somewhere in these stacks," Evers said. "It isn't a lot. We only publish once a month. I can go through them and, if I find anything, I can let you know."

Nolasco handed her a business card. "I'd appreciate it."

They left Evers to her stack of newspapers, and Donaldson led Nolasco downstairs to a classroom on the ground floor, the summer class in progress. Donaldson knocked on the door and moments later, Bill Rector emerged, though not before telling his students in an animated voice to solve the equation on the board for two extra points on their next quiz.

Rector, too, looked to be midfifties but carried himself younger. He had an easy smile and inviting features that, Nolasco presumed, led to a good rapport with his students. "You're the detective asking about Michael Montemayor."

Nolasco detected a familiarity in Rector's tone. "You remember him?"

"Sure. I had him for sophomore geometry. I called him 'the mayor' once because he had the same name as the former mayor of Seattle, but he asked me not to call him that."

Interesting. "Did he say why he didn't want you to call him that?"

"If he did, I don't remember the reason."

"What do you recall about him?"

"Different. Quiet. Not quick to smile. I had a lot of trouble bringing him out of his shell. He was smart though. Very smart."

"Transcript says otherwise," Nolasco said.

"Mostly Cs and Ds," Donaldson said.

"Transcripts are often just a measure of someone's interest in a subject, not their acumen. He did well in my class, and I encouraged him to apply himself."

"What was his response?"

"Hot and cold. Some days I thought I was getting through. Other days, he just shut off like he wasn't listening."

"Did he have problems with any of the other students?"

Rector shook his head. "Not that I ever saw. He kept to himself a lot. Like I said, quiet."

"What did he look like?"

"Sad," Rector said. "He looked sad. Always. On a rare occasion I could pull a smile out of him, but it wasn't often."

"What did he look like physically?"

A shrug. "Typical sophomore. Nothing that stood out. Average height, weight. Dark hair. Some acne. Not a bad-looking kid but not memorable."

"What about friends? Anyone he hung out with?"

"Boy, I don't recall anyone, but I'm not the best person to ask."

"Who would be?"

"I imagine Michael. Can I ask what this is about?"

Ordinarily Nolasco wouldn't say, but he hoped to shock some additional information from Rector, who so far was the best source he had. "We're investigating the deaths of some young women in Seattle twenty-five years ago."

Rector glanced at Donaldson. After a beat he said, "Wow." He said it as if trying to digest a full meal in just a few seconds. Then, for emphasis, he said it again. "Wow. Not what I expected," he said softly. "You think Michael had something to do with that?"

"Do you think the boy you knew could have done something like that?"

Rector again paused before answering, which meant he thought about the question, if only briefly. Then he deferred, as most would. "I can't say, Detective. My world is numbers and equations and algorithms. This is well beyond my expertise. Like I said, Michael was different, quiet. But I don't recall anything about him being violent."

Nolasco handed him a card. "If you think of anything."

Rector gave Donaldson a look like *How the hell am I supposed to teach a class after getting punched in the face with that?* He pulled open the door and stepped back into his familiar world, calling out, "All right. Who thinks he or she solved the equation on the board?"

Donaldson turned to Nolasco. "You really think this student could be a killer?" He was clearly anticipating the ramifications of the school having a serial killer as a member of its alumni.

"It's an investigation. We're covering every base," Nolasco said. "I'd appreciate any information . . . Maybe the name of another teacher who still lives in the area. A friend . . . Anything at all."

But Nolasco could already tell Donaldson wasn't thinking in those terms. He was thinking of the practical—the negative media attention.

Nolasco walked from the school to his car, having reached another dead end, one of many in this investigation, but this time he had no idea what to do next.

CHAPTER 37

Tracy spent much of her morning going through the material in the boxes in her office, reviewing task force member notes for bits of information she may have overlooked, or not considered pertinent or in context. She took some notes but found it difficult to concentrate. Nolasco hadn't called. Tracy took that as a negative. If Nolasco had been handed a picture of Michael Edward Montemayor, even as a fourteen-year-old, he would have called. She had to assume Nolasco had struck out.

Whoever Montemayor was, he was disturbed on a level ordinary people would never understand. Was it because he had been rejected by the man who should have been his father? Or because his mother had also abandoned him, though not of her own free will? He was clearly bitter and angry at the women Edwards had seduced. Had he seen them as rivals to his mother, the reason Edwards had spurned her? Or was it as Santos and Nabil Kotar had said: Montemayor wanted to send Edwards a disturbed message about justice?

Kins, Tracy's former partner on the Violent Crimes Section's A Team, believed a person could be born evil—with a gene that made them kill other human beings. He didn't buy the nurture argument, that the desire to kill was something that developed as the person experienced perhaps psychological or physical abuse. To support his nature argument, Kins said humans were the only species on the planet who killed without reason or purpose. Then primatologists at *National Geographic* had filmed chimpanzees plotting and working together to brutally beat to death another chimpanzee, for no apparent reason. If that was our genetic evolution, maybe Kins was right. Maybe the ability to kill was something within every human being.

Late that morning, Tracy's desk phone rang. The receptionist told her a woman was on the phone with information related to the Route 99 Killer but wouldn't provide a name. Tracy had a sense she knew the caller.

When the call clicked over, she said, "This is Detective Crosswhite."

"Detective, it's Marilynn Edwards."

"Marilynn. What can I do for you?"

"My husband wasn't completely honest with you when you came to our home to speak to him," she said, sounding uncertain, her voice shaky.

"No?"

"He has additional information you may find helpful to your investigation."

"What kind of information?"

"If you know my husband, then you know he won't discuss it over the phone. Are you available to come back to the house?"

"I can be there within the hour."

"I'll see you then."

Tracy disconnected, wondering what more Michael Edwards had to tell her and where it might lead. But she didn't want to play the "what if" game, which was a waste of time and only led to disappointment. Better to just find out what Edwards had to say and take the information in whatever direction it went, if anywhere. Her desk phone rang a second time.

"Tracy, it's Augustus Cesare. Just getting back to you on Henry England. I didn't find any indication he lied on his police application. Schools, employment history, credit card, drug history. Everything checks out."

Tracy had forgotten to contact Cesare to tell him to call off the dogs. "I'm sorry, Augustus," she said. "I should have told you we spoke to England last night—or rather early this morning."

"You drove to Ellensburg?"

"No. He drove into Seattle."

"Into Seattle?" he asked, and she could hear the anticipation in his voice.

"He's not our guy," she said and explained what had happened. "I hope you didn't spend too much time on his application."

"No. That's all right. Good to have a purpose again. Better to be doing something other than twiddling my thumbs. So where does the investigation go from here?"

She thought of Marilynn Edwards. "Not sure. Hoping we catch an unexpected piece of information that provides a solid lead."

"Sorry to hear. If I can help . . ."

"I appreciate it," Tracy said. But she knew Cesare already had one foot out the door, and no doubt his mind as well. "Enjoy your retirement," she said.

Tracy gathered her purse and jacket from the bottom drawer of her desk and started for the door. This time her work cell phone rang in her back pocket. She checked caller ID. Nolasco.

"Another swing and a miss," he said. "Montemayor never got his picture taken. All four yearbooks have a silhouette. Also spoke to two teachers who were here back then." Nolasco told her what each teacher had to say. "Nothing definitive. Easily forgotten. Like I said, a swing and a miss."

"We might have another strike left. Marilynn Edwards called."

"What did she have to say?"

"She said her husband wasn't completely honest the other night when he and I spoke, that he has more to tell me."

"I'd like to get my hopes up, but . . ."

"I'm heading over there now. I'll keep you posted. Where are you?"

"Twenty to thirty minutes away," Nolasco said. "Depending on traffic."

Tracy disconnected and signed out a pool car. Now more than ever, she hoped Michael Edwards had something worth saying, something that would pivot the investigation toward a solid lead.

Roughly thirty minutes later, still trying to stay even keeled, Tracy pulled down the narrow road leading to Edwards's home and parked in the driveway. She knocked on the door and stepped back. She noticed a camera mounted in the corner above the door she hadn't observed before. Something else seemed different from the prior visit, but Tracy couldn't quite put her finger on what that was. Marilynn opened the door, looking somber and tired.

"Marilynn," she said. "Are you okay?"

Tracy knew the investigation was likely taking as big a toll, if not more so, on Marilynn Edwards as on her husband. This latest information had to be enough to put her over the edge.

Marilynn stepped back.

Tracy hesitated, again sensing something not right, then stepped inside and closed the door behind her. Marilynn's gaze lowered to the floor as she led Tracy into the living room. The former mayor sat at the end of the couch closest to the plate-glass windows offering a view of Lake Washington. He looked like a defeated old man.

"Hello, Detective."

The male voice came from behind her. Tracy didn't turn. Not immediately. She recognized the voice. And when she did, the final pieces of the puzzle came together quickly. She realized what had been different about the home from her two prior visits. Something she was intimately familiar with herself. The alarm system in her own home. Dogs barking. The two Chesapeakes had not alerted. They had not barked.

In a flash she recalled the conference room table in the FBI's offices and Amanda Santos explaining the biblical reference to the Angel of Justice and the Angel Raguel.

> *In the Old Testament an angel represented retribution—the Angel of Justice's role is to bring the wicked and the sinners to justice for their crimes.*

—

Nolasco entered his office and checked his voice mail, then his emails. No call, email, or text message from Crosswhite advising what more Michael Edwards had to tell her. If it had been something worth pursuing, she would have called. Just another false hope in a day full of them.

He popped in a piece of mint gum and settled at his desk, making phone calls and reviewing information that had come in on several cases. Minutes into his task he received a call on his work cell phone. He recognized the high-energy voice immediately.

"Captain Nolasco, this is Bill Rector from Lincoln High School. We spoke in the hallway this morning."

"Of course. Mr. Rector. The math teacher. Did you remember something else?"

"I did. It came to me a little later in the day, after I spoke with Evelyn Evers. I understand you spoke to her also, and, well . . . you can imagine the information remains more than a little shocking."

"I can imagine," Nolasco said.

"Evelyn told me she was going through archived newspapers for the time period Michael was a student here, to see if maybe he was in a photograph."

"Did she find something?"

"No, but it triggered my own memory. Remember I told you Michael was a good student, just unmotivated?"

"Yes."

"And that I tried to reach him?"

"Right."

"Well, I did get through to him . . . for a while anyway."

"What do you mean?"

"He really took a shine to computers."

"Computers?" Nolasco said.

"We were just starting to integrate them here at the school, and Michael really took to them. By senior year we had a computer lab and a computer club. I told Michael I thought it would be a good skill for him to have on his resume, and he should at least give the club a try. He did, for a while anyway."

Nolasco felt the tingling sensation in his gut. "Do you have a photograph of that club?"

"I do. I went back and checked the yearbook and there he was."

"Montemayor?" Nolasco said, not quite believing what he was hearing. Not sure whether to trust it. He'd stood from his chair.

"It isn't great, as you can imagine back then," Rector continued.

"Can you email me a picture of the photograph?"

"I already took the picture with my phone and just wanted to confirm your email. I'm not sure what the quality will be like . . ."

"Go ahead and send it," Nolasco said.

"I assume to the email on your card?"

"Yes."

"I'll stay on the line until you have a chance to consider it. If the quality is poor, I'll have the yearbook sent up to you."

"Thanks. I'm ready."

"It saddens me. You know? To think Michael could be responsible."

"I'm sure it does," Nolasco said, anxious to get the email.

"Okay. It's sent. Michael is standing in the back row on the far right."

Nolasco stared at his computer screen. When he didn't immediately get the email, he refreshed the page several times.

"You have it?" Rector asked.

"Not yet," Nolasco said.

"I wonder if the file is too big," Rector said.

Nolasco hit the "Update Folder" button repeatedly. Nothing came through. He checked the junk email folder. Nothing.

"Nothing?" Rector asked.

"Not . . ." The email popped up at the top of Nolasco's list. "I got it," he said. "Hang on; I'm opening it."

His pulse pounded. Rector had not attached the photograph but embedded it in the body of the email. It came through so large only a portion fit within the window. Nolasco moved the cursor over different sections of the photograph, seeing perhaps a dozen students either seated or standing around desks with keyboards and computer terminals.

"Do you see him?" Rector asked. "Back row on the far right."

All of the students were smiling. All but one.

Nolasco moved the cursor to the names of the students beneath the picture next to the tag line: Lincoln Computer Club. He read the name of the student in the second row on the far right. Michael Montemayor. His hair was black. He had no facial hair or glasses, but it was definitely and undeniably him.

"Son of a bitch," Nolasco said under his breath. "Goddamn son of a bitch."

"You see him?" Rector asked.

Nolasco shook his shock. "I have to go. Thank you." He hung up and called Tracy, pacing and repeatedly swearing. The call rang through immediately to her voice mail. She'd turned her phone off. Why would she have turned off her phone? Had to be on another call. Maybe trying to call him.

Nolasco looked back to the photograph and thought again of what Tracy had said. The mayor had additional evidence to provide. He called her number a third time. Again, his call went directly to voice mail.

He had a bad feeling. He pulled his car keys from the drawer in his desk and sprinted from his office.

CHAPTER 38

Everything made sense. Just a moment too late. Not an artist. Not medically trained as the task force and she had postulated.

To bring the wicked and the sinners to justice for their crimes.

A police officer.

"Mrs. Edwards, if you would be so kind, I think you'll find a handgun in a holster beneath Detective Crosswhite's left shoulder." Augustus Cesare had a service pistol pointed at Tracy's head. "If you would remove it for me. Carefully. Don't do anything stupid, Detective."

Marilynn Edwards stared at Tracy. "It's all right," Tracy said. "Do as he says." Marilynn stepped forward and removed Tracy's Glock.

"Barrel pointed at the floor, please. And do not even think about putting your finger on the trigger," Cesare said. "We don't want any accidents."

Marilynn handed the Glock to Cesare. He took the weapon and slid it into his waistband at the back of his pants. Tracy noticed a laptop open on the table behind him; the screen showed the front of the

Edwards home from the front porch down the narrow drive. She'd been correct about the camera. She hadn't failed to notice it on her first visit. It hadn't been there. The Edwards home had the best alarm system in the world. Their dogs.

"Now, Detective, your cell phone, if you would?"

Tracy reached into her back pants pocket.

"Easy," Cesare said.

She handed over the cell phone.

"If everyone would take a seat, please. I'm sure you have a lot of questions, Detective."

Tracy moved to the end of the couch, Marilynn to the middle, Edwards remained seated on the far end. Cesare remained standing. He glanced at the laptop screen. "Just need to be sure you came alone, Detective."

"I let dispatch know where I am, Cesare. It's routine practice. They know I'm here."

"I'm counting on that, Detective. I just want to be sure no one else shows up until the time is right. They would have no reason to come now, would they? Not unless you were to alert them."

He was right. Tracy had advised dispatch of her intended location, but unless she called and gave them a reason, dispatch would not send units to the house. Cesare sat in a chair across from them.

"So, what's your plan, Augustus? Where do you go from here?" she asked.

"Me? I am officially retired, Detective. I can go anywhere in the world."

"So why not do that? Why not just leave?" Tracy recalled the evening she'd spent in the motel room with the Cowboy, with a rope around the neck of his would-be next victim. Her only goal had been to keep Kotar talking long enough to have the chance to disarm him or have someone unexpected come. That was her goal now.

"Because you reopened my case," Cesare said. "The great Tracy Crosswhite is on the trail of the Route 99 Killer. I'm honored. But I also couldn't take the chance you'd figure it out and come after me."

"No one figured it out before. What made you think I might?"

"Because you aren't a dumbshit like Moss and Nolasco. I gift wrapped Edwards for Moss. All he had to do was follow the evidence, and he would have seen the connection between the mayor's special assistants he slept with. The women he used the way he used my mother. It was more than enough to destroy him." Cesare shook his head.

"But Moss didn't follow the evidence." Tracy said.

"No. I can only imagine Mr. Mayor here had something hanging over Moss's head, and Moss buried the information to save his ass."

"Is that why you stopped killing? Because Moss didn't deliver the information?" It had been suggested by Santos.

"I stopped for a number of reasons, Detective. I'm not one of those perverted, demented men who got off on the killing."

Tracy begged to differ, but she kept her opinion to herself. *Keep him talking.* "Why kill all the prostitutes? Why so many?"

"I'm sure you think it was just practice. That's the common assumption about serial killers; isn't it?"

"Was it?"

"Killing was just a means to an end. Sure, I needed practice to know what I could get away with, but I had studied other serial killers and knew I needed to create hysteria to get the public and the police interested. To get the killings into the news. To ensure SPD formed a task force, singularly focused on figuring out why the killer was killing, what the angel's wings meant. Once I did that, I'd start to kill the women who the mayor here had slept with and took advantage of." He pointed the gun at Edwards. "The task force would see the connection, and the publicity would expose him for what he really is." Cesare took a deep breath and exhaled. "When I realized that wasn't going to happen . . . I had no reason to kill if the mayor wasn't going to suffer for it." He looked at Edwards, and Tracy could sense Cesare's anger and frustration were building. "People like you never get caught; do they?" Cesare said to Edwards.

When Edwards kept his gaze down, Cesare moved to the end of the couch and stood over him. "Do they?" he said more forcefully. Edwards and his wife startled. "Answer me."

"No," Edwards said in a soft, hesitant voice.

"No, what?"

Edwards paused, his expression one of confusion. Then he said, "No, sir?"

Cesare laughed. "Did you hear him, Detective? He just called me sir. The child he sought to have aborted." He looked back to Edwards. "I want to hear you say, 'People like me never get prosecuted.'"

Edwards swallowed with difficulty and said softly, "People like me never get prosecuted."

Tracy needed to draw Cesare's attention and his anger away from Edwards. "Why kill so many women?"

"You weren't listening, Detective."

"I was. You said you wanted him to suffer."

"I said killing him would have been too easy. I suffered for years because of him, and I wasn't going to let him off easily. I wasn't going to just kill him, not before I had destroyed him and everything about him. I wanted him to know he was the reason those women were dying. I wanted the information to come out that he'd slept with the final four, that he'd used his position of authority to abuse and take advantage of young women, the way he abused and took advantage of my mother. I wanted him to be publicly humiliated, to ruin him and his family's reputation. To expose him for what he is."

"I didn't take advantage of Rosie—"

Cesare whipped the pistol across Edwards's face, blood spraying. "Don't! Don't you dare say her name!"

Tracy lunged, instinct. Cesare recovered and pivoted. "I don't think so, Detective. Sit down. I said, sit down!"

Tracy sat.

Cesare took several deep breaths. "I gift wrapped the information for Moss to discover, but he didn't do anything with it. He just set it all aside."

Santos had been correct. Cesare stopped, in part at least, because he didn't believe his message would be delivered, or that anything of consequence would happen to Edwards.

"His father buried my mother's pregnancy to protect him, and Moss buried my killings to protect him. I suspect you know why?"

"Edwards had information Moss took drug money. I'm assuming Moss knew if he went to Nolasco with the connection to Edwards, Edwards would burn him, and Moss would be facing prison."

Cesare shook his head at Edwards. "I considered killing you back then, but then I thought it better to let you live with the uncertainty. You knew you'd slept with the women who were dying. You knew you were responsible, and yet you didn't have the moral fortitude to step forward. I knew you wouldn't. Men like you never do. I wanted you to live with that knowledge, that you had killed those women, and with the possibility that someday I might resume my killing, and maybe come for you."

"Is that why you stopped?" Tracy said, again gaining Cesare's attention.

Cesare looked to be giving her question some thought. "In part."

"You got married and had two daughters of your own."

"Leave them out of this," Cesare said, his gaze intense. He looked like a man on the edge, a man struggling to hold everything together. "I thought I'd moved on." He raised his voice and turned to Edwards.

"I thought I'd put you out of my mind. Then I got divorced, my wife got custody of my daughters, and Weber held that press conference and said you were reopening the investigation. I took it all as a sign."

"What kind of sign?" Tracy asked.

"That I wasn't finished yet. That I hadn't finished what I'd set out to do. I saw the reopening of the investigation as an opportunity to finish what I had started. To give my life some meaning and purpose."

Again, as Santos had said.

"Finish it how?" Tracy asked.

Cesare smiled. "You came here because you and Marilynn figured out the connecting thread to Mr. Mayor; didn't you?"

"How did you know?"

"I followed you to the Kubota Garden. Hell, I've had nothing but time on my hands. I saw the two of you together and figured either she or Edwards had to have told you about my mother. Am I right?"

"You're right," Tracy said.

"And from there I assumed you would use my mother's name to find my real name. My given name." He looked again to Edwards. "After everything you did to her, she still wanted me to have your name. She still loved you. Michael Edward Montemayor."

Not knowing Cesare's intentions, Tracy didn't tell him Nolasco hadn't found any photos of him at Lincoln High School.

"I guess now we've all finally come to the conclusion," Cesare said.

"And what is the conclusion, Cesare? How do you see this all ending?"

"You came here to confront Edwards about the affairs he had with each of the last five women and told him you would go public with that information if he didn't cooperate. He then told you those women threatened to expose him and go public with their accusations. That they intended to ruin him. With your reputation, people will believe that's what happened, that Edwards had those women killed to save his reputation. But Edwards always was a slimy, calculating bastard. You underestimated him. He was armed. He killed you, then shot and killed his wife, before taking his own life. You're all going to die, Detective. That's my means to an end. And the Angel of Justice will finally have been served."

—

Nolasco didn't have time to wait for SWAT or for backup. He might already be too late.

He shuffled down the stairs to the fourth floor, feet pounding on the metal steps. He almost slipped but kept his balance and spun himself around the landings. The thought of waiting for an elevator never entered his mind.

He burst into HR and started for the cubicle at the back, not seeing the top of Augustus Cesare's head as he approached, not that he had truly expected to. He knew where Cesare was. "He's gone," someone said from behind one of the cubicles. "Cesare. If that's who you're looking for. He's gone."

Nolasco caught the end of the sentence already on the move to the elevators. He was sprinting now to the secure garage, hitting the "Redial" button for Tracy's number. Again, his call went to voice mail.

He backed his Corvette from its space, tires squealing, then slapped the gearshift into drive and sped from the garage. On the way to Mercer Island, he called the SWAT sergeant, told him what he believed was transpiring, and instructed him to assemble the SWAT team somewhere close to the access road to the former mayor's home, but not to move without his order. He knew it would take time. That he'd beat them to the home, which he intended. He didn't call and ask for backup for the same reason. He didn't know what he was getting himself into, what Crosswhite had got herself into. If, as he suspected, Cesare was at the

mayor's home to finish what he'd started, it wasn't just for Tracy to witness it. He was going to end his killing and the investigation in grand
style. If police officers came barreling down the road to the mayor's
house, it would only expedite the executions. Crosswhite was smart
and resourceful. She'd kept the Cowboy talking for more than thirty
minutes, then, somehow, convinced him to walk out of that motel
room of his own free will.

But Nolasco had a bad feeling this time she'd be trying to tame
a completely different animal. Cesare was disturbed and thirsty for
revenge. Damned if Santos hadn't been right after all. Cesare had killed
those women to send a message. He wanted to punish the mayor. He
wanted retribution. He wanted justice.

And if Nolasco didn't get there in time, Cesare was going to get it,
and more.

He stepped down on the accelerator and wove around cars.

—

Cesare smiled. "You look worried, Detective. Don't be. I've made sure
you get your due. You get credit for solving another cold case."

"And how did you do that?"

"Before the mayor took his own life, he typed a detailed confession
and printed it out. It's sitting on the corner of his desk in his office.
Even a moron like Moss couldn't ignore it. Amid the ramblings of
a demented and sick mind, the mayor admits to the affairs, to their
threats, and to having had the women killed. He even gives specific
details about each of the killings, details only the killer would know,
including, of course, the angel's wings."

Tracy pushed her nerves aside and told herself that she'd been down
this path before and survived. She'd been in that motel room with the
Cowboy pressing a knife to his next victim's throat. She'd managed to

talk him down. Talk them both out of the room. She'd done it then. She would do it again.

What was the alternative?

She wasn't going to just give up. She would not quit. Not on Dan and not on Daniella. She'd buy time, as much as she could. She'd rely on her training. Keep him talking. Serial killers were narcissists. They had big egos.

But the Cowboy, in his own demented way, had at least made sense. Cesare was not making sense. These were the ramblings of a cornered, demented man. She suspected he knew it, but didn't care. He wanted just one thing. Justice.

"No one is going to believe the mayor is a killer, Cesare."

Cesare scoffed. "Not the mayor they think they know. That's the reason for the suicide note and the confessional. They'll come to realize Michael Edwards isn't the man he portrayed himself to be. He's amoral. Unethical. Dishonorable. It happens all the time in society. The public persona is not the private persona. Our heroes fall all the time. They are not who we think they are."

"So the angel's wings are not the Angel of Death. You represent the Angel of Justice?"

Cesare smiled. "I told you the great Tracy Crosswhite would figure it out."

"You have a problem, Cesare."

"Do I?"

Try to make him think of another plan. Confuse him. Make him think his current plan won't work. Engage, stall, stay alive. "If the mayor is amoral, unethical, and without honor, he wouldn't kill himself. Men like him never do. They believe they can talk their way out of the worst circumstances. It's like you said. They never get caught. They never get punished. No one is going to believe the mayor would confess to being responsible for the killings and throw away everything he worked to protect."

"Ordinarily he wouldn't, but what choice does he have with a dec-orated detective in his home confronting him? He's reached the end of the road. He's realized this was the end. And in the end, he does what all cowards do."

Cesare looked to the mayor and chuckled. Tracy used the oppor-tunity to break eye contact. She noticed movement on the laptop com-puter screen. Someone coming down the driveway.

Nolasco.

—

Nolasco parked his car on the dirt-and-gravel road where it could not be seen from the house, then got out and hugged the hillside, hoping the overgrown bushes, vines, and tree limbs would conceal him long enough to reach the house. He couldn't risk making a mistake. He might have just one shot at this.

He recognized the familiar black pool car parked in the driveway. The night he and Tracy confronted the mayor, they'd left Edwards's home via a staircase along the side of the house. He moved quickly in that direction, using the parked car for cover to get there. He went along the side of the house, careful to pause and look inside windows before he crossed in front of them. As he approached the backyard, he remembered the dogs. Big dogs. Where were they now? Their barking would echo halfway across the lake.

He peered between the cyclone fence's wood slats into the mayor's backyard, what he had called Disneyland for his grandchildren. More like Michael Jackson's Neverland. An exterior that exuded joy and hap-piness. But beneath all the boats and Jet Skis, the pool, and the other toys was something much more sinister.

Nolasco released the latch atop the gate and stepped through it. No dogs barked or charged him. He moved to the covered porch and outdoor living area. The television was on, tuned to a Mariners baseball game. The sliding door leading to the movie room was open. Nolasco stepped inside the room and moved to the carpeted staircase, his gun at his side. He climbed the stairs from the lower level to the second level, hearing voices. Tracy. Augustus Cesare.

She remained alive. Maybe the mayor and his wife also.

Time to end this.

—

Tracy struggled not to look at the computer screen behind Augustus Cesare. Cesare focused his wrath and attention at Michael Edwards. She hoped they stayed there. Nolasco moved to the back of her pool car, using it for cover.

So he knew. She didn't know how, but he knew.

"I would have liked to have destroyed you in your prime," Cesare was saying to Edwards with a look of utter disdain. "Not the shell of the man sitting here now." He turned to Tracy just as Nolasco sprinted from behind the car to the side of the house, out of camera range. Cesare looked to the monitor, then back to Tracy.

"He's an old man, Detective. An old man brought to the precipice of guilt by you. By your investigation. He fears meeting his maker. He fears the fires of hell that await him and believes the only way he can avoid them is by unloading his conscience, expressing his sorrow. The way my mother used to go to confession and the priests would absolve all her sins. Blah, blah, blah. It's all in the note, Detective. But I think we all deserve to hear it, don't we?"

Cesare moved back to the mayor and put the barrel of the gun to his head. Edwards flinched. "Unload your conscience, Mr. Mayor. Confess your sins."

Edwards closed his eyes and licked his lips.

"I'm giving you a chance to avoid eternal damnation before you die." Edwards mumbled something.

"I can't hear you," Cesare said. "Neither can God."

"Why did you become a cop?" Tracy asked.

He glanced at her. "Don't try to distract me, Detective."

"Computers," she said. "Did you create false transcripts? A work history?"

Cesare didn't immediately answer. He turned and again glanced at the laptop computer screen, distrusting. Then he looked to her. "All of the above. False birth certificate, false Social Security number. Everything I needed. It wasn't hard."

"Why?" Tracy said. "Why the police department?"

"To watch," Cesare said, a devious smile forming on his lips. "To be close to those hunting me. To control the narrative. To provide the information that should have led the task force to the mayor."

Where the hell was Nolasco?

"And Dwight McDonnel?" she asked. "Why direct the investigation to him if you wanted the evidence to point to the mayor?"

"I had to give the task force someone to concentrate on while I moved on to the mayor's special assistants. McDonnel had a penchant for prostitutes on the Aurora track. It was just a matter of following him one night and finding one he slept with."

"You left behind your DNA."

He shrugged. "It didn't matter back then. Now, they'll assume the fragmented DNA belongs to just another john, that the task force was, once again, mistaken."

Cesare didn't know. He didn't know the fragmented DNA led to a half brother of Jonathan Michael Edwards, to him.

"The mayor's written confession will take care of the mistakes, Detective. And the brass wants this case resolved. They were willing to accept McDonnel as the killer to put the investigation behind them.

They will accept this." Cesare smiled. "I've had years to think this over. I've thought of everything."

"Not everything," Tracy said, seeing Nolasco's head emerge from the staircase well and trying to keep Cesare's attention on her.

"Really? Tell me, what have I missed?"

"The dogged tenacity of a man who wanted justice even more than you."

"Freeze, Cesare," Nolasco said.

Cesare turned his head, then spun back and took aim at the mayor.

CHAPTER 39

Tracy watched Nolasco squeeze off three shots. Two hit Cesare's back, the third, the side of his head. The force of the first bullet knocked Cesare off-balance and his aim off target. The bullets punched two holes in the plate-glass windows behind the mayor before he toppled onto the carpeted floor.

Tracy rushed to kick away his weapon, then cuffed his hands behind his back, though he was clearly dead. She did her best to block the view from Marilynn Edwards, who was shaking and whimpering on the couch and didn't need to see this. With Cesare secure, she moved Marilynn from the room, seating her at the kitchen table, then moved the former mayor. In the other room she heard Nolasco on the phone, advising someone to stand down, likely the SWAT team sergeant, and telling him to let dispatch know shots had been fired, one victim. He asked for a CSI team and for an ambulance, as well as the medical examiner.

With the former mayor and his wife in the kitchen, Tracy returned to the living room. Nolasco lowered his phone. "Ambulance and CSI are on the way. ME also. I told SWAT to stand down."

Tracy looked at Cesare on the floor. "You always were a good shot," she said.

Nolasco smiled but without joy. His smile might have been ironic. They both knew Nolasco had once held the highest shooting score at the police academy—until Tracy went through as a recruit and beat his high score with a perfect one. It was one of many things that had, over the years, caused animosity between them that now seemed trivial.

But Tracy suspected Nolasco's smile was more out of resignation. He would have to answer a lot of questions to explain how the killer could have been a member of his task force.

"How did you know I was here?" Tracy asked.

Nolasco told her about the teacher who recalled Michael Montemayor. "I recognized Cesare in the picture. When I couldn't reach you and my calls went straight to voice mail, I figured something was wrong. I just hoped you could keep him talking as long as you kept the Cowboy talking, so I'd have a chance to get here."

"Thanks," she said. "But I don't think he was going to give me the chance to talk my way out of this one."

Nolasco looked to the kitchen, to where former mayor Edwards now sat. "He had no idea what he'd sowed, did he?"

"He didn't care," Tracy said. "He never had to care or take responsibility. Everything was always handled for him by his father. But to answer your question, no. He clearly had no idea it would come to this."

Within ten minutes, multiple patrol cars and additional pool cars crowded the drive and narrow access road to the Edwards home, along with the CSI van. The ME's van was also en route. A familiar voice drew Tracy's and Nolasco's attention to the front door. Marcella Weber stood in the entry, talking to a uniformed officer holding a clipboard. Weber signed the sheet on the clipboard, handed it back, and stepped down into the living room with the million-dollar view and the body of Augustus Cesare.

"What the hell happened?" she said.

"How much time do you have?" Nolasco said.

"Give me the *Reader's Digest* version."

Even that took more than half an hour for Nolasco to explain. Tracy added information only she had been privy to, what Cesare had admitted in her presence, and the typed confession he said was in the office near the computer. She was happy to let Nolasco speak and take the credit. This was his investigation. Always had been.

When they had finished, Weber said, "We can't bury this."

"No, we can't," Nolasco said.

"The press will wonder what brought Cesare here. They'll want to know the mayor's role in this."

"It's high time that comes out," Nolasco said. "If we had this information back then and had acted on it, we might have saved a few women's lives."

They did have that information, Tracy thought but didn't say.

"The best thing we can do to prevent speculation and innuendo is to open up all the window shades and let the light in," Tracy said. "Come clean and let the chips fall where they may. The mayor has blood on his hands. He did that himself. You try to cover for him, and the entire department will suffer."

"Where is he?" Weber asked.

"In the kitchen," Nolasco said.

"Alone?"

"At the moment," Nolasco said. "He isn't talking, but his wife is being interviewed in their bedroom by one of my detectives." Marilynn, worried about her two dogs, first searched and found them in the shed in the backyard, likely drugged. They had slept through the entire affair. Even now they looked groggy and occasionally stumbled as they walked.

"She's talking?" Weber asked.

"For now," Tracy said. "But her first priority will be to protect her children and her grandchildren. She will shield them from all of this."

"Not her husband?" Weber said.

"Definitely not her husband," Tracy said.

Weber looked about the room, then said, "I'll need to bring in FIT." Meaning the Force Investigation Team, which was standard procedure in an officer-involved shooting. FIT investigators worked with SPD's Office of Professional Accountability to investigate whether the use of force complied with SPD policy.

"You saw what happened?" Weber asked Tracy.

"Front-row seat."

"You'll both be put on leave until this is sorted out." She sighed, likely anticipating the shitstorm to come. Then Weber left the room for the kitchen and Michael Edwards.

A uniformed police officer entered the living room. "CSI sergeant and the ME are outside awaiting instructions."

Tracy and Nolasco walked outside. Nolasco reached into his coat pocket and pulled out a pack of cigarettes, but he stopped before shaking one free. He considered the pack for a moment.

"You want me to get them up to speed while you have a smoke?" Tracy said.

Nolasco looked at her, then at the assembling crowd. He handed her the cigarette pack. "Do me a favor, Crosswhite?"

"Captain?"

"Throw those out."

EPILOGUE

Weber kept the press at bay until after Mike Melton confirmed a direct match of Augustus Cesare's DNA with the fragmented DNA at the fourth victim's crime scene. Melton told Tracy he had confirmed Cesare's DNA with Jonathan Edwards's DNA, as well. A half brother. No doubt.

"What about Michael Edwards?"

"We were told not to run the swab you provided."

"What? By whom?"

"Weber."

Tracy wondered what Weber was playing at.

FIT investigators had interviewed Tracy about what had happened at the crime scene, and whether she had witnessed Nolasco discharge his weapon. She told them if Nolasco hadn't discharged his weapon, the former mayor would be dead and probably her and Marilynn Edwards as well. She spent the rest of her time before going on leave filling out reports and reading the reports prepared by CSI and the ME.

After five days, Tracy and Nolasco had still not been cleared to return to duty, which both found curious, though Tracy was enjoying her time at home with Daniella. On the sixth day, Weber called and ordered them both to appear at a press conference that afternoon. Neither was told to be prepared to speak to reporters.

"I have a bad sense about this," Tracy said to Nolasco as they made their way to the room adjacent to the pressroom. "Weber told Melton not to run the mayor's DNA swab, and now neither of us is being asked to speak."

"We got our guy, Crosswhite. I'm focusing on that."

Four o'clock in the afternoon, they stepped into the conference room. Weber entered with the assistant chief of criminal investigations and Mayor Charles Garcia. Garcia approached and shook Tracy's and Nolasco's hands.

"Congratulations, Captain, Detective. We're all glad to finally have this behind us."

Tracy found his choice of words curious. It seemed the matter was far from behind them. In some respects, it was just getting started.

Bennett Lee, the PIO, poked his head into the room. "Are we ready?"

They filed out of the conference room to the pressroom, which was packed with reporters and the victims' family members. Anita Childress, Greg Bartholomew, and this time, Bill Jorgensen, were also present. So were Faz and Del. Cameras whirred and clicked as Tracy, Nolasco, and the others took positions behind the podium. Garcia stepped forward.

"Thank you for coming," Garcia said. He acknowledged the families seated in the first row and apologized for the earlier "mistake." He didn't blame anyone. He owned it. He said DNA was always tricky, but he finished on a positive note. "Today we are, once and for all, able to tell you with certainty that the Route 99 serial killer investigation has come to a close. This time there is no mistake. The Washington State Patrol Crime Lab has definitively concluded the DNA of Officer Augustus Cesare is a direct match to DNA recovered at one of the crime scenes. Moreover, before he was shot and killed, Cesare offered a full written confession, providing information only the Route 99 Killer would have known."

"Written confession?" Nolasco uttered quietly to Tracy. "What is he talking about?"

Tracy had a sickening suspicion she knew exactly what Garcia was talking about. She glanced at Weber, but the chief of police would not meet her gaze. "She found the confession Cesare put by the computer."

Nolasco gave her a sidelong glance.

"They had to have changed the name at the bottom to Cesare instead of the mayor."

"Many of you are aware of the incident at former mayor Michael Edwards's home," Garcia continued. "We are grateful that both the mayor and his wife were unharmed, and we believe it best to allow him to explain the situation. Mr. Mayor?"

Tracy looked to Nolasco, who had shut his eyes, perhaps knowing what was to come. She knew also.

Michael Edwards entered from the opposite side of the stage. His wife at his side. Marilynn held his hand. Another bad sign.

Edwards didn't look like the teetering old man in the living room of his home. He looked like the slick politician who had once directed the media with a cocksure attitude. He stepped to the podium using a cane. His face, bruised and cut where he'd been pistol-whipped, instantly evoked sympathy. "Thank you, Mayor Garcia. I'm sure you all have questions, and I've prepared a statement I hope will answer most, if not all of those questions. You're probably wondering why Augustus Cesare came to our home last Friday."

Edwards cleared his throat. "Augustus Cesare was not his real name. His real name, confirmed on a birth certificate, was Michael Edward Montemayor. My son."

The press stirred. So, too, did Tracy. Was Edwards actually going to tell the truth? Had Marilynn threatened to expose him if he lied again? Tracy tried to temper her thoughts of justice finally being done.

"When I was in my early twenties, Rosenda Montemayor Alvarado was our family maid. Rosenda initiated an affair to which I succumbed. At some point, she claimed to be pregnant but said her intent was to seek an abortion. My family provided her with information about a facility and funding to get an abortion. She left our employ and the area. I never saw her again. I assumed she had returned to Mexico and fully believed she had the abortion. When Marilynn and I met, I advised her in full of the situation and that I believed it was in my past. I had no further contact of any kind with Rosenda."

More lies. My God. The man could spin lies with such sincerity. Tracy watched and listened intently.

"I understand that, as Captain Johnny Nolasco and Detective Tracy Crosswhite closed in on Cesare as the killer, he crafted a confession, admitting to the killings, and provided his reasons for his killing spree. I want to make perfectly clear I had no idea Cesare was tied to any of the killings or his reasons for doing so. I didn't know he was my son or that Rosenda had not had the abortion."

Tracy shut her eyes. She knew what was to come.

"I am deeply saddened by this tragedy and wish to convey my heartfelt condolences to everyone who has suffered because of his actions. As you know, I am no longer a public figure. My wife and I have, for years, avoided the public spotlight and sought only the quiet comfort and solitude of our three children and our grandchildren. We seek peace now. We do not intend to comment further on this matter or on the investigation, except to say we are deeply grateful for the dogged determination and incredible police work of Captain Johnny Nolasco. Captain Nolasco's initiative and his fortitude brought him to our home and saved our lives. Were it not for him, we would not be standing here before you."

Edwards's voice cracked and he reached for a handkerchief to dry tears that did not exist. He was delivering an Academy Award performance, making himself another victim to those seated in the first row. Despicable.

"He's going to walk," Tracy said under her breath. "The son of a bitch is going to walk."

After a few more words, the former mayor and his wife left the stage, still holding hands. Edwards, intentional or not, glanced at Tracy from the corner of his eye as if to remind her of her place. Marilynn never made eye contact. When they were no longer in public view, Marilynn let go of her husband's hand and stepped away. Tracy didn't fault Marilynn for the illusion. She knew Marilynn hadn't done it for herself, and she hadn't chosen to support her husband. She'd chosen to support her family. Her grandkids would continue to come to her home, to their Disneyland. She would not allow her children or her grandchildren to suffer the same indignities she had suffered.

Mayor Garcia introduced Weber, who stepped to the podium and asked the media to respect the former mayor's privacy. When the reporters asked questions about the confrontation at the former mayor's home, Weber answered along the party line, and when she couldn't, she said there remained an internal investigation, and she couldn't comment on specifics or provide details.

Tracy considered Anita Childress, whose expression looked like Daniella's when her little girl was being force-fed something she disliked.

Weber concluded the conference without inviting Tracy or Nolasco to speak, telling reporters they would not do so due to the ongoing FIT investigation, though she said she wanted them present to receive accolades for putting an end to the investigation. More bullshit. She wanted them to know and adhere to the party line or neither would be reinstated.

They left the stage. Tracy and Nolasco hurried after Weber.

"What the hell was that?" Nolasco said to Weber. "That isn't what happened."

Weber said, "What happened was a task force twenty-five years ago either failed to detect the importance of certain information or deliberately ignored information clearly spelled out on the tip sheet. Information that would have saved lives. What happened was a task force had a serial killer directing the flow of that information. That was your task force, Captain Nolasco. You were in charge. Would you like me to make that public?"

"Cesare gave those tips to Gunderson. Gunderson buried them," Nolasco said.

"The buck stops with you, Captain. I tried to save you the embarrassment of questions about the killer working directly under your nose, someone you could have identified if you had done your job."

"The mayor got to you; didn't he?" Tracy said. "The same way he got to Moss Gunderson all those years ago. He told you if you didn't go along with his story, he'd expose you for taking the drug money from the Last Line task force."

"We've been down this road before, Detective. I believe we reached a dead end. It will again. If it doesn't, if you go running to the papers with what you believe to have been the real story, I will place the blame for the failure to catch the killer directly at Captain Nolasco's feet, as well as those task force members who remain, including Vic Fazzio. If I burn, they'll burn with me. The decision is yours."

Weber gave them both a wicked *try me* gaze before she left the room.

After a long minute, Tracy looked to Nolasco. "Your call."

Nolasco scoffed. "My call? I know there's no love lost between us, Crosswhite, so does the chief. It's why she said she'd also implicate Faz. She knows you won't burn him. Not for anything. Not even to finally be rid of me."

"You're wrong, Captain. So is she. I wouldn't burn you. That's not what partners do."

Nolasco sighed. He looked like a man resigned to his fate. "Let's not fool ourselves and think we're going to go out and have a kumbaya moment, okay? We both had a job to do, and we did it. We got our guy. That's the most important thing. It's over. Cesare is dead. The families have closure. So do I. Time to move on." He took a breath and started from the room, but he stopped at the doorway and turned back. "Just so you know. I wouldn't have burned you either."

Nolasco walked back through the pressroom, Tracy following.

"Detective." Angela Waylon, the mother of one of the victims, who had spoken to Tracy at the earlier press conference, stopped Nolasco.

"My daughter, Cathy, was one of the victims."

"I'm sorry," Nolasco said.

"I wanted you to know that my husband, Cathy's father, died two nights ago, but I had the chance to tell him that Cathy's killer had been found, that you'd killed him. I wanted you to know my husband died peacefully. Thanks to you."

"I'm glad," Nolasco said. "Thank you for telling me."

"My husband did woodwork in retirement. He made these pens." She opened one of two boxes in her hand. Inside was a beautiful wood pen. "I brought one for each of you. I wanted to thank you for what you did, and I thought maybe, when you used the pen, you'd think of Cathy, and of our family, and remember that what you do matters."

"That's very kind," Nolasco said. "It means more to me than you'll ever know. Thank you."

He took one pen, glanced at Tracy, and departed.

Tracy took her pen and thanked Waylon. She made her way to her office. Faz and Del waited inside. They'd both been in the room at the press conference.

"What just happened?" Faz said, looking and sounding incredulous.

"Closure," she said, and she looked at the box in her hand.

"Bullshit. That wasn't closure," Del said. "You know the truth. I know the truth. Go to Anita Childress again. She'll get the story out like we got it out before."

"Maybe not closure for us," Tracy said thinking of Angela Waylon and Nolasco. "But closure for those who needed it most. We should respect that."

"You don't believe that. Not for a minute," Del said.

"In this case, there are more important things than the truth," Tracy said.

"Such as?" Faz asked.

"Family," she said. She thought of Dan and Daniella, but also of Faz and Vera, and of Marilynn Edwards. She'd do as Mrs. Edwards had done. Tracy would swallow the truth, to protect her family. To save Faz, Daniella's godfather.

"I'm thinking of calling Dan and having him meet me for dinner and a couple of bottles of wine. You got any pull at any Italian restaurants in Fremont?" she said to Faz, alluding to Antonio's restaurant, Fazzio's.

"Not me," Faz said. "But Vera? She's got an in with the owner."

"I'll give Kins a call too," Del said. "He and Shannah should be there, huh?"

"Be good to have the gang back together again," Faz said.

"That's the most important thing; isn't it?" Tracy said.

ACKNOWLEDGMENTS

A s previously mentioned, with each novel I give myself a challenge.
I believe it forces me to write better and to produce more intrigu-
ing novels in the Tracy Crosswhite series for my loyal readers to enjoy.
This particular challenge started with my editor, Gracie Doyle, asking
me to write a short story for Amazon Original Stories. Since I was
in the process of writing *What She Found*, an involved novel about a
missing investigative reporter and the four explosive stories she was
pursuing, I decided to tell the backstory to that novel, which involved
Seattle Violent Crimes detective Del Castigliano's first homicide case.
Thus, I wrote "The Last Line." Though it does state on the Amazon site
that "The Last Line" is a short story, many of you loyal readers were
not happy it was so short or with an ending that didn't wrap up in a
nice bow. I took that as both a compliment and a lesson learned, and I
advised my readers to just hold on, that more was coming.

Thankfully, many of you did hold on, and *What She Found,* Tracy #9, became a bestseller.

One Last Kill, Tracy #10, is the final piece to the trilogy within the now ten-book series. It can be read on its own, but also as part of the trilogy and the Tracy Crosswhite series. Writing three stories that piggyback off one another but that still can be read individually was a challenge for me. I had to keep track of all the details in not just one story but three. It proved more difficult than I anticipated. If I made any mistakes, they are mine alone. I hope this struggle resulted in better stories for you, my loyal readers, and you got a kick out of this, sort of like watching a television series within the series. I also hope new readers found each story a good read.

I want to thank all my readers for your patience with and your loyalty to the Tracy Crosswhite novels. The Tracy Crosswhite novels will continue on, hopefully well into the future.

Luckily, I have a great team to help me.

As with all the books in this series, I simply could not have written this one without the help of Jennifer Southworth, Seattle Police Department, Violent Crimes Section. Jennifer has been invaluable, helping me formulate interesting ideas and advising me of daily police routine, as well as the specific tasks undertaken in the pursuit of a perpetrator of a crime. I look forward to working with Jennifer on additional novels and am so grateful to have her on my team.

I also want to thank Alan Hardwick. Alan is a Renaissance man. A talented musician, he is a member of several bands I have heard a number of times, as well as a writer. He was a Boise, Idaho, police detective and founded that department's Criminal Intelligence Unit. In Edmonds, Washington, he served as a sergeant and acting assistant chief of police with the Edmonds Police Department. He was a member of the FBI Joint Terrorism Task Forces and the Washington Homicide Investigators Association. He now runs the Hardwick Consulting Group and is a heck of a lot of fun as a travel companion to conferences. I'm grateful for his assistance and look forward to further collaborations.

To the extent there are any mistakes in the police aspects of this novel, those mistakes are mine and mine alone. In the interests of telling a story, and hopefully keeping it entertaining, I have condensed certain timelines, such as the time it takes to have DNA analyzed.

Thanks to Meg Ruley, Rebecca Scherer, and the team at the Jane Rotrosen Agency. They are literary agents extraordinaire. They do just about everything to make my life easier, and for that I am eternally grateful. They are some of the best people I know.

Thank you to Thomas & Mercer, Amazon Publishing. I'm losing count of the number of books I've written for them. People ask me how I'm putting out more than one novel a year. The simple answer is I work every day, and I love what I do. But I also get a lot of support from my writing team at the literary agency and at Amazon Publishing. This is the tenth Tracy Crosswhite novel with Thomas & Mercer, and the team has made each novel better with their edits, comments, and suggestions. I take each suggestion seriously.

Amazon Publishing has sold and promoted my novels all over the world, and I have had the pleasure of meeting the Amazon Publishing teams from the UK, Ireland, France, Germany, Italy, and Spain. These are hardworking people who somehow make hard work a lot of fun. What they do best is promote and sell my novels, and for that I am so very grateful. I've seen several of my novels on billboards in Times Square in New York City and in the *New York Times* Sunday book section, as well as all over the Amazon pages. My publicity team never ceases to amaze me with their out-of-the-box promotion of my work.

Thanks to Sarah Shaw, author relations. Thanks to production managers Rachael Herbert, Tamara Arellano, and Tricia Callahan; and Adrienne Krogh, art director. It's getting redundant, I know, but I love the covers and the titles of each of my novels. Thanks to Dennelle Catlett, and congratulations again on her promotion to head of publicity, Amazon Publishing. Dennelle is always there, always available when I call or send an email with a need or a request. She actively promotes me, helps me to give to worthwhile charitable organizations, and makes my travel easy. Thanks to the marketing team, Andrew George, Erica Moriarty, Lindsey Bragg, and Rachael Clark, for all their dedicated work and incredible new ideas to help me build my author platform. Their energy and creativity are astonishing. They make each new idea a great experience. Thanks to Mikyla Bruder, head of Amazon Publishing, and publisher Julia Sommerfeld for creating a team dedicated to their jobs and allowing me to be a part of it. I am sincerely grateful, and even more amazed with each additional million readers we reach.

I am especially grateful to Amazon Publishing's associate publisher, Gracie Doyle. Gracie and I work closely together on my ideas from their initial formation to print. Beyond that, we have a lot of fun when we get together.

Thank you to Charlotte Herscher, developmental editor. All of my books with Amazon Publishing have been edited by Charlotte—from police procedurals to legal thrillers, espionage thrillers, and literary novels—and she never ceases to amaze me how quickly she picks up the story line and works to make it as good as it can possibly be. Thanks to Scott Calamar, copyeditor, whom I desperately need. Grammar has never been my strength, so there is usually a lot to do.

Thanks to Tami Taylor, who creates my newsletters and some of my foreign-language book covers. Thanks to Pam Binder and the Pacific Northwest Writers Association for their support.

Thanks to all of you tireless and loyal readers for finding my novels and for your incredible support of my work all over the world. Hearing from readers is a blessing, and I enjoy each email. Recently I awoke to my phone buzzing and found 150 emails from students at Greenville High School in Texas who read *The Extraordinary Life of Sam Hell* in their dual-credit English class. What a hoot! Thank you for your emails.

Thanks to my mother and father for a wonderful childhood and for teaching me to reach for the stars, then to work my butt off to attain those heights. I couldn't think of two better role models.

Thank you to my wife, Cristina, for all her love and support, and thanks to my two children, who have started to read my novels, which makes me so very proud.

I couldn't do this without all of you, nor would I want to.

ABOUT THE AUTHOR

Robert Dugoni is the *New York Times*, *Wall Street Journal*, and Amazon Charts bestselling author of the Tracy Crosswhite series, which has sold more than eight million books worldwide; the David Sloane series; the Charles Jenkins series; the stand-alone novels *Her Deadly Game*, *The 7th Canon*, *Damage Control*, *The World Played Chess*, and *The Extraordinary Life of Sam Hell*, for which he won an AudioFile Earphones Award for narration; and the nonfiction exposé *The Cyanide Canary*, a *Washington Post* best book of the year. He is the recipient of the Nancy Pearl Book Award for fiction and has twice won the Friends of Mystery Spotted Owl Award for best novel. He is a two-time finalist for the Thriller Awards and a finalist for the Harper Lee Prize for Legal Fiction, the Silver Falchion Award for mystery, and the Mystery Writers of America Edgar Awards. His books are sold in more than twenty-five countries and have been translated into more than two dozen languages. Visit his website at www.robertdugonibooks.com.